The
Quantock Hoard

By
John M. Barrett

Published by

John M. Barrett

49 Beadon Road, Taunton TA1 2DL.

Copyright reserved May 2000

ISBN No. 0-9539128-0-9

Typesetting by John M. Barrett

Printed and bound in Great Britain by

The Taunton Printing Company

Units 11 & 12, Belvedere Trading Estate,

Taunton, Somerset, TA1 1BH

CHAPTER 1

The Drillers - Date 17/7/76

Jack Martins arrived at the 'Fox and Feathers' public house, just as Burt Stevens and Ray Hayman had received their pints of bitter and moved across the bar room to sit at a small table near the open window. One of only two windows open in the room, which was not allowing the sun, shine through. Every time the door opened, a gentle breeze came into the room, giving a cool respite for whoever was sat there. The weather had been the same for over a period of six weeks now, hot and dry. Every where in the Southwest of England had suffered from the intolerable dry heat. All around the area was parched, with the rivers and streams at an unusually low level which had not been seen since many years before. For the two drillers who had been working in the heat of the morning, the coolness of the small room was a welcome relief, and something they had been looking forward to since mid morning when the heat began to break through the early morning mist of the day, as it had done so for every morning they had been on site.

They felt the soothing coolness of the breeze as Jack had entered the bar, Burt Stevens reached for the beer mug in front of him.

"Have I been looking forward to this!" He remarked, as he lifted the froth topped mug to his parched lips to take a long generous swallow. He placed the vessel back onto the table showing the contents had shrunk to just over half a pint. "There was a time, just about an hour ago, when I thought I was about to pass out, what with the heat of the weather, and the fumes and heat from the exhaust of the rigs engine, but the thought of a drink here at lunch time, kept me going".

Ray Hayman meanwhile, had been looking around the bar to see if there were any of the regulars they had seen and spoken to when they had frequented the pub before, since they had been working in the area, and had at the same time seen Jack Martins enter the room. With a nod of his head in the direction of the bar to his workmate, his voice low but loud enough for Burt to hear. "Gaffers here, and just gone up to the bar".

Burt turned his head towards where his workmate had indicated. "What's he doing here, now? He said he was coming late this afternoon with the wages! I suppose him and his Mrs. are off to the beach for the weekend again instead of tomorrow morning, making a full weekend of it in their caravan down Cornwall way. Well not to worry, if the 'Golden Eagle' shits now instead of later this afternoon, we will be on our way home not to long after he has left, and that's for sure!"

"Have you both got a drink?" Shouted their boss from across the bar room.

The other five or six people in the bar looked up towards where they heard the sound of his loud booming voice, thinking perhaps there was some one they knew, who was talking to them and, offering a free drink. Seeing the offer was not directed at them they turned back to resume the conversations they were having before they had been distracted.

Both men raised their glasses which were now empty. As soon as Ray had seen Jack Martins enter the bar they had emptied their glasses with astonishing speed. Knowing the first thing he would do would be to offer them a drink as he had always done since they had worked for him. It had become a kind of firms ritual. He came over to where they were sitting and took the offered glasses from them as they were held out towards him."What's the grub like here? I'm famished, I left home in a hurry this morning, with just a cup of tea and a biscuit for breakfast.The county surveyor wanted to see me about the work we have been contracted to do after we finish here. Why now, and why he seemed so insistent it was so urgent, I don't understand, this work we are doing now, will take us at least another four weeks or so,at least. But then, I suppose when it means a continuation of work in our own area for a while it pays to keep him sweet, when we

1

don't have any travelling away from home for a while".

"The food here is pretty good, we had a ploughmans lunch yesterday, and will have the same today, they make a well filled plate with quite a portion of trimmings around the cheese, we have ordered ham as an extra with the pickle it's reasonably priced, as well as filling".

Moments later Jack martins returned from the bar with the drinks and placed them on the table in front of his workmen. The landlord told me that the barmaid collects the money for the food when she brings it to the table, something about keeping the bar money separate from the food money, different tills or some such thing. I will pay for yours when it arrives at the table, O.K.! "The lifting of glasses and the word "Cheers" was their only response to his generosity.

Jack Martins had been in the drilling game for over twenty years, things had been hard when he had first started up on his own. He had left school at the age of fifteen, and started working at a local tannery, but in a short time he could see the work was not for him. He had left school at the end of the Christmas term, and spent the first few months out side in the open pulling sheep skins out of the tannery vats in freezing cold weather. It was not very pleasant work, his arms and hands immersed in cold briny water, most of the time, and at the end of the day when they were looking forward to finishing, there would be a lorry load of sheepskins to unload, covered in salt and smelling, and nearly always wet, or at least damp, and heavy, the salt content within the fleece made any cuts which never seemed to heal and dry, smart like blazes.

Then as the weather became warmer in the spring, he found himself more and more inside the tannery itself, working in the hot drying rooms pegging out skins which had been cured and "Chromed" ready to send to manufacturing companies to be made into various types of garments, from gloves to sheepskin coats, or even rugs. But the thing that vexed him most was, that all the older men working there seemed to be getting the jobs to do outside, while all the winter it was all the "so called" young trainees such as himself and others of his own age, had to suffer all the cold and inclement weather, and cold brine vats. It seemed to him there was too much unfairness in the place, for him to want to spend any long length of employment in the conditions he was experiencing there. The over riding clincher to the decision was that towards mid summer he discovered he was only receiving one third or less than the older workers were getting, while he was doing exactly the same amount, and type of work it was also about that time he had heard from a friend, was to be a position as a trainee driller, coming up in a week or two, with his friends employer. The local county council.

The following week he saw the position advertised in the local paper, applied for it, and was successful. He took to the work immediately, if it was due to the type of work itself or the out doors life in winter and summer, no one could say with any degree of certainty. He was quite a tall person when he had started on the rigs, but by the time he reached twenty one, he was six feet six, and about eighteen stones of solid muscle.

He had decided to finish on the county council after a period of five and a half years, but had learnt the skills needed for percussion and rotary drilling.

He had decided to terminate his employment there when the opportunity of work, with top wages in the middle east, was offered to him, due to someone who he had known while working for the county council, had obtained contracts out there.

He stayed, for four years, with paid home leave, every nine months.

Time went by, and he eventually returned home to England, with a good healthy bank balance, which he decided to make use of.

In thinking of his future, he bought himself a reconditioned Shell and Augur percussion rig, setting himself up as a self employed driller.

In time he made use of all the contacts he had made over the years in the drilling field, and managed to land a few lucrative contracts. He now owned two shell and augur percussion drills and a mobile rotary, core drill. With two, two man teams with himself left to run the business side of the operation, although, he still did field work when the opportunity presented it's self, all in all, he had done quite well for himself.

Three quarters of an hour later all three were back at the site of the drilling operation, set up in a field near a wooded area off of the main beaten track, with the entry gained through two gates which led to two quite large fields, which left the rig standing quite concealed until entry into the second of the fields was gained.

Burt Stevens was in charge of the rig on site. At forty six he was six years older than Jack, he was about a foot shorter, but there the physical difference in build ended.

He was built like a pocket battle ship; a bull like neck, with shoulders and upper torso reminiscent of an old square rig sailing ship, but where Jack was quite a handsome figure; Burt was as rough as they came, when he smiled, which was quite often due to his nature, and weird sense of humour.

A gap due to two missing front teeth on the top row, showed he was not too particular about his appearance; and those which were left were loose and discoloured. His nose had been broken years before in a barroom brawl, while in the army, at the time of national service, when he had been stationed in Gibraltar, serving in the 'Royal Engineers'.

But as a worker he could hold his own with anyone, once he decided it would be to his own advantage, and was one never to be taken advantage of. He had on many occasions worked a much younger man to a stand still. Ray Hayman was a complete contrast to the other two, twentysix years of age, and a Rugby football fanatic. He would travel to where ever Bath City were playing, when ever a chance of a free weekend happened and while working with Burt that was quite often.

He had long blond hair which hung down to his shoulders, but with a complexion of some one who came from the Mediterranean. While at work he dressed as the other two, which at the present time, because of the weather was shorts and sweatshirts. But outside of working hours he was very much into the fashion of the times, and had a well stocked wardrobe at home, where he live alone in his rented two floored sectioned. Before they started the engine of the rig to commence drilling Burt had useda string line with a lead weight on the end of it for depthtesting, and had just pulled it out of the ground after testing the depthof the bore hole, and counting the knots which had been tiedevery five metres on the line.

"How deep are you now?" Jack had asked as he withdrew it from the hole.

"Just over twenty metres, top and subsoil measured bout a metre, and since then we have had nothing but red clay, and the deeper we have gone the harder it has got".

"Have you tried using the cruciform chisel?"

"We were working with the chisel up until lunchtime, because of the hardness of the clay, but it was still hard going. Before we left we put the claycutter back on with an extra sinker weight, then poured ten gallons of water down the hole to see if it would soften it enough to make it easier, and perhaps make better progress than we have up until now, we can only hope for the best".

The rig had been working for about thirty minutes or so, and progress had increased by a good two and a half metres then stopped. Red clay slurry on the arms and legs of Ray Hayman, enough to make better progress than they had done earlier in the day. After a few more drops of the clay cutter Burt could tell by experience they had hit bedrock, and winched the claycutter up, unscrewed it, then put the cruciform chisel back on with the extra sinker weight still attached.

Jack by that time was looking around to see if he could find any of the other markers the surveyor had put in the ground where they had to do the rest of the drilling. He was just in the process of walking towards where he thought he could see a yellow painted marker stake sticking up in the ground when he heard Burt's voice shouting that he had hit bedrock.

"What's the difference in depth from the last bore holes when you hit the bedrock?" Jack enquired as he began to walk back towards the set up rig.

"Quite a bit I think, Hang on a mo' I have my note book in the tool compartment of the rig. I will just get it out and tell you exactly".

By the time he had retrieved it, Jack was at his side. "The last one was deeper by fifteen metres or so, the difference all together from when we started the first, averages only about three metres over all, except for this one, and that is perhaps due to the slope in the ground".

3

"Oh well not to worry, just keep going with the chisel for another thirty minutes and if you make little progress in depth in that time, seal the hole, move the rig to the next nearest peg, then bag up the samples. Both of you can pack up and call it a day after you finish that, it's too hot, and late now to start another bore hole. I'm just going to look around to see where the other markers are and then, I will call it a day. I'm on my way for a break, this weekend in Cornwall. Are you going to come in all day tomorrow or just the morning on overtime?"
"No we both decided to have the full weekend off, to take a break from the heat.

The two men continued working for about ten minutes, just raising the chisel and letting it drop onto the rock below, without seeming to make much progress at at all. Burt was standing pulling the lever working the cable, while Ray was leaning against the 'A' frame support of the drill rig. Suddenlythere was a loud crashing sound of metal, and a hissing and whirring sound as the cable wound off of the drum dangerously fast. The rig began to lurch and shudder as if it had a life of it's own. Ray had watched in disbelief as the steel bore head disappeared, and the ground opened up in front of him......

CHAPTER 2

The First Time - Date 14/3/79

"Can I come to you sir, no sir, not you. The young man wearing the grey polo neck sweater just behind you."

Peter Jones looked around him, then back to the woman standing on the rostrum, then made the gesture of half pointing to himself, unsure of what to do. "Yes that's right young man, I mean you". She smiled warmly at him.

Peter Jones swallowed, and felt a cold shiver at the back of his neck, but at the same time his face began to blush, with the heat travelling from his hot dry throat then down his chest. He had been to these meetings just three times before. He had seen other people respond to the person on the rostrum. What was it they nearly always said.... something?..... "Bless you," that was it," he spoke. "Bless you friend". His voice sounded half it's normal volume. He had seen them go to other people, but now one of them had picked him out. 'Don't panic' he thought to himself, just see what happens,.....just see what she has to say.

Looking at her, he estimated she would be somewhere in her early fifties, a well built person, her hair was a shining silver grey, tied up in a bun at the back of her head. She was wearing a flower patterned dress, of various colours on a light green background, which hung quite loosely on her, but never in any way was it frumpish, it suited her well. Around her neck she wore a double string of pearls, which seemed to enhance her neckline, and colour of her skin.

The 'Medium' closed her eyes, put her hand to her forehead, as if she was thinking hard, or had a headache. She opened her eyes, her hand came down onto the altar part in front of her, and picked up a glass of water which had been placed there for her before the service had started, she took a sip, then focused her eyes back onto him. She closed her eyes again for a moment then opened them. "I have someone here. They are building up in my mind's eye.... It's a lady,.....a lady of about forty five.

Closing her eyes again she leaned slightly to her left, and seemed to be listening with her right ear with intense concentration. "Oh, I see my dear. She says she is showing herself to me as she would have looked before she was ill with lung cancer, she says she lost a lot of weight prior to her passing, but insists she is fine now, and she feels no pain at all. She is also telling me she was fifty eight when she passed over to the other side of life....she also tells me it was some six years ago she passed over......hold on, I am getting thename of Peter, some thing about her son,.... I keep getting the name of Peter.

The woman in front of him, now seemed to concentrate with all her power, her lips were pursed tight, with furrowed lines across her fore head, as if she was trying to understand some one talking to her with difficulty, or as if she was a little hard of hearing. Then suddenly her eyes opened, and looking at him a smile on her lips, while at the same time her voice became soft and gentle.

"It's you! You are Peter, she has told me she is your mother, she tells me her name is Peggy, but every one in the family had a pet name for her, every one called her 'Aggie', am I right love".

Peter was almost speechless, and could only nod his head and answer "Yes" With a lump in his throat. "She is now telling me you are the last of the family left on the earth plain, every one else is there with her, your father was his name John or Jim, I could not catch the name clearly, also she says something about a Mac or Max, and all of your other relatives". She seemed to become thoughtful for a moment, as though she wanted to say something specific to do with him, but half decided it may not be for the best at that moment, instead she asked. "Are you in a developement circle at the moment?"

"No....., well I am not sure what you mean, I have not been coming here very long."

"Well not to worry, I will speak to you after the service, and explain a few things to you. But for now, I have some messages from the other side from your mother. She is telling me now that the link has been made, and there is better communication between this world and the next for her. She is surprised, that the efforts they have tried from the spirit side of life, have finally succeeded in influencing you attending a meeting of this nature. As I say, she is surprised, but pleased you are here. One thing is, that for you to attend a church outside of christenings, marriages, and funerals, has been a complete reversal of your attitude on religion. She had tried to come through on the other occasions you came here, but was unsuccessful."

Peter Jones, was listening to what this woman was saying to him, but not really taking in fully what was being said at that moment, he was still amongst other things, taking in what she had told him about 'Max' being with his mother. Max...,Max was his younger brother, he had died in the hospital, he had been seven years old, just two years younger than himself at the time, if he had lived he would now be twenty two, he had been knocked down in a road traffic accident while, coming home from school. The woman told him a few more things, small things, but when put together, made quite significant evidence that what she had told him could be the truth, and had half conceded the information he had received in all probability, could as he saw it, only have come from his late departed mother, although he was in truth still finding it hard to take in fully. Then, just as she finished off her messages from the other side, as those who regularly attended the services called them, and about to go to another person in the congregation, she suddenly turned back to him. "Oh! There's one more thing, your mother has just asked me to tell you that "Tramp" is there with with her as well. She helped him when he passed over, and he knew her right away, Dolly and tramp are with them most of the time....is Dolly another dog? No, She has just told me Dolly is a tabby cat, well she is telling me they can come and go as they please there, with nothing to hurt them, so don't be upset any more. There are lots of other dogs around, and they all need love and companionship, the same as tramp had, when the time is right, one of them will 'choose' you, and you will not feel any disloyalty to Tramp when that time comes. Remember love given freely, is always returned ten fold and is everlasting from any animal once they adopt you."

The last thing the woman had told him hit him like power from a thunder bolt. In a shaking, and choked voice he thanked her, while at the same time fighting hard to keep back the tears in his eyes, tears of mixed emotions, sorrow, but at the same time they were also tears of joy.

The emptiness, he had felt over the loss of 'Tramp', since his passing had been unbearable at times. He had been given Tramp, from a neighbour, when just a puppy of ten weeks old, he was only a cross bred mut as some would say, but as the years went by the medium sized brown and white shaggy coated dog endeared himself to everyone he came in contact with. Quite often, Peter and Tramp could be seen regularly out and about together in the mornings and evenings. He seemed to know when Peter was on his way home from work each evening, and would be laying down in the hallway waiting for the door to open, jump up to greet him, and nuzzle his pocket for the titbit he would always have there for him on his return. They had always been close but, but when his mother passed away, they became inseparable.

Tramp had almost reached his sixteenth birthday, there had been just six weeks more to go, and he would have made it.

Towards the end of his life Tramp had deteriorated rapidly, the 'vet' had done all that was possible to do for him, and relieved what he could in the way of pain. Where as he had been eager for his walks in the mornings and evenings, it became a struggle for him just to go out into the garden to do his business. His back legs became weaker with every passing day, until Peter had to lift and support him out of his basket, and carry him outside, inwardly Peter knew he did not have long, and really, he was being selfish but up until the last, he could not bring himself to do the obvious, though heart breaking, final act of love for him. It was a Saturday morning when he came down the stairs, carrying tramp down from his bedroom in his basket, he had made the decision, in the night watching his breathing becomemore laboured, that he would do the last, and kindest thing for him, and have the vet, him put to sleep to release him from any discomfort and pain he may be in. That morning even now, when he thought back, was one of the worst days in his life. He had never said any thing to anyone, but it compared on a par, with the time he had lost his parents.

He could remember vividly, phoning the vets surgery, and being answered by one of the assistants, and after explaining to her the reason he was calling, was told there would be an extra charge for treating the dog at home, which they called a, 'A call out charge'. He wanted to see Tramp pass as peacefully as possible in his own house with him, and in familiar surroundings. He agreed to pay the fee when the vet came.

He came back from the telephone ,and could see Tramp was panting heavily, he sat on the floor next to him, tidied the blanket, and talked to him, he was sure old tramp understood every word he spoke to him. Picking up Tramp's water dish he put it near his mouth, and gently flicked water into his mouth. Tramp's tongue curled around his mouth, looked at Peter, a paw came came up slowly, a look of love and thanks from man and dog was exchanged, that could only be understood, by an animal and ananimal lover. It was only moments later Tramp had given a sigh, then taken a deep breath, exhaled it, and was gone. Peter got up composed himself, telephoned the surgery, to let them know the vet would not be needed and that Tramp had died just a few moments before, put the phone down, went back to where he lay, knelt down lifted Tramps head in his arms then broke down, tears streaming from his eyes sobbing his heart out. He had buried him in the garden, and planted a lilac sapling near the spot where he lay. That had been six months before, but was still as vivid in his memory as if it had happened only the day before.

CHAPTER 3

All three men stood looking at the billowing powdery dust which was surrounding the rig in the still hot air, it hung around the area like a large pinkish red cloud at sunset, completely covering the 'A' frame, part of the rig, leaving the engine end of the rig just visible.

"What the hell has happened Burt, has the cable snapped or what?"

"I Don't know for sure. There was a terrific crash and the rig began to lurch and tilt as if it had a life of it's own, the next thing I saw Ray moving as if lightning was chasing him, I'v never seen anyone move so fast in all my life from a standing start." He turned to face Ray, and the look on his workmates face made Burt burst into laughter.

"What was it Ray? Did you see what happened?"

"Don't know for sure Jack, all I saw was the ground open up in front of me and all the equipment falling down it, and making a hell of a noise at the same time, with the rig shaking and tilting side to side, I thought the whole lot was about to go down, rig and all, I just moved out of the way before I went down with it."

Burts laughter helped to take the nervous tension out of the situation, as all three walked towards the rig after the dust had settled down and made the area around the "A" frame clear enough to see if they could see if there was any damage done to the rig it's self.

They approached the site of the hole immediately in front of the "A" frame, although the the clay dust was still blowing around the the hole, they could see it was about five feet in diameter, with one of the "A" frame supports dangerously near the edge.

"How the hell has that happened, and how safe is it to walk around the edge of the hole and rig?" Jack was concerned for their safety and, and the precarious position of the rig, there was still sounds coming from the hole, as lumps of hard clay were still falling away from the sides.

"There's only one way to find out and that is to have a look and see. Have you still got the length of rope you usually carry in the back of your landrover Jack? If you have we could use the safety harness out of the tool chest, and if we tie one end of the rope to one of the vehicles, I will wear the harness, and walk to the edge."

"Are you sure about that Ray?"

"Of course I am, if the edge does collapse the rope will hold me, won't it?"

"What's it like there Ray? Can you see any of the equipment?"

Ray was at that moment on his hands and knees, his head leaning out as far as was possible over the open hole looking into it's depth.

"I can't see a thing, it's still to dusty and dark down there to see very far down. But the ground around the hole seems solid enough and, not giving away or anything, I think it's safe enough for you to come over and have a look. Gingerly he rose to his feet, his left arm reached for the nearby "A" frame support, after steadying himself he gave a couple of jumps around the edge of the hole. "Yes it's safe enough, you can come over and have a look for yourselves. Look". He again jumped up and down, just to prove a point.

After joining Ray and sussing out the situation as best they could, all three decided it was imperative they moved the rig, in case any more ground did collapse. Twenty five or thirty minutes later this had been done, and the rig was a safe distance away from the hole, having played out the cable to almost it's full extent, so as to enable them to winch what ever they could salvage from the hole from a safer distance. Eventually after a long period of trial and error they had managed to winch up to the surface the cruciform and sinker weight, dragging it well away from the open hole. But the steel liners were still down there. They were costly items, Jack had told his two workers there would be a "backhander" for them if they could get them out.

That was all the incentive Burt needed but, suggested it would need all three of them to accomplish it, plus, they would need more tools than were on the site at the present time. It was now beginning to get late in the afternoon, and at Jacks suggestion they all agreed to go to his home to pick up the tools they thought would be necessary to recover the liners from the depth they were at.

One and a half hours later they returned to the rig site. Burt had telephoned his wife to inform her of the situation and, how he thought they would be involved in the recovery of the liners for perhaps a couple of hours or more, making it later for his return home than usual.

Jack had explained the situation to his wife 'Ruth' on their arrival, and explaining they would have to put their trip to the coast on hold for the present time but, if they managed to recover the liners early enough, they could then carry on with their planned trip, just a little later than originally anticipated, or at the worse, early the following day. For her part, although disappointed with the news, she suggested perhaps it may be a good idea if she made up a snack and a pot of tea for them before they returned to the site. A suggestion that was welcomed by all three men, as they went out into the garage to sort out the equipment which would be needed.

On their arrival back onto the site, the dust had settled and the hole was clear but, when they peered into it, they could not see any of the equipment as visibility was poor due to the darkness and depth of the hole.

Covering the top of the hole with the tarpaulin sheet they used to cover the engine of the rig with, when it was not in use, they shone a beam from powerful torch down to see if the liners could be seen, and how deep the hole actually was.

After their eyes were able to focus properly from sunlight to the light of the torch beam they could see the bottom, and just about make out the top of the drill head and part of the liner screwed into it.

"Well" Ray spoke, the sound of resignation in his voice. "Somebody has got to go down there, there is no way, we can fix the recovery tool to the head from up here, is there! and, we don't know the extent of damage there might be to the linings below the well head, with all the sounds we heard when the collapse happened there could be damage to the liners below the well head, and if there is, it will have to be a case of lashing and tying the sections one by one to retrieve them".

"He's right Jack, have you any ideas as to how the safest way it can be done? I think Ray has just volunteered for the job".

Jack was silent, for a moment, his mind working out how the task before them could be safely accomplished, then turning to Ray suggested an idea he had formed in his mind."Use the harness again, and lower you down with the rope tied to the winch cable on the back of my 'Landrover'. What do you think Ray?"

"That's O.K. by me" Ray spoke with confidence, but was feeling he had wished he had kept his mouth shut, and answered, just so as he would not lose face.

Burt turned to his drilling partner, and with a friendly pat on the back suggested it might be wise to put his overalls and hard hat on, before going below.

Everything had gone like clockwork. Ray had been lowered the way Jack had suggested, except for a few small knobs of hard clay hitting him on the shoulders and hard hat with no harm done, he had fixed the recovery tool to the well head, and shone the torch he had carried with him, past his dangling feet to see if the liners were still in one piece and joined together, they seemed to be but he was unsure, due to the angle they seemed to be standing against the side of the hole, and while he was hanging there it was difficult to manoeuvre himself enough to get a better look below his legs while holding and directing the torch beam at the same time. He gave Burt a shout, for Jack to start to winch him up to the surface, and thought no matter what may happen they would have to take the risk that they were all together and try raising them once he was back on the surface.

As it happened they were not able to raise them all up in one go, as they were being raised there was a grinding sound and then a loud clattering, just as the first of the three metre sections had cleared the surface of the hole, both Burt and Ray saw at the same time the part of the second section where the liners were joined was fractured. The weight of the rest below the fractured joint caused the fracture to widen.

As they saw the problem both men tried to attach a rope for support beneath the tear to hold it long enough to separate the top sections, but it was to no avail, suddenly the second section had torn away and dropped down the hole, with the lower sections of liners with it.

Again there was the sound of clattering and crashing, as the rig had been brought back and set up over the hole with railway sleepers supporting the the 'A' frame uprights and the ground around the hole, the first section hung swinging suspended in the air by the cable. Even though the rig engine was on, the sounds the liners made as they fell seemed louder than anything they had experienced on the job before.

The rig was switched off, the three returned to the hole in the ground, a small eddy of dust hung around the top of the ground and gently blew at right angles from where they stood.

"Shit! It had to happen, didn't it! Why the first two sections? Why couldn't it have happened on the last two instead? It seems that this just isn't our day."As Burt finished his outburst he reached over to swing the hanging liner away from the hole, Ray reached over at the same time to assist him, from below them there was the sound of metal as the liners were still moving, probably the last movements as they settled at the bottom of the hole, as they listened Jack had a sinking feeling in the pit of his stomach, wondering how much more damage to the liners had been done now, due to the second fall to the bottom of the hole. All three agreed the initial fracture must had happened as the liners hit the bottom of the hole when the initial cave in had occurred, the lower cases had hit the bottom sending all the stress of the impact travelling up to the very top section."Well with the one we have here, that leaves eight still down there, and it won't be easy to recover them as we first thought will it?" Jack turned to Ray.

"How do you feel about going down there on the rope for a second time?. Still have the bottle for it, or would you rather one of us took a turn?"

"Yea! No problem the sides are solid enough, there were only a few lumps which came loose, and I should think that most of what was going to fall will have already come away from the sides by now, what with all the bumping and suchlike as we pulled the liners up before they came apart".

Burt was about to add he would be willing to go down, if Ray did not want to go but, was more than a little relieved when Ray had answered that he did not mind going down again, so he said nothing except, for Ray not to take any chances while he went down again and, any sign of trouble he should signal with the torch should he start to become uncomfortable about the situation in any way.

As Ray reached the bottom of the hole, he immediately understood why it was that he had not been able to see the bottom of the hole clearly the first time he had hung on the rope in the harness. It was because he could only see part of the scene he could now see, the clay had fallen through a section of rock the chisel with it's double sinker weight attached had broken through, and with the aid of his torch saw a large section the size of a family saloon car had fallen into what seemed to be an old abandoned mine tunnel of quite wide proportions. What he had initially thought was the bottom, was in fact the fallen spoil of clay and large boulder sized chunk of rock, which had landed in a heap in the now visible mine tunnel, not realizing there was a mine passage below him he had taken the heap of spoil for the bottom of the hole.

Burt was laying flat on his stomach peering down below him, waiting for Ray to signal with three quick flashes of the torch light, to let him know he had reached the bottom, and to let Jack know to stop any more cable and rope playing out. When suddenly he saw the continuous beam of light disappear. His first thought was the torch had gone out, and being unaware of the situation of the tunnel began to get a little concerned for the safety of his friend below him. He shouted down to where his friend had gone, asking if every thing was well but no reply came back. Cupping his hands together he bellowed as loud as he could, but still there was no reply from Ray.

Jack seeing Burt seemingly in a panic over something stopped the decent of the cable, and putting the winch out of gear, he then hurried over to where Burt lay.

"What's the matter Burt has something happened to him down there?"
"I don't know, the bloody light went out just now and I can't get any reply back when I shout down there to him".

Both men waited on the surface, and shouting down at intervals, watched and, hoped to see the torch light come back on, Burt's concern for his partner Ray, was showing by now, in his face and actions. He turned to Jack.

"This is no good Jack, while we are both up here he could be in real trouble and in need of help really bad". The look of concern had now become etched onto his face, causing a nervous twitch at the corner of his mouth while at the same time his tongue poked through the gap in his teeth, as had always happened when he became concerned over something which was bothering him.

He reached over to the winch cable and pulled it towards him as he did so, there seemed to be no weight on the end of it, it swung towards him with ease. "Oh! shit! Where is he? What's happened now. There's no weight on the end of the cable. Well this is no good, We have to do something". He got up, walked a few paces turned, and then went back to the hole, to have another last look, hoping to see the light of the torch beam, but saw only the darkness that was there moments before. Turning he started walking towards the vehicle.
"I'll put my overalls on, you start pulling the cable up, and put one of the plastic bag ties at head level before you do so, you can tell how far to lower me when I am harnessed".

* * * * * * * * * *

Meanwhile down at the bottom, Ray had moved to the side of the spoil heap, and had taken the harness off, so as to give him the ability to crawl backwards down the large rock and spoil heap, to see exactly what it was he had discovered below ground.

When he felt his feet step onto the firmness of the passage floor and moved away from the large rock and scattered lumps of clay. As he shone the torch beam around him, he could see that the fall was about twenty five metres or so from what looked to be an entrance to what seemed to be a cavern of sorts, he shone the torch beam directly from where he stood and moved towards it, as he did so he saw part of the passage he was in had been tunnelled by hand, the tool marks on one side of the passage made it evident that there was originally a small natural passageway that some time in the past had been widened considerably. He recalled how as a child he had heard tales of the past, of how contraband had been smuggled from Bridgwater docks to Taunton, and beyond, using various routs, such as the river Parrot, and Tone and then onto the highways at discrete points along the way. This place he thought, could well be one of the holding and distribution places smugglers of the past had used.

He walked to the opening he had seen from the passage, the beam from his torch aimed straight in front of him as he came to the opening the ground sloped down at an angle of about forty five degrees, and formed a ramp downwards in front of him. On each side of the entrance were naturally formed walls which rose to the height of two double decked busses, one on top of the other. The ceiling was flat and level. He could hear, nothing, the silence was eerie, he had been in caves before but this one felt different, there felt no sense of dampness one usually associated with caves and caverns. No sign of stalagmites or stalactites. Aiming his torch at the side walls and ceiling, he could see they were smooth, not shaped with tools smooth, but a natural smoothness, as if in a time period long ago, the whole of a large portion of rock had just sunk and left the unnaturally even and smooth sight he now saw before him.

Moving down the ramp into the chamber, while at the same time shining the torch beam all around him, he caught sight of something in the beam which first startled him and, then made him curious, for right in front and at the far end of the cavern was a long stone object, he went forward to take a closer look but, began to feel uncomfortable about the place, a cold shiver travelled quickly up his back, making a prickly sensation, which made him shudder involuntarily.

He then decided it might be better to make his way back to where the breakthrough and, fall-in had occurred. Turning around he saw he had travelled about thirty five metres into the chamber and had not reached halfway to the far end where the stone object was situated. As he walked the shaft of light from his torch hit the side wall at an angle and, as it did a dark triangular shape seemed to appear there. At first he was taken aback due to the distortion which occurred as he moved the torch back and forth in his hand. His heart seemed to stop a beat, a flush of heat surged around his chest, then his brain told him what he had seen, as it did he gave a shrug to and a half smile to try to convince himself he had not been frightened for the short time the event had happened. "Another doorway, passageway, whatever, an entrance anyway". He thought to himself. Then he realized at once why he had walked by, for some reason the entrance was made at an angle and it was only when he had walked back shining his torch back where he had come from a recess in the wall could be seen, it was as if the part of the wall had split and formed a triangular arch, for a moment he took a stride towards it but decided he had better return to the entrance where he had come in.

Hurriedly he made his way back to the bottom of the fall-in, as he neared it a tenseness he had while in the cavern on his own seemed to leave him the nearer he came to it. As he reached it he saw the linings had split in two or three places, and partially buried but, with a bit of effort knew they could be repaired, and used again, once they could get them to the surface. As he stood contemplating which would be the best way they could retrieve them there was a noise from above him looking up he saw Burt his head hanging over the side of the hole shouting something down to him, and waving his arms around.

Eventually after scrambling up the fallen lump of rock and clay, he reached the top of the heap, and only realized then, the harness was not where he had left it hanging. While Burt was yelling down to him, asking if he was all right. It felt strange to hear him after the complete silence of the tunnel and cave he had just returned from. The harness was lowered to him and he returned to the surface, only to receive a right barracking from both men, after explaining to him how they had been so concerned about his safety after seeing the torch beam disappear, and no answer from him when they had been shouting to him.

After apologizing for his thoughtless action, he began to tell them what he had found below them.

"We'll have a look around down there after we get the rest of the gear up here. What do you say Jack?" Burt did not relish going down there, but had to admit he was curious after hearing what Ray had described to them both, the tunnel, cavern and arched entrance within it, and not least the large stone object he had described to them.

Ray had ventured his initial theory that it could well be something to do with the smuggling that he had heard of, which he had heard tell was pretty well organized in the early eighteen hundreds. Burt had agreed he thought it may be possible he was right, he also as a young boy had heard of the smugglers activities in the region. Maybe, just maybe, he thought there might be something in the tales he had heard as a child, and it could be Ray had indeed stumbled on one hidden and forgotten hide-out.

CHAPTER 4

Psychic Cold

Peter Jones had spoken to the medium that evening those years before and had been told if he continued to attend the meetings on a regular basis, there would probably be an opportunity to sit in an open circle and learn a lot more about the psychic and spirit world, he had somehow been influenced to attend the meeting that evening, as he had since the first time attending them. She also told him, she did not know the reason why he had been so influenced, but was sure it was more than just to receive the messages from his mother. She also felt that the amount of information and the clarity of it was the result of the work on the other side, and not solely due to her ability as a medium and, sensed in some way there was quite an importance placed on the communication that evening, she rarely had such accurate information to impart to a person in a church congregation. Mostly she had always been on a one to one basis with a sitter to be so accurate, with the different vibrations of a packed congregation, it was, to say the least unusual. More than that she did not know, and could only advise him that when the opportunity came for the chance to sit in an open circle to take it, and see where it might lead him, but always remember, if he did carry on with her suggestion, developing gifts of psychic ability, and spiritual progression is not an easy task, but the rewards in the end are well worth the patience, dedication, and hard work involved. She ended the talk to him by saying that if he remembered that any gift or gifts that he may develop should be used for the benefit of others, such as healing, and perhaps even proof of 'The Here After' the rewards would be ten fold but not always in the material sense.

There was an open circle running at that present time, which he decided to attend, still with an open mind, but the longer he attended the more his attitude changed, and began thinking there was, 'indeed' more to what most of those attending had already believed, and that there was only one truth, but as always there had always been more than one road to whatever that truth was.

But, this road seemed to suit him more than any he had known before. He began to like the personalities of those of a like mind to his own.

He had been attending the open circle for approximately seven weeks, when he had been approached by a couple attending the same church as himself. He had come to know them quite well through the church and open circle. They told him they were going to try to reopen a closed circle which they had belonged to for some years, but due to the main medium's husband being taken ill for a period of four months they had to close it because there was no one who felt competent to run it without her. He was now well again and they asked her if she would be willing to start the circle up again, if, her husbands health was up to it. She had immediately agreed to their request. But they had found out that due to the fact of new commitments, on the same evening they would hold the circle, some of the original members could not attend, and the meeting could not be held on any other evening. As he went to the same church, and open circle as themselves and, seemed quite serious on learning, they thought they would ask him if he would like to attend when it started, also, they told him some of the other people who attended the open circle suggested he might be interested, so they had made the offer for him to join. After some thought on the matter he had decided to accept, when he next saw the person the following Sunday.

There were eight others in the circle, held and run in the house of the older medium, a Mrs. Chandley who had been in the spiritualist movement for over fifty years, and had taken an active part for forty of them. When younger she had travelled all over the Southwest giving demonstrations of clairvoyance and had built up a tremendous reputation in her earlier years for accuracy in communication with the spirit word.

Peter who had expected to see a round table, as was nearly always portrayed in films of seances ect; was surprised to walk into a medium sized sitting room with chairs arranged in a circle and, a glass of water placed by the side of each chair, with a large glass bowl in the centre on the floor filled with water.

He was also pleased to find there were four others in the same position as himself there, and sitting in a closed circle for their first time.

Before starting the development proceedings everyone talked for a while getting to know each other, and as luck would have it they all knew each other by sight from the church meetings they attended, even though it was just, by sight, they came quickly together as a friendly group. The first evening went off quite uneventful, they sat down for a period of meditation, during which someone went into a trance and spoke to them for about a quarter of an hour. While this was happening Peter was unsure if the person who was supposedly speaking to them through one of the sitters of the original circle was genuine, or the sitter was somehow faking the procedure himself, and was just wanting to be the centre of the scene there. He decided as he had no real knowledge of what was genuine and, what was not, he would have to take what had happened as genuine, but kept an open mind just the same.

The content of the talk was much the same as could be heard in a Sunday service, and could be heard from any minister of the cloth, of any denomination. With the largest emphasis on love to each other, the state of the world and what could be done to put things right. The evening over he was not too impressed on the whole, but decided that it was his first time and maybe he should not be to judgmental of the evening, but he did enjoy the conversation afterwards with the others, with tea and biscuits. There was a nominal charge of one pound each, for the refreshments and heating, and other expenses pertaining to the circle night.

Peter Jones attended the weekly meetings regularly, and as time went on began to feel some benefit from them, more so on his outlook on life rather than anything to do with psychic progression, although, some of the others there were beginning to do quite well in that field and better he thought than he was, one couple who had started the same evening as himself, a husband and wife were becoming very good at giving clairvoyance, and had some small success at hands on healing after church services on Sundays when there would be quite a few others practising the 'Healing gift'. Another sitter had the beginnings of a 'psychic artist' without having had any formal training whatsoever in the art field. Another seemed to produce poetry and automatic writing at the drop of a hat, which to say the least was very profound in content, two others had dropped out, probably due he thought, to the fact that things were not happening for them quickly enough, and in the way they had hoped and expected. Leaving Peter and a young widow of his own age, not doing very well at all in the things that they thought to be the object of going to the development circle for, besides inner fulfilment.

He had tried healing but, no one seemed to benefit from it that he could see, and was beginning to think that anything in the healing or clairvoyance field was not going to work with him, and he in turn started to become disheartened and almost ready to call it a day himself. It was only the fact that he was becoming friendly with the young widow there, which kept him attending the circle.

Eventually he mentioned what had been going through his mind to her, and when she had replied that she had been feeling the same about things herself but, had gained so much in the way of support, from what she now believed, that she would have felt uncomfortable to leave the circle, just because things were not happening as quickly as she wanted, she just felt that in time there would be something happen that would lead her onto what ever it was she was supposed to do, and that perhaps one of the things she was being taught by spirit was patience. It was as she had finished speaking the word "patience" the memory of the mediums words returned to him. "Hard work and patience!"

It was barely more than a couple of weeks later while in church a medium who had been taking the service came to him in the demonstration part of the service and told him she could see a red Indian guide standing next to him, and that he was saying he was his 'Door keeper' and for her to tell him that he was understanding the doubt that had been going through his mind about his progression spiritually and in the psychic field, and was saying he must be patient for a little while longer, because those in spirit had been working along with him for quite some time now and there would be just a little more time needed for him to be capable of doing what those in the spirit world had been working towards. To show faith in him he was going to tell the medium his name (the guides) and asked her to write it down and to place it in a sealed envelope, and leave it with someone in authority in the church, and in time he would give his name while in circle, then he must check the envelope and see the name given is the same, and the way it would be done would leave him in no doubt of the authenticity of the present communication.

A few weeks later found Peter sat relaxed in a chair in the circle, with the others. The opening prayer had been said asking for the usual things, such as peace, enlightenment, and healing for those in need, and finally protection from harm for those sitting, from any evil or dangerous influence that evening.

Mrs. Chanley was sitting opposite Peter nearest to the sitting room door, to keep her eyes on the proceedings. Because of her experience and knowledge of things that can happen during a development circle. Also, that she was clairvoyant and clairaudiant, was a large contributing factor which made everyone there feel safe, relaxed and at ease. Nothing could harm them with out her sensitivity, seeing or hearing anything harmful to them entering the circle, or near the vicinity of it, should anything happen, she would detect it and know how to dispel it, and would then close the circle for the rest of the evening.

Peter, eyes closed, breathing at a soft and even pace was going through the stages of relaxing to meditate. Roughly ten minutes had passed, when he felt or sensed, without any fear at all, (although, the hair at the back of his neck seemed to stand up slightly) there was someone behind him, it was just a feeling that came over him, without any way he could explain it. As it was happening he felt his legs begin to grow, heavy from his feet and ankles spreading to his knees, the heaviness began to become more intense, then it seemed to become a more of a paralysis of his body, creeping up until it reached just below his chin, he tried to move his legs and arms but, no matter how he tried he could not budge them at all, it was as if there was an unexplainable weight surrounding the whole of his body, which was keeping him in the same position he was sitting in. He did start to become a little frightened, and tried to muster every ounce of concentrated effort, in one last attempt to move but it was to no avail, he could do nothing about it, but accept the condition.

He was not in a panic of any sort, but, was a little concerned at what was happening, with no means of stopping it.

The next thing was a coldness, again starting from his feet and gradually following the progress of the earlier condition, until he could feel the cold had reached his solar plexus and then stopped. He slowly opened his eyes, and looked across to where Mrs. Chanley was sitting, and she was looking at him, and seemed to know what was happening, and looked quite unconcerned, motioning with her eyes, and with a smile and a nod of her head, conveyed to him every thing was as it should be and he should not worry.

After that he closed his eyes and was feeling quite unconcerned for himself, confident by Mrs. Chanley's assurance the situation was well under control. He started to relax again and as he did so there was in his minds eye, and right in front of him a green hexagonal disc about the same size as a fifty pence piece which seemed to start rotating in front of him about the height of his forehead, as he concentrated on it, it seemed to draw him and, he seemed to follow it, as he did so it grew larger and larger until it seemed he went into it, or it surrounded him, he felt comfortable as if he was enveloped in warm soft velvet blanket.

Mrs. Chandley as was her roll in the circle kept a close watch on Peter, waiting for signs of what she knew would start to happen next. As they started she gently and quietly leaned over and touched the two people each side of her and, motioned them to do the same to the person on their left or right to bring them out of meditation, everyone immediately saw as they looked around the circle and focused their eyes on where Peter was sitting, what they later described, as a smoky like substance emanating from his nose, mouth, and solar plexus, swirling across the floor until it reached about waist high, the red and dim meditation light gave a luminous translucent surreal effect to the phenomenon, and as they watched, they could at the same time smell a musky perfumed odour, which as time passed, seemed to change from a heavy to a light flower scented fragrance. The swirling 'smoke' continued for some thirty minutes and then began to disappear. But during the time it was at it's maximum density small faces could be by everyone in the room manifesting within it, and at one point Mrs. Chanley seemed to be listening intently.

"Well everyone, we have all, except Peter been privileged to have and see our first Phychic manifestation together, and, I have been given, instructions by Peters guide who has told me his name is 'Two Bears', and who is a north American Indian, those in spirit have conveyed to me they have hopes with the use, and, permission of Peter to progress along similar lines to Join our circle to advance and help us in our spiritual progression, and help with the development of our gifts even more."

After the the development circle had finished, Mrs. Chandley had asked Peter to stay behind for a short while telling him she wanted to speak to him on what had actually happened that night, and to tell him some things his guide had wanted him to know.

They both sat in her kitchen at the table face to face, she had made a cup of tea for the both of them as he took the first sip from his cup she began to speak.

"Your guide has given you his name just as he promised, and in circle in such a way to dispel any doubts, as he also promised. "He has told me the way they engineered tonight's proceedings had taken time, mostly due to you having to progress spiritually, and that it had been just the start of their ultimate goal. After tonight when you were told by the others what had happened while you were in a trance state, and not as you had first thought asleep." She gave a quiet laugh, as she saw the embarrassed look on his face. Don't worry it happens quite often in that way the first time. But, from now on you will know when anything like it is happening again, believe me. He has said that the experience we have all had tonight is just the start of a deeper understanding of spiritual awareness, he has been with you ever since and, before you entered your present life on this earth plain. From now on he wants you to meditate regularly every day on your own at the same time if possible, so it will produce an awareness, and conditions for you both to work together, to convince people with absolute proof that there is life on other plains of existence after death in this life, and by various ways to prepare others for that journey, without fear, and with knowledge, that the way one lives now determines the level at which plain of existence we go to after this life." Peter Jones's life changed completely from that night.

CHAPTER 5

The Altar

The men returned to the site early the next morning. With the use of scaffold tubing, they built a frame, above the hole and attached a pulley wheel in the centre of it. Then by using a long length of cable, and the winch from the Landrover made an improvised bosun's chair lift, with a length of sawn off scaffold plank as the seat.

Using Burts knowledge, and a little knowhow of electrics they used a lift switch from the tail lift off of a lorry, with a roll of electric cable, which they left hanging loose, so as to have control of the seat and rate of decent as they lowered themselves below the ground, it worked fine for both lowering and raising the chair.

Ray had managed to recover the liners, by attaching the recovery tool down below the hole, they were now back on the surface, in all it had taken a little over three hours, with the result after inspecting the liners recovered, they found the damage was not as bad as it first seemed and all could be repaired with little problem.

A short time after that they were all down in the passage which led to the cavern Ray had told the of. When they reached the cavern, they lit four camping gas lamps and placed two of them around the area near where the ramp finished, the other two were placed strategically towards the middle of the cavern.

After this had been done they could look around and see everything in a lot more detail, Ray had, described to them what he had seen there when he had first entered the cavern, but now with the place illuminated more than he had been able the first time with just the light from the torch he could see at once the place was far larger than he had first realized. All three were silent, and still because they were unsure of what they should do next.

Burt was the first to move and started walking towards the stone block, the others followed. As they came nearer to it they all shone their torches upon it.

"What do you think it is Jack, it looks to be like an old sort of coffin, or something of that nature at anyway?" Burt began to walk faster as he came nearer to it.

"It's a lot darker coloured stone than the granite around us, It must have been transported here from elsewhere". When they had all reached it they stood around wondering how it came to be there, and were surprised at the dimensions of it as they stood next to it, it was about four and a half metres in length, by two and a half wide and two and a half in height.

As they looked they saw carved into the top, was a five pointed star pentacle, and from each point on the star there were channels that ran to the edge of the smooth flat topped surface, from each of the star points, starting at a depth of half a centimetre and finishing at the edge of the block at a depth of about three. Where each groove finished at the edge of the block, below it was a recess of about ten centimetres shaped in a half circle.

"What do you make of it Burt? Look at the sides of the thing, there are all kinds of writing here, I have not seen anything like it before, have you in your travels abroad?"

"I can't say for sure, but some of it reminds me of Hebrew, but, to be honest, I am not sure I know it is nothing like the old Egyptian, although, there are some drawings, but I can't make out what they could be about, or the meaning of them." "How about you Ray? Have you seen anything like this before or not."

"It's definitely not Egyptian. I have some plates and other souvenirs I brought back last year when I went on holiday to Cairo, there's nothing like that on them and that's for sure."

The three of them stood in silence looking at the block, each had their own thought's as to what it was before them, and each unwilling to voice them at that time. They had all looked at it, and inwardly had come to the conclusion it was some kind of altar. How long it had been there they could not guess, or who would have used it, they could only come to one conclusion and that was, they all felt uncomfortable near it.

Moving away they decided to go back to the tunnel and see if there was another entrance to the cave, by following the tunnel wherever it went. After walking past the place where the fall in had happened, for about thirty five metres they could see there had been a roof cave-in, sometime in the past, and the cave must have remained hidden for a long time. Picking up a large rock Ray gave the part where the fall-in had happened a hit, the sound it made was as if the amount behind where they stood was as solid as the sides of the passage. He looked at the other two. "I don't think we will get much progress if we tried to go any further clearing what must be laying behind that lot do you?"

They had returned to where Ray had seen the partially concealed archway on his first visit, the entrance was only wide enough for one person to enter at a time, until one was fifteen or twenty metres into a kind of low passageway and then it began to widen while at the same time the headroom increased to about ten feet giving ample room enough to allow two abreast with ease. They continued walking until they came to an area of about ten by ten square feet, and as they did, there facing them were two large strongly built doors. One of which had large iron studs, with hinges to match, the other was exactly the same, but had a large iron grill door as well, which was fixed securely by a large locking device set into the wall.

"What the pigging hell have we got here?" Whispered Jack, more to himself than anyone else there.

"Could be something worth having behind that lot" Was Burt's excited whispered answer to Jacks statement.

Since entering the tunnel, and then being confronted by the doors in front of him, Ray was beginning to wonder, just, exactly what it was they had found there, it seemed to become more stranger by every passing minute.

They all moved forward and looked closely at the door without the iron grill. They saw that right in the centre there was what appeared to be a plaque, about a foot square or so, with more writing and symbols similar to what they had seen on the stone altar. Trying the door they found it would not budge, there was a door knob, but as they tried to turn it they found it would not budge either, even when all three put their shoulders against it, still it would not move.

Burt turned towards the other two, "Well there's nothing more for it, I'll go top-side and get the large crow bar."

"Hold on! Hold on now! Lets think about this first, maybe we had better stop where we are for the moment, and get somebody from the council, and tell them what we have found here."

Burt and Ray looked at him in silence, and then at each other, Burt was the first to speak.

"Bugger off Jack! Let's see what we have here first, before letting some asshole with authority from sticking their nose in here, once they get a whiff that there maybe something of value here, they will have us out of here and away from the site quicker than a dog can smell a 'bitch on heat' sharing the same basket in a wooden kennel. Then, the next thing you know the place will be crawling with archaeologist's, council brass, and police, then we will never know what the fuck they find. I say, sod em, let's see what's here first, before we say anything to anyone. What do you say Ray? Do you agree with me?"

"Too bloody right! Let's wait and see what we have behind the doors before we think of telling anyone what we have found down here." Answered Ray.

Jack was unsure what to do for the best, he knew what he should do in the eyes of the law, but his two workmen were also friends, and he did not want to go against them, and cause ill feelings between them now, or for the future.

"Come on Jack, it's all right for you, your not short of a bob or two. Let's have a fag and talk it over." Burt took out a packet of 'Senior Service' and offered the packet to the other two.

After a couple of puffs of the cigarette he had taken from the pack his he eventually came up with a solution which he thought might keep the other two satisfied.

"O.K.! We will carry on, but by rights we should inform an official of some kind but, it's not only

18

that. I don't like the feel of this place, what with doors with bars on the outside of them, and studs, and on top of that, a bloody great lump of rock with carvings, which, no matter what way you look at it, could only be some kind of an altar, it's a little more than strange, or unusual to say the least." He looked at the studded door with the plaque they were standing in front of. "And what should we be making of all the strange writings and suchlike connected with this place".
"I must admit I don't get a good feeling about everything we have found here myself." Ray remarked."Oh Shit! You guys have been staying up to late at night watching to many horror movies. Whatever has been going on here, happened a long time ago. Lets face it, it's just an empty cave now, even the writing and symbols we have seen don't make any sense to us, and the way I see it, would'nt make any sense to anyone else these days, I think it's just some mumbo jumbo, that someone has dreamed up and, it's putting the shits up you, just as it was intended to have the same effect on anyone, who might have stumbled on the place any time before us. Don't forget when all that mumbo jumbo stuff was going on, the fear and superstition would have been all part of it, and if it was something to do with smuggling the ones in control over whatever it was they were up to, used it, I am sure to good effect to keep anyone who just might have stumbled onto the entrance of the place away in fear of what they might think they had found, think about it, what could be more of a deterent than fear and the atmosphere of the place back in those days of superstition with the fear of the unknown. Just look how you two have reacted! I think it's that simple. Even now, here you are in the later half of twentieth century acting with the superstition of centuries earlier. Come on! Get a grip of yourselves and lets see if there is anything worth having behind these doors."

A few minutes had gone by, Burt had returned to the surface to fetch the crowbar he had spoken of. When he returned he had also brought a hacksaw and a few blades, plus a fourteen pound sledge hammer.

While he had been gone, Jack and Ray had used the time to look around the area they were in more closely, with the hand torches, and on inspection saw that whoever had done the building and tunnelling had worked extremely hard. Everything had been done with the uttermost quality of workmanship, from the standard of work to the materials used.

"Whoever did this must have had a fair bit of dosh back in those days, whenever it was." Ray spoke aloud to himself.

"Yes, I think you could well be right. Look at the doors, they look as solid as the day they were put here, still as solid as rock. The wood does not seemed to have deteriorated at all. "Jack walked closer to the iron bars of the grill door and took hold of them in both hands and gave a tug, but there was not even a movement of them, even when he tried with all his strength, there was not the slightest give for all his effort, moving around he looked at the edge of the grill frame, and could see that they were somehow embedded into holes into solid rock and could only assume the spikes had been heated and then hammered home, making them fit while hot and soft, and then cooled securing the frame into the rock in a tight fit without any play what ever.

They saw there were two fire brand holders above the two doors, and above them on the ceiling were thick soot marks covering a large area indicating a long period of use.

"Which door shall we open first?" Burt inquired of the others.

"Take your pick, I would try the one without the iron grill bars myself, it looks the easiest of the two. I'll hold the crowbar in the door jamb, while you hit it Burt." Ray walked forward, bar in hand and forced it into the side of the door.

Opening the door took a lot more effort than any of them had expected, even with the five foot long and two inches thick bar to use.

Fifteen minutes later saw the door partially broken away from the sides, after creaking and groaning from the efforts, and work of all three.

"Keep the bar pushed in as far as you can keeping the door forced inwards, while I hit it as hard as I can with the sledge, it might give a little more then, well, enough for us to see inside the room at least."

Burt it seemed had taken charge of the proceedings, while the other two seemed happy enough about it, by carrying out the instructions as he gave them.

Drawing back the hammer as far back over his shoulder as he could, he swung it with as much force as he could muster, against the top, left hand side of the door, and about three inches above the hinges, there was a mighty crash as the hammer hit the wood, the door gave away suddenly, the weight of it as it as it did tore at the top hinges pulling them clear from their fixings, it then seemed to swivel tearing the lower hinges away in the same manner, while at the same time gave out a screeching groan. As this happened. Burt with the momentum of his swing and the sudden giving of the door, went crashing through, along with the falling door, and ended up sprawled headlong on the floor, in front of the other two, feeling a little foolish and embarrassed.

He got back onto his feet, and stood with the other two, sledgehammer hanging at his side, but still firmly gripped in his hand, he watched as the beams of torch light from his workmates torches flashed around the room they had just gained access to. Before they could enter inside the room, Burt had placed his hammer against the side of the now open doorway, bending over the door with the intention of picking it up and moveing it out of their path before entering the room itself. His hands gripped the top of the door and he attempted to lift it, but it just would not budge more than a couple of inches off of the floor."Bloody hell! Feel the weight of this sodding door! It must weigh a ton." Upon looking more closely he saw it was four inches thick and made of solid oak. "There's one thing for sure, they built it to last, what do you think something like this would cost to make today."

"You could'nt find the wood seasoned long enough anywhere to be able to make it." Jack retorted, humour evident in his voice."All right smart ass, let's see what we have in the room, besides some seasoned oak for sale, now the door is opened." Moving past the other two, now, with his torch in hand, Burt was the most eager of the three to look around the now opened room, he stopped after just a few steps.

"What the bloody hell is that?" His torch beam had picked out something on the wall, and he had immediately walked towards it."Look at this Jack? What do you think it is, and what is it made of?"

On the left hand side of the door a little way in was what appeared to be a large plaque. As all three shone their torches upon it they could see it was about two feet in height by approximately eighteen inches across. There was writing much the same as they had seen earlier on the stone 'altar', but in the centre was a figure of a human. As they looked the could see the writing or whatever it was, seemed to be inlaid, and stood proud on the plaque. It looked black in colour, and Burt surmised it could possibly be silver, the rest of the plaque with the exception of the figure standing proud and black as was the writing, was green and made of copper.

"What, or who, do you think 'He' is supposed to be Jack! any ideas? I have not seen anything like that in any history books at school, or any other time have you?" Ray had begun to feel more uncomfortable with every minute that passed, since they had entered the room.

As they walked deeper into the room they could smell a distinct musty odour, more associated with a dark damp cellar, and yet there was not a sign of dampness anywhere, that they could see.

Ray Hayman could not shake the uneasy feeling he had, since before they had entered the room, something was not right about it all, in what way he was unsure, but there was a nagging feeling he could not explain to the other two, or himself for that matter. "What" he thought to himself "was that thing they had seen on the wall?" He could not get it out of his mind.

Leaving the other two to wander around the room, he decided to return to the plaque to have a closer look, he felt sure in some way it might throw some light on what they had discovered so far. After he had returned, and looked at it more closely.

There was the writing surrounding the figure, but as he looked more closer he could see there were symbols they had not seen before on anything down there surrounding the writing, which until his closer look he had taken for a kind of border of the plaque itself, but could now see that it was not the case, it was obvious to him now the writing and symbols were all part of the plaque, and were both sectioned off with lines, similar to those he had seen in various newspapers, with diagrams of astrological charts, they were not the same but, yes, he thought there was a distinct similarity. Looking again at the centre of the plaque he could see it was indeed a figure, and somewhat human in appearance, but he was close enough now to distinguish the features of the head and face, and what he saw agitated him even more.

The figure, arms outstretched, holding what appeared to be a tree gnarled and twisted, with all manner of horrific beings, some humanoid, reptilian, and animal, all had partial human characteristics in one way or another. But to Ray they had one thing in common, it seemed to him as he looked at them they all belonged to something out of a nightmare.

The face of the figure was the most grotesque, partially human, but devoid of any expression other than to portray an inactive malice and capability of evil destruction that lay dormant, waiting to be revived.

"Come back over here, and take another look at this, you two, have a closer look." He shouted at them.

"What the matter now Ray? It's only a bit of bloody metal." Burt seemed to be getting fed up with him, he had returned with Jack and stood with an exasperated look on his face. "What are you on about now?"

Ray pointed to the plaque, "Take another look up closer, then tell me what you think."

Burt and Jack stood looking at it for a few moments, "What do you think Jack, it's pretty old by the look of it, I suppose it might be worth a few pounds or so to an antique dealer if it was cleaned up a bit?"

"I don't know, but I have heard somewhere or other, that cleaning anything of an antique nature can devalue it's worth quite a lot, if it is not done professionally, and if we can get it done, how are we going to explain where it came from."

"We could find a way around that somehow."

"How does that sound to you Ray? See! we have have got a bit of cash already for coming down here, what with a bit on the door, and this metal picture, and who knows what else we might find of value after we look around a bit more."

"No! you don't understand what I mean. Can't you feel anything about this place at all? Just look at the plaque and what it contains in the content of it."

"Oh! Bloody hell Ray! What's the matter with you? It's not about that writing again is it! I'v told you it's just a load of tripe and superstition, forget about feelings and all that bullshit. I told you before whoever it was had the place, and whatever they had it for, are long gone, dead and buried, and let's face it, when have you ever heard of the dead hurting anyone!"

"Oh yea! What about that 'Egyptian Pharaoh', do you know the one I mean? About how when they opened the tomb and, there was a warning on the entrance about disturbing the tomb, and how someone died because of a curse or something, right!"

"Oh come on, I can remember something about it, some guy was bitten by an insect or something, it went septic, and he died of blood poisoning, it could have happened to anyone, and if I remember right, that was back in the twenties, and before penicillin. The locals of that time made up some story about a curse, so they would not violate the tombs of those that were buried in them, just the same as I have been saying about this place, they used fear and superstition, and who knows perhaps there may yet be a person buried here, we have still got to look around down here some more." Burt thought to himself. Hey! Yes, that Carved block down here perhaps there is someone buried beneath it, and it is a headstone after all. Anyway, Jack! You must have heard that before. Go on, you tell him, I'm right aren't I?" He turned to Jack in the hope of support, but received only a gesture of an open arms and a half shrug of his shoulders. After a short while talking on the subject there was an eventual agreement, to carry on looking around the room they had gained access to.

"I'll carry on looking with you, but I still say we should bugger off out of here. I for one won't be happy until we are back on the surface, and that's for sure. Three beams of light from three torches penetrated the darkness of the subterranean room, and with the light from them they could see that it was roughly twenty feet wide, by thirty five in length, the height was roughly the same as the area outside where, where they saw the two doors facing them, The area also seemed a bit

21

confusing to them, the floor of the room from where they had entered, rose slightly, and seemed to reduce the size of the room visually, making it appear smaller than it actually was, walking slowly the light beams playing around in different directions, on the walls and recesses which tended to distorted their vision, as they tried to focus where their light beams fell. Then as their eyes adjusted to where they were, and the shadows began to take on form, they began to reveal tattered material hanging from iron hooks which had been hammered into the wall to their right. Suspended from the ceiling, was a chandelier of wood which resembled a wheel of a cart, with candle holders set into what would have been the rim. As they looked they could see there was still remnants of candles in them, which had been placed there by hands of someone unknown, long ago. All three said not a word, but kept playing their beams left and right of them, revealing some benches and tables, which were rough in appearance, but sound in construction, numbering sixteen in total, all were bare. The beam of Jacks torch revealed a small wooden table set against the wall opposite the tattered clothing they had already noticed. There was something on the top of it, that drew his attention, he walked towards it. Burt saw him move in it's direction and followed.

"What is it Jack?"

"There is something on that small table, I was just going to take a look to see what it is."

Burt said nothing but, followed him to it.

On reaching the table they saw there was a box about the size of a biscuit tin, Burt picked it up and saw it was made of wood and covered in a dark tanned waxed leather. Beside it stood a bulbous earthenware unglazed vessel, ten or so inches in height, with a long necked spout to it.

"These have to be worth something Jack!" As he spoke he picked up the vessel, and found it was quite heavy for it's size. He gave it a shake, it seemed empty.

"Could be! but have a look at this!" Jack had picked the box up and was holding it in his hands while he looked at it closely turning it over. He shook it while in the beam of Burt's torch.

"Does it feel like there is anything inside it?"

"There's no sound of anything rattling inside, but it feels heavy as if it is not empty, but I can't see a lid anywhere, he turned it over again in his hands.

"Here let me have a look!" Reaching over he took the box from Jack, and after looking at it carefully he saw what appeared to be two grooves along one of the sides. Placing the palm of his hand and pressing and pushing each way, he found a section moved along the grooves, until a click sounded releasing a lid which folded back, but was still attached to the now opened box, as the lid was fully opened two small metal pins that were hidden until the lid was fully opened dropped from the sides to form legs and hold the lid in line with the sides to make what seemed to be a small metal inset work surface. The inside of the box revealed eight small compartments, each with it's own lid, with small round button knob handles, which appeared to be made of bone, to lift them off with ease. After taking the lids off of a few of the compartments, he was disappointed to find a powder like substance of various colours and textures. Putting a pinch of some between his finger and thumb he sniffed to see if there was anything familiar in the smell, but could smell nothing at all.

"What do you think it is?"

"I don't know. could be something to do with cooking I maybe but, it seems too earthy to have anything to do with cooking of any kind."

They placed the objects they had been looking at back on the table where they had found them, then looked around the area where they were but, could find nothing more of interest to them, then decided to go back to where Ray was now standing, shining his torch beam directly ahead of him, towards the far end of the room. On seeing the others coming, he pointed with his free hand saying there's something at the far end of the room but, I can't make out what it is, but it looks quite large, from here."

All three converged on the spot Ray had picked out in the light beam of his torch, and saw what they had all taken for one large object, was in fact three large chests, similar to what 'seamen' of the eighteenth century may have used. The three men stood around them saying nothing, looking at each other and then back to the objects in front of them. Jack was the first to move, kneeling down in front of them he ran his hand along the surface of the nearest to him. "They are leather bound the same as the small box we were just looking at Burt, waxed in the same way as well."

"Take a look at them Ray! I'll bet that they are sea chests, and what we were saying at the beginning is right, this place 'was' used by smugglers, and this could be some of the gear they had stowed down here and had to leave here when the room caved in, look they even have the keys still in the locks". Burt excitedly pointed to the chest nearest them.

Ray was silent and still hesitant to admit he had been wrong about the feelings he had been getting about the place, even though it did look with the chests in front of them, Burt was probably right in what he had said before. Except for the writings, and symbols. "What about all the writing and such like we have seen here?"

Burt thought for a moment or two, then laughed, "Simple they are old style writing from abroad, like from old charts and stuff which, they had brought back and could not, or would not get rid of."

What about the altar or headstone thing then?"

"Copied from something they had seen abroad. When they were bored or had time on their hands, who knows? All that matters for the moment is there are these chests here, with keys, and they are waiting to be opened. So let's get on with it!"

All three chests were identical, three feet in height, two six in width, by four feet six in length. Each one was bound with metal straps, and identical to what could be seen in many a sea side museum, up and down the length and breadth of the British isles, and illustrated in children's treasure and pirate story books of the eighteenth century. They were all round topped, and covered in leather, which had been cured, tanned, then waxed to a shining, though cracked, aged perfection, which had resulted, no doubt, to the condition they had remained in for so long. Except for the dusty rust on the iron straps, there seemed little to show in the way of deterioration, and were in a remarkable state of preservation.

Kneeling down beside one of the chests, Jack tried the key in the lock but, found it stuck, perhaps he thought from a long time of unuse or possibly dirt or rust or both. Burt impatient had meanwhile tried another with the same result. Resorting to the age old 'fixing kick' to the side and below the keyhole, and then trying again, there was a sudden loud click as the key turned, and the chest was now unlocked.

Burt looked at the other two with him, with his hands on the lid of the chest gripped each corner nearest him, he began to lift, slowly the lid gave forth the sounds of groaning, as the movement fought against time and corrosion on the hinges, slowly the lid began to open with all the effort he was putting in, eventually it was open. Peering inside they could see the top was covered with a leather inner cover, fitting completely over the inside of the chest. The covering was fixed down tightly by four leather buckled straps, which were fastened at the rear of the chest. With fingers trembling with excitement, and hearts pounding with expectation, Burt and Jack began undoing the straps.

As the last buckle came loose and the straps came free, Burt drew the waxed leather covering from the top of the chest to reveal five sheets of rolled parchment, each tied with red ribbon and sealed with sealing wax, and as they carefully lifted them out of the chest they saw the tied, and waxed knot was stamped with a miniature impression of the figure and symbols they had seen on the plaque, as they had entered the room earlier. They carefully placed them on the floor away from them and out of harms way. As they were placing the last one on the floor Ray took it from Jack. "Here let me have a look at that" He looked at it for a few moments. "There you are it's that figure again. Now do you still say it's something they have brought back from abroad? Or is it something a lot more sinister? I say we should get out of here now! Before we get ourselves into something we will regret later."

The other two seemed not to hear him, so intent were they on finding out what more there was to be found in the opened chest. Burt reached into the chest and pulled out a bundle of what appeared to be clothing, and could see there was more beneath. As he continued to pull them out, the first was black in colour and felt soft, and of a velvet texture, there were more, numbering ten bundles in total, the colours being red, black, green, and dark brown. Each bundle held seven individual garments, not unlike a monks habit, and each was tied loosely with half inch gold coloured rope.

"It seems to be clothing of sorts, well preserved, but just bloody clothing." Burt's disappointment over the contents of the first chest was obvious to the other two there with him.

"Come on Burt! Not to worry there are still the other two chests yet. let's see what they hold before getting disappointed, Jack seemed to be taking every thing in his stride now, without thinking of what he had said earlier about informing the authorities.

Moving over to the next chest, and taking the same procedure as before, but with less time taken, the lid was opened and, the buckled covering undone, and when that was accomplished, the three stood peering down into the chest. "Bloody Nora! will you look at that lot". Chuckling, Burt reached down into the chest and brought out a plate, a dark grey in colour, handing his torch to Ray standing beside him, gave the plate a rub with his thumb, trying to see what it was made of. Then produced a penknife from his overall pocket, gave the plate a slight scrape on the edge. "What do you think it is made of? Silver or what?" Ray asked.

"I would say it's silver and, feel no doubt about it. Let's see what else we have in here."

"Look on the back of the plate to see if there is any assay marks there, it may give the date and silversmith's mark." Ray had been his quiet self up until the discovery of the contents of the second trunk had been revealed, but now even his interest had been aroused, and even he began to become exited which had already affected the other two and pushing his earlier fears for the moment to the back of his mind, Burt handed him the plate he had been looking at. "Here you have a look and see what you think old son."

Ray took it from him and looked at it, felt the cold scalloped edge on it. "Hey! did you notice there was a name on the outer edge of this plate. It says Jane Coulder."

Burt lifted another plate out of the chest and exclaimed. "Here's another one, saying James Coulder. Look they have all got names on, here's another with the name Mary Curtis, there must be sixty or seventy of them here they all seem to have names on them. They must be worth a mint, there's loads of stuff here." His head down into the chest he began to move things inside it around, as he did so there was a dull clattering, as metal bumped against metal.

"I have loads of things at this end as well. Loads of little bowls, goblets, candle sticks, they all seem to be made of the same metal as the plates you have there." Came Jacks voice amid the clattering Burt was causing, while Ray was playing the light beam from his torch around the surface of the chest revealing all the things they had spoken of. It was obvious that who ever had packed the chest had taken care to pack it as carefully as they could, to enable them to get the large amount of items in there.

While Ray was looking down through the neatly stacked piles of table ware and such like, he could see where the things had not been disturbed a long similar coloured metal box, the same as the metal that had covered and surrounded it. What's that below where your hand is?" He asked Jack, while pointing towards it with his free hand. Immediately Jack began to clear the things away from the top of the chest to enable him to get a better view of it and get access to it. Eventually it was within his grasp.

"What's that you have there?" Burt inquired of him as he tried to lift the box out.

"I don't know, but it's bloody heavy, whatever it is!"

As he began to lift it from the bottom of the chest, goblets and other metal objects began to clatter and clank together as the space vacated by the lifted object, was filled by the disturbed stacks falling sideways.

As Jack had almost got the box clear of the top of the chest, Burt reached over and caught hold of one end of the box and helped Jack clear the chest altogether. "Phew! there's some weight here all right Jack, you should have waited for me to help you, a rupture would be no good to you at this stage of events, you could have ended up dropping a 'bollock' as well as the box, and what good would that do any of us. As they laid it on the ground, next to the opened chest, they saw immediately it was in fact a replica of the stone altar in the large cavern. It had the star pentacle, and within the pentacle was engraved the same figure again they had seen on the wall, around the sides were the same as in the large altar, the writing and even the recesses were reproduced but, set in them were small bowls identical to some they had found in the chest moments before. The box measured approximately eighteen, by twenty four, inches and in depth about sixteen, and was made of solid silver, the engraving had been done by a master silversmith, that much they could tell by the detail, and except for the gruesome figure in the centre could have been classed as a work of art.

"Well, this is definitely silver but how much weight is it all together I am wondering, whatever it is there is a fair bit of dosh for all of us, if we use our noggins, and keep quiet about what we have found here until we can find a buyer for it."

The box was on the ground, with Ray and Burt knelt down beside it while Jack was holding his torch the beam covering the the object which now held all of their interest.

"Open it up Ray, and let us see what is inside that makes it weigh so heavy" He pointed to the side nearest him. "There are hinges here so it must open from your side. Can you see a catch or lock there?"

Ray instead of answering caught hold of the sides of the lid and lifted, it opened with ease, to reveal the contents within. The reaction of all three was none other than stunned disbelief. A sudden dryness came to the throat of Burt as he tried to speak to the others, and only managed to blurt out in a husky whisper.

"Can you all see this lot? I think we have just hit the jackpot here!"

Ray was knelt down, while Jack was stood bent over the the box the beam unwavering as they were seeing exactly the same as Burt. Laid out neatly, were four gold medallions, the size of jam pot lids with gold chains attached in a tray, which was divided into sections, and obviously made to accommodate them. Burt lifted out one of the medallions and commented on the weight, as he held it in the light beam of the torch. "Will you look at this, it's solid gold and heavy as hell, and there are four of them with chains to match." Ray saw and remarked that each of them had one of the symbols they had seen on the altar, and plaque as they had entered the room. Each link of the chain was at least half an inch in length and an eighth thick, when held up with the medallion hanging they saw there was a drop of about eighteen inches of doubled chain all four were the same except each one had one of the different symbols they had seen on the plaque.

Lifting the tray out of the top of the box, and placing it on the ground there was revealed yet another tray, without any sections, but was filled with rings, bracelets, and what could be clothes fastenings of some kind, each again had the motif they had seen on the other things, but slightly smaller than the medallions all were made of gold with precious stones of all colours encrusted in them. Running along the edge of the tray was, a smaller box three inches wide by a foot in length, Burt lifted it out, when he opened it he saw a double edged pointed dagger, with the hilt made of solid gold and, it too was encrusted with precious highly polished gem stones. The blade was smoothly polished and, glinted brightly in the light from the torch. Inside the box was lined with soft tanned black leather."Feel the weight of this thing." Burt had taken hold of the dagger and lifted it from the box, and in a shaving motion had scraped it gently down the side of his cheek, "See this! It's still razor sharp after all the time it's been laying in this box." Where the stroke of the dagger had gone there was a bare clean shaven patch, a complete contrast to the rest of his stubbled face.

"Why has all this been left here, and no one tried to get, or recover it? The value of what we have found here for the gold alone would have kept a large family for generations and, when you think of the poverty in this area alone in the Victorian times, it just does not make sense that all this was here and nothing of it was known, not even in any folk lore, or legend of buried treasure in this vicinity. The more I think about it the more uneasy I am about the whole place and every thing in it".

Jack and Burt seemed unaware of Ray speaking to them, so engrossed were they in what they had found, and was before them. To them he was just a sound in the background talking, and had not really heard the words he had been speaking to them, as they continued to search through the chest to see what else was there.

Ray moved away in silent thought from the others to one of the nearby benches, fumbled in his pockets for his cigarettes and lighter, deciding that the way he was feeling he would have a smoke, and think what he was going to do, as at that moment he was wishing he had never found the cave at all when he had gone down for the liners. As he looked over towards the other two, he thought they looked to be obsessed with every thing that was in the chests, as each in turn were trying on the rings and holding other items into the torch light to view them more closely.

He was watching as Burt had lifted the second tray out, he had seen as he left them, when there was a gasp from Jack, just as Burt had placed it on the the top of the first tray after it had been lifted clear to enable them to see what was beneath it in the bottom portion of the box.

In the bottom wrapped in a black satin cloth, Jack had just withdrawn a life sized mask of gold, of the head of the figure they had seen in the plaque and, various other articles of jewellery they had seen since, with tiny holes cut in the eyes so that it could be worn by someone.

"It's solid bloody gold, the same as everything else we have found. Where the heck can we sell something like this, without coming unstuck? What do you think Jack? Melt it down and sell it for scrap! Look how thick the metal is, God knows how much weight there is here."

"Let me feel, how heavy it is." Was Jacks only remark on the questions Burt had put to him.

A cigarette dangled from his mouth, the ash curled in a downward direction as it had burned away while his mind had been in deep thought, over what, he, wanted to do, and what the others would be prepared to do. Almost ten minutes had passed from the time they had seen the mask, and talked to each other about the best way to dispose of the things they had found in the two opened chests, and they had now moved to the last of the three unnoticed by Ray. When suddenly he was jolted out of his dream like state of thoughtfulness.

He turned his head towards his friends, still reacting to the jolt he had received, to see them both holding each other by the shoulders, and jumping up and down, and ending up doing an excited jig together. suddenly they stopped, and started to look around, realizing for the first time he was not there with them, and wondering where he was and, only then did they see him sat on the bench.

"Come over here old mate, and have a look at this lot, and for Petes sake stop looking so bloody well pissed off." Burt waved his hand gesturing with the torch light towards him and waving it around the room, and in his direction.

Ray got up, and was going to say what he had been thinking to himself while on his own, but, as he saw the excitement of the other two, he decided it would be a waste of time. He walked over wondering what more they had found, to have got them into such a state but, was completely unprepared for the sight that met his eyes when he looked into the third open chest, a sight that would remain with him for the rest of his life. By the time he reached the chest, Jack and Burt were knelt down, their hands buried deep into gold and silver coins, from the Roman to the mid seventeenth century periods, and from every country known, although he had no knowledge of what countries most of them were from, he could tell they were quite an age as coinage went, some he could tell were European, and quite old. But also stacked into the chest in rows one on top of the other were ingots of solid gold bullion which took up over half of the room in the chest. Each measured eight inches in length, three wide by two and a half thick.

"Rich man! Bloody rich that's what we are going to be! Ever so bloody stinking rich! Richer than any stinking rich there has ever been in one go. This morning I hardly had what you would call the 'proverbial' pot to piss in, and now, we have hit the biggest Jackpot, of chance for riches, there has ever been. We have just got to make sure we don't 'fuck up' on this, we have to think, just what we are going to do next, to cash in on this lot for ourselves." He looked over to where Ray was standing, staring into the chest, a glazed look upon his face. He laughed. "Bath City Rugby Club! You could buy the bloody club, and purchase any player you wanted for it, with your share of this little lot Ray. For God's sake cheer up and smile, this sort of thing only happens once in a lifetime and now it's our turn."

Jack stood up from where he had been kneeling, and tossed a few of the coins he had been holding in his hand back into the chest. "What we have here must be worth in today's currency a few million, or more. How the hell can we keep it, and get it changed into today's money, and work for us without anyone finding out where it came from, because, if we were found out, we would not get a penny piece, and probably, be prosecuted in the bargain Burt?"

Burt was only half listening to what Jack was saying, while holding and guessing to himself, the weight of the gold ingot. He placed it back into the chest with the rest of them. Only then did he answer.

"First things first Jack and, the most immediate problem we have is to get all this gold and suchlike up and away from here, then safely hidden. To be frank, I think for the best it would be better hidden somewhere at your place. It would be safe in the sense that nobody could see us unloading it from the Land Rover's there and, it is country lane driving all the way back from here, and even better your place is isolated, and has a long driveway to it, and even more important yours is the nearest. What do you say?

Jack gave the suggestion some thought, and could see the logic in what had been said, then agreed. "I don't mind, if you both agree that is! What do you say Ray? Would you be happy for the stuff to be hidden at my place for safety, until we can figure out the best way to get it changed into money for the three of us?"

"I don't care one way or another what we do with it, let us do what ever you want, and get out of this place for good once and for all, is what I say."

"Right! that's it settled then, let's start moving the stuff now."

CHAPTER 6

It had taken four and a half hours of hard work to get everything above ground, and another three to move and store it in Jacks large garage come store room. They had put as much of the gold bullion and coinage as possible into strong rock core sample bags. The chests filled with the clothing, and the replica of the altar containing the things they had found in it, were placed against the back of the garage wall. They then covered it with a large tarpaulin sheeting they had at hand. The third chest they had moved and placed it along side the other two, after refilling it with the gold and silver bullion they had loaded into the rock core sample bags because of the weight having made the chest too heavy to move when it was full. They then covered everything with a tarpaulin sheet they had at hand. Piling on top of it for good effect, some coils of cable and sample bags, with any other drilling equipment they had in the garage, making it look as if the mud covered articles covering the valuable items below would look as inconspicuous as possible, it was, after all, where the drilling equipment was usually stored, and would not look out of place should anyone come to the garage for any reason.

When they had finished, they realized they had worked through the night. They all sat down in the garage on what ever they could find, to have a smoke break and to talk over what to do next, before returning to the site.

As they came out of the garage they saw that dawn had broken. There was a golden and orange glow in the sky, as the sun was breaking over the hills, a damp freshness in the air, and early morning dew thick on the grass, dampened their boots and, made the bottoms of their overalls wet, as they made their way towards one of the vehicles they had used, to bring the valuable cargo from the underground room. The morning mist was evident and, quite thick in parts, mostly where the road crossed the stream, or ran alongside it as they drove back to the site.

* * * * * * * * * *

Burt rubbed his eyes, stretched his legs in the confined space of the Land Rover, they had left Jacks vehicle behind at his home, deciding to drop him off there on the way back later after finishing at the site that morning, he looked across the fields as Ray drove, there was an excited feeling within him, of dreams that had always seemed impossible to fulfil, a slight grin of contentment played around his lips, his tongue moved around inside a dry mouth, protruding every so often through the gap left by his two missing front teeth, he looked over at the others. "How about we stop for a fried breakfast when we finish on the site this morning. It won't take long to clear every thing up and cover the hole with the steel sheeting, and I will be ready for something by about then, because all I will want to do when I get home is shower and then hit the sack for a few hours, and not have to wait for the Mrs to make me some breakfast. What do you say?"

The others agreed whole hearted with his suggestion, and carried on with their own private thoughts of the previous day and nights events.

"How are you feeling this morning Ray? Feel any better? No more heebie jeebies about the place? see, I told you there was nothing to worry about all the time, although, I will admit to you now, there were times when it was a bit strange, and I did get the shivers about the place a couple of times, but that was mostly when you started talking about the place, but the thought of anything we might have found down there made me push it to the back of my mind, and now!....With what we have back in Jacks place, don't you think it was all worth it?" He laughed affectionately as he finished speaking, giving a gentle punch on his workmate's arm.

Upon reaching the site they stepped out of the vehicle. The air was crisp and fresh, all three felt tired and grubby after the past twenty four hours of exertion, and had decided earlier that once back on site they would make the hole safe by covering it with steel sheets they had brought with them, and then secure the equipment there, around the hole so, should anyone happen to walk near it all they would see would be a pile of sheeting, covered with cable and sacks and, not suspect the hole was even there.

When all of this was was done they returned to their homes. They all decided to take the Sunday off and, return to the site the following Monday morning and be satisfied with what they had stowed away back in the garage, and start the week as they would normally. Then whatever was to be found in the unopened room, with the iron grill, after they had opened it, they would inform the authorities then, and they, could do what ever they wanted, without realizing they had already taken all they wanted from the site early on the Saturday morning. They all agreed it should work.

Ray was feeling fine but felt a bit foolish about his reactions to the place, after having the rest of the weekend to think it over rationally. A few drinks in "The Running Stag Inn" and after the Pub closed, did wonders for him. Especially as the female company he had spent the rest of his night with, had been the culmination of quite a few weeks of trying to "pull" the party, he could not believe his luck when his past efforts fell into place, and she fell into bed beside him for the Saturday and Sunday nights. With the wealth they had found and his success with the woman he had been trying to pull for so long, he was feeling really lucky , he smiled to himself, at the memory of her as she had got out of bed that morning and after, when they were in the shower together accompanied with the spontaneous laughter. Yes he thought the weekend sure did hold a bonus for him, and the prospects of the coming weekend held much the same, lucky for him he thought, the work around Taunton should last him well for the time being, and after....well...let's just wait and see. "What's the crack for today." The smile of his previous thoughts still on 'his' lips.

"Jacks meeting us on site and we are taking it from there, or so he said when I phoned him last night."

They had arrived on site and were in the process of pulling the steel plates off of the hole, that they had placed there the Saturday morning, when Jack arrived.

"How long have you been here."

"Just arrived." Was the answer from the two workmen in unison.

"Have you seen anyone else around this morning? Farmer or anybody?"

"No not a soul quiet as a grave yard here!" Burt had a smile on his face and looked at Ray as he spoke.

"Oh!...Shut up and give it a rest Burt!" Ray picked up a lump of clay and threw it at his mate in a friendly gesture, just missing him as he ducked out of it's way. All three laughed together.

"What do we do now Jack? Carry on as usual?"

"No! We will leave the rig where it is, and then later, after tea break and the morning sun is up and every thing is dry, I will phone the 'County Council Surveyors Office' and say we have had a cave in and have managed to get out all of our gear from down below, while doing so discovered what's down there, and except for breaking the door in, we will tell them the place is as we found it. It's hard dry ground down there, so nobody can tell we have been in the room and taken away every thing we found down there, we can say that when we saw the things such as the furniture ect. down there we realized it was old stuff and would be of obvious interest to the 'Local History Department'."

"That sounds good, let's stick to it. You happy with that Ray?"

"I'll go along with what ever you both agree."

They just hung around passing the time, and not really doing anything until lunch time. As an after thought, they reasoned, to phone anyone before would have conflicted with the time they knew it had taken them to get the equipment from the bottom and the time it had taken drilling before the cave in, and that it had happened that morning instead of the Friday before.

Ray was sat on a railway sleeper usually used for a bedding support for the 'A' frame on soft ground, which was relatively clear of mud or clay, eating a cheese and tomato roll he had bought in a garage, while filling up with diesel that morning on the way to the site. While Burt and Jack

29

sat on the ground with their backs against the wheels of the Landrover for support eating cheese rolls, also bought that morning and, drinking tea they had made using the gas ring and kettle they always used on site rather than filling flasks.

"How are we going to sort out all the gear we have found and turn it into money Jack? Have you any ideas?"

"I have one or two floating around in my head. There's an old friend I know, who has a lot to do with importing and exporting antiques and such like, he may be in the know of where we can sort something. I know for a fact he has done some shady deals in the past for a few people. Not long ago he did a deal for a couple of ground workers by getting rid of some bits and pieces, what it was I don't know, but it was stuff they found while excavating near some old Roman villa over towards Dorchester way, they made a good deal out of it by all accounts, with some yank, a private collector, or something like that anyway. If I just pump him a bit without giving anything away, he might be inclined, unwittingly, to point me in the right direction at least. But it might be best to let everything die down around here first, before start to even think about doing anything."

"I understand what you mean. But it would be good to say to the Mrs. we could have a holiday in New Zealand this year, we have been saving for the last three, and the way things were going it could have been another at least two or even more before we had the money for a month over there, what with the cost of living going the way it has in the last year or so. It's just that her sister is over there, and they have not seen each other for almost twenty years or so. Anyway a holiday would do us both a world of good."

"Well that should not create much of a problem now. With everything we have back at my place, just say when you want to go, and if you want I will let you have a couple of grand, or whatever, until such times as we can sort out something with the other lot."

"Is that all you do all day, sit around drinking tea and scoffing. No wonder the 'County Council' jobs take so long and get over budget. If that's how you work."

All three turned around, and saw walking towards them the assistant county surveyor, a large grin on his face, and holding a clip board with papers flapping in the breeze, wearing a white shirt, sleeves rolled up, and a tie flapping as he walked towards where they were sitting, trousers with knife edged creases, and a pair of brogues. Looking completely out of place as he came up to the three sat eating and drinking.

"How goes it Jack? Any problems."

Jack Martins and Phil Grainham were on good terms and had known each other for years though the course of their work, and occasionally through social functions.

He was five nine, blond hair that had started to turn silver grey and sporting a bald pate, and forty seven years of age, married with one daughter, who was married herself just over two months before. The wedding of which Jack had been invited and, had attended, and the last time the men had seen each other, due to the fact he had taken more duties in the office, and thus reducing time he could spend in the field, as was normal before the restructuring of the county council office administration. "Not a problem exactly Phil, but there's a bit of a mystery down below ground where we have sunk a bore hole." Jack then explained to him the events of the Friday before but leaving out about what they had found, as had been agreed amongst themselves, saying it had happened that morning instead.

Phil Grainham walked across to the site of the cave in and looked down. "You say there are caves and rooms down there?"

"Well they are all caves really I suppose, but two have been made into rooms with doors."

"Also, there's a bloody great, what we think is an altar, with all this writing on which we can't understand." Burt chipped in.

"Come on! your pulling my plonker." Phil Grainham knew of Burt's sense of humour, from the times they had met before.

"Take a look for yourself. I shit you not. It's down there large as life." He caught hold of the scaffold frame and gave it a good tug. "It's safe enough Phil and, works better than you probably think."

"I don't know, and it's not for me to say, but I don't know what the County Safety officer would make of it. It might be all right but knowing him, I doubt it."

"We were going to ring the county office, after we had lunch, the main thing was to get all of the equipment out in case it collapsed again, and would have had to write off what was down there, but as you can see it's all up on the surface now and the size of the hole is quite large and the walls are pretty solid, probably because of how dry it's been. I suppose you can tell them now, when you get back, it will save me having to leave here and to use the public phone in the pub a little ways down the road."

"I was going onto somewhere else after I left here, but seeing what you have told me I had better inform somebody about it, but I am not sure who. Someone in the County Historical Records Office, or County Museum I suppose.

Anyway if I report it to Wilmot the county surveyor and leave it in his court. Nothing like this has happened to me before." With that said, and advising them not to go down to the bottom of the hole again, before someone from the council was there. He made his way back to his car. They saw him drive past the gate which led to where they had set up the drilling operation, then disappear behind a small wooded area, on his way back to the County Hall.

"What did I tell you?" Burt remarked as Phil Grainham drove past the gate of the field they were in. "Now the place will be crawling with brass from the county council, you wait and see. If we had not acted as we did we would not have got a brass farthing out of the place below. What do you think Jack? Do you think he swallowed what we told him about finding the place below today, instead of Friday."

"No reason to think otherwise Burt. There is no way they can tell the three chests were ever there. All we have to do is stick to our story. They will, I'm sure be chuffed enough to have that wall plaque and those benches with the leather bound box, with the sections containing the powder on the table down there, and what ever there may be, behind the other door."

Just over an hour later, as they had finished setting the rig in position to sink the next bore hole, Burt saw two policemen walking towards them."

"Here we go! It's started." Burt's comments made the other two look towards where he had indicated.

"Hello! Which one of you gentlemen would be Mr Martins?"

Jack introduced himself, and was told they had been sent to secure the area, and wait until some other people from the county offices arrived, and that they would not be long behind them.

"Why? It's not going anywhere! Burt shot back. The two constables did not seem to have a sense of humour at first, but soon warmed to the drillers, once they understood Burt's sense of humour, with one of them giving it back as good as Burt could give it. After they had been there for a quarter of an hour, and the drillers had started the engine of the rig ready to commence drilling at the spot of the next yellow peg, three others arrived, an archeologist and two assistants, and immediately asked them to switch of the engine, for fear the vibrations could cause a cave in. Just as the introductions and and questions about what it was they had actually found down below were concluded, two more people arrived Phil Grainham accompanied by the county safety inspector, who immediately took a look at the 'bosun's' chair they had erected, and felt it was quite safe to use for the purpose of what they had used it for, and also very ingenious to say the least.

They had all got down to the bottom of the hole and waited in the passage until the last person, who was Ray, came down, before moving into the cavern they had been told of by the drillers. The archeologists were amazed and excited by what they had seen after entering the large cavern. They were puzzled by the writings and symbols and took photographs of them, and measurements of the altar, with the hope of finding something to compare them with, in the county museum, or archives records office, and perhaps be able to decipher what they actually said.

A short while later they were in the room with the tables and benches, after a brief examination of them and a cursory look around the room they thought it might be a good idea to open the room with the iron grill.

"Try not to damage the iron door too much if possible, it could be invaluable for using as an exhibition for the local history section of the museum." The archiologist seemed to be more worried about damage to the ironwork of the door and the grill being damaged than gaining entry to whatever lay behind it, was the thought Burt had. He took from the bag they had left down there from the last time they had opened the oak door, a hack saw.

"Are any of you three a locksmith."

The three he had spoken to looked at each other, not really understanding he was having a joke with them. With all their academic qualities it seemed they only knew of skills which were needed, with straight forward excavations and documenting finds ect. He moved towards the bars with the saw, and began to size up the situation of the grill and how best to tackle the job of freeing it from the locking device set into the wall, without having to resort to the use of the iron bar they had with the sledge hammer on the previous occasion.

"What do you think this could be? It looks like a key of some kind. Do you think it could be a key for the lock in the grill gate?"

They all turned towards where the voice had come from, and saw one of the assistants to the archeologist holding a 'T' shaped nine inch piece of metal, with triangular teeth set at differing angles the archiologist took it from him. "Where did you get this? It looks similar to an old type of barrel lock key but these teeth are a new one on me."

"It was laying on the floor near the wall there." He pointed to a spot some ten feet or so behind them in the passage where the area opened in front of the two doors. They had all walked past it, but their attention was so much on the doors in front of them while holding the torches to illuminate the way they were walking, no one thought of looking down on the ground as they came into the area. It was only because he had stepped on it while moving back to let Burt and the others through to the gate area.

Moving forward past Burt, the archeologist, 'key' in hand, looked at the box set into the wall, saw what he thought could be the keyhole and inserted the 'T' shaped key into it, he tried turning but it would not budge one way or the other, he then tried to withdraw it but it would not come out, seeming to have jammed tightly inside the box. "Give the box a bang, it might loosen it." Burt suggested remembering secretly to himself the difficulty they had in the other room with the chests.

"Here use this!" Jack held a hammer out to the archeologist, he had got from the tool bag, as Burt had made the suggestion.

Eventually with a little banging and a drop of lubricating oil also found in the bag, the key turned until the iron door was loose and away from the box, screeching as it swung out freely towards them. The inner wooden door took about the same time and effort as the previous wooden door, but without Burt doing his leaping fall into the room, and just swung inwards, after a little persuasion with the iron bar into the door jamb.

As he saw the door begin to give, Ray Hayman began to get the feelings of trepidation he had felt before, to the extent his heart began to pound and his legs began to grow weak and tremble uncontrollable. He wanted out of there, some sixth sense seemed to scream at him that there was something not right about everything going on in front of him and he should not have come down there again with the others. He was in the act of turning to go back, when his limbs seemed to move in slow motion, he stood half turned, but his eyes were transfixed and looking at the opening door, it seemed to open slowly inch by inch, with every jerk of the bar, Burt had then dropped the bar to the side of him leaning it against the wall next to the door, then putting his hands forward and against it ready for one final push to open it wider. As he looked at the others there, they seemed unconcerned, the complete opposite to how he was feeling, and seemed to be concentrating on Burt's efforts to get the door opened. He tried to shout at him to stop but, could not produce a sound before the door was open wide with one concentrated push.

The door was fully open, and in that instant there was a rushing in his ears, as though all around him a gale force hurricane had appeared from nowhere, as he stood and looked around him the others were falling to the ground, like skittles in a bowling alley, but it all seemed to be happening in slow motion to him, he felt weak as if, he himself was going to black out, but he fought against it with every fibre of his being through fear, and fearing if he did succumb as the others seemed to have, he would be lost. In what way he did not know, but some kind of animal instinct, call it what you will, but it was telling him to fight with all his being.

The roaring continued in his ears, he began to become dizzy and confused, but still he continued to fight, he did not know how he was doing it, but still he fought. Then suddenly he felt as if he had been hooked by a thousand fish hooks within his body the pain he felt was excruciating to him, it felt at the same time there was a dividing of himself, as if something was being pulled from him. Something which was vital and part of him, and what ever that something was he instinctively knew it was part of the individuality of himself and, if he gave in and succumbed to the division he would have to follow, if he gave up. He felt the fear again but more intense than before, what ever it was he was fighting from being taken from him seemed to become insoluble, and unstable, he knew he was falling and could do nothing about it anymore, a cold and, what felt to him to be a physical blackness seemed to try and enter his mind, he tried to focus on his surroundings as he fell onto the ground, screaming in pain, the feeling was similar to fish hooks pulling at him until it seemed he was in a state of mind where by he could take no more pain. The roaring continued all this time and as his body twisted convulsively on the floor then the roaring it seemed reached a crescendo, the pain increased at the same rate, then there was only what could be described as a tearing apart occurred with his physical body and the something soluble as this happened, there was a complete silence and the pain was gone. Then a feeling of motion, although he could see nothing, there was within him a feeling of a new awareness, the next thing he was engulfed into the centre of brilliant colours, such as he had never seen or experienced before and was beyond any definition of describing, then he felt the feelings he had felt before of the experience when the was door opened moments before. The colours all were around him with indescribable brilliance, he felt the sensation of being carried, or just blown around. Carried along as a leaf in the wind, but still he felt the complete sensation of his own individuality, circling, sweeping along in eddies, twisting, turning, up, and then down, still, with all the sensation of movement, then he was in the centre of a kaleidoscope of colours the patterns ever changing, and then suddenly he found he was in a whirlpool the colours of which secmed to be alive and focusing upon him as he flowed through it. Then in an instant he was in a tunnel of white brilliance with no form other than it's own brilliance and as he travelled through it, it seemed to give off an energy he felt he needed and seemed to attract, he felt comfortable, then in a blink of an eye he lost all sense of human form, but remained conscious of his own being and, individuality. Eventually there was a stillness, a feeling of peace, a sense of floating movement around him, in a thousand directions at once, yet he knew they, like him belonged to the same source and consciousness, which he instinctively knew was within, and around him at the same time. Then came a revelation of a profound understanding of life it's self, yet he could not fully grasp the significance of his understanding in an ordinary human or physical sense, something he knew, a past memory locked into his mind, the door to which could not be opened fully, just a mirage of his latent knowledge in front of him, but out of focus and not seeing it clearly enough to be able to understand any meaning to it. But above all, thcre was within it everything he felt thought and saw, a feeling of love, total and absolute that came, and was received by him, and was then returned to whence it came, having nourished him with a total feeling of peace, love, and contentment.

All these things occurred within a time span he could not understand and found, as his mind tried to calculate time as a relevant fact of measurement, found it was not possible while in this new state of being he found himself in. Expanding and contracting in the system of the things occurring, that to him was as if a memory of years before was happening and yet simultaneously was past, and yet still to come, the knowledge and abilities he gained made him able to understand these things as he thought of them, but as the thought moved on to something else the the the understanding vanished.

His mind then seemed to focus eventually on what had happened to him, and how he came to be in the state of being he found himself. He then thought of his friends, and immediately a heaviness came upon him, and the memory of the open door and falling outside of it and the pain he had endured, then in the instant of thinking it, he found himself above and looking down on them, seeing their motionless bodies in front of the opened door. As he watched a feeling of misery, and fear took hold of him, a darkness around them all that seemed to become more darker the more he watched.

"Now! Now! before he can return, the more we have the sooner we can become strong and all return again." He heard the voice strong and insistent with an authoritative tone and, as if it had the power of commanding instant obedience.

Within the darkness he could see shadowy forms moving, darker than the surrounding darkness. Then he felt the essence of what he knew to be himself being drawn back downwards towards where his body lay motionless, as he did he had the sensation of light surrounding him as he moved slowly at first and then with increasing speed, through the dense and endless plane of darkness. As he moved nearer to his body there was all around him voices babbling high and low, whispering, shouting, and screaming, a crescendo of sounds coming from all directions, they all seemed to have a sense of urgency about them then suddenly his decent stopped the sensation of light around him began to increase, so much so it began to dispel the darkness around him. Looking down he saw the bodies of his friends begin to move, and stretch, he shouted to them but they seemed not to hear him. "What" he thought "is happening there."

"What the hell happened?" It was The voice of Jack Martins, Ray saw him as he sat up rubbing the back of his head, slowly he got to his feet, picking up the torch as he did so, shining it around he caught sight of Burt in it's beam, then walked over to him. "Are you all right Burt?" At the sound of Jacks voice he began to stir, sitting up he began to rub the front and then the back of his head, he looked up at the light beam squinting, and then at Jack, a look of puzzlement on his face. "I'm all right except I have one hell of a headache, and a mouth like a vultures crotch, and my legs feel a bit queer, except for suffering like I am, and not having been out on the piss earlier, I'm fine."

Within minutes everyone, except Ray Hayman, were on their feet.

"What's the matter with Ray?" Burt had come around more by this time and could see he was still laid on the ground, and looked to be unconscious, he went over to him.

Ray Hayman continued to watch, as they all began to crowd around his body as it lay on the ground. He could hear Burt's voice, saw him kneel down and begin to shake him, "Some thing is wrong with him he won't come to!"

Jack came over and started to speak to him, while Burt continued to shake his body.

"Here let me have a look at him!" One of the police officers proceeded to administer first aid, made sure his air way was clear and felt his pulse.

"Well, he is breathing, and he has a strong enough pulse, what happened to him, has he fallen and hit his head on something? Come to that, what happened to us all? I just blacked out and the next thing I knew was, I woke up on the floor." The policeman tending Ray's prone body, turned around to look for his colleague.

"What about moving Ray how can we get him up to the surface, while he is unconscious?" Burt was getting in a bit of a panic now, about his work mate.

"That's no Problem, the problem is what has happened to him for him to be still unconscious." Jack turned to the Archaeologist. Have you experienced anything like this before?"

"No never! But, I have never been in the same situation before. I normally work above ground on open excavations. This is the first time for me working below ground."

"Have you any idea what could have caused us to black out as we did?"

"Methane! Methane gas! It sometimes happens in old wells, tunnels, tunnels and sewers, it can in the right conditions build up in enclosed spaces." One of the policemen had spoken while looking carefully to see if he could locate any injury on Ray, to account for his present condition.

34

"I don't understand it, I have looked all over but cannot find any injury on your friend, that would leave him in this condition. He is not prone to fits or anything is he?"

"Yes he could be right, methane gas is caused by rotting matter, and what is in there would more than likely be the cause of it." One of the assistant's to the archeologist was standing outside the open door his flashlight shining into the darkness, and everyone could look into the room. What was there made them gasp and stand frozen to the spot, disbelief registering on every face. For all around the room, sitting, laying, in all kinds of positions were, skeleton remains, partially covered in tattered clothing, and of what remained, one could see by the attire there were both male and female skeletons of what were once people.

Ray had also moved from the vantage point where he had been looking down on his earthly body, and as he did so he could see surrounding it a dark and what to him seemed to be a shadow of a deep shade of dark brown, as he consciously tried to move closer to it the light he could feel around him seemed to make him repel away from it with a feeling of repulsion, quickly he turned his attention to the room and at what the others were seeing, it was just as he had taken a quick look that there was a feeling about him he did not understand, as if he had started to tremble, then there was the rushing sound again and the next thing he was in the tunnel of light he had been in before only this time there was someone else there as well, he could not make out any identification of who it might be but knew it was someone, he was sure, he knew. As he came closer they beckoned and he was just content to follow as they moved further into the tunnel and the light without any fear. Then there was suddenly a flash of coloured brilliance, and the person he had been following was gone and he found himself back inside the front of the hallway of his apartment confused and alone.

Later when everyone had returned to the surface, and an ambulance had been called to take Rays body into hospital, Burt and Jack with the assistance of the two policemen had been making the area safe before they left. Suddenly there was a rumbling and a crashing sound, then the earth began to tremor beneath their feet, everyone ran as fast as they could away from the site of the hole. After a few moments everything became quiet again. When they cautiously returned the hole was no more, where it had been was just a depression in the ground of about two or three feet deep by fifteen in diameter. Some one remarked "It's completely collapsed."

* * * * * * * * * *

Six months later, Raymond Hayman was still seemingly in a coma at a private hospital, with his own nurse in attendance. A matter of two months later his life support was switched off and he was pronounced dead, while all the records of his stay there mysteriously disappeared. The archeologist and his two assistants had finished on the county historical department, one had emigrated to U.S.A another to Canada with their wives and children. Philip Grainham was promoted to Chief County Surveyor, and moved house to the outskirts of Taunton. The two police officers were still stationed at Taunton, and were now both sergeants. Jack Martins, in partnership with Burt Stevens purchased the farm and field where the drilling operation had occurred, and the surrounding land of some seven hundred acres, after the sudden demise of the farmer and his entire family, due to a road traffic accident.

CHAPTER 7

Peter Jones looked at his wrist watch and saw he was a little earlier than he had expected, by just over ten minutes.

It had taken less time than he had thought to walk from the car park to the town centre, where he had arranged to meet his wife of three months after she had finished work. He decided while he was standing there, he would pop over to the cash dispenser before she arrived and draw out some cash, so as they could go straight on to the stores and finish off the last of their Christmas shopping. There were only two or three small presents to buy now, and then they would be ready, with all the hectic preparation behind them.

This was to be their first Christmas together in their own home, although from early Christmas morning he would be at his in-laws for dinner and tea. But that did not concern him over much, because Abigail and himself would have the rest of the Christmas period together on their own.

It had been strange how things had turned out, from the friendship as they attended the development circle with Mrs Chandley, then as time went by the friendship became more until they had both gone away on a day trip to Weymouth, on the church's annual outing. They had spent the whole day in each others company, mostly alone and away from the rest of the coach party and, at the end of which, they had both known there was more than an attraction of just friendship, both accepted what they had known secretly of the feelings they had for each another for quite a while, but had been afraid to speak of it to one another for fear of the others rejection.

Abigail because of the fact of her being a widow and, Peter because he was afraid that she might not be ready, or want to start a new relationship with commitment, he was not sure if she had come to terms with her late husbands passing, as it was hardly mentioned by her since they had become friends. But in the end body language and eventually a kiss and cuddle on the sea front that day solved all problems, and shortly after they became engaged and married, with the blessing of Abigail's dead husbands parents, who attended the wedding service on his side of the church, to add their blessing, to the marriage.

They had moved to an old terraced house and with the help of friends had just about finished doing repairs and redecoration. Resulting in a small but comfortable home, for them both, and with the money Abigail had through her husbands insurance, her savings and what Peter had, they managed to pay off more or or less outright for the house. True it was not much to look at when they viewed it with the estate agent in all it's faults, but after reading the surveyors report confirming the structure was sound, a mention of cash in the sale, and they had managed a very quick acquisition of the house. In nine months from the time of them viewing the house they now had a cosy comfortable warm home together. Luck, with hard work and, good friends, had smiled upon them.

Returning from the cash point he stood there waiting, watching every one who came by, glancing up and down hoping to see her, he looked at his watch again and saw it was only just on the time they had agreed to meet. His hands in warm gloves and wearing a thick woollen jumper under his short car coat, his top half of his body was like toast, but he was finding his legs, feet especially were freezing, he stamped his feet hard on the ground, and swore the first thing he would buy himself was another pair of thermal socks, the same as he had been wearing to work at the building site while plastering. As he watched others go by him, he looked at their faces, and wondered if his looked as red as some of those passing him by, as he stood stamping his feet.

Suddenly he saw her coming towards him, the familiar white knitted fluffy Angora hat perched at an angle, and the smile of Abigail beneath it.

"Been waiting long?"

"No, but it sure is cold when you stand about." She reached forward and planted a kiss on his cheek. It was the usual greeting from her now whenever they met, and he was now used to it and had begun to look forward with a kind of delight to the greeting.

"Where shall we go first? Any ideas?

"I saw a gift shop when I was on my way here to wait for you. It's back in the direction you have just come from and, there is a cafe next door. What do you think about having a hot drink first before we start shopping?"

"Now that does sound like a good idea. But what about money?" She smiled at him. "It makes things easier when you have some and I have very little at the moment."

"All done. I was early arriving here and drew out the amount you said we would need and a little extra just in case we decided to have a meal out before we go home."

"Fish and chips from the chippy will do me. Is that all right with you? I would rather get the shopping done and then go home to the warm and eat them. Then spend the evening by the fire, maybe watch a little T.V.. Or we could hire a vidio from Blackmores Vidio Rental it's on the way home, and if we do, remember it's my turn to choose the film this time."

"Oh no! Not one of those true life things again."

"Come on none of that, you admitted you enjoyed the last two we watched." Abigail playfully thumped his arm. He lurched to the side in mock pain.

"There! You you see what happens if I argue with anything you say. I get duffed up."

She laughed and put her arm in his as they made their way towards the cafe and gift shop.

As they drew up at the curbside the flashing lights on the small Christmas tree in the window seemed to be welcoming them home. The silver star was still at an angle where he had brushed against it earlier in the morning, and had forgotten to straighten it when he had returned from work that afternoon, he had changed from his work clothes earlier, then drew the curtains and switched the fairy lights on before driving into town to meet her.

Abigail opened the door while he held the carrier bags with the things they had bought, she bent down and picked up a scrap of paper, which turned out to be a envelope torn in half. She turned it over and saw there was something written on it.

"What is it? A Christmas card? It was not there when I left earlier to meet you." All he saw was that she had picked up something white.

"No it's a note from someone. Let's get the things in the carrier bags away, and then see what it says after, there is a telephone number on it what ever it is. I hope no one is coming around tonight. I was hoping to spend the evening on our own just you and me together."

Coming down the stairs after taking the presents they had bought and deposited on top of the wardrobe until the they would be wrapped in Christmas paper, he saw Abigail at the foot of the stairs with the note in her hands.

"What does it say? Who is it from?"

"It's for you. From someone called Ken Barber, at least I think it's Barber, the writings not too sharp. It looks as if it was scribbled outside the door with out resting it on anything. It's written in pencil. Here, you look and, see what you can make of it. There's a phone number here as well."

He took it from her. "Ken Barber?.....Ken Barber? I know that name, but I can't recall where I know it from. It's a local call number, and all it says is would I give him a ring......Says it's important and would appreciate it. God the writings terrible, can't make out what else it says."

"Well! Give him a ring. Then we can find out who he is."

"After we have eaten, we don't want cold fish and chips. You get the plates while I see to the knives, forks and the cruet. Do you want any sauce with yours or not?"

"Dad! There's someone called Peter Jones on the telephone for you." A young teenage voice which could have been male or female shouted loudly.

"Hello! Peter, I'm sorry about the note, all I knew was your first name and where you lived and I was not too sure about that to start with. Can you remember me? We worked on the same job together for a few weeks in the summer. I was the chippy at the house on the Albone Estate renovation job For the council? Where there was a fire which had started in the kitchen and eventually spread upstairs to the bedrooms. Can you remember me?"

"Ah! The Albone Estate. I remember now. I knew the name but could not remember where from. That's right, there was a bad fire and the house had to have a complete renovation job done to it, we worked there for about three weeks. What can I do for you? Is it an urgent plastering job needing to be done? Only if it is I'm absolutely stacked up with work. I do know one or two others who may be able to help you out if you are really stuck."

"No!...No!....It's nothing to do with work. I don't even know if ringing you will do any good anyway. It's just that when we were working together, some of the others there were talking about religion and all that one lunch time. Well your plasterer's mate at the time said you were in the spiritualist church movement or, whatever it's called and you knew something....or understand something in the way of ghosts, spirits and that sort of thing. Well!......That's what he said....,to be truthful I did not pay a lot of attention to what was being said at the time, because I was reading my newspaper and only caught parts of the conversation, but remembered what he was saying to the others there. It was the time you had to go for some more materials in the lunch hour and they had finished talking on the subject by the time you returned."

Peter was a bit taken back at first. Not expecting the conversation to be about the subject of his religion, so much so it was the last thing on his mind. "Yes it is true. I am a spiritualist. But it is not only about ghosts and spirits. It encompasses a lot more than what was probably discussed at that lunch time. "What is it you want to know? Where the nearest church is? If it is you would be welcome there without having to be introduced by anyone or anything like that, it's always an open service for whoever may want to attend."

"Well no,...it's not that. I don't really know how to ask you. Is it possible for you to see and advise me, on what to do for my daughter and her husband. They are both at their wits end. I have them staying with me at the moment because of what I need to talk to you about. I can, come and see you. As a matter of fact it might be better. I have told them to leave the matter with me, and told them I would get in touch with someone who may be able to sort out what has been happening, or at least point me in the direction of some one who may be able to help them. Would it be possible to see you this evening for a short while? I would not ask but I am really desperate and worried for them both."

"What exactly is it that is causing them so much bother. Can you tell me now?"

"It's where they are living. There is something going on there and it's frightened them, so much so they refuse to stay there overnight, and can only stay in the place for a few minutes at a time, and will not even enter the place alone, at any time. That's why they are staying with me at the moment."

Peter quickly thought over what he had been told, and decided that perhaps he had better have a word with Abigail of what they should do. "look Ken I will have a word or two with my wife about what you have told me. Then I will get back to you. Give me about ten minutes or so, and I will ring you back. Don't worry, what ever it is, I am sure if I can't help you I am sure I will be able to find someone who will be able to.

"What was all that about Peter?" Standing near him and catching the end of the telephone conversation, and percieved by the perplexed expression, while deep in thought, his hand still resting on the receiver. Abigail held out a cup of instant coffee she had made while he was having the conversation with Ken Barber. Her voice and movement brought him out of his speculative thinking.

"I am not sure to tell you the truth. Something about his daughter and son-in-law, and where they have been living, and how he has them both living with him because they are afraid to stay in their own house over night."

"Who is he? Did you find out?"

"Yes, he is a carpenter who was working on the same house I was on. A renovation job on the Albone Estate, back in the early summer. Can you remember? The house had been almost gutted by fire. It was the first time I had worked with him. I knew the name was familiar, but could not remember him until he mentioned the house on the Albone Estate.

"Why did he want you to telephone him?"

"He asked if he could speak to me about a problem his daughter and son-in-law have been experiencing in their home. Apparently the others on the site had been having a talk one lunch time in the house, when I had been at the builders merchants. Alan Cook, you remember him? He was labouring for me at that time while I was working for the local council, he was only there for the three weeks while I was doing the plastering, you remember I asked him if he wanted to work with me on a self employed basis but he was quite happy working for the council, and stayed with them. Anyway, he mentioned I was a spiritualist and was actively involved with the church. He asked if he could see me this evening, I told him I would have to speak to you and see if it would be convenient. What do you think? He did seem concerned and worried. I don't suppose it will take him long to tell us what sort of problem it is. I told him I would ring back in ten minutes and let him know if we could see him this evening. What do you say? Do you agree?"

"I suppose so. I hope it does not take too long, remember the vidio has to go back tomorrow. It would be a shame if we did not have time to watch it tonight."

"Ken Barber arrived still wearing his work clothes, a thick quilted shirt, donkey jacket and denim jeans.

"Come on through to the sitting room, it's warmer in there we only have one coal fire here at the moment. Central heating is the next job to be done in the new year when we hope to have the cash to pay for it outright."

Ken Barber looked around the sitting room as he came in, seeing that everything had obviously been refurbished. New plaster on the walls and new doors and double glazed windows.

"See you have done a lot here." He excaimed.

"Yes we had too, we stripped everything out and started with the shell and had to renovate everything from top to bottom. Lucky enough we had a few freinds in the building trade. Saved us quite a fair sum of money in the long run, we could not have done it with out their help on the money we had alone. It took most of our spare time for this year to get it the way it looks now."

He stood back and looked around obviously pleased with the end result. A look of pride about him. Then remembered Abigail was standing near the fire as they had come in. He introduced her to Ken.

"Some of my freinds and I did most of the building side of things, but the furniture and fittings is what makes it a comfortable and impressive home for both of us, and the credit for that goes to Abigail here. As he spoke so he put his arms lightly around his wife's shoulders giving a gentle pull towards him.

Ken Barber sat in the chair which was offered to him, and all three sat around the area of the fire feeling the warmth, as fingers of flame licked their way around and upwards as the heat was drawn up the chimney, he sat staring into the fire watching as small jets of flame came from the already burning lumps of coal with a splutter and hissing sounds, occasionally there were loud cracks from the couple of logs which had been placed on the top of the coal fire, and were spitting as the sap within them began to ooze from under the burning bark as the heat below made them smoulder before they would begin to burn. The loud cracks within the fire as it was burning and slowly reducing in size, these things he noticed while at the same time he tried to get his mind together so as to be able to explain to Peter what he had come to see him about, and to speak of the instances which had been related to him by his daughter and son-in-law. But to which he had no witnessing of and, was unsure if they were imagining everything they had told him, although when they had pleaded for him to let them stay at his house until they could find somewhere else to live, and by their actions and manner they did seem to be desperate. His daughter had not slept she had told him, for over a week and was at that moment on medication, and on sick leave from her employment.

"Well Ken. What is it you want to ask me, or tell me about?""About a year ago my daughter and her husband moved into a rented apartment, everything was fine for about six months, nearly seven actually, and they were happy and content and getting on with their lives, working and saving to enable them to put a deposit on a mortgage for a house of their own. Simon her husband had the opportunity to work shifts, he works as a lathe operator at an engineering firm locally. The work was divided up into three shifts, he volunteered for the night shift for the sake of quite a rise in his take home pay. Well you know how shifts work, to keep the machines as fully operational as possible, and night shift always pays more no matter what type of work is being done.....After he had been working for about six months or so, he began to notice a change in my daughter Karen. She began to get depressed and fly off the handle over the least thing. He tried to talk to her, but she would walk away from him and sit in silence, and would not converse with him at all. To cut a long story short he advised her to go and make an appointment with her G.P., but all that did was to stir up a hornets nest within her and a blazing row ensued. At this point he thought there was no benefit in arguing any more and, he did not know what else there was, he could do. Threatening that if she did not see her doctor he was going to pack his belongings and leave. That seemed to do something inside her, and she began to snap completely, she broke down and in tears, and begged him not to go. It was only at that point and after he had consoled her enough that she calmed down and felt she could tell him what the matter was with her and, why she had been behaving so towards him."

Peter and Abigail had listened intently so far to what had been said and both could not see what it might be leading to, or would have been anything they might be able to advise him about so far, but were coming to the same conclusion as the son-in-law, perhaps his daughter could benefit from some kind of orthodox medical treatment. But thought it might be better at this stage to say nothing and, just to listen to what else he had to say.

"Carry on Ken."

"What she told me I found hard to believe at first. But I could see she was serious, and as far as I could tell was, telling the truth. Things, she said were happening when he was with her and when he was not. First objects would disappear from where she had known without a doubt she had put them, the first she could remember were her car keys, she usually put them on the kitchen key hook rack with all the others connected with her work, and house, which they used frequently, as they both normally did when they came home. On the first occasion she had intended to get the shopping to make Simon some late tea before he went to work, she had gone for the car keys and they were not there. She hunted high and low for them, in her pockets, her hand bag even retracing her steps to the car to see if she had dropped them or left them in the ignition, but still they were not to be found. After giving up looking for them she went to the drawer in the sitting room where they kept some spares. Then she went to the supermarket as she had planned, assuming that somehow she had just misplaced them somewhere after coming in from parking the car and coming into to the house. The rest of the evening she did some washing in the machine, switched it on then left it, while she settled in front of the T.V. for the rest of the evening. Simon had left for work, she had switched of the T.V. and retired for the night. She had switched the bedside lamp on, and there on the bedside table were the missing keys she had been looking for.

At first she could not understand how they had got there, being sure she had not been up the stairs let alone going into the bedroom when she had come home from work that day, but logic being what it is she assumed eventually that she must have, and had with an absent mind placed them there. That was the first instance she could recall. But the days and weeks went by and all kinds of things began to happen, but nothing seemed to happen when Simon was there, until about a month ago that is. When things started happening which both of them saw and heard in the place, and that is the reason they are both staying with me until they could find other accommodation. Now it seems in the last day or so things are happening to them at my house. I was speaking to a neighbour about what had happened with Karen and Simon and the reason they were staying with me temporarily. The neighbour then mentioned there was something similar on the television a month or so before about someone, another family, in Germany who had experienced a very similar thing and it had lasted for over eight months or more and they had to get a priest in and have the house blessed and so on. Apparently it it did the trick and has stopped now and after the priest did whatever priests do, it just seemed to stop, but the family had researchers there, and there were all kinds of reports and photographs taken while things were happening. They said on the program, the researchers put the occurrences down to some sort of charge or power or something like that which somehow caused the things to happen around one of the family members. Such as things moving and disappearing and turning up in the oddest of places. Except for a few differences it seems that what has been happening to Karen and Simon, is much the same thing as was happening to the family in Germany. If it is the same, I was hoping that you might know what is going on and, perhaps what we can do about it.

Peter and Abigail sat looking at each other unsure of what exactly they could say to him as he finished telling them of the experiences his daughter and son-in-law had told him of. Peter was the first to break the silence.

"How long have have they been living with you since leaving their home?"

"Just over a week now, for the first few days they were fine, but now since things have started to happen in my home she has become much the same as before they left theirs." "You have told us of things happening. What kind of things are we talking about, and how often?"

"Different things, such as objects disappearing and reappearing elsewhere. There have also been things appearing that they have not seen before and, did not belong to them. The last morning they were at their home they went into the kitchen in the morning and on the kitchen table there were a dozen or so old copper pennies with small beach pebbles strewn around them. They both say that they just appeared there and there was no way any one could have placed them there overnight, the windows were shut, and when they went to bed the night before the doors back and front were locked, with the security chains in place. Plus the fact they live on the third floor and facing a well lit main road."

"Do they still have the keys to the flat? Or have they handed them back to the apartment owners."

"They still have six months on their tenancy agreement, and unless they can find someone else to take it over they have to pay the rent as usual."

"Who else knows of the experiences they have had at the apartment besides yourself."

"No one else, except the neighbour I have mentioned to you and, they have agreed to say nothing until the matter of them finding somewhere else is completed. They have kept it quiet for fear if anyone else heard about it they would not be able to transfer the tenancy agreement. A bit unfair in some respect but understandable considering the financial commitments. I mentioned that perhaps if they went and spoke to the apartment owners they may cancel the agreement, but logically speaking I think they would just prolong the discussions until the time was up anyway, and they would still have the bill to pay at the end of it.

"Well if what you say about things now happening at your home now it does not seem to be much point in what they do as far as they are concerned."

Ken Barber left that afternoon after they had talked for a while longer and, had decided if his daughter would agree to accompany them to the apartment the following evening with her husband, to see if there was anything they could find out about the place that would account for the recent disturbances. Also to see if anything would occur while they were there. Peter was still not convinced of any "Paranormal" activity had been going on there, he was always suspicious of anything told to him second hand, and always felt it was better to look for rational answers before accepting anything else. But at the same time he could not dismiss what he had been told by ken Barker out of hand, as a publicity stunt of any kind, simply by his nature as he had related the facts to him as he had been told them, and admitting he had not witnessed anything concrete there, or at his own home personally.

The following day being a Saturday, and a free day from work, as far as all there were concerned, he decided to agree to see if a visit with the daughter and son-in-law to the flat could be arranged.

It had taken a lot of persuading on the part of Ken Barker to coerce his daughter and son-in-law to return to the apartment in daytime, and were totally adamant they would not stay after dark, and eventually Peter received a call from Ken Barker to say they would at least return there with them but they would leave immediately should the least thing happen out of the ordinary, and not return.

Unlocking the door with the key Ken's daughter then pushed it open and stepped away to allow Peter and Abigail to enter first. As they entered they felt nothing suspicious in any way and carried on into the first room which happened to be the sitting room, there seemed nothing out of place and was in quite a tidy condition, Peter walked over to the T.V. set ran a finger over the top and saw there was quite an amount of dust accumulation on his finger. Not an over an unusual thing he thought to himself if they had not been in the house for a week and mif they were experiencing the things they had described, and were experiencing a quite considerable amount of mental anguish the thought of house work would not he reasoned be on the top list of priorities for the couple. As he looked around the rest of the room he saw the amount of dust was about the same in quantity as on the television, not puzzling but acceptable in the circumstances. He turned to the couple who's flat it was.

"Take a look around this room, is everything in the same place as you usually put them, the pictures, vases, anything, is it all more or less as you left it the last time you were here."

After a quick look around both confirmed that it was the same as they remembered it, except for the clock on the mantle piece, it, had stopped but that was because they had not been there to wind it up. Deciding there was not much more to be seen Peter Jones decided he would take a look in the kitchen where the last reported incident had occurred.

He entered and could not feel anything different from the sitting room. Simon hung back for a while with his wife not really relishing entering the room, but slowly they came into the room to join the others, their eyes looking around and, seeing the place as exactly as they remembered leaving it, having taken their own personal belongings out as they fled the building. After the last experience of the coins on the table, which were still there for them all to see as ken had described to Peter.

Silently and turning to those behind him Peter motioned for them to stay where they were. He walked on into the other rooms alone, after returning to the sitting room, then on to the other rooms in the apartment, he returned to the others.

"There doesn't seem to be anything to be alarmed about that I can see or sense at the moment. I suggest, if you are willing that we should all return to the sitting room sit down and try to relax for a while. Perhaps you have some tea or coffee still in the house from when you were here last." Simon nodded. "There is some tea and coffee in the cupboard in the kitchen and the mugs are on the mug tree near the kettle, but we have no milk. Peter reached into his pocket and took from his wallet a five pound note. "If we stay here will you and Karen walk to the corner shop and get some? I noticed it as we arrived and was still open and, probably does not close until late this afternoon, if there is no sugar in the house get some as well, and a packet of biscuits of your choice might not go amiss."

While they were gone Peter spoke to ken to explain that his plan was to try and make Simon and Karin as relaxed as possible and to get them talking on any subject they could, except why they were there, and see what, if anything may happen.

"What kind of things are we talking about? Things appearing and such like?"

"To be honest I just don't know. I think it may be best to play it by ear, and if anything does happen we must take it from there."

Simon and Karin had returned coffee had been made and served, biscuits on a plate were in the middle of a coffee table in front of them. Everyone was settled in the sitting room, and because of the way the conversation was going they both were not now so unsettled about being in the house as when they first arrived. Time seemed to go by and then it started to become dark, and as it did so they both started to become nervous about being there. Peter was sure they would be all right if they stayed, but suggested they they returned to their own homes for a break and meet later to decide if they would be willing to accompany them there again later. In the mean time they could talk it over with each other and tell him how they felt about it later, adding they had now been in their home for almost three and a half hours and nothing had happened in that time.

As they were filing out into the hallway, continuing talking they stood still for a moment as Simon opened the door for them, and as they were all huddled in a bunch to walk through the door, a loud wrapping was heard coming from the direction of the bedroom, the talking immediately stopped, and as it did so there was the sound of something falling onto the floor in the kitchen. Each of them stood looking at each other except for Peter, who immediately on hearing the sound of the noise from the kitchen went straight in there. On the floor he saw a saucepan on it's side, the handle sticking up towards the ceiling, as he watched it began to rock gently, the handle eventually swaying from side to side but not coming in contact with the floor. While he stood there Abigail came along side him joined by Ken whose arm came onto Peter's shoulder, while he stood behind them both.

"What's causing it." He looked at Peter as if he was about to answer him in the same tone as he had asked the question, as if he was enquiring about some interferance on a T. V. screen.

"I'm not sure but it certainly isn't anything to do with Simon or Karen. Can you feel the cold here? Compared to where we have been sitting that is. There must be a ten degree difference at least, and your son-in-law switched the central heating on when we first came in and has only just this moment switched it off."

Abigail then turned away and went back to the front door to see where Simon and Karen were, and found them out in the hallway well away from the the entrance of the apartment waiting for the lift, she could hear down below in the lift shaft the sound of the lift doors opening and closing continually.

As she saw them she could see straight away they were in a panic to get out of there, they began to walk towards the stairway, as she came up to them Karen began crying with a look of pure fear on her face, fear of what was now happening, the more Simon tried to comfort her the more she became hysterical. Abigail directed her and Simon to the stairs then told him to get her away from the building as quickly as possible. As she saw them disappear down the stairs she turned to rejoin the others in the kitchen.

Walking through the door to the apartment she could hear all kinds of noise going on from where she had left her husband in the kitchen, as she approached the kitchen door, it slammed shut and as it did there was total silence from within the kitchen. Cautiously she tried the door, pulling it by the handle it would not turn and the door would not budge.

Peter and Ken stood motionless watching the saucepan rock too and fro on the kitchen floor, they both noticed Abigail as she turned and walked out of the kitchen. Ken more than anything wanted to turn around and follow her out, but seeing Peter was not going too, he somehow found the courage to stay with him, it was not long before other things began to happen, the kitchen drawers slid open and the contents such as cutlery and cook books and anything else they contained seemed to fly out and onto the floor, saucepans began to move, banging against each other making a terrible noise in the small kitchen, plates, cups and glasses spewed out of the cupboards bouncing and then scattered all over the floor around them, but strange as it may seem there was not one thing broken, and nothing flew anywhere close to them. A thing Peter immediately realized as he stood in the mayhem going on around him. Another thing had also occurred to him at the same time was the considerably increasing drop in temperature in the room. How long the events had been happening when he saw from the corner of his eye Abigail returning and the kitchen door closing so quickly, but not slamming shut and as it was closed there was an instant silence which prevailed in the room.

Ken his heart pounding, turned and was about to move towards the door, perspiration had formed on his face, cold chills of prickly fear were travelling over his body, he had an involuntary bladder function, leaving the front of his trousers with a dark stain as the warm urine he had no control over ran down the front and insides of his legs.

"Stay there and don't move." Peter could sense a presence in the room, and as he did so he felt there was no malice with who or whatever it was. Feeling that what ever was happening was due to wanting to draw their attention to it for some reason. He put the fear of the few moments before to one side, and listened with in his mind, as if he was in one of the evening circles of Mrs

Chanley, and asked in a prayer for help and assistance for the situation they were in, and within a short space of time there seemed to come into his thoughts the words "Help me". He knew then he had been right, the words were clear and explicit with a kind of echo to them.

"Who are you?" How can we help? What is your name?"

As Peter had spoken Ken could see in front of him a kind of brightness with no actual form to it, similar to a bright shadow in front of them both. It looked to him reminiscent of the brightness a mirror would make on a wall when reflecting light from a window inside a gloomy room, but forming in the centre of the kitchen directly in front of them, alternating from a brightness to a smoky translucency, that in some way made it impossible for him to focus his eyes on it with any degree of optical stability. He just knew it was there, and though still with a degree of the jitters he was now content with the situation, because he could see Peter seemed to be able to understand what was going on. Although his eyes were closed, and could not see what he could.Peter stood still, his eyes closed talking in and out, as if he was in conversation with someone in the room with them. Ken under any other circumstances would have felt embarrassingly uncomfortable, but waited listening, with his his mouth open and breathing shallow, and his heart beating heavy, to what Peter was saying unsure, of the out come of the ethereal experience. Suddenly the brightness before him began to fade until it was there no more.

Peter stood for a while after it had gone silent and still, suddenly he slowly opened his eyes, turned immediately towards Ken, rubbing them as if he had just awakened from a good nights sleep.

"Are you all right?" He asked now rubbing his face with his hands.

"I feel all right now. But have to admit, it's something I would rather not experience again. What was it? What was it all about?" He looked over towards where the brightness had been. "There was something here.....a light, it's crazy but I saw it, it was there all the time you were talking." He looked closely at him slightly embarrassed. "Did you know you were talking? I could not hear everything you were saying but I did hear a couple of sentences here and there. You sounded as if you were having a conversation with someone."

Peter smiled and patted Ken on the shoulder. "You are right. I was! It was unusual but much the same as I have seen others do before when I have been in church, but some how there was a difference, a subtle difference but it was there, another thing is, when I have gone into trance in a circle or in a church service, I can remember nothing of what I have said seen or heard. But this time I can remember everything. Although, I could see nothing except a light. A bright and vibrant light around me and the words were spoken to me from inside of it. There was also a feeling of despondency coming from the voice I heard. I don't think there will be any more occurrences here to frighten Karen or Simon, now a link has been made. If we all go to your house I will try to explain everything."

Three quarters of an hour later when every thing was calm over what had happened in the kitchen, and Simon and Karen had been half convinced by Peter, when he had told them he was more than sure there would be no more distressing activity if and when they should decide to move back into their apartment, due to what had taken place in the kitchen while he and Ken had been there, but there was still a little ambiguity over his words and conviction it would be the end of any happenings they had endured there in the recent past.

Simon asked. "Was it anything to do with us in the apartment, something we had done unwittingly?"

"The only thing you did was to move in there, and had not realized what was happening when it first occurred. Not your fault in any way we can know. As time went on the contactee for the sake of a better word, became frustrated as his efforts to attract your attention seemed to no avail, thus he tried to make you seek help in hope Karen and Simon would get assistance from someone who would understand what was going on and would be able to communicate with him. Which was the only thing he could do, and as it has now turned out he has managed to succeed."

Karen and Simon could not believe what they were hearing, still believing the the manifestations and things which had happened to them in their home could be for the reasons

Peter was explaining to them. Still halfway expecting something to happen while they were at Ken's house while still talking of the reason for the strain which they had been enduring for the past months.

As Peter listened to Ken and his family talking he was waiting silently for the opportunity to speak to Karen and Simon, unsure of how they would take what he was about to say, when he got the chance. Eventually there was a lull in the talking which gave him the chance he had been waiting for.

"There is something I have not told you of yet. I have been unsure of how to tell you, or how you are going to take what I have to say. While Ken and myself were in the kitchen, and as I told you, I did communicate with whoever it was causing the disturbances. The first thing I heard was a voice that said 'Help me' The words were clear and distinct. The way they had been spoken left me in no doubt whoever said them was in a earnest and troubled state. He told me he could not understand what had happened to him. I was about to tell him he was deceased, but for some reason I held myself back from saying so.He told me his name, and that he had at one time lived in the apartment some time before, he had seen others move in and leave, he had tried to contact them, but no matter what he did he could make no impression on them, he tried to touch, speak, anything he could think of, but they seemed to have no knowledge he was there. When you both moved in he had all but resigned himself to the fact you would be no different from the others. But, while you were out one time he moved about as he usually did. Seeing a bird come to the window he moved towards it, and in doing so walked near the table with the statue on it. Forgetting for that moment the state of his existence, and had forgotten he had no solid form and in a sense subconsciously put his hand out to steady it on the table, and as he did so it fell onto the floor. It puzzled him how he had done it, because in the past when ever he tried to touch anything or anyone there was never any reaction at all. He tried again for weeks but could not repeat anything similar, and could not understand how he had done it. Then came the day when Karen had told you Ken, of the keys. When she eventually found them on the table in the bedroom, while at the same time she was sure she had not been in her bedroom that day. When she had hung them on the key hook he had just thought to himself he wished he could hide them from her, it was just an idle thought at the time he told me, and then they were in his hand. It was then he discovered when he thought with out any conviction of achievement he acquired the result of what he wanted, and deduced if he used his actions and thought's in a negative way, for some reason he began to get positive reactions in our physical world. I asked him how long it had been since he had found himself in the state he found himself in now, he replied he had no idea and, had no sense of time passing. I told him with your permission I would be willing to hold a circle in your apartment with some of my friends to see if we could help him in some way. How would you feel about that?"

Karen and Simon did not answer him, but just looked at Ken who was as surprised as them at what Peter had said. The silence was broken as Ken spoke.

"I don't know the ins and outs of what happened in the kitchen when we were in there, but I know there was something going on, I trusted you, even though in truth, I wanted to get out of there. What ever it was, it seemed to me you knew how to act and what to do. As it happened everything ended well." Turning to his daughter and son-in-law he added. "If I were you I would go along with what he has said and, do what he thinks is necessary. Finish everything once and for all, and as long as I and yourselves are not involved in whatever he has to do there, then I say let him go ahead."

CHAPTER 8

August 1994

The Detectorists

Philip and Trevor Reed were twin brothers, they had parked their car on the edge of the now empty hay field, the hay had been cut and baled, and transported to a barn for winter feed, leaving the grass short cropped and perfect for them to use their metal detectors on. The farm belonged to a Fred Buller, and they had managed to get permission to detect on the field earlier in the spring when they had seen the farmer ploughing up the field next to it for potato planting that season.

They had a few days on the ploughed field before the planting had begun, and had asked if the could detect on the field he had set aside for feed hay for the coming winter. He did agree but told them they would have to wait until the autumn, as he was anticipating getting two cuts out of the field instead of the usual one. Once he had harvested the second cut, then they would be welcome to try out their hobby, and see what they could find.

He told them they would be welcome to look in the woods situated at the the top of the fields at anytime, but they had declined the offer at the time because the thought of picking up 'twelve bore' cartridge cases all day was not a prospect they enjoyed while out for a days detecting, experience in the past, in other woods had shown them, in wooded areas they were the bane of all detectorist's.

Philip happened to be in the area delivering parcels. He worked for the G.P.O. on the parcel deliveries, and had seen the harvesting of the hay was in full swing earlier in the week. He had told his brother, who went to see the farmer as soon as he had finished work the following day, and asked if they could do some detecting at the weekend to which he had agreed.

Philip Reed was feeling quite pleased with himself, he had decided to give up smoking just over a year before, and had put the money he would normally spend on cigarettes into his savings account, but keeping it separate from any other savings he had. It had stayed there mounting up and he was quite surprised when he had a bank statement of the amount he had saved in what seemed a relatively short time, and was amazed at how much he had been spending on the weed. He had kept adding to it until he had enough saved for a top of the range detector with accessories included in a package deal, without spending all he had saved.

Having tried it out earlier that week soon after it had arrived in his garden where he had made a test area with coins ect. planted for some time now at different depths under his lawn, and knowing the location and depths had been really pleased with the results, and it's performance. This was the first time he had 'field tested' it and was quite excited, with the hope of some good finds. He had also decided to keep his old machine as a backup, and for doing fair grounds after they had come and gone. Both brothers had been keen detectorists for eight years now, after seeing some one using one on the foreshore of a beach in Cornwall while on holiday. They had both bought second hand machines soon after, and 'upgraded' them as time went on. Since the start they had been keen, and found time for their hobby whenever they could. They had found a few interesting items, including coins ancient and modern. Phil was the first of the two to decide to purchase a new machine, and Trevor not to be outdone had secretly ordered one, the same model as his twin brother had purchased, after seeing it in action, and admiring the results of the day on a beach.

There had always been a standing wager that whoever found a "Victorian" shilling first, should one be found on a days detecting, would win a five pound note off of the other. The wager always added to the search, and made the brothers joke to each other whenever they had a positive signal from a target in the ground.

After an hour or so they had found a few old nails a couple of musket balls, a handful of mixed pre-decimal coins and a George the third sixpenny bit, a bit ground weathered and bent, but he was more than happy with it because he had not found anything so small and buried so deep before. Trevor had found a horse brass he was quite pleased with, thinking it would look quite nice after a cleaning and polishing and mounted with some others he had in his collection already, and had found at other occasions.

Phil decided he was about ready to stop for some refreshments and signalled his brother with a whistle and and his hands together forming the letter 'T'. Both brothers made their way back to to where they had left a flask and some sandwiches in an old army small pack they had in the family for years, hanging on the gate post at the entrance to the field. Pouring tea from the flask Trevor casually remarked. "There must be a rotting carcass of of some kind inside the woods near where I am searching, perhaps a dead fox or badger even. When the wind changes a smell comes right across to were I am, it made feel quite sick at one time, I am glad there is not much wind today, and not constantly blowing my way"

"Did we bring the O.S. map with us today, or is it still at home?"

Trevor looked looked across to his brother as he handed him a plastic cup of tea from the flask. "What do you mean we? I thought you were going to bring it from the house, with you when you left this morning."

"Damn it! I put them all in the satchel, and must have left them on the shed bench when I picked up my digging tools this morning. That's what happens when I rush around, they must be still be there, on the bench where I left them."

Trevor casually got to his feet and walked towards the parked car.

"Where are you going?"

"It's a good job I had my batteries on charge all night in there, and one of us can wake up with a clear head in the morning. What would you do without me? I sometimes wonder." He returned carrying the satchel and dropped it on the floor in front of his brother's feet.

"Take your pick, there's a new O.S. map in there besides the old one we usually have, I thought the details on the old one have become a little worn and there are parts almost worn away, so I bought a new one, let's face it the other one is over eight years old now and then it was second hand when we got it. I saw the new one in the shop as I passed it a week ago I thought we would be coming to this field sooner or later this month and thought it would be handy. I will take the price of it out of the kitty when we sort out the rest of the things we are going to get, such as the rechargable batteries we need."

Philip searched around in the satchel until he found what he wanted. He opened the new map his brother had bought, then one of the copies they had bought from the records office of local history, finding the field they were now in, and the surrounding area he began to compare the two. Then he stood up holding the new modern map in his hands and glancing down at the other laid out on the ground, he had weighted down with some of the coins and objects he had found so far that morning.

"Look Trev! On the map dated 1900, it shows the path running further over towards the hedge you have been detecting near, than the modern map. There must have been some alterations made to alter it's course for some reason in the past, and instead of showing it running along in side this field, it shows it running along the other side of the hedge along and inside the woods, and then enters this side seventy yards or so further along, towards where you were when we stopped for a break." He knelt down and placed the new map over part of the old Victorian copy, and began to trace his finger along the path in the old copy. "If you look along here, and follow the path it meets up eventually with the path shown on the modern map, leading to the old church behind the woods. Why don't we walk along inside of the woods, where the original path was? If it is not all there there might be still remnants of it we can still see. Once in the woods we could see perhaps where the original path entered the field we have been detecting in, and then follow it all the way down to the main road. What do you say? Shall we move out of here and give it a try.?"

"I suppose it would hurt to give it a try. Thinking about it, I did find most of the Victorian and Geogian coins lower down the field than up. Possibly I had left the old original path lower down where it would have joined the main road, and as I swept up towards where you were would been moving away from it, and out of line of the dropping zone.

The brothers then continued on with their lunch break, while at the same time showing each other what they had found so far on the field.

With their metal detectors over their shoulders and the two different maps in Phil's map pocket of his ex army surplus combat trousers, they made their way towards what they perceived to be the old path way behind the hedge and inside the of the wooded area. A lot of nettles and wild parsley was growing profusely in the area behind the hedge in quite a broad swathe measuring approximately Fifteen feet or so wide, travelling as far as they could see, along the hedge row, giving conviction they had found the pathway marked on the old map.

As they walked along, there was what appeared to be remnants of an old stone wall which had long since crumbled in places, and covered with earth, which rabbits had burrowed into, leaving their excavated soil mixed with the stone work which had fallen away, or caved in due to the rigors of time and weather, but mostly hidden by the overgrown hedge of bramble and blackthorn, with the odd elderberry tree holding it's own as it always seemed to no matter where situated, some of the berries were sparse and still hanging where earlier there had been purple ripe clusters, while most had been devoured by birds or fallen to the ground after the gusting breezes had loosened them once they had ripened, to be consumed by the rodent wild life.

They travelled along until they saw the wild vegetation begin to clear away from the side of the hedge until there was a stretch of long grass, yellow and brittle, dried from the heat of the sun, bending over and beginning to fall flat towards the ground, mole humps were dotted here and there. Then suddenly there were weeds in clumps at at the side of the hedge, which had obviously been made up with what ever was at hand, and built up reaching to halfway in height of the rest of the hedge they had travelled along, tied here and there were lengths of barbed wire, which had been woven into the hedge and twisted around stakes of hazelwood, then anchored to blackthorn bushes in the hedge. Tied around higgle dee, piggle dee. Also, to make a crude form of netting, were lengths of binder twine made to improvise as a rough form of a serviceable net fence, although nothing stylish, it would however serve the purpose of stopping any live stock from straying into the field they had been detecting in, into the wooded area.

"Thats's just got to be where the path entered the field shown on the old map. See! it's about seventy yards from where the modern path is marked here."

Turning around Philip Reed could see there was an area that came down the wooded hillside, a clear area of about twelve feet or more wide, which was directly in line with the filled in gap in the hedge where they were standing. "What do you make of that?" He asked his brother. Kneeling down on one knee, he looked towards where he had pointed, and then back to where the barbed wire was in the hedge, then turned to where they had just come from.

Trevor looked to where his brother had indicated, not quite understanding what it was he was supposed to be looking at. "What do I make of, what?" He asked, puzzled. "That depression in the ground! See! It's too wide to be just an ordinary track or footpath, and the depression is worn, not by water erosion, you can tell by the way of the direction and the depth, when you look at it from ground level. Look at the trees that are in it's path, I bet there is not one that is more than one hundred years old, Well, not much more anyway and at most, I would say the majority would have to stretch to be even a hundred. But when you look at the trees around the depression, they must go back to at least two hundred and fifty at least and some are probably a lot older."

"So!....I still don't see the point you are trying to make."

Philip did not answer his brothers remark, but had got out the maps again. "Well I'll be buggered." He spoke softly to himself.

"Well what is it? What do you find that is so interesting about some old, and some not so old trees and such crap? What is there on the map? An old fort, earth works or the site of an old manor house or what?"

"There's nothing on the map and that is what so interesting." "How the hell can nothing on the map be so interesting? Come on Philip let's stop farting around and get onto the path now, and do some detecting before the days over."

"No Trevor! Wait a moment, listen I think we may have inadvertently stumbled on something which would not be on any maps, of the past or the present, we could get hold of."

"Such as what?"

"Such as an old, very old cart track, and if I am right we may be extremely lucky to have found it." He knelt down on the ground and placed the maps so as they were overlapping again as he had before, so the details on them could be compared more easily. "Look here, this is about where we are on the map." He then lightly drew a faint line with a pencil he always carried with him of what he considered to be an ancient cart track through the woods. "If we assume it is what I think it to be, and follow the direction of it, look where it is heading, and where it has come from."

Trevor looked, but could still not understand what his brother was driving at, and looked blankly at the maps.

Philip stood up and walked across to the fenced topped hedge, his brother picked the maps up from the ground folded them and handed them to him.

"If I am right and I am more inclined to think I am, it's probably the cart track which would have led up through the woods to what once was the site of an old Dominican Priory. All anyone knows for sure was that it was in the general direction of the church at the far side of the woods. There are parts of the church built with stone, some say, might have come from it, and evidence that some of the old farm houses around the area have some of the stone from it as well. But because of the time that has passed since the church was built, the actual site of the priory has long been forgotten and lost, and nobody knows for sure where it was located but, I feel it strong in my water that this could be the original track that led to it. Don't forget it was way back during the reign of Henry The Eighth that the dissolution of the monasteries took place, most were raised to the ground, and, if you think of the depression in the ground here, leading to the field we have been detecting in, it would lead down all the way to the old coach road from London to Taunton, Exeter, and so on."

"There's a lot of if's and but's about it all, but if it was where you say it could have been, then.... surely someone would have found it, or traces of it, in all the time which has passed since then. What about the farmers when they have ploughed up fields and dug ditches for drainage, tree felling, anything to do with altering the landscape in any way, why hasn't some one in all that time found anything, let's face it a Priory is not the same as a medieval hovel, of which today, would be almost impossible to find the remains of, even if the general location was known?"

Philip did not answer, but was looking up and down the hedge where he stood, then he began walking back towards where they had come from, with his long handled digging tool in his hand, until he came to the part of the hedge they had seen the remnant of wall. Looking around more closely where the fall in with stone and earth were uncovered, he moved slowly along until where he could see the the hedge undisturbed in any way, and began digging into the earth and vegetation covered hedge row, it was not long before there was a clang as his digging tool hit stone, within a minute he had cleared away and area of about two feet in diameter. Then stood back to look at it. His brother looked on quite puzzled at what he was doing, but let him carry on without saying a word.

"Well what do you think that is?"

Trevor was getting a little peeved at his brother by now. "So it's a bloody wall. I could tell that at a glance. Do I get a silver or a gold star to put in my note book to show mum, teacher. For gods sake tell me what the bloody hell you are going on about before I go doolali."

"Trevor! Don't you see anything? Can't you see what's here besides just a wall? Look how well the stone work was dressed, and the position they are all laid down. When we were looking at the rest of what we could see, we could not tell whether it looked like anything we see here because it was all hidden, and what we could see was just fallen rock, earth and vegetation, it was not clear whether it had just been banked up, and the stone thrown in for support, when the field had been cleared of stones in the past. Now we can see this part of the wall in all it's splendour. Why, and who, has gone to all the trouble to build a wall such as we see here, way out in the middle of nowhere, with well dressed stone?"

"You tell me because, I still don't have a clue what you are driving at."

"Think! What kind of people would have done that sort of thing in the past! Monks! That's who. I think that this might be a boundary wall, or what's left of it at least. I also think the depression in the ground that goes from here into the woods leads to somewhere in there which is the site of the priory, or abbey, which no one knows the exact location of, and to answer your earlier question, of, why farmers ect. have never found any trace of it is, because I believe it was built in this woodland, and has been hidden, and it has never been cleared since then! That is what I meant when I said about the trees each side of the depression being older, a lot older than any within it. I believe it may be worth detecting along the depression and into the woods, to see if we do turn up anything medieval, then perhaps we could look around there more closely in the woods while detecting, for anywhere the earth has been disturbed by such things as rabbits, foxes or badgers, who knows, perhaps we might find such things as pottery shards, or anything ecclesiastical."

"So! If that's what you have worked out about the place, can we now get back onto the field, or the so called track you say might be here and start detecting again. Then perhaps you may find a crucifix that might have fallen off of a monk while he was out jogging. Come on now, Phil! Give it a rest about monks and Priories, all we came out for was just to get a bit of detecting done in the field while we have the chance, lets get back to it before the days over."

"You can carry on in the field if you want, but seeing as we already have permission to look in the woods I'm going to give it a go, along what I think is the cart track, and see what if anything I can turn up. If only we had started earlier in the year when the farmer gave us permission to look in here we would have noticed what the possibilities were and not wasted most of the time on beaches and footpaths. Picking up his detector and digging tool Phil started to walk towards the suspected cart track.

"Oh well! Detecting in the field or in the woods does not really matter I suppose, as long as the detectors are switched on and we are sweeping ground with them, I might as well follow, and two machines are better than one but, don't call me over unless you find something worth looking at, but more than likely it will be mostly twelve bore cartridges, we will be finding, and they don't exactly make my day. Perhaps your theories might pay off so just this once I don't mind giving them a chance."

As the brothers entered the wood, there was an immediate coolness around them, the canopy of green cut out the strong sunlight, and rising heat of the morning, making the air around them feel fresh and clean, flashes of golden yellow brightness penetrated the area around them here and there, from the gaps in foliage above them, as they swept their detectors in even sweeps to the left and right in front of them. They were oblivious to any sounds other than those coming from their earphones. A rustling in the undergrowth, the fleeting movement of a mouse as it scurried away to safety, the heavy flapping wings of a wood-pidgion as it crashed it's way through the foliage above them, none of these things were heard by the brothers. So intent were they listening for even the slightest of signals that might be given off by their machines via the head phones, indicating there was perhaps some small metallic object of interest or value to them buried below them waiting to be found, and see daylight for the first time, perhaps in centuries.

A couple of hours had gone by with out much in the way of interest being found other than a few coins and cartridge case ends. Slowly they travelled on, stopping to recheck an illusive signal here and there along the nine to twelve foot depression, as it wound it's way deeper into the gloom of the woods, they saw it began to level out, then after about seventy yards there was still no sign of it petering out, although if they were to look around them with a little more attention to their surroundings, they would have noticed there was a marked difference in the age and position of the trees around them off of the suspected cart track, and the distance between them became more thickly covered with bramble, hazelnut, and stinging nettles in places.

Keeping to the 'cart track' they carried on along the level part of the woods, while concentrating as before on every bleep of their machines. Trevor after digging to a depth of seven inches pulled from the hole a small silver coin, rubbing it between his thumb and fore finger became excited, as there in his hand and in quite good condition was a coin he thought could be of Henry the Seventh silver penny.

"Here let me have a look." Philips voice was tinged with excitement, as he took the small coin from his brothers hand, as it was held out to him. He took a close look and immediately knew it for what it was and confirmed his brothers suspicions. "See what did I say? I just knew there was more to these woods than we thought, when I noticed that depression earlier. So what do you say now?. About all the if's and but's you were on about when I first mentioned what I thought about the depression."

"O.K.! O.K.! So there might be something in what you have been on about, but one coin does not mean a lot, it could be just coincidence, and nothing more."

"That I will admit but look at what Monarch it is, and where we have found it.

Both men looked around them, there seemed to be a hush, and the only sound was the gentle rustle of leaves as a cool breeze fanned them, at the same time there was a feeling of excitement and hopeful expectancy of perhaps more interesting things to be found. As they were stood still talking about the find they became aware of the singing of a song thrush somewhere deeper in the woods, faint and then loud as the wind blew the sound towards them, then eased of as it changed direction in such a way, knowing where it was perched, and giving sound to the woods, they could not accurately discern.

"There is hardly any sign of a depression around here. What do you say we go back to where the depression can be seen and sweep the area hap-hazard, and then if we find anything of interest in one part we, can peg and line it, after some lunch and see what else may turn up. What do you say?"

"Come on then. Let's get started." Trevor after his find of the silver penny was eager to start detecting again.

It was one of those situations that happen so quickly, and yet it takes the mind so long to comprehend. First came the flies, then wafting to and fro on the breeze, the horrible stench of rotting flesh, the odour of which enters the nostrils with such power, the brain becomes confused for a moment, the mouth opens allowing the full force of of the stench to be inhaled, making the full impact on smell and taste senses simultaneously. Such was the sudden impact on Trevor he could not stop himself from gagging, then ultimately brought everything he had eaten earlier in a sprayed heap on the ground in front of him. Standing bent double the flies buzzing around in clouds, his detector lay on the ground covered with half digested vomit, while his hands were holding his stomach as he carried on retching.

Philip at this time had stopped sweeping his detector, while in the process of swapping his own recharged batteries into his machine, when he casually looked over towards his brother. He saw he was bent over double with his detector on the ground retching for all he was worth, in uncontrollable spasms. But it was not his brother that held his attention, for directly above him was suspended, only inches from the top of his brothers head, should he have been standing upright, was the head of a body which was suspended from a thick branch of an oak tree by the ankles, hanging upside down, arms stretched out at right angles as in a crucifixion. Lashed and kept in position by a length of ash sapling of about seven feet in length, swaying and with a partial twist, as it started each direction of it's gentle wind induced swing. The flesh or what remained of it, green, black, and blue with putrefaction, large empty sockets where the eyes once were, which had been picked clean by carrion's of the air, leaving the edges torn and ragged as they had taken their fill from the softer parts of the hanging body. The swarms of flies and maggots moving on the surface and around the close vicinity of the body gave the impression that what was once human flesh had been somehow transformed into a hive of variable coloured and industrious movement as insect life intent on using it for their own purpose of survival and continuation of their own kind. The sight made more grotesque, hanging there, amidst the beauty of various coloured leaves and trees with the flickering of golden shafts of sunlight around it.

"Trevor! Trevor! Come away from there, come over here, hurry."

His mind was working twice the speed as normal, and yet the words would not come to his lips as he wanted, but just a lot of garbled sentences hurled in the direction of his brother. Which made Trevor hearing the sounds and confusion in his brothers voice while feeling the way he was and not understanding why, he instinctively ran towards where Philip was standing and shouting. Vomit spittle still flowing from his mouth as he ran, after retrieving his detector vomit and all, from the ground.

Minutes later detectors in hand, both men were running through the wood as fast as they were able, the vision of the suspended corpse vivid in their minds as they went, both unable to feel safe until they were out of the woods.

Eventually they made their way along the road in the car to a public house and told the landlord what they had found in the woods and asked him to telephone the police.

The landlord after assessing that they were still in some kind of shock offered them a brandy each, which they downed in one swallow.

CHAPTER 9

August 1994

The Policeman's Lot

Detective Sergeant David Royston Mitchell, held his breath then plunged his head into the sink once more, holding it under for as long as he could beneath the water which he had filled with two trays of ice cubes, the cold water brought on an instant numbness, which seemed more intense than it had the first time and then a sudden tightening pain due to the cold water, which immediately started to bite into his scalp, the skin seemed to shrivel under his hair with the cold, while his face and, nose especially went numb. He opened his eyes while his head was submerged and felt the cold bite intensely on his eyeballs, eventually the cold and need for air forced him to lift his head out. Arms straight and rigid he held on to the side of the basin, through stinging eyelids he looked into the mirror in front of him, sticking his tongue out he felt the rough dryness of it against the roof of his mouth as he retracted it. The furred whiteness, a contrast, to the red veins in the whites of his eyes. He felt rough, he looked rough, he bowed his head and looked to the toilet at the side of him, it looked a lot smaller this morning than it had the night before when his head was over it, his stomach gave a rumble just before he broke wind again. He caught hold of the chain and drew it up pulling the plug with it, the water drained, as it was almost empty a gurgling sound came, matching the way his stomach was feeling. Straightening his back he reached for and gripped the chrome plated taps. He shuddered as cold water continued to drip from his hair and run down his back, goose pimples covered his bare arms and body. "Good God Mitchell! You look like and feel like shit." He reached for a towel and began to dry himself, groaning as the vigorous rubbing made the pain within his head throb more.

He had been out the night before for a celebration drink or so he had tried to convince himself, with some of his colleague's at the station. He had come home with a skin full and was now suffering the consequences. It had started as a celebration, but in the end it was a case of him using the drink to cover what he was really feeling, empty, alone and totally depressed.

There was little of the evening he could remember after the first two hours, except that there was a lot of laughter around him, and he was laughing too, but not really taking part in the festivities, just committed to ride the laughter ripples, as it were, and be there. There was not a lot he could accurately remember about the later part of the night, it all seemed to him now, as if he had been just a distant observer, within the bouts of laughter it seemed. The only thing constant in his mind, what patches of the night he could focus his memory on were of conversation's he would listen to, smile, nod his head and answer yes or no as he swayed on his feet, looking back it made him feel a little foolish now with some of the scenes he could remember. Such as, when he found himself on the floor, having fallen over a table as he tried to reach the end of the bar in the corner, so as to be able to lean against it for support, but mostly he thought now was he just at that time wanted to be on his own. He never did reach the bar, come to that, after he had been picked up off of the floor he was half dragged and then carried out to the car park of the public house, to a waiting taxi with two of his colleague's who he could remember insisting to the taxi driver they would come with him and, should he have an accident they would make sure it would not be in the car. He remembered his head out of the window for most of the journey, and the soothing but giddy feeling coolness on his face as the taxi sped it's way along the road. There was not a lot he could remember about his arrival home, he remembered someone fumbling in his jacket pocket for his door keys and opening his door, more or less carrying him to and laying him on the couch, but who it was he could not remember, it was all just a hazy collection of out of focus and muffled voices. Then later, when he could remember the spinning ceiling, it had only lasted for a moment or so, then came the queasiness in his stomach, and the journey on his hands and knees when he made his way across the floor to the bathroom. Then the trek later as swaying and mumbling to himself he found the couch then the spinning ceiling again just a few moments before he closed his eyes and drifted into a drunken slumber.

He remembered while he had been under the water for the last time, it had been years since he had felt as he was feeling that morning, and swore with determination it would be years, if ever again, that he would do the same as he had done the night before. How many drinks had gone past his lips he could not remember, but it was never worth it for the way he was feeling at that moment.

The cause of his self inflicted illness was because three days before, he had received in the post his 'Decree Absolute'.

As had walked to his gate on the way to work. He had taken the letter from the postman and without really looking at it, had placed it in his pocket and had forgotten it. It was there until lunch time when he had pulled his wallet out, to pay for his lunch, and saw the address of his solicitor on the reverse side, knowing instantly what it probably contained. He opened it, and as he read it anyone who was there could have told it was news he was not over excited, or happy about.

After news of the letter had got around to his colleague's and knowing his feelings on the matter someone suggested it would be a good thing for him to have a night out than stay on his own all over the coming weekend, insisting it was their duty to rally around, as they put it, to try and cheer him up. But he knew from past experience, having seen similar situations in the past, it was just an excuse for them to have a booze up without wives, it was as they termed it "a male bonding of consolation." As the cold water had gone down the plug hole he scooped out what remained of the ice, and threw it into the toilet bowl. He then washed and shaved, and while watching the wash basin empty for the second time, the mini whirlpool swirled around the basin, he was thinking as it gurgled, it was as if he was watching his life go down at the same time, a kind of postscript to his married life.

After his head soak, wash and shave, he dressed himself, made some coffee, then sat at the breakfast bar in the kitchen. The paper with confirmation of the decree absolute was in front of him on the bar. He sipped the steaming coffee, and in the quiet of the kitchen his mind began to go back the years, from when he had been married, to the present day, and try as he could, he just could not see how things had gone down hill so much and ended in divorce. How it had gone wrong, or even when, he could still not understand, even to this day what had actually happened with their marriage. Had it been a case of 'Gaynor' not content with him being on call at all hours? If that was so, she had known him for three years before they had got married and always seemed to understand then the unpredictable inconvenience of the job, also as he got promotion which caried the extra responsibilities it involved along with it there was still no sign from her she was coming discontented. Anyway if so, what else had she expected, it was all part of the job, and they had a comfortable living for all the years they had together out of it. Some how things had come to a head, and it had come as a complete shock three or four months after their daughter Erica had married her young husband, who had waited until he had passed his doctors exams, and was now in a practice in his native Canada with his young wife. Although, now looking back he could see there were signs of her being discontented before then, but had foolishly put it down to her going through the menopause after having had to have a hysterectomy, which at the time of her having the operation they had been told it was possible menopause could occur soon after.

The old saying of putting something down to experience, could not work in his case, experience would be when you know where you have gone wrong, and he still did not have a clue where that was. All he had to show for twenty plus years of marriage was his house, a daughter now living in a foreign land with a foreign husband and, a life of her own, an ex wife, living god knows where, with God knows who. He looked around the room, at the furniture and fittings they had chosen together, nearly everything he could see held a memory of some kind or another, whether it was the choosing of them, or disagreement over the purchase price, one or the other of them had paid at the time, but there was always some memory attached somewhere. But eventually they had ended up with a home they had been happy and comfortable in. He had even begged her on the telephone on the few occasions they had spoken before the divorce to at least try and talk over what the problems were, and the suggestion to see a councillor, but all she would say was there was no point because she had fell out of love with him, and wanted to start afresh somewhere else. To do things she had always wanted to do but had never had the chance while she was married and bringing up Erica.

She had insisted all along the break up was through no fault of his and had even seen her solicitor and instructed him that she wished him to proceed with a divorce on the grounds of an irreconcilable breakdown of their marriage.

He had kept his personal life separate from his work, so it had come to the others at the station that things were not well at the Mitchell house hold only at the time of the decree nisi.

He was wondering what to do for the rest of the day, looking at the kitchen clock he saw it was well past lunch time, a lot later than he had first thought when he had got up. It was the first full week end he had free for quite a while, as he sat at the kitchen bar looking out of the window the sun was bright and there was no sign of rain to come. He pondered whether to mow the front and back lawns, he could see they needed cutting but with the hangover still with him he decided to put the task on hold until the following day. He heard a clatter of the cat flap in the kitchen door behind him, and then saw Millie, his sole companion in the house, run up to him, rubbing herself against his legs. "Hello old girl. I had forgotten all about you, hungry is that it?" He went to reach down but as he did so the blood ran to his head, making it throb even more, getting up he went to the cupboard, the cat followed brushing against his legs as he did so. He opened a tin of cat food and put a quantity into her dish, then placed it on the floor before her. She instantly began to feed, he stroked her affectionately behind the ears, her rump came up, and tail curled back and then stood rigid for a while, he left her then, as she settled down to eat her food purring with delight.

He decided after he had fed the cat to take a walk down to the village store for a newspaper, thinking the walk in the fresh air would do him good, and make him feel better by the time he returned home, he was wrong his head was a bit clearer but his stomach was still upset. He was sitting back in the kitchen the paper open in front of him on the breakfast bar, as he turned the second page over the telephone rang. On answering it he heard the voice of Alistair Loverage, a detective inspector at the station. "Dave I am sorry, I know it's your weekend off, but I have to call you in. There has been an incident at Stoke Croft woods, apparently, a body has been found there. The superintendent has called everyone in, and leave has been cancelled for those who are available. We have to take over the investigation at the scene. The local uniform are there as we speak. The Super has told me to have you come in if you were available, to assist in the investigation. I will pick you up in fifteen minutes sorry to spoil your weekend."
"When you say body, what do you mean, just dead or dead with suspicious 'C's'?"
"I don't know any more than you at present, but apparently the people who rang sounded a bit confused, and seemed in a panic, and said something about the body was hanging in the woods."
"Hanging! More than likely a suicide, wouldn't you say at this stage Alan?" Loverage hated his given name and preferred to be addressed as Alan by his colleague's at the station.
"We only had the call ten minutes ago from the local village policeman, and he has have not been in touch with us since then. There might be more on the car radio as I come over to pick you up, we'll see, and if there is more information, I will fill you in if I do receive any update on what is there, when I see you." "I will get changed while you are on your way here." Dave Mitchell went upstairs to the bedroom, opened the wardrobe door, his eyes immediately fell on a couple of dresses his wife had left in the cleaners and were forgotten about until he had gone to the same cleaners to pick up a pair of trousers and jacket he had cleaned a month before. When he had

picked them up the assistant had told him the dresses where still there from when she had put them in for cleaning, he did not want to say anything about the separation and pending divorce to anyone at the time still in hope of a reconciliation could be made between them, and just said he would pay for them and took them on at the same time as his slacks and jacket. One of them she had worn at the police ball a couple of years before. It was black with red shoulders, with white lace down the front of it forming a 'V'. He remembered how stunning she looked in it and how he had been so proud and still in love with her, when he had seen the looks of envy on some of the visiting guests, and police from other towns. He had the same thoughts every time he went there, she had seemed so happy then, they both, were for that matter, well he knew he was. "How!" He had asked himself once more, as he had so many times since. "Could things get out of hand? When did the changes start to happen?"

He was as much in the dark now as when it had first happened and could not see himself coming to terms with the divorce and loss of her, and was still in love with her now as he was on the day they had been married. That was how he saw things at this moment in time, and could not imagine any change in the future as far as he could see.

His thoughts then turned to his daughter, who at the time of the separation was as confused and upset as himself, but due to circumstances and distance away from them both, had moved on with her life with her husband and, and then had come along a one year old grandson he had not seen yet and advised him that perhaps he should do the same. Since it had all happened she had kept in regular contact with him through the post and a telephone call every two months or so, and each time the contact was made she always asked if he had heard from or even seen her mother, to which the answer was always the same, except for contact through her solicitor he knew nothing of her where about's, or what she was doing, or who she was with if at all there was anyone. Although before the break up she always insisted there was no one else she was involved with.

On the way down the stairs he heard the car, and a toot of the horn to let him know it was there. Arriving at the scene, the police barrier tape was being put up, showing the extent of the activity there since the grim discovery. Eight or nine uniformed police officers were on the scene also preparing for a fingertip search of the immediate area.

"With all the uniforms here it does not look as if it could be a suicide Dave. I wonder where the body is?"

"There's Herbie Slater coming out of the woods on the path towards us it must be over there somewhere. He has probably just finished his part on the body and will tell us when we reach him."

Herbert Slater, was the medical examiner and always seemed in a happy mood, no matter what, or who he had to make a medical report on, whenever, the two detectives had met with him through the course of their work. Except in cases they had investigated in the past in connection with the deaths of children through ill fated consequences, and only one of those was a case of murder having been suspected and later confirmed. His warped sense of humour was his private safety valve, to cover any feelings he may have about the body he was called to investigate for the police force to pronounce that death had taken place. But everything that day seemed different with him, he looked nothing like his usual self.

The two detectives watching him as they were walking up the hill and came closer to him saw the the difference immediately remarked as much to each other.

"Hello Herbie! How goes it with you today?"

"Alastair,...Dave,.....The body is up there, in the woods behind me, you will need a gauze mask, I have left a bundle of them with the constable at the entrance to the woods."

"Is it that bad Herbie?"

"Worse than anything I have seen in over twenty five years in this business and the first to hit home through my 'Dead' humour. If you understand what I mean?" After a few more words to the two detectives he was on his way back to his car saying he was on his way home for a good stiff whiskey to get it all out of his 'system'.

Masks on, the two detectives walked from where the constable distributing them had directed in the direction of where the body was found.

"My God Dave! Herbie was not wrong when he said we would need the masks, we have them on, and we are still thirty to forty yards away and I can still smell it from here."

After measurements and photographs had been taken, the body was taken down and 'body bagged' for transport to the morgue for the attention of the pathologist, and a forensic scientists examination. Later when the body was being carried away by the ambulance men to the ambulance. Loverage spoke to the policeman holding the tape for the ambulance men to walk under.

"Who found the body?"

"Those two over there." He replied pointing to the brothers who where at that time standing and talking to Fred Buller, who had declined the offer of a cigarette from one of the brothers, who had decided a packet of cigarettes was more than called for after the shocking discovery of the body in the circumstances they had found it. He had declined with the usual tone of a typical none smoker when asked if he would like one, he saw saw the detectives walking towards them. "Looks as if those two might be wanting a word or two with us three".

The two brothers turned towards the detectives as one

"We have been told it was both of you, who found the body."

Loverage had closed in on the brothers while Dave Mitchell spoke to the farmer, while at the same time edged him away from the others, indicating he wanted to speak to him away from them.

"How well do you know them?" He asked.

"Only what I told the other policeman when he came to my farm to tell me what they had found up here in the woods." They seem decent enough blokes, they had asked me for permission to go metal detecting on my farm land earlier in the year, and had to wait until I had finished harvesting it, and I just gave them permission is all. They came for the first time this morning just as they said they would, that's about it."

"What field are we talking actually talking about?"

Fred Buller pointed to the field the ambulance men had just walked down into.

Dave Mitchell thought for a moment. Then looked at the field, then back to the woods where they had found the hanging corpse. He thanked the farmer, saying they appreciated the time and trouble he had been put to waiting for them to see him, and he could carry on with anything he might want to do providing it was not in the vicinity of the area they were in at the moment, because it had to be swept for any evidence they could find to shed some light on the body found in the woods. Adding they would probably want to take a written statement from him later, but it was not that important at the moment and did not want to hold him up any longer than necessary. When he went across to where Loverage was questioning the two brothers he could see he had just about finished with them. He stood to the side and waited. Then as they were about to leave he asked them to wait for a moment, then turning to Loverage he spoke to him in a low voice so as the brothers could not hear what was being said, then he turned back to them. "Why is it you started in the field and ended up in the woods where you found the body."

The brothers explained about how they had come up with the decision to look inside the wood after comparing the old Victorian map with the modern O.S. map and how they could see there was a discrepancy in the path on the maps, also after finding the gap in the hedge began to think about Phil's theory that they had by chance stumbled upon what Phil thought could be a cart track. They then told of the theory they had of what else could be in the woods, an Abbey, or Monastery, and how the wall could have been the boundary. Loverage gave Mitchell a wide eyed look and a partial smile. Then he had a sudden thought. "When you were using your detectors did you find anything on the surface of the ground which could have been dropped recently?"

"No nothing." They replied.

He asked them for their addresses, and then told them they could go but, they could not do any more detecting there for that day. To which they replied. "We'v had enough for now anyway."

The two brothers looked sheepishly at each other. Both remembered what they had seen there earlier, gave a shiver and said it would take a long time before, if ever the went detecting again in the field, let alone going back into the wood on their own, they gave details of what the police detectives wanted and then made their way to their car, parked where they had parked it earlier that morning, before driving it away when they telephoned the police station from the village.

Loverage and Mitchell took a further look around the crime scene, spoke to the, uniformed officers as they had made a search of the area to see if there was anything significant found that might help in some way in their enquires, there was nothing of interest. A police photographer had made his way to the woods and had cleared away his camera away and the tripod he used to photograph the corpse and area around it. Mitchell knew him well, and had often spoken to him in the police canteen and when he had been on other crime scenes, although they were nothing much in comparison to what they had to deal with now.

"What kind of person could do this to another?" The photographer asked Mitchell.

"Don't know? But seeing as you do, what was a person is, no matter how it looks to us, still was a person who had feelings, a family, friends, there is nothing he can do so it's in our court to try and find who has done this thing and bring them to justice." As he had looked at the hanging form he felt at the time an inner compassion for it and, for those who would be mourning the death of a loved one, in such horrific circumstances.

Deciding to leave the scene in the hands of the uniformed officers and, wait until later when the area would have been thoroughly searched and see if there had been anything worth while found which might be of help to their investigation of the heinous crime. They drove back to the station, and for quite a while both men were silent in their own thoughts of what they had seen.

"What do you think about it Dave?" Loverage asked.

Mitchell remained silent, trying to think out the words to express the way he was feeling, they would not come, no words could express the way he was feeling or to answer in the way he would have wanted. Instead he answered, as it came into his mind, blunt and to the point.

"Well!....A bloody body of a male, hanging in a wood without any clothing on, or identification, and with the mutilation that has been done to it. There must be one hell of a sick mind running around loose, and I hope to God we catch him within the length of time he must have been hanging there.

"No Dave. I think there's more to what was in that wood than just the work of a maniac, although, I can understand your logic of what we have seen. It may well as you say been the work of some one with a sick mind, but I cannot get out of my mind that which ever way I look at it there was something more about the way it was hung there and mutilated. I don't think it is just a case of it being just a hanging, I think there is more to it than that. It was not just hung but positioned. Think! Why were the arms spread-eagled, why upside down?"

Dave Mitchell turned his head towards Loverage. "Satanic? Is that what you mean! Either way, whatever way you look at it, it would still be like I have already said a sick mind, except if you are in the view of something occult, Satanism, let's, say then we are really up the creek without a paddle. I don't want to even begin to think along the lines that this murder is the work of more than one person with all the added problems it would entail for us, such as where would we start, how do you go around finding out where such people if they existed practice whatever it is they practice. No I can't see what you have said holds water other than some individual has taken it on himself to make it look as if there was more than one person involved in the death, and perhaps have tried to throw a red herring in our path,I suggest we wait a while before we start talking about things occult. It's probably the results and actions of a sick and depraved mind, is what we have seen there. Why we use such as animals to describe what we have witnessed today makes you wonder why it is humans use such words such as 'animals' to describe the things we have seen on the poor unfortunate person we have just left in that wood. There is no wild animal that would be capable of inflicting something like that on their own species. Only civilized human's could be capable of such evil. Don't you agree?" The sight of what he had witnessed in the woods he knew would never leave him.

CHAPTER 10

September 1994

The Abduction

Mrs. Mary Jane Willard was a matronly figure, and had a simple outlook on life. Her parents were devout followers of Catholicism, she had been taught at at a convent boarding school. Which had instilled in her a deep sense of ethical codes which she had adhered to all of her life. Time had not been unkind to her, it could have been that she took life as it came, resigning herself, to what ever was her lot, and kept herself busy most of the time. She was also a person who would make time for anyone who would come into her life, a greeting with a smile and a kind word, was as natural to her as water runs down hill, ready to discuss a happy event, or a problem with equal attention. She would give advice freely when asked and never repeated anything told to her in confidence, at the same time she could never be called a busy body of any kind.

She was still an attractive woman for six years into her fifties, and when young must have turned many a male head. Her husband Robert John Willard had died thirty years before, their love was of a very deep and gentle nature. Having courted for three years, which at that time was about average, they had married at the local Roman Catholic church, with relations coming from all over the country, due to the splintering of the family during the thirties, the males travelling from the north east in search of employment, then to settle in various parts of the British Isles where ever they were lucky enough to find it. Then came the second world war, when her father had enlisted into the Royal Navy, served on many a ship involved in action, entering as a rating, and by the end of the war finished his service as a C.P.O.. On demob he found work in Taunton through the recommendation of a fellow N.C.O. he had known and served with. His friend who had returned to Taunton and resumed his profession as a chart maker/printer at the Hydrographic Office based there.

His friend had informed him there was a vacancy in the security section, and told him that if he would like to apply he would put in a recommendation for him, and with his qualifications and service records he was sure it would be possible for him to obtain the position. After visiting his friend the weekend after receiving his letter, and liked the Taunton area, he applied and was successful. He moved from Plymouth to Taunton, found accommodation, then later had brought his wife and daughter to settle there permanently.

Both her parents had died, leaving her totally alone, and still a widow. There had been opportunities in the past to remarry, but she had always declined, feeling that if she would have been letting her Rob down in some way. Also she did not think the feeling of her happy courtship and marriage could be repeated, so for the rest of her life she was quite content to live with the cherished memories of a happy courtship and a short but wonderful marriage. This she felt was quite satisfactory, and above all she was more than content with her life, keeping busy with her roll as a member of the 'Woman's Voluntary Service' and many other outside interests.

A friend had called to visit her one evening and mentioned in passing, a cousin of hers was a house keeper for a Father Doyle her local priest, and due to the fact she had met with an old boy friend she had gone out with in the early fifties and who had gone into the forces to do his national service, and as in so many other relationships in the past, he had met someone else while serving abroad, they had broken up, both to go their own ways. Each had married eventually, but had since both lost their partners, and through a chance meeting had gone out with each other for old times sake and found through the time spent together there had been a spark of the past in both of them they had rekindled and their relationship had become serious. Culminating in the decision to remarry, which had put the priest in the situation of having no one to do for him once they were married. Not knowing why, she had commented to her friend that something of that nature would suit her very well. It had only been a comment in passing, and as they moved on to other topics of conversation she had forgotten it with in a few moments.

A couple of weeks had passed, then one morning there was a knock at her door, and standing there was her friend and Father Doyle. She had been taken aback at first, as her friend had introduced him explaining since the conversation they had when she had told her of her cousins forth coming marriage, and she had mentioned that she thought the position of a house keeper could be of interest to her. She had since seen Father Doyle who was still finding it difficult to find someone suitable for the post, and had mentioned their conversation together to him.

She had invited them in and had talked about the matter over tea and biscuits. He had said he would really appreciate it, if she would consider the post of house keeper for him. He also told her he had been in touch with her own parish priest and had mentioned to him he was considering asking her if she would accept the position. He in turn had told him if she could be persuaded to accept, in his view she would make the perfect house keeper, and with that purpose in mind he had asked her friend to accompany him so he could speak to her on the matter. On leaving that day they had come to the decision for her to think the matter over for a day or so and he would visit her again in the hope she would accept his offer.

When they had left, and over a period of a few days she had thought over the situation with every thing it would entail, such as leaving her house in the central area of Taunton and moving to the outskirts, making shopping and being able to see her friends whenever she wanted difficult. During the period of her thinking it over, and the days passed she gradually came to the conclusion perhaps it might be a good thing after all, no doubt she would make new friends and still be able to keep in touch with those she already had, and on top of that her friend who had mentioned her to Father Doyle lived in the same vicinity, so it would not be as if she was moving to an area where she would not know anyone. When they did meet again and she told him she had thought it over carefully and had decided to accept the post offered. Father Doyle was visibly elated as soon as she had told him of her decision.

Three years had passed when Father Doyle had been asked to take over a larger parish in Liverpool. An inner city parish which offered a challenge. That, and also, the fact he had worked in the area as a young priest when he had first entered the priest hood, plus it was only a short distance from his family and friends of many years standing who he had grown up with. All these things considered he felt obliged to accept the post.

On taking the house keepers post three years earlier she had at the same time sold her house and banked the proceeds and had not much reason to spend it other than to have a holiday once a year in Cornwall or other parts of England for a two week period, or other small personal things, and as her wages went straight into her bank savings account she found herself well off considering all things. In her mind she began to think about what she would do, when Father Doyle did leave. She was unsure of her position at first when she found out that he was going to leave the area, but he soon put her mind at ease, saying that as soon as he had heard of the new parish he was offered he had spoken immediately to his superiors concerning the matter, and was assured there would be no difference to her status there and they would be more than delighted if she would stay on and carry out the work she had done for him for his replacement when he arrived.

The replacement came with the name of Father George O'Connell he was a little younger than Father Doyle, but as soon as she had met him she knew there would be no problems. As he stood in the doorway in the pouring rain and soaked through his first words to her were. "This is the first rain yours truly has seen in nine months, since before I went to Africa. The lord was sure set on me having a clean start when I came to England. Twenty minutes I was waiting outside the station for a taxi to bring me here, until some kind soul tells me the rank had moved from where I was standing, to the other side of the station. Why was there still a taxi sign on the wall I wondered, for silly idjits like you see before you no less, and that's a sure fact."

She looked at him and wanted to laugh, seeing him standing there, a black trilby style hat, the brim soaked and hanging limp over his fore head and ears, with the rain dripping from it as if he was standing in a shower, in a bathroom. A lightweight raincoat which might have been shower proof at one time but in no way was it appropriate for weather that day, having absorbed the rain water so much it had become water-logged to such an extent the water was running down him like a waterfall. "Come in Father." She stepped back from the doorway, and watched as he began to take his raincoat off, he stood for a moment as he realized the water was now dripping all over the Parker block flooring inside of the house, seeing this happening he began to apologize.

"Oh! don't you worry about that, I have a mop and bucket handy, and it will be none the worse for a drop of rain water. I will show you to your room so that you can get out of those wet clothes, and then you can get yourself around some stew and dumplings I have prepared for Father Doyle and yourself."

"Is Father Doyle still here then? I was hoping he would be. It will be a big difference here from what I have been used too and I don't mean just the weather. The part of Africa I have just come from is far from safe for Europeans now, it breaks my heart that I had to leave the orphanage there, but who knows what the combatants there would have had in store for us, if we that were of the church had stayed. We have to do the best we can with what tools we have, and in the end the sword proved to be, for now, more mighty than the pen, and the word of God could not be heard."

His face took on the look of pain, as he if by talking about his last appointment which had left scars, he had rekindled memories which filled him with chagrin. He seemed to return suddenly to the present, saw her as she had watched him, his eyes watery, he looked away bending to pick up his luggage case, as in his heart he felt the empty pangs of guilt over those he had been forced to leave and did not want to convey his inner feelings to someone who could not fully appreciate the frustrated emotions torment and anger that was still present within him. "Chaos!" He muttered "evil motivated chaos."

She did not know what was in his thoughts, but could tell there was something which was undoubtedly troubling him.

"Father Doyle is out at present he was here earlier and was hoping to be here when you arrived today. He was called out to a family who have suffered an unexpected bereavement, he went just over an hour ago, and should be arriving back shortly. If you will follow me I will show you to your room where you can change and dry yourself and, freshen up. By the time you are finished and ready, Father Doyle should be here and I will have dinner ready for you both."

Three days after his arrival and after Father Doyle had taken time and care to introduce him to as many of his flock as possible in the time they had together before taking up his new appointment in Liverpool. Things began to set into a routine, Father O'Connell found his housekeeper a gem of a person. He was to find his housekeeper and himself had a lot more in common when they had been in each others company for a while. He could see they would become strong and sturdy friends, they both had a lot in common humour wise, which had been one of the things that had helped break the ice more easily than had they not. Everything settled nicely with them, and in a short while they made a good team together.

It seemed nothing was too much trouble for her where he was concerned, and often did a lot more than was normally accepted as a house keepers chores. She considered her duties to her employer as paramount, fussing over him like an old mother hen. The house was kept spotlessly clean and tidy, and if at times Father O'Connell made somewhere untidy, there wood be nothing said, she would just put whatever it was away and clean up after him. Many a time as he was walking out of the gate to visit someone in the home or hospital, or any other duties he was required to fulfil in his duty as a priest, she could be seen in the garden digging, weeding, planting or harvesting some fruit or vegetables for the pot or for deep freezing, using some fresh and being able to have them when they were out of season and knowing that they really were fresh from the garden, and then into the freezer within an hour of being picked or gathered. Even doing a spot of painting and decorating was not beyond her scope of accomplishments. Including the three years with Father Doyle she had been housekeeper there for eight years and was totally content, not wishing to change anything with her present life or position at all.

****

The time was approaching seven thirty in the evening, the light was getting to the point where shadows and colours were beginning to blend together as one. The dusk chorus had just about come to an end, as an occasional chirping was heard in the far distance, the house sparrows had flown under the eaves of the house for the night and silence began to descend, an individual bird gave out it's last message before the darkness prevailed and then settled to wait for the following dawn to awake from a contented slumber and start a new cycle of searching for it's food.

A short while later the silence was broken by the screeching cackle of a blackbird taking flight in alarm, from an old yew tree it had regularly chosen to roost in for the night. The tree stood about five metres from the house of Father O'Connell. The outside door of the porch was open, and illuminated by a large coloured glass window set into the inner door, as the bird had taken flight and had flown across the open doorway, it gave off flashes of colour, from it's usual dull plumage, reflected from the stain coloured glass window. The porch was a six foot extension to the house, with a pointed roof and five feet in width, covered in mineral felt and under sealed with tar based pitch, the rest was made of pine wood, and darkened with wood staining for weather sealing.

Fallen leaves from a large distant sycamore tree rustled as the cool evening breeze blew them along the path leading to the porch and eventually making them swirl around inside of it, to be built up into a heap on one side of the inner door. As the gentle breeze grew stronger the surrounding area began to drop in temperature.

But, for the figure standing motionless in the shadows, waiting for his accomplice to arrive from the other side of the garden, it was a welcome relief due to the perspiration running down his face, an indication to the tension of the situation, and adrenaline his body was producing, while in pursuit of the dishonest activity the pair were engaged in.

They had both arrived together and had carried out a search of the garden for anything of value they could sell, once they had it in their possession. They had found a shed at the bottom of the garden which after forcing an entry had rewarded them with quite a few things of value, including an almost new electric lawn mower, strimmer, petrol powered rotavator and various other small but expensive items of value, which they had loaded into a wheelbarrow, also found in the shed, then taken to a Ford transit they had parked in a layby a short distance from the house, with just a field with a low hedge laying at the end of the garden, offering little chance of being seen coming or leaving the place.

"Anything happened since I have been gone?"

"Nothing much, just some old biddy around the corner in the kitchen washing up some dishes, she has probably finished by now. The priest is in there," He nodded towards a window a little way from where they were stood. "He's sat down writing at the table."

"There's a ladder in the back of the shed in the garden, how about if we get it and get in upstairs, there is a window open and it's in the dark part of the house. If we are careful and quiet they won't know we are inside, we have done it before, could be trinkets and jewellery in drawers up there. What do you think, shall we give it a try?"

"No! We only ever do a place once and, there is some good gear in the sitting room, it would be a shame to leave it for a few trinkets which may or may not be there, in case we are heard or seen and then have to scarper. Let's just wait a while longer to see if they go out like they have every other time we have watched the place at this time of the week. If they do go out they are usually gone for at least an hour and a half, and that would give us plenty of time to search the house properly and take what we want, upstairs and down."

"That's all very well but what if the old biddy does not go out tonight? She has stayed in the last couple of times we have cased the place."

"We just flog what we have found in the shed, you said there was quite a bit of good gear there. Then forget about the rest."

The two thieves waited in the shadows getting more impatient as the seconds ticked into minutes, until a quarter of an hour passed. With the tension and anxiety mounting, one of the two could not stop himself having to leave his companion to relieve his bowels some way down the garden behind the shed, making use of leaves from a nearby cabbage patch.

It was not long after his return, they could see through the window the priest rise and move away from the table, as Mrs Willard came into the room with her top coat on and carrying a large black hand bag, they stood for a short while talking and the two watchers saw them leave the room together, and the sitting room light went out.

"They are on their way out by the looks of things, come on lets get ourselves away down the garden and watch them leave from there." One of them whispered.

As they began to move the outside light went on, making both thieves throw themselves down onto the ground near a low hedge which ran at right angles to the porch doorway. Hugging the ground they moved cautiously towards the cover and dark shadow thrown by the yew tree, and lay there as still as could be, and half holding there breath as the occupants of the house walked by them, no more than ten feet away. Everything was so silent, they could hear clearly the conversation the priest and woman were having as they walked by them, one of the two on the ground slowly put the sleeve of his jacket up to his mouth to muffle the sound of his breathing, so loud it seemed to him, he was afraid one of them would hear him as they walked by. They turned to their left and behind a white washed wall and as they proceeded their voices still rang out loud and clear in the night air. As the sounds of the voices and footsteps diminished the two moved back onto the foot path and then one of them went straight into the lit porchway and tried the door, while the other kept watch near the yew tree. As he turned the handle and pushed, the door opened easily, having not being locked, turning he beckoned silently to his companion and they both entered the house, closing the door immediately behind them.

****

Father O'Connell after walking with Mrs. Willard to the church, went immediately to the vestry, while his companion made her way to the notice board to pin up details of a forthcoming jumble sale, which was to be held at the church hall the following week. She then left the church to make her way to see a friend, she had agreed to spend the evening with her to help in the icing of a cake for her daughters anniversary party planned for some time in the next few weeks, which was also to be held in the church hall.

The evening service was over. After standing at the doorway as the small congregation which had attended the evening service left, he locked the door and made his way back to the vestry.

Sitting down on one of the chairs there, he poured himself a schooner of sherry as was his habit every evening after services. He looked forward to his treat as he called it, just the one glass every evening before he made his way back to the house. In the quiet of the vestry and alone with his private thoughts, it kind of rounded his day off, he always told himself.

He had raised the glass to his lips and taken a large sip, after about three seconds he felt the warm glow as the golden liquid caressed his throat and coursed it's way down into his chest, eventually after a few more sips, he was warm, content and very relaxed. He continued sipping from the glass, his mind thinking of things to be done in the near future, and of the things he had come to terms with from the past, which he had sadly but finally accepted were beyond his control, and was now endeavouring to make his presence in the Catholic comunity mean something for the less fortunate he came in contact with through the many charities he had become involved with.

He was unaware of anyone in the church besides himself, until his eye caught a flicker of movement through the half opened vestry door. Puzzled he got up from the chair, with the intention of seeing who was out there, thinking, it was one of his parishioners who had wanted to speak to him on a personnel problem after everyone had left.

It had happened before on more than one occasion, but usually they would have spoken to him as he was standing next to the exit, and would have asked him if he would see them at home or have a word or two with him in the vestry, but even then, they usually mentioned their request to him as they came in, while he was standing at the door which he always did as people arrived.

Thinking quickly, he could not think of anyone who he had seen come in and had not gone not out as the church emptied. He placed the half emptied glass on the table then walked towards the doorway.

"Who's there? Can I help you?"

The only answer was silence. Pushing the door until it was fully opened, he heard a slight bump as it hit the side of the wall, he moved forward to enable him to have a better view into the interior of the church, and caught sight of a movement down the far side near a pillar and a doorway which led to the bell tower. "Who's there?" He called again, and moved into the centre isle and towards where thought he saw the movement, everything was quiet and he was beginning to think it was just his imagination and was mistaken. He was half way down the isle when he saw the door was open and slightly ajar, he could remember he had definitely locked it with the key before he went to the vestry.

It was only then he realized there was indeed something wrong, and there was someone in there with him. Stopping half way he began to look around in every direction, heard a scuffling and a squeak, such as rubber makes on a polished floor surface towards where he had thought he had seen the movement before.

Raising his voice he asked who was there and what and what they wanted, and that if he did not get an answer right away he would telephone for the police. There was still no answer, as he was about to turn with the intention of walking to the telephone in the vestry, he had a sensation of movement behind him, but before he could turn to look he felt a blow behind the right ear. There was darkness as all feeling left him, his legs buckled then he felt for an instant he was falling, then nothing as he lay unconscious on the floor.

First one then another figure knelt down beside him, one felt for a pulse at the side of the neck of his victim. Not a word was spoken, moving quickly around as a team one of them picked him up by the legs while the other grabbed him under the arm pits and lifted him effortlessly out of the church and into the night, then into a van parked in the church car park.

After, one of the men returned inside the church, locked the entrance door, removed the key then walked to the vestry putting the key he had taken from the front entrance onto the table, saw the half emptied glass there and picked it up, drank what was left then washed the glass in the small sink leaving it to drain on the draining board. He then looked around the room, saw the cupboard open where Father O'Connell had taken the bottle of sherry from, picked up the bottle from the table and put it in the cupboard next to the communion wine. He then took from the back of the door Father O'Connell's jacket which he had worn to the church that evening and placed the cassock on the peg instead. Making his way to the side entrance of the church, he left, locking the side door and taking the key with him and made his way back to the waiting van. In the vehicle he turned around to see the priest had been trussed up securely by his companion, leaned over and gave the ropes a tug. Settled in the drivers seat he started the motor and the van began to move and then drove away from the area of the church. Two and a half miles on as the van passed over a small hump backed bridge that spanned a stream, a key arched through the air landing with a plop in the middle of the fast flowing water.....

CHAPTER 11

The coroners inquest had just closed, and a verdict given. Murder by person, or persons unknown. The clock on the wall showed the time of twelve forty five p.m., as every one left the room.

Dave Mitchell along with the other witnesses had given his evidence to the court of all accounts leading up to and since the discovery of the the body in at 'Stoke's Croft' woods. The cause of death was given as multiple injuries of which there could be no definite individual cause of death but an accumulation of various aspects of the injuries, from loss of blood to heart failure due to the injuries inflicted. The time of death could not be more accurate than three to four weeks, and this was only a rough guess by the pathologist due to the deterioration of the body tissue. The reason for the inquest was a formality in one sense and, to put on record that the death was in fact murder.

There was nothing said about the injuries which had been inflicted upon the deceased, other, than they multiple, but because Mitchell had seen the body in the morgue, he knew the true extent of the horrific injuries on the body found in the woods.

The death of the deceased had not occurred where the body was found, and the evidence, which was not given to the court, was that the body had been mutilated and disemboweled elsewhere, and then taken to where it had been discovered, and displayed in the most horrific of circumstances.

Mitchell stepped down the steps leading from the hall where the inquest had been held. He squinted in the bright sunlight after spending a little over an hour in the poorly lit room where the inquest had been held. The brightness seemed to put a spring in his step, and an itchy feeling in his nostrils making him sneeze in rapid succession, after the sneezing fit had finished he put his handkerchief into his coat pocket then made his way back to the police, station some one hundred and fifty yards from the courthouse.

Stepping through the front doors, which had just received a complete rub down and then revarnished, back to the dark brown they had always been for as long as he could remember. He saw the desk sergeant, who was known by everyone there as 'Tubby Brown' behind his back, but as Sergeant Brown to his face. He could see while he waited for the security lock to click open, so he could enter the inner precincts of the station, the sergeant was in a bit of a quandary, and being as polite as he could to an elderly lady, who was complaining about a neighbour throwing dirty disposable nappies over her garden fence, and saying she wanted a policeman to stay with her, to catch them when they did it again, and in doing so she would have the perfect witness when she prosecuted them. He heard him reply that it just would not be possible and made a suggestion that she tried to catch them doing it with a camera, and if she managed to she could bring the photograph to them, and they would be able to handle it from there for her. But without any proof of them committing an offence there would not be any chance of the police force prosecuting.

The door opened and Mitchell could not hear the ending of the conversation, but had a wry smile on his face as he walked through.

He walked into the passage and up the stairs to the C.I.D. department, with a nod and a greeting here and there to other officers coming and going.

Passing the door to the canteen he could see that it was beginning to fill up with officers who were changing shifts, there was a smell of curry wafting out of the room, he knew there was curry and rice on the menu that day. The aroma started his taste buds producing saliva, while his stomach began to rumble reminding him he had not had anything to eat for quite some time, and something to eat might ease the rumbling at least.

"Maybe I should have a plate of that for lunch." He thought.

He made his way to the office where he found D.I. Loverage sorting through some papers on his desk in front of him.

"Hello Dave. There's a fresh pot of coffee made, go on over and help yourself, pour one for me while your at it. I am just sorting through these papers on local missing persons. It seems there has been another body found near Bridgwater, not quite the same condition as ours, but there is something strange about it, there is nothing more I can tell you for the moment.

Bridgwater C.I.D. have been on the phone to us. After theirs was discovered, they remembered ours, and think there could be a connection between the two. I have found three possible candidates for ours, by height, weight, and age, although, age is a bit suspect with the decomposition, but the M.O. thinks he was between thirty five and forty five, he can't be more specific than that, until they have done more tests, and the results from dental records will be in later this afternoon, or early tomorrow morning.

I have been looking to see if there are any photographs of the missing, but have only managed to find six, and they were reported missing from up to two years ago, and there are none that I can find of recent reports with those we have turned up so far. Do you know of any existing photographs that are more recent, of reported missing persons?"

Mitchell leaned over to where Loverage had placed the photographs and picked them up. "Where did you get these? I looked in all the missing persons file cabinets in the file room and could not find any there, except for years back."

"I suppose someone from records must have dropped them off up here, they were in an envelope marked 'Missing Persons Photographs'. Perhaps some one knew you were looking for them and found them after you had gone, then had them sent, or brought them up. Top dog says we are to work alongside Bridgwater, and he's O'K'd it from them, for us to see exactly what they have turned up at their end. We have to see a D.I. Marshall there after lunch today. He is on late's and won't be there for an hour or so, he was difficult to get hold of this morning not being at home when they phoned him. Anyway how about some lunch? are you hungry? It might be wise to have something in the canteen before we go. What do you say?"

"I'm game. I could smell curry as I passed the canteen just now, and I am ready for something to eat anyway."

Loverage looked at his watch and saw it was almost ten past one.

"If we go now, and leave after about one thirty, that will give us about twenty minutes to eat lunch, which should be fine, provided we get served quickly."

With a quick attempt to tidy his desk top, both men made their way to the canteen.

They both had the curry meal with banana fritters to follow, which had been eaten within the twenty minutes. Walking towards the car drinking cups of tea they had got from the dispenser, dumping the plastic cups in the bin outside near where the car was parked. As the officers were approaching the slip road leading to the M5 motorway, a message for their attention came over the car radio, informing them to disregard the instructions to travel to Bridgwater, and instead make their way to 'Blunders Farm', Weston Zoyland. D.I. Marshall had already made his way there and, would meet them and would be expecting them when they arrived.

"Do you know where that might be Dave?"

"Not the farm but, it must be somewhere on the Weston Zoyland road and the road is straight foreword when we turn off of the motor way at Brigwater. We can radio there and get directions when we are on the Weston Zoyland road."

As the two officers came over the brow of a hill they could see in the distance, and to their left, a few police vehicles pulled off of the road and into a lane which was close to a farm house. There seemed to be a lot of activity going on, and there were quite a few police officers in uniform walking up the lane towards the farm house. It looks as if we don't need to radio for directions after all Dave. There, is probably the place we are looking for." He was at the time leaning forward as if impatient to see whatever there was going on, although as they came down the hill their view was restricted the closer they came to the turn off to the farm. By the hedge at the side of the road as they came to the turn off, they saw at the side of it a wooden sign with Blunders Farm burned into it by a hot iron.

After seeing it and turning in they were stopped by someone in uniform, after explaining who they were, and why they were there, showing their warrant cards, he let them pass, and saying for them to be careful as the track was uneven, suggesting they park up into the side halfway down and walk the rest of the way.

They could see what the policeman in uniform had meant, the track it seemed was mostly used by tractors and four wheeled drive vehicles, easily seen by the state of the track, the middle was covered by long grass, which had been brushed forward by the other police vehicles which had preceded them down there.

As they brought the car to a halt on the lay-by they had been told of, they radioed back to their H.Q. in Taunton saying they had arrived at the location they had been given, and were about to meet D.I. Marshall from Bridgwater.

An inflatable tent had been put over the body and area around it. Loverage and Mitchell made their way towards it and saw a person who seemed to be in charge of the investigation look over in their direction as they approached the tent. Before they could introduce themselves, he had offered his hand and introduced himself as the officer they had been told to see.

After introductions were over they made their way to the tent to view the body. D.I. Marshall had not mentioned anything about what they were about to see except it was female. It came as quite a shock to them when they saw what was on the ground in front of them, the body, or what was left of it was stripped of flesh. From the head to the bottom of the feet, and no hair visible anywhere. It was it seemed to them impossible to say if it had been male or female, such was the state of the carcass on the ground before them. Except for the internal organs there was nothing to see but bone, which looked as if it it had been out in the hot sun for ever. The skull and other bones were of an unnatural white with nothing in common with any skull they had seen, not a hint of yellow or shades of anything normal, one would expect to see.

"What the bloody hell have you got here? What could have caused something like this?"

"One other thing about this body is not only is it female, but it's a pregnant female." The young D.I. looked down at the still form on the ground as he spoke to the two Taunton officers. "The other body was it like this? It's as if it has been picked clean by something!"

"No that was completely different again. It is back in the morgue in Bridgwater. You can see it later when we finish here,was there anything similar with yours?"

Loverage turned to the younger D.I. Then to his sergeant, he was for that moment at a total loss for an explanation.

"What do you think Dave? Any ideas? Because this is a first for me. It's like something out of a science fiction movie" "We tried to move the arm and when we touched it, it just turned to powder. How we are going to get it onto a stretcher I just don't know. Watch this!"

Marshall was wearing rubber surgical gloves, he caught hold of one of the fingers of the corpse, and as he did so, the detectives saw it crumble before their eyes, ending up as powder in the grass.

"It seems that even with the slightest touch something happens and it just crumbles. The other parts, the internal organs look as fresh as...as, I don't know?.....As if what happened, took place a matter of minutes ago. So we have no idea who she was or how long ago death actually took place, or how. Especially how!"

Dave Mitchell, while the others were talking was looking around the ground closely.

"Who discovered the body? Was it the farm owner? Did he come over close to have a look at it before he got in touch with you? Because except for the trails in the grass we have made, there are no others around that I can see except for those I presume she has made when she came here, and she has not come from the direction we have, I noticed there were tracks in the grass coming from the far side of the field, away from the actual farm house. So I was thinking how did she die, if she was in the state we see her in now it would be impossible for someone to just dump her body, and if she was killed on the spot here, how was it done, it just does not make sense, unless you or the other uniformed police have walked on the same place as any one else who might have been with her when whatever occurred for her to end up as we see her now and I am damned sure that would not have happened.

All three officers were with the mortuary attendant, wearing face masks and disposable overalls, and shoe coverings viewing the body which had been found on the outskirts of Bridgwater. Again in an isolated field, just as they had seen the one earlier, but a distance of over four miles apart. The difference with this body was the dehydrated state it was now in. Because as the young D.I. had told them when it had been found it had all the signs of someone who had suffered a massive heart attack, or a stroke, something sudden at any rate, in other words natural causes. It was a few hours later after it had been on the pathologists table and they pulled away the sheet covering it, the sudden and unexplainable deterioration of the body was first seen, until in the end it had finished up looking as if it had lain in a desert sun for a considerable time period, shrivelled up and leathery to the touch, not that anyone wanted to touch it with their bare hands. Nothing had been said to those who had first come into contact with it, but they had all been placed into quarantine and had been told it was a precaution, as there were fears that the man may have somehow contracted an extremely rare tropical disease, which he had eventually succumbed to, and they would only be in quarantine until a short period of time had passed, and with the evidence so far it seemed there would be no danger to them at all.

But all those with the knowledge of what had actually happened to the body of the deceased, were in a bit of a quandary not knowing what had exactly happened to have caused the condition. "What makes you think that our victim is somehow connected with yours? Ours is not exactly as mysterious as those you have, the wounds on ours are pysically explainable."

"Have you seen the latest report from your pathologist on the body you have?"

"What latest report are you talking about?" Loverage looked at his sergeant.

"Have you seen anything of a later report?"

"No! But I can remember seeing an envelope on your desk with the pathologists handwriting on it. When we were tidying up before we left to come here. It was in the 'in' tray and I thought it was the original one and you had put it in the tray by mistake, I did not look at it, I just put it in the other tray with every thing else we have."

Loverage turned again towards Marshall.

"Do you know what was in the report?"

"Not the exact wording, but I know there was something strange in it by what was said by our pathologist to us, when he had mentioned to yours about what had happened with the deterioration of our first body. Our's got in touch with yours to see what if anything, there was about the deaths that could connect them. seeing as how they were both found in country areas and baffling conditions. After explaining what had happened to ours, your pathologist did a second examination and closer examination and found like ours there were things he could not explain with sound logic and sent a fax over to him with the updated results, I thought you knew!"

"If I had seen the envelope from him we would have, but I thought that part of the investigation was over with. We will take a look at it in the morning there is nothing in it that will make a lot of difference to what we can do now. Have you managed to identify any of yours by the way"

"No not yet, but we are working on it."

All the way back from the Bridgwater police station there had been silence from both police detectives each having their own private thoughts on what could be done next. As the car came off of the motorway, Loverage was the first to break the silence.

"What do you make of the situation Dave? Any theories or ideas of what could be possibly going on? I have racked my brains from the time we have left Bridgwater, and I keep coming back to the same conclusion. Is it possible that something has escaped from some M.O.D. research establishment laboratory. You know like a virus of some kind that is top secret hush, hush, stuff, from what we have seen today it is the only thing that makes sense to me, and if it is, I think we have a lot more to worry about than just a murder enquiry!"

"How do you mean?"

"Well, if it is something hush, hush, shall we say, then who is going to be straight with us and let us know the truth, if there has been a balls up some how, and a biological virus has escaped, and what if, what we have seen so far is only the tip of the iceberg. What if there is more to come, as you said today the woman made her own way into that field and, there was, no sign of other tracks except hers around."

Mitchell was at a loss as well, and told him so.

That evening after Mitchell had finished for the day and was sat at home in front of the T.V. set in his sitting room thinking over what had seen in the field at Weston Zoyland, and not really coming up with any real explanation of what had happened to the dead woman to cause what they had seen happen when the Bridgwater officer had touched it.

Then while he was half watching a program on the television and still thinking of the conversation and Loverage's theory about the M.O.D. angle, he felt what he could only describe as a prickly sensation at the base of his neck which travelled up the back of his head, like a form of stactic electricity, and as it did he had a most peculiar feeling. As if some one was watching him as he was sat there, he half turned in his seat, so real was the feeling and looked behind him. There was no one there, and he felt silly for a moment, but minutes later he had still not shook the feeling of. He rubbed the back of his head and neck and that seemed to work. He gave a sigh and got up from the chair, thinking the day was beginning to get to him, deciding to call it a night and go to bed, he moved to the television and switch it off, and as he moved towards the door on his way out of the room he felt the feeling again only this time it was a much stronger feeling. It was as if there was someone there watching his every move. He gave an involuntary shiver as he walked through the sitting room door, as he was shutting the door he stopped and opened it again suddenly, but saw nothing and no one, he felt foolish, and shaking his head muttered to himself the day's events were getting to him worse than he thought. Telling himself he would feel better in the morning and not to be so stupid. He went up the stairs to the bathroom to get ready for bed.

The next morning as he drove to the station, the feeling returned. But now it was as if there was someone in the car with him, the feeling stayed with him until he had got out and walked into the station, and until he met other officers he began to get upset with himself, and put it down to imagination. Instead of going to the C.I.D. part of the building he went to the wash room area and gave himself a cold water rinse to try and shake himself out of his foolish feelings, and now, it seemed to him annoying imagination, and clear his head for a fresh start to the day.

CHAPTER 12
The Prisoner

Father O'Connell saw a red mist that seemed to intensify with every throb within his head, eventually he managed to open his eyes, his mouth felt dry his lips were cracked and sore. He tried to sit up but found it was difficult, because he was laying on the ground, his hands and legs tied. After much effort he did manage to sit up, and saw he was in what appeared to him to be a small damp cellar, with just a single low watt light bulb giving a dim glow from the ceiling and hanging from two feet of wire flex. He was feeling cold, and uncomfortable, due to the fact he had been laying on cold damp flag stones.

As he looked around he could see there were no windows, just bare brick work, stained with dark damp mildew and lighter streaks of mould mixed with the crystallized salts out of the mortar, which like the brickwork, was crumbling with age. Not a stick of furniture was to be seen, something skittered across the floor, but he could not make out what it was, because of the poor lighting.

Where was he? But more to the point! Why? He still felt uncomfortable sitting in the position he was in, after he had struggled to move from the laying position. He began to wriggle and slide himself along the ground until he was against the wall, where with a lot more effort he managed to raise himself into an upright position, with his back against it, to try to give some kind of support to himself, even though, with his hands tied as they were, it was still uncomfortable with, the numbing cramp he could feel in his shoulders. Every so often, he would try to shift his body and arms slightly to try and relieve some of the pain but without any relief forthcoming when he did so.

How long he remained there after he had regained consciousness he did not know. He could remember the events that had happened in the church, but was still confused and could think of no reason why anyone would want to kidnap and keep him bound up as he now found himself. "Could it be for money? Have they been in touch with the church? The Cardinal even?"

No matter how he tried to rationalize the reason for his being there, he could not come up with an answer. It had even come into his mind to wonder if he had been taken hostage by some middle eastern fanatical religious group, who for some reason had infiltrated mainland Britain, to commence their hostage taking efforts in reprisal for one thing or another.

He could hear the faint and intermittent sounds of footsteps above him. They sounded muffled, and far away. He called out but no one came, "Probably to far below to be heard." He thought to himself.

Cold, worried, and hungry, he sat there drifting off into a semi sleep, but could not rest his mind or body, the cold and dampness of the place seemed to penetrate every part of him, his body ached all over in his cramped position, he came close to crying out through the pain and hunger, drifting in and out of a restless sleep.

Eventually, he began to find solace through prayer, asking for help through the 'Blessed Virgin' that, he should find strength and courage to carry him through his present situation.

After a while, how long a while, he was unsure, he felt a feeling of peace which seemed to enter into him, a warmth, which seemed to carry within it an inner energy. Which, was nothing to do with the physical world, but it numbed the cold and dampness. It seemed as all feeling had left his body, and he could feel nothing of the pain and hunger he had been experiencing moments before.

It was as though he had consciously moved his mind away from the pain his body was in, and in doing so, had left his body, although in his altered state of consciousness he had not fully understood what had happened. The feeling was of being without his body, and yet he knew it had been accomplished through prayer in some way, and some how he had been able to rise above his problem, by awakening this inner consciousness which in turn had enabled him to rise above his physical problems to aid him in his immediate survival. All that concerned him at that moment, was he was at least not where he had been, with all the pain and discomfort associated with it.

He was not sure how long he could sustain this condition, because he had never experienced anything similar before, and all he was concerned with was, he was afraid he would slip back into the state of feeling pain again, and was also conscious of the fact, it was far from a normal state of being.

He remained in this state for a long time. It could have been hours or days he had no concept of time, but remained in a kind of dream zone of reality, and dreamed of one thing after another, eventually in his mind, with such a realism and clarity he was floating on his back in a warm sea, with bright sunlight all around him, he watched as sea gulls glided and swooped around him, he began to take on a welcome interest in them, with the ability to view them with a clear and defined focus, saw their eyes as they looked back at him. The perfection of silky feathers of their wings stretched out burnished, defined in the sunlight, he began to feel an affinity with them as if they were his companions and friends, where ever he was.

What he was doing there had not even entered his mind. All he was concerned with, was that he felt comfortable and content to stay there. All thoughts of his actual physical predicament ceased to exist for him.

Then, as suddenly as he found himself in calm waters, the situation began to change, waves began to buffet him, he could feel himself rise and fall, then felt himself being bumped along a beach, large pebbles dug into his sides, his arms and legs seemed to be coming apart, he could hear above him the sounds of the rushing sea, the screaming cries of the sea gulls above him. They seemed to be screaming in sympathy for him, as his body continued to be pounded up the rough stone beach he seemed to have no control over it as the sound of the sea was roaring in his ears.

Then suddenly! Amongst the roaring sea, and the cries of the gulls, there came lights, muffled voices each side of him, every part of his body was racked with pain, as he at the same time realized the cries of the gulls were his screams. The sound of the sea became the footsteps of the two men supporting him between them with his legs dragging along, echoing, with the shoes on his feet scraping along the rough stone floor of a passageway.

There were the sounds of voices shouting at him, but his senses were reeling between consciousness and passing out.

A feeling of nausea and distress returned to him, affecting his stomach, mostly due to the lack of food and water. He felt himself being dumped roughly onto a chair, almost falling off, until one of the men who had dragged him from the room where he had been tied up gave him a prod in the ribs, and pulled him upright against the back of the chair. His head was pulled off of his chest, where it had drooped as soon as he had sat down. He felt something being forced between his dry cracked lips, knocking his teeth, and a rough irritable sounding voice say, "Drink."

Putting his hands up to the vessel which the other person had put to his lips, he realized his hands were free although they were stiff and cold. He commenced to drink with voracious gulps, wasting some down the side of mouth and chin. The vessel was empty in no time at all, as he finished the last drop it was taken from him. After he had finished he wiped his mouth with his hand, and in doing so found he had at least five days of growth of beard on his face, which at first he found hard to believe, it did not seem that long since he had been taken by whoever his kidnapper's were.

"Where am I? What do you want of me?" He groaned. Then he spoke clearer, his voice hoarse, the water he had drunk moments before helped to quench his thirst but had done little in the way of easing the dry roughness of his sore throat.

The questions from his confused mind went unanswered.

Both men who had brought him to another room from where he had been tied up, then walked to the door, leaving him slumped in the chair. Frustration began to take him over again. As they were on their way out of the room he shouted at them as best he could. "For God in heavens sake, what do you intend to do with me? I have had nothing to eat for days."

As the door was shut and bolted, he could hear them laughing as they walked away from the door down the passage outside away from the room leaving him there.

After they had gone Father O'Connell, after rubbing his arms and legs to try and get some life into them, realized the dampness and smell pervading around him, was not just due to the dampness and conditions he had been held in, but the fact that while asleep, or whatever state he was in, which in no small way had seen him through the period of time he had been held there, was in fact, the result of him being restrained, to the point he could not carry out any of his bodily functions. Even though he knew it could not be helped, he felt total humiliation for himself and, a seething anger towards his captors.

He was alone again and took the chance to look around the room he was in now, and saw that compared to the one he had been held in initially, there was at least a difference of sorts. It was still the same in condition as the other, a cellar with brickwork ect, but at least he was not tied up now, and there was an iron bed frame, another two chairs and a small wooden table. "Well!" He thought "It does not look like they have any intention of disposing of me, at least for the immediate future anyway. Perhaps negotiations had been made on his behalf in some way and they had moved him from where he had been held while they continued and perhaps later he would be taken somewhere else for release."

When all the initial shock and pain of being dragged from the other room had subsided, he began to think and consolidate his thoughts, and reason a little more rationally. He began to think of what chance he may have of escape. As he took stock of his new situation, he saw that to escape from the room he was now in was as unlikely as the other room, pretty well impossible, he had heard the bolt drawn into place, and a key being turned as well when the two men had left so he did not bother to try to get up from the chair to see if it could be opened, and the fact he felt so weak anyway reinforced that thought immensely. "Anyway!" he thought. He had no idea what was beyond the door other than the passageway, and even if he did manage to get out of the room he knew nothing about the number of people who were involved with his kidnapping. Also the fact he had no idea where he was being held, it could be in an isolated farm house out in the middle of nowhere, or it could be in a basement cellar of a building in the middle of a town, he had no idea at all, the only position for him as far as he could see was to play it by ear, and quickly reason his chance of escape if an opportunity arose to make one.

His thinking was interrupted by the sound of footsteps coming down the passage towards his door, they stopped out side of the room, he heard the sound of the bolt being drawn again then after, the key was turned. The door opened, one of the men the tallest and biggest built of the two walked in with a bundle of clothes under his arms, wrapped in a blanket, while the other close behind him carried a mattress balanced sideways on his head and shoulders which he carried to the bed stead and threw them down upon it.

Seeing the bedding and clothing gave him a sense of relief, thinking perhaps he was right and they may be going to release him shortly. "Perhaps?" He began to think. "They have accomplished whatever it was they had wanted with his abduction, and it would only be a matter of time before he would be released from capture." The only thing that worried him as he thought this was:

"If they were going to free him why had he been allowed to see their faces?"

"Can you stand up on your own yet?"

"I don't know. I haven't tried."

"Well bloody well try now!" The shorter of the two men growled.

Getting up from the chair he felt weak, and a stiffness in his legs, his stomach was aching with hunger, his balance was not all it could have been, but he managed to get to his feet and walk unaided.

The shortest and more aggressive of the two took hold of his arm in a vice like grip. "Come on preacher man." Almost dragging him out of the door before he realized it, while the other walked behind them both, and carrying the clothing they had brought with them. As they walked along the passage Father O'Connell could see just how large both men were, the one walking behind was the larger of the two, but seemed to be the most menacing of them with his silence, and standing well over six feet six, and he could see with the physical body he possessed   would be capable of incredible and fearsome strength. Although both seemed slow in movement, they were obviously adept at at any task that would be required of them.

They led him some twenty feet from the room, and into an alcove, where he could see a shower unit had been installed. "Get in there and clean yourself up. There is everything you will need". He pointed to a small table where the taller one was putting the clothing onto, where he could also see, soap, towel and a razor.

"When you have finished put the razor and blade on top of the towel, so that it can be seen. Then put on the clean clothes. You have eight minutes. We will not be far away so don't get any ideas of escape because there is none."

The two men returned after a while, picked up his soiled clothing and threw them into a black plastic bag, while at the same time he was told they were taking him to meet someone, and would be given the choice over whether he was going to live or die, and adding the choice would be his, and his alone. They spoke in such a completely matter of fact, tone of voice, it took moments for him to realize what they had just told him to sink in.

They led him a little farther along the passage until they reached another door, opening it they pushed him through ahead of them.

It was a large room, or a chamber would be more an apt description, and the like of which he had never seen before.

Hanging around on the walls were tapestries, some of which were illustrations showing animals and people, explicit in all forms of bestial depravity. Scenes of hunting, and battle scenes of the ancient past, and up to the present time. One large tapestry which covered a complete wall, had upon it leaders and kings depicted in full regalia of their period in time, which seemed to him to be placed in a position of honour, he noticed personalities from the recent past such as Hitler, Stalin, and others who's faces he recognized but could not put names to, there and then. Faces of people who had been known for their corruption and evil while in possession of power in their lifetime, along with their evil cohorts. While he looked, every facet of greed, power, and evil, seemed to emanate from them.

There was nothing spared in the scenes around him, the colours of red, black, and gold seemed to be the most dominant, giving the contents an untouchable depth of infinity into the realms of evil. He looked at them again more closely and could not come to any other conclusion, than it was a room dedicated to evil of every generation from time immemorial up until the present day.

But worse than all that he had seen so far in the room, there was one tapestry which he had not at first paid much attention to, but that was because there did not seem to be much on it compared to all the others there. But as he took another look at it, it became to him more menacing than all the others put together. It was not the contents upon it but, the lack of them. It did at first glance seem blank, with just a series of outlines of pictures beginning to show through. Pictures of faces as if seen in a kind of faded negative photographs, not quite able to pick out the features of any of them, but he had the distinct impression they were forming as he was looking at them by minute fractions of a second. It had been positioned completely separate from the rest of the tapestries in the room, as he looked, he felt within himself a feeling of absolute consternation.

"I see you are admiring our decor. The very few we have allowed to venture into this sanctum, always have the same look upon their faces whether in awe, horror, or disgust it does not matter which. The look on each individual never changes, and after a short discussion with you, we will find out, how you, view it."

Father O'Connell was taken aback, he had not seen the man speaking to him enter, and after the initial shock of his voice assumed he had been in the darker shadows of the room and had come out of them as he had spoken.

"I know you must be hungry, and your head is full of questions of why you are here. I will do my utmost to satisfy you on both counts, but first before you ask any questions, please follow me to the guest room we have nearby, where you may eat your fill, of the very best in food anyone could offer you."

While the pair who had brought him to the room stood at each side the entrance of the door of where he entered the room, the third party he had just met and had spoken to him, motioned to him with a sweep of his hand towards a door behind a heavy dark draped curtain where he had been standing. He followed him through the doorway, and saw immediately it was a small room, well furnished and decorated in Georgian style, a table set laden with all kinds of food was situated in the centre.

"Here you are! If you help yourself to whatever takes your pleasure, until I return,.....Shall we say in.....about an hour?" Father O'Connell by this time was totally confused over the treatment he was experiencing now, after what he had endured over the last few days.

"Who are you? What is your name?" He asked his confusion showing.

"My Name? My name is James Coulter, but for anymore you must wait until I see you later I am afraid." He then passed the priest and made his way out of the door they had come in.

All thoughts of rationality went, as he approached the table, the hunger within him took over, as he began to eat his fill, from what was provided in front of him.

CHAPTER 13

Gowendene Manor

September 94

The gates to the manor house were of wrought iron, and had been taken out of one of the many sheds surrounding the house. They were the original set, which had been taken down during the second world war, they should have been sent off to be used as scrap metal, to be melted down to aid the shortage of iron for the war effort in the recycling of metals. But some how it had escaped the foundry, and had laid undiscovered in the back of one of the stable sheds under a fallen roof, until the new owners of the manor house had thought to try and repair it by putting a new roof on and use it as an extra store room for cattle feed.

There were many sheds on the estate, which had been used mostly for carriages and horses back in the late seventeenth and the mid eighteen hundreds, when the wealth of the owners allowed them to live in the style of of the rich and titled.

The achievement of wealth had been accomplished with major dealings in the slave trade of the late seventeenth until the mid eighteenth centuries. The house and estate had been sold in the fifties to cancel out debts and save the owners whatever they could in the way of valuable assets to be turned into cash. The owners then emigrated to Australia, bought free land and started a sheep farming business that thrives to this day.

The house had been virtually empty since that time, there had been squatters who had made use of it through out the seventies and eighties, mostly in the winter months but there were a small number who stayed there on a more permanent basis, but for some reason which no one had been able to figure out, this practice finished suddenly for some unknown reason, and it needed quite a lot doing to it in the way of repairs inside and out. Once purchased by the new owners, extensive work on renovation had started almost immediately on the house and the surrounding buildings.

Charlie Bird had walked the four and a half miles from the centre of Taunton, and had at last reached his destination. He had been told many times before about the place he was now standing in front of, and how there was always a bed and a meal for the night, for those in need, but he had always found somewhere else to doss down, near to wherever he found himself at night.

Since the council nurseries he had used when he had come into the town earlier in the year, were now being renovated and with out heating on in the green houses, a night spent there was really cold even with a sleeping bag, and all he had now was a blanket he had managed to swap a few meager things for, even though the days were still warm the nights were becoming to come in quite cold now. After a few nights there with very little sleep, there was not much in the way of energy, strength and physical effort available, to find any jobs to do for cash the following day.

He put his hand in the pocket of his patched and torn denim jeans he was wearing, and pulled out the five pounds and some small change left out of the ten he had earned that afternoon for knocking down and clearing away the rubble from an old brick coal house for some one in the more affluent part of the town. It had been hard work and had taken longer than he had thought it would, but he had just about finished it before it had become dark. He had been paid ten pounds cash, and although it was not much he was glad of it, after knocking on doors most of the day searching for casual work. "Yes!" he thought, "it had been hard work, with not even a cup of tea thrown in." All the woman was concerned with was, for him to leave everything tidy for her when he had finished, and after she had paid him for what he had done for her and her husband, she then told him she had phoned up someone who had advertised in the local paper, who would be willing to take on small clearing up jobs, and when they had called to see what it was she wanted doing they priced the job at thirty five pounds for demolishing the coal bunker and clearing the rubble to where he had wheeled it to, and another ten pounds to load it up and take it away in a small truck. So it had been lucky for her that he had come along that afternoon, and had agreed to do it for two pounds an hour, before she had rung them back, because, she had not been able to find anyone else to do it for less. He had said nothing, but remembered thinking to himself, "You will have to pay out a lot more than that in the end when your drains block up you tight old git." It was with her fussing and hindering him all the while to make sure he was doing the work the way she wanted, which had annoyed him most, and it was while she had left him for a short while, and he was knocking down the last portion of wall, where the footings were, there had been a large piece of slate covering a sewer pipe and the footings in that spot were quite shallow and not as deep as everywhere else, he had used an iron bar to loosen the bottom and had gone through the slate and sewer pipe which lay next to a rain water tumbling bay, with some of the rubble going into the sewer pipe which the drain from the household waste emptied into.

If she had shown a little more charity towards him and not wanting to get as much as she could for, as little as possible, he would have repaired the drain and not casually covered it over with the remains of the broken slate and put the rubble on top of it.

He had thought long and hard after she had paid him, whether to go to the 'Grey Goose' Public house and spend the evening in the warmth with a few drinks and company and perhaps a pasty from the bar, then spend the rest of the night in an old pill box on the outskirts of the town, which was some times used by others like himself, 'the homeless and down and outs'. But remembering how cold it was there the night before, he decided to give the manor a try for once. He bought himself some rolling tobacco and papers off of a contact he knew, who managed to get it from some one in the smuggling racket, for three pounds fifty, for a pack of fifty grams with papers thrown in, less than half the price charged in the shops.

'Dropping out' had been good for him from the spring and through the summer months for the past two years, with a bit of casual work, pea, bean and apple picking. After six years in a factory in the midlands, he had not minded moving down to the Southwest after the factory had closed down.

He had lived in care all of his youth, and had not had much in the way of ties anywhere, when he had reached sixteen he had to leave the care hostel where he had lived most of his formative years. He was helped to adjust with digs and a job, then after six months the ties to the home faded into the past, as he had got on with his life.

After the factory went into liquidation, he spent a short while looking for work, saw that what savings he had were beginning to dwindle fast, then one day he looked around the flat he was living in, saw there was nothing there to hold him, and as the holiday period of the year was coming up decided there and then to move down to the Southwest, and get a job in a holiday complex at Minehead. Putting everything he owned into a hold-all and knapsack, he caught a coach down to Taunton, where he got a bus to the holiday camp landing a job in the kitchens, as a kitchen hand, washing dishes and preparing vegetables, and any other manual job he was asked to do.

After he had worked in the hot kitchens for six weeks, rushing around doing one thing after another, and with a constant stream of greasy pots and pans to wash, he would go into the town in the evenings, and his free time off to relax, and wander along the beach, then end up for a drink and some conversation in a pub with anyone who would be inclined to talk.

With his past background he sometimes found it difficult to start up a conversation with strangers at that time, but got by in his own way.

Then came the day when he had time off, and had gone into a bar for a drink, he had struck up a conversation, or rather someone had started to speak to him, they had seemed friendly, and seemed to have a good sense of humour. Which after the time at work with all the shouting and bad tempers of cooks in charge of the kitchens, was a good release of the tension, and stress caused by his employment, although it was the same for all menial workers in the job male and female, and not just himself.

After getting to know them for a few days, and being gradually introduced to their friends, he found out they were drop-outs of the normal so called society, and very loyal to each other, living and sleeping rough and doing odd jobs when the chance arrived to earn a little money to help them on their way, sleeping on the beach or in some kind of shelter when the weather turned unpleasant. But the thing he admired most was the way they all seemed to help each other out at any time they could, from buying the odd pint, and offering what they had if it was needed. In a way he began to look on them as 'latter day' hippies.

It was only a matter of time when he thought to himself it might be a bit of fun and an experience to join them, being careful normally, it was one heck of a decision to come too, but decided to himself to work where he was for a few weeks more and get a bit more money in the bank, and when he had the sum of three hundred pounds saved he finished at the holiday camp and took the plunge. He had travelled quite a lot and enjoyed life with so many different friends he had met while living the new life style he had chosen and, was in most respects happy living the way he had for the time he had.

He found himself in Taunton, after coming back with a group of friends who had made their way to a pop concert, for a weekend and while making their way back to the coast saw there were apple picker's wanted in the area and had decided to stay and earn some money for a few days. When the picking had finished and it was beginning to get late in the summer and the winter would not be long in coming the rest of the friends he had made decided to move on, but he decided he would stay a while longer in the area and do some 'door knocking' for odd jobs to earn a little money for a while.

He had so far not had any regrets, except for just recently with the cold, but he intended to move to Exeter after a day or so with friends he had spent the last winter with in a squat, and try to build up a bit of money over the winter with help from some of the work agencies there were there, and do three or four days work a week, he did not need much money to live with the minimum of expenses he existed on. Some of his friends had asked him to come with them to a commune they knew of in Wales again, but he did not fancy going there because the casual work situation was poor and he wanted something in his pockets before the spring of the following year.

This year the weather had started to become colder and inclement earlier than it had the year before, and as time went by the groups of friends began to go their separate ways to squats all over the country that they knew of, to see the winter months out. Charlie was among the last of them to think about leaving, and that was why he was now standing outside of 'Gowendene Manor' holding what remained of the ten pounds he had earned, in his hands.

He stood there, outside the gates on a dark cold evening, as the rain, a constant drizzle, his denim jeans and jacket by now soaked and wet through, feeling relieved now that he had reached his destination, and looking up at the large sign on one of the gate pillars illuminated by a flickering outdoor neon lightbulb:

GOWANDENE MANOR

SHELTER FOR THE HOMELESS

RUN WITH DONATIONS

&

PRIVATE BENEFACTORS

ALL ARE WELCOME.

He walked through the open gate and casually up the stone shingled drive to a large doorway, with an entry and reception sign above.

Walking through it he saw he was in a porch area with double doors, one side of which was open. Immediately to his front he could see part of the inside area, had been partitioned off by a wooden and glass framework. The door to the partitioned room was closed but to the side was a sliding hatch. Marked on a red board in white lettering a sign read 'Reception'.

Sat on a chair in the act of dunking a biscuit into a cup of tea, was a woman who seemed to panic when she had seen him standing there, the biscuit was at her lips and as it went into her mouth, broke off falling to the side of it, and onto a multi coloured blouse then onto the desk in front of her.

Embarrassment clearly showing on her face she quickly wiped away the sodden crumbs of wet biscuit from her mouth and blouse, with a tissue she had taken from her bag on the desk.

After satisfying herself that everything was now in order, and herself and the table was clean of soggy biscuit, with a smile she turned her attention to Charlie.

"Sorry about that. Can I help you?" She asked.

"I was hoping for the chance that there may room for me for me to stay the night."

"Well of course there is, that is what we are here for. Have you come far?" "Only Taunton." "Well that's fine. We will soon fix you up with a bed for the night. There is a small charge for the night I am afraid, but if you have no money, don't worry, we can sort something out with the D.H.S.S. all you have to do is fill a form out, and we can get it paid for you by them." She opened a drawer on the side of the desk and searched through a folder she had pulled out. "Ah, here we are. I knew there was some left in this folder." She pulled out a sheet of paper with writing on it. Then placed it on the desk in front of him. "You just have to fill this in, well the details which are relevant to you, it is for administration purposes and everything you write will be confidential, anyway, if you can just just fill it in while I see about getting a room for you."

He filled in the form she had given him. It only had sections for his name national insurance number and where he was born and next of kin, she checked through the details he had written. After a moment, of looking at the form she looked at him and then back to what he had written. "Are you planning on staying here for long? I have to ask you, because we have an arrangement with the D.H.S.S. in Taunton, and should you wish to stay longer we can arrange a payment for you at this address for as long as you wish, providing you go to the unemployment office and sign on as unemployed. They will deduct payment for lodging here and pay us direct, plus you will be paid some money for yourself from them. It is entirely up to you of course. Why not sleep on it? Then perhaps you can make a decision tomorrow." As he stood there a thought came to him over what she had said about a room. "Just now you mentioned something about a room. Did you mean I would be sharing with others, or a room on my own?"

"Oh! We usually get asked that question. It is a room on your own, it is pretty bare but quite comfortable. We found that it was better when we took over the building for the purpose of taking in guests, that it saved a lot of bother with some of the clientele we had in the past, and if possible to let everyone when they came here for the first week or so, to have a room on their own, and later on if you so wish and, you do accept the offer of staying here and perhaps after making friends with other guests, then we have four, six, and eight person's dormitories, but usually when circumstances allow we have found most people prefer their own room for privacy initially. Ah! Here is someone who will take you to your room. His name is "Willie", and and my name is Moirah. Spelt with an 'H' on the end. Should you want anything meanwhile, you only have to ask." She looked at a watch which hung from a chain around her neck. "If you follow Willie he will take you to your room, and show you where you can have a shower and clean up. Then you should be just about in time to have dinner. That will be in the large hall leading off of the centre of the reception area over there." She pointed towards a doorway behind him. "Ask anyone and they will tell you where to find it, when you come back down the stairs." Turning around she took a key off of a key board, and handed it to the person she had spoken of as Willie.

"Take him to room twenty two Willie."

"Thank you, thank you, yes I will, fine, thank you."

Charlie smiled at the old boy who had shown him to his room for the night. He was he thought in his late sixties, but very active, a small dapper type of about five feet in height, a white pressed shirt, green cardigan with buttons done up, thinning grey hair parted to the side and oiled with some kind of hair product making the scalp through the thinning hair show through. Grey pressed trousers with the creases looking razor sharp.

From the time he started to show him to where his room was, and pointing to everything he thought Charlie should know about, toilets, bath, and shower rooms, plus a room where there was a washing and tumble drying machines should the need arise, there was also a laundry cupboard where sheets and towels could be found, if needed in an emergency. A hand went up to his mouth and his eyes went skyward as he said it. Why, Charlie did not understand at first, it must have shown on the puzzled look he gave him.

"In case you have an accident while you are asleep". Charlie understood what he had meant, and gave a laugh and nodded his head.

"I have not had those accidents since I was very young. But, you never know as you say."

He was also told there would be no extra charge for using the facilities he had been shown, because it was all included in the lodge money. The talking from his guide was none stop, and as he reached his room and went inside he was more than glad to close the door.

After, when he had closed the door, he turned, gave a sigh, closed his eyes and did an arm stretch, yawned, gave a shiver and realized just how cold and wet he was. Picking up his hold-all and knapsack from the floor where he had dropped it when he had entered, he moved to the bed, dropping the hold-all on the bed and the rucksack on a chair next to it. He was all for having a shower but wanted to make sure Willie was not still out in the corridor when he went to the shower room. So he took his time sorting through his knapsack for his razor ect. He sat on the bed after sorting through the hold-all for a clean pair of jeans and a sweatshirt to wear when he had showered and shaved. He had learned when he had first started on the road of living rough it was wise to put anything for wearing in a plastic bag to keep them from becoming damp and uncomfortable, although ironing was out of the question, as long as things were folded and packed with care they were not too bad in appearance, and any wrinkles that might be showing when first put on, soon disappeared when worn after and hour or so with the heat from his body. Looking around he saw that the room he was in although sparse was neat and tidy, and the bed he was sat on he felt would be comfortable.

On the wall was a picture in a darkened wooden frame of a stag in woodland, with the suns rays piercing through the trees giving a misty quality to the scene. He had seen it before somewhere, in a shop, restaurant, or more than likely a pub, but he could not remember where. He walked over towards it and could then see the title given to the picture below it. 'Monarch Of The Glen' Yes he he had seen it before, he remembered the title, but could not bring to mind where that somewhere was. "Oh well, it might come back to me " He thought. He saw as he looked around, the floor was bare boards with a rug next to the bed, and another near the door where he had entered the room. A Green cloth which looked as if it may have been part of a curtain at one time, covered a small table placed next to the window, while, as he looked was continuously being lashed with rain on the outside. Making the reflection of himself as he looked towards it distorted, the wind came in flurries, making the flow of water on the panes into ever changing rivulets, then they were blotted out as the wind gusts moved them away and in turn reflected the lights twinkling outside, from what he took to be distant dwellings making them change, in form, and shades of brilliance and directions. As he watched looking at it, feelings of satisfaction began to overwhelm him that he had made the right decision to make his way out to the manor house after all.

The walls were painted with emulsion and were of a magnolia colour except for the side where the window was situated, which was a light orange, almost peach, giving the room a fresh feeling to it.

Turning from the window he picked up the clothes to wear when he finished having a shower and shave, and made for the room he had been shown earlier by the talkative Willie.

'Men's washroom' on a plaque made him think to himself. "If they have men's washroom marked on the door perhaps there are some women on the same landing." But then immediately thought they are probably on another wing or somewhere else in the house, although he had heard they did in fact take both sexes there.

When inside the room he saw lined up against the wall one side, six washbowls and at the end of them, two washing machines and a tumble dryer. Four shower cubicles were across the room opposite them. He undressed and got into one, switched on the the water and felt the the spray with his hand and adjusted it until it was the right temperature for him, then stood under it and let the water flow through his hair and down his face, while he reached for a plastic container of shower gel which hung from a hook at the side of him, not sure if he should use it or not thinking perhaps, it belonged to whoever had used the shower last, and they had forgotten to take it with them after they had finished having a shower. He quickly lathered up with the foam of the gel relieving his body of the cold he had felt in his room earlier, and was feeling better by the minute as he stood under the sprinkle jet from the rose above him. Rinsing the suds away from his hair and his body, he stayed under for as long as he dared knowing that the meal time was not far away and did not want to be late, and have to walk into the canteen on his own, also thinking there maybe perhaps ten or so others staying there besides himself according to the number of rooms he had seen on his landing alone, perhaps even, someone he already knew from his travels. There were towels hanging on hooks with a notice above them saying that when they had been used to place them in the laundry basket provided near the door on the way out, so they could be put into the laundry the following day.

Charlie after having showered, shaved, and changed, was sat on the chair in his room musing over what had been told him about the long term stay arrangements, and was thinking seriously about giving it a try, and if things stayed as good as they appeared to be on the first impression he had of the place, then he could well do worse for himself. It would all depend on the house rules so to speak, and last but not least would be the problem if there was a curfew on what time you had to be back in the place at night should there be occasions he would want to be out late, or not return there for the night even, well he thought I can find out that in due course, and make a decision then.

His thoughts were interrupted by the sound of a bell clanging loudly, and could only presume that it was the signal to everyone in the place that it was time for a meal. Now quite refreshed after the shower and shave he was quite ready for a meal and got up to make his way to wherever the canteen was.

When he was halfway down the stairs he could see the reception room where he had made out the forms to stay there, and it was only then realized he had not paid any money to stay there for the night. But when he saw there was not anyone there he decided to follow the people who were walking through a doorway opposite it. As he reached the door there was a sign which read dining room an arrow painted on it which pointed the direction, he just followed others who were also walking in the direction the arrow indicated. Every one seemed to be talking at once, except for one person who seemed to be on his own as Charlie was. Charlie looked at the man closer and assumed by his dress and manner he was a 'dropout' like himself, except he was quite a bit older by about twelve to fifteen years, his hair was long brown and sun bleached blonde in places, and braided on each side of his face, and wore a red head band, making him look like a throw back to the sixties, wearing jeans and a hand woven maroon waistcoat jacket with hanging tassels around the bottom edges.

Coming up alongside of him he asked. "What's the grub like here mate?" Trying to strike up conversation with him and to see what kind of answer he would get.

The man he had spoken to turned towards him showing a weather beaten face, and a full set of whiskers, which seemed to be sun bleached the same as his hair on his head. He smiled when he realized it was him, Charlie had addressed, showing a full set of white well kept teeth, answering in a strong Yorkshire accent he replied. Foods not bad. The best I have ever had in any hostel, and I have stayed in quite a few in my time. It's as good here as you will find in any

Bed and breakfast, and that's for sure. I only meant to stay for a couple of days but it's been so good here I have stayed for over a week now. I never dreamt of staying in a hostel for longer than four days before, but with the weather turning the way it has just of late, I am in no hurry to move on anywhere just yet, every thing here will do me fine for a while longer yet. He offered his hand to Charlie.

"The names Choco. On account of the fact I am a little more than partial to a bar of the brown stuff. "Are you here on your own?"

"Yes. I came here this evening. The names Charlie."

"I'm on my todd for now. Do you mind sharing a table with me? At least it will make dinner more interesting to have a natter with someone in the same boat as myself here. Most here are what you may term a bit clicky. Not unpleasantly so, but they always seem to talk of people they know or knew and it always seems to   leave a lot of the conversation wanting."

"No that's fine, it beats eating alone, and it does not look like I know any one here anyway, and you could fill me in on a few things about the place as well. Routine and such like."

"Here we are. Pick up a tray and, then we move over to where the queue starts, is the first thing for me to tell you."

A meal of liver, bacon, carrots and peas, made into what could only be called a casserole, with the gravy thick and onion flavoured, and an ample portion of mashed potato with seasoning which made the mouth water as it was put onto the plate, with jam sponge pudding and custard to follow, was Charlie's introduction to the cuisine of Gowendene Manor.

After the meal Choco showed Charlie where the sitting room was, where they could smoke, talk, and watch T.V. or even play a game of pool. They did a bit of each until they decided it was about time to get their heads down for the night, agreeing to meet again at breakfast, when he would fill him in about staying at the manor for a while longer if he wished.

CHAPTER 14

D.I. Loverage sat looking out of the office window totally confused. On his desk were the reports of the two bodies found on the outskirts of Bridgwater, plus the one found by the two detectorist's at Stoke Croft woods. There was nothing that made sense about any of it. There was the revised report from the pathologist as D.I. Marshal had told him, and the contents were as different from the original as they could be. The body did have lacerations as the original had stated, but everything about it was in reverse order. There had been aspects of wounds inflicted on the body the pathologist's could not explain by conventional means, and had contacted his counterpart in Bridgwater for a second opinion, and to see if he could come up with a different explanation than the one he had reached himself, but only to have the conclusion he had reached, confirmed by by his Bridgwater colleague, as incredulous as it may seem. Somehow the victims injuries had been inflicted from inside, as if it had cut outwards from beneath the surface of the flesh, from where the skin tissue and flesh met, starting from the bottom of the throat down to the lower regions of the genital area, causing even strips of skin and flesh to come apart in ribbons of an inch width by two and a half in length, giving the outward impression of the subject being flayed using some kind of razor sharp mechanical device just once, over the whole body, and then some of the internal organs removed after death had taken place, but because of the manner of the injuries this was only supposition by both pathologists, due to the fact of the condition of the body when found, and apart from that they could not in their wildest of imagination, see how someone could still be alive after being subjected to such injuries, or even remain conscious for any prolonged period of time. Even that was stated on the report, but there was nothing on how this seemingly impossible task of terrible injuries had been accomplished.

Dave Mitchell came into the office, and saw his colleague studying one report and then the other, and throw them with a frustrated action back onto the desk. He looked at Mitchell when he saw him standing there.

"What the hell is going on? Not a thing in these reports makes sense. There is nothing similar in the deaths that could connect one to another except the for the unknown means of the way they have died, with no concise explanation as to how that was.

Except for the bodies and the manner of their deaths there seems to be nothing that we can find that might connect the reason for them being killed. Were they known to each other? We don't even know that, of the three which we have found, there is only one we have been able to put a name to. Maybe there is something, but in all the thinking I have done on the case I still have not got the faintest idea as of yet what that something could be."

"We have the identity of two bodies now." Mitchell held out his hand towards Loverage holding a sheet of paper, we have a match for the first body found at Bridgwater, but that is only half the story, he is one Leon Thomas, another minister belonging to Parkland fields, New Road, Penticostal Church."

"What about the woman?"

"No joy there I'm afraid. There is no report of anyone missing with the description of the woman found at Blunders Farm. Could be a case that she has not been reported missing yet for some reason. Anyway to get back to the other two. Paul Gage aged thirty five, he has been identified as the body found at Stoke Croft woods, married to Angela Gage, reported missing five weeks ago by his wife. He was last seen leaving his church after evening services by a Mrs.....Mrs.......Laver. She was coming home from taking her grandson back to her daughters house, after having him for the weekend and by the report we have, he was walking to the car park behind the church towards his car. She often saw him on the occasions she would be coming home, just leaving in the car or walking to the car park on his way to it carrying his briefcase, and the times were always about the same, or within the span of five minutes.

After not returning home by the usual time his wife became a little concerned, ringing the church she had got no reply, and asked a neighbour if she would look after her two children, a boy and girl, while she drove to the church herself to see if he was inside, or if something had happened to him while inside and he could not answer the phone. She arrived at the church and everything seemed normal. The church was locked and seemed secure, but when she went around to the car park his car was still there and locked up, and no sign of him anywhere. After phoning around to make sure he had not been admitted to hospital for any reason, she reported him missing the following morning at nine fifteen, after he had not returned home all night. She had been inside the church the evening before when she saw the car was still in the car park, using the spare key to the church they kept at home."

"Has she been notified of his death yet?"

"No. We have only received the reports ten minutes ago, and I just happened to be in communications room when they came through and brought them straight here."

"The other one. What do we know of him?"

"There's not a lot really. He was forty three, a black West Indian, unmarried, named Leon Thomas no one really knew he was missing for sure, for a while anyway. The report on him missing was filed by his brother, and was only done after he had not been seen for over a week, and it was only done then when another church member had chanced to see him after he had returned from holiday a little over a week before. It was only when the friend had spoken to the brother and had inquired if his brother had enjoyed his holiday in the West Indies, he had found out he had returned. The brother was a little concerned when going around to his brothers house a few times and not being able to see him there or contacting him by telephone. Then just to make sure he telephoned relatives in the West Indies, Trinidad, to be precise, and found he had indeed returned to England over a week before. He had also been seen the day after he had returned by another neighbour, but they had not spoken very long to each other, except to say he had enjoyed his time in Trinidad, the conversation took about all of twenty seconds, and was while the neighbour had been getting into his car to go to work. In all from the time he was seen by the neighbour and friend and found five weeks had passed.

Some one else had been brought in to take the services while he had taken the holiday, and they are still there covering until, they heard word from him or until he returned from where ever he has been. Of course when they hear about his death it will put a new light on what they will have to do, the least of which would be to appoint a new minister I should think.

His brother was highly concerned solely because his disappearance was completely out of character, and he had feared he might have had a mental block problem of some kind. Not, he says, that there was anything to make him think it. It was the only thing he could think of to try to explain his disappearance, he had not been in any relationship which had not been going well, or anything that could be associated with him wanting to disappear. After drawing a blank at hospitals, and checking his home, to find his bags were not fully unpacked and some clothing had been put in a laundry basket ready for washing. Then only after getting in touch with various people who had known him and coming up empty handed of anything to throw any light on his disappearance the brother reported him missing."

Loverage took the reports from Mitchell and as he did so Mitchell leaned forward and with a lowered voice said. "That's not the end of it!"

"What do you mean?"

"Look!" He took the papers he had just handed over back off of Loverage. Sorted through them until he found what he was looking for.

"When we came back from the scene at Weston Zoyland, I had a thought whether there were any more cases similar to those we are involved in anywhere else in the country. It was just an idea, but I asked control just to fax any details similar to what we have experienced, or questionable deaths which have remained unsolved in the last two years, and this is what came back from H.O.L.M.S. The Home Office Computer Data Base."

"What?....What is it?"

"Take a look for yourself. There are eight similar deaths in the past eighteen months alone. All within the South West. The main thing of concern is. Well take a look at the occupations of them. Of the eight only two are not priests or clergy of some kind. When I received that I went for the hole biscuit instead of the crumbs. Take a look at what I got back and then tell me if there is not one over riding connection that does not stick out like a ten pound lump of coal in the snow, to the hard of hearing."

Loverage took the paper Mitchell held out to him and began to read. After a couple of minutes he looked up to his sergeant. "Why has nothing of this come to light before now?" On the paper he held in his hands were the names of different people, from all over the British Isles. From the very top of Scotland to St. Ives in Cornwall. Found dead or missing, from nineteen eighty six until the present time. They were of different religions, from Christian of every persuasion, Catholic, Church of England, Baptists, to lesser known affiliations, Jew, Muslim, Buddists, every religion one could think of was on the list. A total of two hundred and thirty were on the list and had been reported as missing. All of those missing were ministers and the like, or had held a position within the religion they were followers of.

Of the Two hundred and thirty listed as missing from home, twenty seven have been found dead. That included the two known ministers whose deaths were under investigation of the strange circumstances of their demise by Loverage, Mitchell, and Marshall. The rest were still down as missing persons. Of the total if just five percent were due to anything similar to what they had experienced so far in their investigation, and met with foul play in some way then it would look as if there was something far more involved than any of them had imagined when they first started the investigations.

"Because they are hidden figures! Those details only came to light when I specifically asked for them. In England alone there are thousands of people who go missing every year for one reason or another, to the majority of police forces they are just figures on paper and in files. The only reason we have stumbled on these facts is because of the locality of where the the deceased were found, and that Bridgwater thought there may be a connection between them, and that was only due to our own pathologist wanting a colleague to give a second opinion, just to confirm the conclusion he had already reached about the method used to cause death, in the case of the body found at Stokes Croft, and if he had not with the decomposition of the body when it had been found we would have looked at the death as if it had been caused by some kind of maniac, and not have come this far in the investigation, and would probably ended up filed as unsolved even with the unusual circumstances surrounding it. Until something similar happened again, if it ever did, what would have happened then, because we would still be as much in the dark as we are now. Also the distance and time between the other murders is another factor, it does not seem to be a case of one victim after another in the same area, until ours came to light, usually they have been from upwards of hundred miles at least is the normal distances involved, and maybe at the most those who would be found in the similar circumstances as those we have under investigation, have a distance of at least sixty miles from each one, with intervals of months rather than days or hours as we have experienced according to the information available, that is.

Loverage was thoughtful and quiet for a while, and when he broke the silence, there was in his tone of voice hinged with purpose in his words.

"What we have made of things up until now, it seems, to, me, we have been looking in the wrong direction. It looked at first as if we have some kind of nutter on the rampage. Who has the ability and time to travel, and has a big down on religion, and people who believe in it, no matter what the religion might be, and to him, who ever practices it is fair game for the chop, right? Does that sound right to you Dave? Or do I sound like I am blowing shit out of my mouth?"

Mitchell looked at his superior, was about to agree fully with him, but thought again about what had been bugging him from the first time he had read the reports that were on the desk in front of Loverage, and from the time he had viewed the bodies, and knew Loverage wanted things to be the way he had said, but underneath did not believe his own words, as he was speaking them. "You know there's more to it than that boss. How is he killing them? There has been no evidence of any kind around the areas where they have been found, nothing at all, and could it be more than one person involved?"

"So blowing shit doesn't work on you either, so what more can we do? Except inform the next of kin, of the news they don't want to hear. We had better take a W.P.C. or should I say you had better. I hate this aspect of our job. Every one I have had to do affects me the same as the first. They say one can distance one's self from it once it is over but, it follows me for days afterwards. Not the crime, that is bad enough but, the reactions of the people who have to take the news of a loss of a family member. But with first the loss and then the condition of the bodies when they are found such as those we have seen since we started this investigation. There is never going to be a way of telling it without getting in some way involved at the time of telling. While you are gone I will see what, if anything, I can dig out of the information we have so far. O.K?"

****

Some time later Loverage got up from his office chair, and as he did so he felt his shirt stick to his back, the chair was made of simulated leather, and because of the length of time he had been sat in it that day, going through file after file, and cross referencing each file to see if there was a common comparison, with all the facts known, besides the disappearance of priests ect. But there seemed to be nothing conclusive that could be of interest to them connecting all or part of what they had in evidence, to the individuals who had been found dead in suspicious circumstances, and the strange and macabre conditions of the bodies when they had been found.

He gave an open mouthed yawn with his arms outstretched, as Mitchell returned, and entered the office.

"All done Dave?"

Mitchell nodded, and began to take his jacket off.

"Find anything of interest, such as answers to what we know so far?"

"No not a damned thing unless you call that sole fact a connection to whatever it is that's happening, and the fact that there are no witnesses to anything about the priests, ministers or whoever when they are disappearing."

Loverage looked at his watch. "Don't bother taking your jacket off Dave, it's nearly six I think it might be as well to call it a day." Picking up a bunch of keys from the desk top, and quickly tidying up the surface, placing the files together he put them in a side drawer of the desk and locked it up. "We have been on this practically all day and I for one am feeling quite jaded. What about a cuppa in the canteen then home and a fresh start tomorrow, what do you say?"

"Your the boss, and I am not about to disagree with the day I have had, and a fresh start tomorrow may bring something useful to the surface, but I cannot think what it might be if we do progress a little it seems to get more confusing with every new fact that comes to light."

They had gone to the canteen and were about to leave, when their attention was called by a uniformed constable, who upon finding them had a message from the duty desk sergeant, he had told him to see if they could be found if they were still in the station, and if they were to tell them to come to the desk as soon as possible, because there was someone there he thought they should see.

The two detectives upon arriving at the desk found the duty sergeant in conversation with a man in his early twenties. At the moment of their arrival there, the sergeant excused himself politely, and spoke to them immediately, saying he thought it might be a good idea for them to speak to a woman in the interview room, saying she had come to report a missing person. Curious why the sergeant thought they might be interested in a missing person, and for what reason the sergeant thought it might be worth while for them to speak to her in the interview room.

The reason became clear when the officer explained the person reported as missing was a priest. Upon hearing that fact the two police officers hurried to the room where the uniformed officer had directed them.

On entering they saw sitting with a pronounced worried look on her face was a woman they both estimated would be about forty five to fifty. As they both introduced themselves to her, the

85

door opened again behind them and the desk sergeant poked his head in with a folder in his hand and handed it to Loverage. "That's the preliminary report on the burglary at the house from yesterdays investigations."

Loverage took the folder offered to him. His face a picture of bewilderment, turning to Mitchell he saw that he was as confused as him self.

"What was that about a burglary?"

"The vicarage, or the house where the priest lives. Mrs. Willard here, reported the burglary yesterday morning when she came down from her bedroom to make breakfast for Father....Father, O'Connell that's right isn't it Mrs. Willard? If you tell these officers what you have told me earlier at the desk, they will look into it for you."

As the sergeant turned and closed the door, Loverage was on his heels and out of the room following him into the passage. "Hold on sergeant. What's this about a burglary? I was under the impression it was a missing person enquiry we had been asked to see about. Nothing about a burglary was mentioned."

"Yes, I know, but when she came here this afternoon to report the priest missing I remembered the report of a burglary which was investigated yesterday and thought perhaps there could be a connection to the burglary and his disappearance. I brought the file to you just in case I might be right, and when you found out about it which you would, when you question the house keeper, well you have it there, and you would only have sent for it and I thought you would appreciate it being to hand sooner than later."

"What are you implying the burglars abducted him or what?" Has she told you she has seen someone hanging around the house, or something else has happened before the burglary."

"I don't know any more than I have already said. Make up your own minds about what to think. But I think it may have been a case of the burglars being disturbed, and may even have panicked when or if they were caught in the act by the priest returning unexpectedly. Anything could be possible, but I must say that in my experience burglars tend to scarper as soon as anything looks to be going wrong, such as a house owner returning unexpectedly.

Loverage had to agree with the sergeants last statement. It was true that in most cases anyone caught in the act of carrying out a burglary most often than not did try to make an escape before they were seen. Just a car pulling up outside of a dwelling, or the sounds of voices or key being turned in the lock, was usually enough to make most flee through the nearest open window, or even bedroom windows to make an escape.

"What time was it yesterday when you found there had been a burglary?"

Loverage was looking through the papers he had in front of him as he asked Mrs. Willard for more details. Noting in his mind things listed which had been stolen, large objects such as a television set with a twenty two inch screen, antique frying pan type bed warmer, a turn of the century wall barometer and matching wall clock, with various small objects of value, not great value individually but in total when added together, it would have been a tidy sum for a couple of hours work, although the price they would get would not amount to half of the total value of the goods taken. They would no doubt be happy with the sum they would receive considering the small amount of labour they would have done for it.

CHAPTER 15

Father George O'Connell had eaten his fill, and had taken a drink from the bottle of wine which had been on the table with the rest of the food. He was as confused now as he had been when he had first come around from the blow on his head in the church, those few days before. Looking around he could see there was no chance of escape from the room he was now in than there was from the other two rooms he was in. He was sure those who had brought him there were still in the passage outside, although, he could hear nothing in the way of conversation, being there were two rooms between where he was sat and the passage, where he assumed, the two were waiting should he try to attempt an escape.

At least if the opportunity of escape did present it's self he now had a full stomach, even if he did feel a little bloated and and sick, due to his over eating. When he had started eating he thought to himself it might be wise to eat as much as possible with the thought upper most in his mind of the treatment he had received since his abduction, there seemed to be no way of telling what could be in store for him from one moment to another, nothing seemed to make any sense with the way he had been treated so far, he then began to wonder how long it had been since the man who had called himself Coulter had left.

The door opened and the man named Coulter returned.

"I hope the food was satisfactory, we had to do the best we could with what was in the kitchen at short notice, but I am sure you would have found it appetizing as well as filling. I see you have sampled a glass or two from the bottle of wine it's very similar to a good Madoc, and it is from a local vineyard which supplies us, we have a standing order with them and they supply us once a year.

"Why have you brought me here? What do you want of me?"

The man seemed to take a while before he answered, perhaps thinking of what to say, or how to say it, he put his hand to his chin, gave a slight pinch to the bottom of it, then as if coming to a decision he spoke.

"When we first abducted you we planned to use you in a kind of,.... I suppose.....one could say.....an experimental sacrifice. It was nothing personal you understand, it was just the fact we had need of a priest, to use in a ceremony on ground which had been consecrated, and had been used by us in the past, a long time before your Christian church practices were held there and it will now be of use to us again in the future. We also intended at the same time to test our powers more fully as a group, as it happened we tested similar power on someone else, who we felt could end up as a potential problem to us. They were in the end dealt with, with little effort and, without any problem to us. Of course if he, it was a male person, and if he had been a priest such as yourself or some other kind of cleric or minister, of any other denomination within the Christian church we would have disposed of him in different circumstances, and would have accomplished a lot more than we actually did, but then not to worry there will be others for us to make use of when the time is right again to carry out what we had intended for you, and there are many more priests we can call on to aid with our progress in this world."

He was completely unprepared for the answer the man gave to the question he had asked, and sat motionless, with complete disbelief, at what he had just been told.

"There are some who still want to go ahead with what we originally planned for you, but others who can see as I do, that it could help our cause immensely if you had the opportunity and could be persuaded to work with us, or even join us. The rewards for you would be beyond anything you could envisage. We would have had to wait for a precise time to come around again with the right circumstances to be in place to do what we had originally planned to do with you, and by the time that happens you would quite certainly be dead of starvation.

"What if I refuse?"

"Oh! Then you would be disposed of, for the benefit of our....,shall we say order, although that is not what we look upon ourselves as, an order. We think of ourselves as the rightful inheritors of this world, who have been subjected to all kinds of persecution for centuries, and now after waiting for the right climate, we have returned to do as we wish, and as our hearts, shall we say desire. While we have waited we have been learning what we are capable of, and as things now stand we have built up a formidable force, and nothing can stand against us.

We have conquered death, it has no meaning to us now and we have no fear of it, to us it does not exist. Since our return in just a few years of your time, we have influence in Governments the world over, our people have all but taken control everywhere, without anyone having the slightest idea, soon will come what you in your teachings have called Armageddon. It will come and then we will reap our reward of centuries of waiting patiently for this time to arrive. You are welcome to ask any questions you may have, and I will answer them without hiding anything, because it will not matter one way or another whether you join us or not, you cannot escape to tell of what you know now, or may have knowledge of later. But remember should you join us there would be no turning back, you will in the end have to disregard all you believe in as the truth, and then you will begin to see it is only a shadow of what is in reality the true facts in the order of the way things really are. I will leave you now to think over what has been offered to you in place of death, and to think over any questions you may want answers to later. You will be taken back to the room you have come from by our two friends and left there. Anything you may require will be brought to you, if you knock on the door and request it. There will be someone outside of the door to your room at all times. I will see you at about this time tomorrow, by which time you should have decided if you wish to become a helper, and part of us, or not."

With those words he turned and walked away from Father O'Connell, spoke to the pair outside the door, who came in and escorted him back to the room he had come from with the bed ect. in side.

The walk back to the room was a complete contrast to when they had brought him from the first room to the other, and to have the shower. They talked to him in general terms and as if he was a new friend whom they had just been introduced to. they told him of all the things which would be at his disposal, if he were to join them, but he could not help but to notice as they spoke and smiled at him, there seemed to be no life in their eyes, or any depth of feeling as they spoke. He decided there and then, to play along with them and they in turn kept up the rapport and friendly conversation.

All that night Father O'Connell devoted his time to silent prayer, not really knowing what else he could do, accepting that should things go bad for him, he would not lose faith in his belief, and had put his faith in his maker to see him through whatever the outcome may be the following day.

Early the next morning food was brought to him, with a choice of tea or coffee to drink. Nervous and with apprehension, he slowly ate what he could, although, he felt far from having an appetite, and just ate to make the others, whoever they were, think he was going to join them. "Somehow!" He had to get away. How he had no idea. But felt deep down in his being, he had to somehow escape and inform the 'Church' of what he knew, and to turn any advantage he could get, that could work in his favour to accomplish it.

The two outside opened the door for him and, told him he was wanted by James Caulter in the room where he had last seen him and he was to come with them immediately.

Upon entering the room he saw that Coulter was already there and sat at the table that the day before held the food he had eaten. Sitting next to him was a woman of about thirty years of age, Caulter introduced her as his wife, and said that she always had been. He looked at the both of them with more attention now, and could see Caulter was around the age of forty years of age or so. Quite slim in build but also athletic looking, well groomed, with dark wavy hair, and cut a quite handsome figure. His dress was casual but immaculate. He turned his attention to the woman, who in fact was quite beautiful, long waved brown hair cascaded down well past her shoulders, shiny and clean, she was dressed casually the same as her husband, a black skirt and white blouse, there was a small pendant hanging from her neck on a chain, which the priest suspected was gold, there was some kind of engraving upon it of a face, but he could not tell if it was male or female because of the length of the hair. Her eyes were green with flecks of orange with tints of brown, but the same thing was noticeable in them as Caulter and the other two men, no depth, and seemed to portray a coldness and without feelings within them.

Father O'Connell was the first to speak after sitting down opposite them.

"I find it hard to believe that there is nothing known about you. How can you be sure that is so?"

"We are sure because we have people in governments and local administrations, informants in every public service from police to local governments, hospitals, to well placed politicians, and to the highest level of governments worldwide it's surprising how large a weapon greed can be when used well, you name it and we have ears and eyes working for our cause everywhere. Mostly they are willing participants, but some have been coerced, in ways you cannot begin to imagine, or would even want to know of."

Coulter went on, telling Father O'Connell of things which had been done to accomplish their goals since they had 'returned' as he put it, which the content of, made the priests flesh creep.

When he had finished and asked if there were any other questions he might want to ask. He was too stunned to answer right away. "What more, is there too, tell me." He thought to himself.

The woman turned to Caulter and spoke softly to him, Father O'Connell could not hear what had been said, because he answered her in a low voice himself, while casually tapping his fingers on the top of the table.

"If you look at the world today there is a lot of unrest as you would put it, a lot of what is happening is due to changes which have come about by the influences such as we work with to achieve our aims, not that we have had done much in the way of influencing the things that are happening now, most of that is due to the ways modern living has evolved. With corruption rife in top governments of the world, religious bigots who speak of one thing, but act with only their own interests at heart. Taking scriptural passages from religious teachings of all religions and then using them along with other interpretations which would suit their cause, to stir up hatred, and animosity which have caused the deaths of millions, and when these things occur it produces negative energy which we can then use to further our own power, so you see we are in the end only using what you yourselves produce with wars, uncontrolled famines which cause starvation to those unfortunately enough to be born where they occur, anything that is done without thought for the unfortunate consequences to others, and that negativety has through the ages been building up and stored, and now we have the ability to tap into it and use it as we have done. Thus in the eventual and final course of events, we will be left with only the strong to inherit what is left, and the biggest majority will be with us eventually, those that are not will be left to fight things out between themselves, but will accomplish nothing except to strengthen our position, for what we will eventually achieve, total control, and our right to inherit everything and do as we will."

A confused priest, sat looking at the two in front of him. Could he be hearing what was being told to him and live if he did not agree to join them? Obviously not, was what they had implied, and he was left in no doubt what so ever, they meant every word if the treatment he had experienced so far was anything to go by.

"If what you have told me is true, and I don't disbelieve you now for one minute, that it is. What puzzles me is why you would want me to join you when I stand for and believe in everything you object to."

"Yes that is true, as you believe and feel at the moment, but with a little education and home truths to dispel what you now believe, it is shall I say possible, you could change your mind.

It was something we had been discussing amongst ourselves when deciding to make you the offer to join us. Also there was a time when your church in the past gave people, as was said, a chance to repent before and after what was then the most barbaric of torture, if they had so called repented or not they would still be executed in the name of your holy teachings. So you see, yours is not such a history of benevolence and forgiveness as you would have so many believe, at least with us, you would, have the right to live or die in your own hands. We offer you the chance to live in luxury far beyond anything you could imagine, or the choice of a quick death instead of the kind of death experienced by those unfortunate to be condemned and executed in the past in the name of Christianity, the choice is yours alone."

"What are you saying, that in the past you were all witches or devil worshiper's and executed for your beliefs?"

"No just as today our our existence was unknown it was just the poor misguided or misfits, even finger pointing at specific people who were used to illustrate the power they had within the realms of the ignorant and uneducated. All through the centuries we were even then a society of beings that were well able to look after our own, should anyone have learnt of us they would never have dared to speak of what they had learned through fear of us and, the offer we have made to you would have been made to whom ever it might concern, there were very few in the past who would have rejected our offer when they saw just what they could have if they joined us, greed and power was as common in all ages of the past as it is today. We had complete control of all matters in the past because of the way we worked within the local community, so you see should our secret be discovered they were either with us, or had an accident but, most were prone to go insane once they had seen the power we had, although it was then nothing to what we can achieve today, so you see even then we knew exactly what we were about. The Church through the ages would have known of some goings on, but could never quite understand what, and mostly with a little help from us they would use the old and mentally unbalanced, or people who displayed what you would call uncanny accomplishments such as clairvoyance, or knowledge of healing one way or another, which would not be in keeping with the logic of the churches of the past understanding, unless the church could turn these things to work for them, they would be made scapecoats, to be called such things as the devil's workers, or if someone was not liked for some reason in towns or villages they were pointed out as heretics over one thing or another, then they would be brought before someone in the church, or elected by the church to be an interrogator and, who would prove in some way, the person was in league with the being you call the devil, or had invoked in some way the powers of the devil to harm another person, or cause sickness within a family or cattle of an accuser, and in doing so made their authority seem to be for the benefit of the poor individual, and the punishment meted out in the name of, the so called 'saving of souls', making their punishment, and authority seem just. The end punishment made people keep anything they thought would be detrimental to them in the eyes of the church to themselves, and to all outward appearances they strayed little from the path of to what the church would consider sacrilege in their eyes. In other words, the punishment was used to keep anyone from straying from what the church decided was the right path, thereby keeping power and influence for themselves through fear of punishment to those they considered could under mind their authority, and power. No different than the methods we employ now to obtain our goals today. Of course there were in the past those who stumbled on our existence by accident, and of those some refused outright our offer of joining us and, were dealt with in a quick and final way, leaving our secret intact as I have already told you earlier, for us to continued our work and progress towards this time, when everything is now in our favour for complete domination of this world.

The priest had listened to Caulter as if he had been spellbound, as the mans voice seemed to rise and fall, he felt it was better to let the man talk. He had already made his mind up as to what he was going to do earlier, and having already made his decision on what he was going to try to do, he let the man speak on until he had finished.

When he had finished, he asked what exactly he had meant when he had told him there was nothing he could not have if he joined them. He was answered in one word.

"Anything."

"We will leave you for one hour to think over what we have said, at the end of which we must have your answer, one way or another. Join us and live, or refuse and die. If you let us know truthfully, one way or the other, should you refuse, your death will be quick and over without pain but, should you try to deceive us then you would die in pain you could not imagine possible."

As the husband and wife left the room, someone else a woman he had not seen before came in with a tray with coffee milk and sugar and cup and saucer. She told him to help himself then left.

Alone, Father O'Connell thought to himself what he would have to do, when he told Caulter he was willing to join them, he must make it as convincing as possible, then make his escape at the first safe opportunity, then to inform his superiors immediately of what he had happened to him and what he had discovered in the process.

After what seemed more like three hours instead of the one which had passed, Caulter and his wife returned. Caulter's wife looked the same as when she had left expressionless, and as if she was in a semi dream state, although, her actions of walking and, everything else about her seemed normal.

"All I want from you now is your answer, what is it to be?"

He took a deep silent breath, steadying himself to answer as convincingly as he could, while at the same time in his mind said a quick and earnest prayer for help in anyway it was possible to escape from the situation he was in.

"I have thought over what you have said to me, and am willing to accept your offer to join you." His heart was pounding and he felt his face flush with heat as he spoke the words.

When he had given his answer, the woman turned to her husband, and spoke to him, again in the same low tone she had used before, while as before Coulter while being spoken to, softly tapped the table with the fingers of his right hand.

While Father O'Connell could again not hear what was being said, just a word here and there, and again nothing that he could make any sense of. When she had finished speaking both the man and the woman seemed to grow excited and, it showed in both their eyes while at the same time their manner towards him changed immediately, from seemingly friendly to a cold and indifferent attitude. As one they rose from their chairs, while they did so, Caulter's features took on a look of pure animosity and evil.

"I warned you to be truthful, before we left earlier, but it seems you have not heeded my warning to you. I know every thing you had in your mind now, but had to give you the chance as was your right by our law, just as I was obliged to do, to give you the choice of a quick and pain free death. Thank you for the anticipation of looking forward to making your death as painful as we can priest, the next time we meet will be most pleasurable for me, and then we will see just how the faith in what you believe helps you when you need it most." With that said they both turned walked to the door and were gone.

The two heavies came into the room caught hold of the priest and dragged him back to the room where he had woken up when he had first arrived. As the door was slammed shut he could hear them laughing loudly in the passage outside of the room. He looked around the room a cold shiver of fear began to take hold of him as he began thinking what they had in store for him. He then started to think how he might thwart their plans by escaping, slowly he walked to the door to examine it more closely, then suddenly it opened, the larger of the two men he had seen leave the room came in carrying some lengths of rope, roughly pushed him onto the floor and tied his arms and legs leaving him on the floor, laying on his side. His task completed he turned from the priest walked out of the door, switching the light out as he went, with not a word spoken.

CHAPTER 16

When Charlie and Choco had decided to retire they had both made their way to their respective rooms, Charlie came in sat on his bed and decided to have a last 'rollup' for the night, and think to himself what his plans could be for the near future. His thoughts were interrupted by the sounds of clattering metal in the hallway, followed by a knocking on his door. Opening it he saw standing there wearing the same clothes he was wearing earlier that night, Willie, holding a mug towards him through the opened door.

"Here you are, some nice hot drinking chocolate to turn in with, help yourself to sugar, it's on the trolley here."

He pointed to a large stainless steel bowl standing next to an urn on the trolley he had pushed around, knocking on doors and offering the beverage, to the people in the rooms on his way.

Charlie took the offered mug and helped himself to sugar, placing the spoon back onto the trolley, thanked Willie, and started to close the door before he could start up a lengthy conversation going, but it was not necessary, it seemed Willie was in a hurry at that late hour, probably Charlie thought he wanted to get his head down after a day of activity around the manor doing all kinds of odd jobs there. As he finished with the sugar from the bowl and placed the spoon on the trolley he was already on his way to the next room.

When he had finished with his drink and a smoke he decided he had, had enough for the day, and as he began to feel tired he got up from where he had been sitting on the bed and walked towards the door where the light switch was, and turned the light out. Returning to his bed he looked towards the window and saw the rain had now stopped, as he looked for an instant he saw a flash of light which seemed to sway, it could have been a torch or a lamp, he saw the light again, but for a little longer period, then another and another, they all seemed to be in a line and heading away from the area of the manor grounds. He waited watching the the lights until they all seemed to blink out one after another as they reached a certain point. He wondered to himself who it could be wandering around out there at that late hour. He tried to think of the geography of the manor house and what was out there in the area he had looked onto, but because it was dark and raining when he arrived and, he was unsure of where his room was situated in the house and, what direction it overlooked he did not really know what was out there. He watched for a little while longer but saw nothing more, moved away from the window to his bed, undressed and got into bed, he was asleep within moments of his head hitting the pillow.

That night he slept as he had never slept for as long as he could remember, so much so he found it difficult to awaken in the morning.

When he came down for breakfast, Charlie saw his new acquaintance of the evening before was already sat at the table they had used the night before when they had eaten dinner. He saw Charlie enter the dining room, and gestured for him to come over when he had got a tray and his own breakfast from the counter.

Two slices of bacon, egg on toast and a portion of beans was Charlie's fare which he brought to the table that morning, to be washed down with a steaming hot cup of tea.

"Sleep well?" Choco spoke between a mouthful of much the same as Charlie had got for himself, except for the portion of beans which seemed to take up the larger part of his plate and was swimming with tomato sauce.

"Yes, a real good nights kip. Just what the doctor ordered, but I found it hard to get up this morning I slept so sound."

"That's the one thing I have found with this place, you always seem to get a sound nights kip here. I expect it is due to the country air out this far from the town, plus, a good bed to kip in."

During breakfast and after they told each other a few things about themselves to each other. Such as where the came from, and about who they knew that the other might know, but as it turned out both came out with names the other could not recognize.

Eventually the conversation turned to the immediate plans Charlie had decided on, and that was; as he stated to his new friend, he was more or less deciding to spend a couple of weeks at least at the manor, or until he could sort out more precise plans on where he was going.

"First thing you have to do, is to go into town to the 'Unemployment Office' and sign on as unemployed, you can't do anything about staying here for a prolonged period until you have done that first."

"Is there a public transport service in this area to catch into and return from the town, or is it a case of shanks's pony again?"

"There is no public transport, but there is transport laid on from the manor to and from town four times a day for those who want to make use of it any time. I have to go into town myself today, to collect a bit of cash from someone, so if you want to come into town with me, eat breakfast and be ready in half an hour then we can both catch the transport in, and return in time for dinner this evening, they have to go into town for supplies and such. They know that those of us who have to stay here don't have any means of transport. There are I have been told some here who have got themselves work in the town since staying here, and return for the necessity of a roof over their head, until they get enough bread together to get a flat of their own, but there are others, they are what short time stayers such as ourselves refer to as 'rezzies' in other words those who are staying here more or less permanent and seem to be part of the mainstream of activity here. Seems to me there is some kind of...of....what's the word I want, community, I suppose, much more I don't really know, except to say they all seem to keep very much to them selves." Choco nodded his head to the far end of the dining room, "There are some still here, I have tried to strike up conversation with them since I have been here but they are not forthcoming with any answers on what they are about, so let things be is what I say, the place will suit me for the time being at anyrate."

They caught the transport laid on by the manor into town and during the drive they became more aquainted with each other.

It seemed Choco had come to the Southwest some years before in eighty eight, to 'Stone Henge' for the summer solstice celebrations and had been nearly arrested because of local feelings and the law and disputes with the site heritage laws which had recently began to come to the fore. He had lost his 'Varna' and then later due to personal problems had split up with his 'lady' along with the wares they had made in the previous winter period in a 'New Age' winter encampment in Wales. He had settled in Devon for a couple of years living in some woods without any ones knowledge he was there. 'Living rough, was he had said, quite nice in the summer months, but could get cold as winter set in. In his dugout dwelling with a tarpaulin covering for a roof and a small fire inside, was quite comfortable. There was food around growing wild if one knew what, and where to find it, and as he did know there was no real inconvenience to him. He kept himself busy most of the time and every so often when the feeling took him he would take a walk to a nearby town, for a chat and some company, or do a bit of field work to earn a bit of cash. He did not need much for his needs, just tobacco, tea, coffee, flour and suchlike. He was fine content and happy, until the owners of the land he was on found him there, it was he thought too much for them, that anyone could be happy and content at their expense while living the way he was, and wanted him to leave. Their excuse, he was trespassing and a likely fire and health risk through rubbish and sanitation, even though he had been there over two years and there was no sign of him having lived there apparent.

Charlie and Choco had been dropped off in the centre of the town with three or four others who were staying at the manor who had also used the transport. They were told by the driver, the transport would be returning to the manor, from where he had dropped them off, at five thirty, to enable them to be back for the evening meal and the last transport should they not be able for any reason to catch the transport then, there was a last lift of the day at ten p.m., should they miss that then they would have to stay in the town or make their own way back, and go through the rigmarole of reregistering the following morning, so it would be in their interest to at least catch the last lift back at ten.

Charlie stepped out of the back of the van and saw the large clock in the centre of a large red bricked building, that once was the centre of the town market back in the twenties, but now marked the centre of the town.

Choco pulled from his pocket a navy blue bobble hat from the pocket of his combat jacket he had worn that morning, placing it on his head, and pulling his jacket collar up as far as it would go. Turning he walked to a shop awning to shelter from the rain which had started as they were halfway into the journey to the town.

"Every time I have to come into this town it starts pissing it down." He looked up to the heavens, and saw the dark grey clouds which seemed to look darker from the west. "Looks as if it is in for the rest of the day by the looks of that lot coming this way."

"Which way do I go for the job centre?"

"I will show you, where it is, or point you in the direction, once you walk up past the super market you will be able to see when we reach the road entrance, it's on the same side of the road and, you can't miss it. Don't forget once you have signed on you have to ask them for a B.1. form and bring it back to the manor and fill it out, and they will see to everything and send it in for you, you should get a payment in about four days time. When you have finished there, which should be about eleven or so, if my past experiences are any thing to go by, come out of the building and turn right keep going until you come to the traffic lights cross over and then with the town clock behind you walk to where you come to the turning into an arch way the Portcullis is at the end of it, the sign is hanging over the door you can't miss it, I will be in the bar room."

Having said that, Choco hunched his shoulders, his head tucked in and down, and with a pat on Charlie's back he was off. "See you later!" Was his parting cry, as he went on his way into the lashing rain.

Charlie having signed on as unemployed, and clutching a few forms and a booklet with aids to find work, and a rolled up B.1. in pamphlet form, sighed with relief as he stepped out of the building an hour later. The weather had become worse, the blustery showers had now become a full blown cold on the face storm, after a few steps into it he found himself walking as close to the shops as he could, most of the shops had by now withdrawn the awnings which had been present earlier because of the stronger winds, and lashing wind driven rain. He saw as he walked with his head down, the water running in torrents down the pavements, matchsticks, cigarette buts, paper, and plastic bags, blocking and stopping the drains from functioning properly, causing large and deep puddles to form. Pedestrians passed him making his journey like a game, as they dodged from side to side, avoiding streams of water overflowing from the gutters above them, because the extreme heaviness of rain in the down pour was so excessive, and could not flow fast enough down the drainpipes. At the same time a child oblivious to the weather walking in every puddle it could see, and being chastised by it's mother for splashing water on her legs and skirt.

It was not long before he was wet and cold, the rain trickling down his neck front and back. He thought of standing in a shop doorway until the worst had passed but, as he looked up at the sky he remembered what Choco had said about it being in for the day and by the look of things had to admit he was probably right, and continued walking.

Standing in one of the many shop doorways, sheltering from the rain was a young man of about seventeen, possibly a college student, his hair hanging down the side of his face wet and limp, with a look of complete misery about him. A billboard hanging from his shoulders advertising special reduced prices for all garments in a denim store, and special bargain lunch time meals for a French bistro in rainbow patterned letters.

"Which way to the Portcullis pub mate?" He inquired.

"Go on for another fifty yards, then first left."

"Lousy weather!"

"Yea! No let up for the past hour and a half now, another ten minutes and that's it for me, then they can stuff the board where ever they want after that."

"Don't blame you pal." Charlie replied as he continued on his way. The boy leaned out as, if keeping his eyes open for someone.

The portcullis it seemed, had let time pass by without seeming to change with the times. A sign hanging with the paint peeled and flaked, held from the wall by a rusty ornate bracket. From where he stood it looked as if the swinging sign would not last the storm, and looked as if it had been there since the Monmouth rebellion in the sixteen eighties. There was however a crude attempt at some time to do a bit of renovation, pointing around the crumbling brickwork, but had been given up after a short space of time.

He opened the door more than glad to get out of the terrible weather conditions outside, when he had stepped inside he saw there was an inner door, with all around the sides a wooden partition, with stained glass windowed sections from about five feet in height reached a low ceiling yellow with nicotine stained whitewash completed a small cube like entrance to the bar within, opening the inner door he entered and, saw in front of him about a dozen or more tables with people sat at them. The buzz of conversation which could be heard by him as he had opened the door slowly came to a stop, heads turned towards him, and eyes viewed him with obvious suspicion, as to who he might be, while some heads strained forward to see, who if anyone, he was with.

As he stood there, he felt totally alone and unsure what to do as he viewed the characters he saw before him, and had the feeling he had unwittingly stumbled upon a later day Fagins den.

The silence was broken by a voice from the far side of the room.

"Over here Charlie."

He looked over to where the voice had come from, and saw across the smoke filled bar, Choco, half standing with his hand raised.

The heads turned to the direction of Choco's voice, then back to Charlie, hands reached for for glasses in front of them on the tables they were sitting at, while slowly the hum of conversation began to start up again, quickly reaching the loud buzz he had heard upon entering the room. He made his way through the tables and chairs until he reached where Choco was sitting.

Charlie was introduced to three men who were sitting at the table with his friend, a nod, smile, and a quick shake of hands, and the introductions were over. It seemed that by the simple acceptance that he was a friend of Choco's was the same as a club membership card, and everything was O.K. as far as they were concerned.

Choco handed a ten pound note across the table to Charlie.

"Get Yourself a drink and one for me as well, mine's a pint of best, you have whatever it is you drink. He looked at the three with him to see if they wanted a refill of what they had been drinking. All three declined, saying they would be getting on their way in a short while.

Standing at the bar Charlie could see within the dim lighting of the place, decoration and hygiene, were the less important aspects of the watering hole he was in.

Behind the the front of the bar were mugs of all shapes and sizes hanging on hooks, made from glass, pewter, or earthenware. on the shelves themselves was what could only be described as a collection of different types of miniature alcoholic drink from all over the world, numbering a hundred or more. Hanging around the inside area of the bar were naval hats of different countries, even some from the second world war, German, Italian, as well as British and American, all were covered in a thick layer of dust and cobwebs, giving the appearance of a corner of an attic which had laid undisturbed since Victoria last sat on the throne of England, and the last time a duster had been used in the place. Every thing in the room had the yellow tinge of nicotine stains, from wall to ceiling which seemed to have accumulated over the same period of time.

His observations were interrupted, by two hundred and fifty pounds of mobile lard, contained in what could only be described as a tailor made black string vest. It could not be possible he thought for it to be bought from over the counter in a high street department store. Two eyes that seemed to belong to another face, small and piercing, a red and white patterned neckerchief around the neck, a bald shaven head which shone with the reflection from the forty watt bulb above it. The lips moved and a gruff but friendly sounding voice which reached the deep brown

eyes asked: "What will it be cider or beer?" Implying it seemed to Charlie, that was about all was sold in the establishment, and except for a few bottles of spirits with quantity measures beside them and with the absence of any optics, he thought to himself "It probably was."
"Two best bitters please."
"Pints, or halves?" "Pints, please.
"Pints, coming up."

He reached down below the counter, and then brought up two pint mugs by the handles, held them up to the light bulb, and seemed satisfied they were spotlessly clean and offered them to Charlie to look at.
"You see that, every glass and mug in here is sparkling clean before the drink is poured into it, there is nothing worse than a dirty glass with drink in it, even with the pipes as clean as they are here. Never mind anything else you will never get a dirty glass or mug or bad ale in this house."

He turned and pointed to a notice Charlie had not seen.

The Management stipulates that should

any customer be served with a dirty

glass in this establishment, they will

be entitled to free beer, or cider

(of their own choice)

for a period of one year.

****

Also,

pub grub is sold here, providing it comes in bags and called

crisps, nuts, or pork scratchings.

Hot Pies and Pasties must be ordered a week in

advance, and paid for at the time of ordering.

Signed: Gus. Proprietor of

The Portcullis Inn.

CHAPTER 17

Mitchell had switched off the television because there seemed to be not much of interest to him on it. Sitting in his armchair he suddenly had a thought, he had not seen 'Millie' since he had returned home, an unusual event to say the least and began to wonder where she was. He had fed her that morning as usual and as soon as she had eaten she had gone out of the cat flap on the front door, instead of going upstairs and on to his bed as was usual for a nap for a while, before going out into the garden.

He went to the front door and checked that the flap was not stuck in some way, found it was working perfectly well. He opened the door and shouted her name. He heard from the side of the house, a meow, as she answered him, then he saw her appear from around the corner walk a little way towards him, gave a couple more cat cries, but would not come any closer to him as he stood in the doorway. He then tried to coax her with a dish of her favourite cat food, but to no avail, for some reason she did not want to come any closer, perplexed at her actions he wondered if there was another cat she had become friendly with and was loath to come indoors for a while longer. Placing the dish on the doorstep he called her again but still she would come no closer, he took the dish of food to her and placed it on the ground in front of her, she then began to eat as normal. He decided to let her be and leave her to come in when she decided she wanted to.

As he returned inside the sitting room he was undecided what to do, picking up a magazine he quickly thumbed through it, then threw it back onto the table.
"It's the job." He thought to himself. "It's getting to me."
He decided there and then he needed a change, and company other than those at the station. In an instant his mind was made up and knowing of the public house, which was only a short distance away he decided there and then he would take a walk to it and have a drink or two, and perhaps take his mind off of the case for a while. He had been there one or two times before, but only on a Sunday when his daughter and her husband had come to stay with him. It had saved him having to cook a Sunday lunch and having to clear away and wash up dishes afterwards, but it was a long time ago since that had happened. "Perhaps, the trip there and some company would do me some good." He thought aloud to himself.

Standing in the bar of 'The Harvest Moon' he glanced around, he recognized some of the people there as neighbours, from the area where he lived. He had seen most of them around as he was going to, or returning from work. Most times it it would be just an acknowledgement of a raised hand or nod of the head, such it would seem was the way of the people in the neighbourhood of where he lived, friendly but not imposing.

A tap on the shoulder made him turn around to see a man he knew to be a neighbour who lived at the end of his road, and who he would always take time out to have a friendly chat with while Mitchell would be working on his garden, usually he would have an old black Labrador with him, but he had not seen the both of them about now for quite some time.
"I saw you standing there on your tod, and thought to myself I had not seen you here before, and there is nothing worse than going to a bar for a drink and not really knowing anyone to talk to, so, if you want, why not come over to our table and join the rest of us, we all live in the same area, but if you have come out just to be away from home and want time to yourself, that's all right as well, so what do you say?"

Mitchell had taken a liking to the man from the times they had talked together in the past and and after a little hesitation agreed to join him with the others.
"We have just being having a laugh, winding up young Jimmy Edwards there." He nodded his head towards the bar at a young man of about eighteen years of age who had passed Mitchell as he had walked from the bar to the table.
"About how he has just volunteered for the Royal Navy, and how he should have settled for the Army, because he was as sick as a pig when we all went to Lyme Regis for a days fishing on a

hire boat there last year, and we had not even left the harbour at the time."

They all laughed, seemingly at the memory of the lad bent over the side of the boat being ill and doing what all sea sick land lubbers are prone to do.

Mitchell stayed with the group at the table, and had an enjoyable evening, with the topic of conversation being from light hearted banter to, sport, micky taking, to the state of the country, and what more would happen in the way of taxes, unemployment, and pensions for the retired.

During the evening Mitchell found out the reason for not seeing the the man he now knew as Shephard around with the dog for quite some time. The dog had suffered with arthritis in his back legs and joints badly, and eventually a diseased kidney and in the end had been advised for the sake of the dog, it would be the best and kindest thing to do would be to have him put to sleep, which after a short time longer with him he had reluctantly done. Shephard it seemed was now in the process of getting another dog from the R.S.P.C.A. kennels. There was one there he had seen, he told Mitchell, a cross labrador, and had not had a very good life until he had been taken there by one of the inspectors, due to having been ill-treated, for the best part of his two years of life. He was happier now he had decided on another dog, he had taken time to come to the decision, but was looking forward to having another canine companion in the home again, he had missed his old dog and was not ready to adjust his life to take on another right away after his loss, but now felt the time was right to give a good home to an animal, and receive the companionship it would bring also with all the new characteristics the dog would bring with it.

Mitchell left before closing time, saying he had enjoyed himself, and would look forward to coming there again in the near future.

Returning home he looked for Millie at the side of the house and seeing she was not there, picked up her empty dish he had left for he earlier, and went inside. After washing it at the kitchen sink he was on his way to the sitting room when he saw her curled up at the foot of the stairs. She saw him and immediately got up onto her feet and stretched herself and came over to him and started to rub herself against his leg and purred loudly while she did so. He reached down patted her gently on her head and smoothed her back which made her rear end raise as she always did, making the sound of her purring rise in volume. He picked her up and saw that she seemed to be back to her old self again.

Looking over to the clock in the hallway he saw it was well past eleven o'clock, a quick shower and, then to bed he decided.

It was after he had showered and was in the process of drying himself, he happened to look into the bathroom mirror and saw his reflection, and something else, a movement, a shadow seemed to darken the area in the reflection behind him, and as it did so the temperature in the room seemed to drop dramatically, while at the same time sent a cold shiver through his body. He seemed to slow down every action of drying himself, it felt as if he was carrying out the functions, but somehow in actual fact seemed some how able to observe himself doing so in minute detail, it only seemed to last for a portion of a second, then he was back to normal speed, he stood still, wondering if what he had experienced had actually occurred or the effects of the few pints he had consumed earlier that evening. But the coldness he felt was still there, and there seemed to be in the bathroom a silence he had never felt there before. He put the towel he had been drying himself with on the towel drying rack on the wall nearby, then put his towel robe walked out onto the landing, as he did so he gave an involuntary shudder, as if, as is said, 'some one had walked over his grave.'

As he walked from the landing to the bedroom door, he heard an almighty screeching scream and saw his cat Millie go tearing along the landing, down the stairs and seconds later heard the sound of the cat flap clatter loudly as she made her exit at astonishing speed.

He was to say the least dumfounded by the speed at which she had moved, he had never in all the time he had her, ever, seen her move with such speed and agility. He had often thought when he had seen her attempts to catch a bird in the garden, which, to most cats it would have been second nature, he would watch and know the bird would be well away before she could reach it, and what he had just witnessed was a revelation to him. She had always ever since she had lived with him been pampered and, exercise was not one of her strong points as she was for the most time lethargic to say the least. Happy and content with comfort, warmth, and food.

That night he he had an uneasy sleep, waking up at least three or four times during the night, and each time he had a strong feeling there was someone watching him at the side or the foot of his bed, the first time the feeling seemed so real he had reached over and switched on the bedside lamp but saw there was no one there, but the feeling would not go away. Eventually he had awakened to feel Millie, she had returned home and had climbed onto the foot of his bed to spend the rest of what remained of the night with him curled up along side his feet.

By the time the dawn of day filtered through the curtains the feeling had left him.

For the next few days as he continued to work on the case he and Loverage were involved in, but there were moments when he kept turning around with the impression there was someone following him, or when stood still he would experience a sensation as if some one was standing near him. Until one day as he was walking down the corridor in the station he was sure he heard a voice distinctly call out his name loud and clearly, he turned around and found there was no one else in the passage way other than himself at the time. At this point he came to the decision he had been working too hard, and with nights of restless sleep thought he could be heading for a break down of some kind. Coming to that conclusion he decided it might be wise for him to have a break from the job, and to take a short break holiday.

"What do you mean a break?" Loverage sat in his chair looking incredulous at his sergeant.

"I don't know, but I have not been feeling myself of late, and at times have been feeling unwell." He was feeling stupid as he spoke to Loverage, unsure of himself, or, of how he felt. "Unwell! Here we are in the middle of a God almighty murder investigation, and you say you are unwell. How are you unwell? What is it headaches, migrain, or what? Have you seen a doctor?"

"No, I don't know exactly what it is, but something has been happening to me!" His hand went to his forehead, fingers spread wide and began to push his hair back, while his face seemed to contort in exasperation, he turned sideways away from Loverage for a moment, then turned facing Loverage and placing both hands on the table with fingers spread wide in front of him looked at his colleague straight in the eyes. "I don't know exactly what it is, as I have said, but it feels as if I am cracking up, whether it is due to the cases we are on, or the divorce, or what. All I do know is if I don't have a break or ease up, or something! I will have had it!"

Loverage after listening to to his friend and colleague, could see there was something he could not understand bothering Mitchell, and must have been going on for some time unnoticed by him. He was silent for a moment then in a lowered tone of voice quietly asked. "Come on now Dave, what has happened to make you act this way?"

"I can't explain it really, it's like feelings. It started first a few days ago, perhaps a week, maybe a bit longer. It's as if I am never alone, as if there is someone watching me all the time, and I am being followed, but when I turn around there seems for an instant a fleeting shadow, nothing specific, a movement, or the feeling of movement. At first I put it down to imagination, and getting uptight with the job, and all the pissballing about we have done, and getting nowhere. But, in the last three days I have heard, or imagined I have heard my name called out loud, when there has been no one around to call it out, that was when I decided, enough was enough, and the best thing might be to have a weeks holiday and rest up for a while and then see perhaps if everything returns to normal again."

Loverage for the first time since they had been on the murder investigations looked at his friend and could see he had changed from the outgoing and confident detective, to a seemingly altogether different person. He was puzzled by the fact he had not noticed the change in him until the last few moments, due probably he thought to the effort and concentration he had been putting into the investigations, and had taken for granted Mitchell was the same, and had not perceived the change which had been taking place. But now he saw things were grim with him and he seemed to be falling apart in front of him. He stood up, reached over to Mitchell touching his arm.

"Come on 'Mitch'! Let's get you down stairs and see if the S.M.O. is still here and let him take a look at you, perhaps he can help. Things can't be so bad that they can't be put right. Let us go and see what he has to say, and what help is available. I am sorry I was such a pain in the ass to you just now, but now that you have mentioned it to me, it's obvious there is something wrong. Let's just go and see if he has any answers to your problem, and also find out what the possible cause of it could be. Perhaps, it is not at all as bad as it seems to you now."

Both police officers managed to catch the M.O. as he was just about to leave the station evidence room, after depositing some blood samples from a suspected drunken driver who had been involved in an accident resulting from a stolen car chase driven by some youths who were now also at the station in custody.

"I just can't understand what things are coming to, four kids the youngest is just eleven the eldest has just turned fourteen, half out of their heads on cider stolen from a supermarket, taking and driving away a Granada, with a police patrol car in pursuit they decide to park it into the boot of a Jaguar parked at traffic lights, and the driver of that vehicle, who was much the same way on whisky, who is in the cells going ballistic, saying he was driving competent enough, and it's all down to the kids that he is here suspected of drunken driving, and as how he would not have been breathalised even, if it was not for them going into the back of him. The country has gone crazy."

The M.O. saw Mitchell and recommended after an initial examination, that he be placed on sick leave, and that he should make an appointment with his own G.P., taking with him a letter he would give him, when he left the station to go home.

Doctor Wentworth, Mitchell's G.P., after a full examination diagnosed he was suffering from stress, which he suggested could have been brought on by a combination of a heavy workload combined with the effects of his divorce, and suggested he take at least four weeks off of work and take the medication he would prescribe for him, all being well he thought things would improve enough in the time off for him to return to work after the period of sick leave, but suggested he should make a further appointment to see him in ten days time to see if the medication he would give him had made any improvement to his condition. He finished the consultation by saying he felt rest and medication he was sure, would bring the improvement required for him to return to work in that time, and could find nothing more to concern him other than the symptoms he had earlier diagnosed as stress.

It was two days later after seeing his G.P.. While he was sat at home in his armchair having finished a meal of fish and chips he had bought from the nearby 'chippy' and enjoying a cup of tea. He was looking out of the window watching some children kicking a ball around on the small green space outside, using a coat and jumpers as goal, thinking to himself things did'nt change so very much, even in now in the days of sophisticated games and computers, kids would still be doing the same things as he had done when young, although, boredom was it seemed a lot more rife than it was then, leading to vandalism which could be seen on most estates in any town now. Better he thought to see something he could watch and, they could enjoy while at the same time keep them from causing problems anywhere, which did not cost the earth for parents.

After about ten minutes watching them, he got up from his chair with the intention of pouring himself another cup of tea from the teapot which he had left on the table in the middle of the room, away from the window he was looking out of. As he picked up the teapot he noticed the small jug of milk was not on the tray and realized he must have have put it back into the refrigerator unconsciously earlier, after pouring the first cup for himself. He laughed silently, thinking he must be beginning to improve, he was always forgetful and absent minded around the house, before he became unwell.

He was walking towards the kitchen, and as he reached the the passage the front door flew open banging hard against the passage wall to it's side, there was at the same time a resounding crash as the glass panel smashed, and then sound of broken glass being smashed again as it fell onto the bare polished floor of the passage, then sliding and scattering everywhere, ending as a complete mess of broken glass on the floor. A gust of cold air rushed through the passage with the sounds of a gale's force, making the glass lamp shades hit the ceiling and breaking both shades and light bulbs, showering particles of glass along towards where Mitchell was standing. He winced as he felt small particles of the lamp shade and bulb glass hit him around the face with stinging force, which at the same time felt as cold as ice. Within a matter of seconds the wind ceased as suddenly as it had started, then the front door slammed shut leaving the gap where the pain of glass had been. Through which he could see the children shouting and playing with the football, oblivious to what had just happened fifty yards or so from them. Then, in the deathly silence which followed there was clearly defined a figure of a man, surrounded with a shimmering blue light. As he looked at the figure manifested before him he thought him vaguely familiar, but as he was still in state of shock after what he had just experienced he could not recall who it was, or where he known him.

"Be careful, and open your mind, but be cautious, always, above all be cautious."

He was unsure if he heard the voice in his head or if it was spoken aloud. Mitchell's mind was in a whirl, and he could not think rationally as it was happening in front of him, he just stood there. As the figure had appeared, so within the same instant of time it had disappeared, with the words spoken still ringing in his head, echoing over and over until there was the silence of just moments earlier.

Even though it had happened with such force, and unexpected he had not at the time felt threatened or frightened in any way, there seemed not to be enough time for any rational feelings about what was happening at the time, still in a semi stupor his hand went to his face where he had felt the broken glass from the lamp shades struck him, expecting to find it lacerated, with blood on his face and clothing, but there was not a drop, and not a trace of damage to himself any where.

Turning he walked calmly to the kitchen, sat on a kitchen chair for a while. He was perspiring profusely, although, inside he felt calm as could be. As he continued to sit, with a glazed look about him, he noticed the handle on the cooker he had broken weeks before, and had been meaning to repair it for well over a month but had just not got around to doing so. After he had noticed the handle his thoughts seemed to sharpen up, and he felt the need to go to the passage again to check on what had really happened, and to make sure it was not a figment of his imagination, due to the tranquelisers he had been prescribed.

Standing in the passage he could see the damage in front of him, the hanging, and smashed lamp shades, glass all over the floor and the window missing in the front door, while a gentle breeze blew down towards him, showing it had not been due to any imagination on his part, or due to the prescribed tablets. He had known in his heart of hearts it had really happened. But he was afraid in some sense to admit to himself after it happened, and wanted it all to have been untrue because he could not explain what had really happened. The children were still there.

After realizing he had indeed been a party to a strange and unusual experience, while at the same time he understood what he had been experiencing over the past week or so was no doubt in some way connected to what he had just experienced, and therefore came to the immediate conclusion he had not as he had been thinking, "going off his head". For the first time, since his first experience's which had led him to see the M.O. and then his own doctor, as the realization dawned on him, his powers of reason and deduction began to come into play. His first question to himself was: "What did it all mean?" He tried to think of what he should do next, he did not want to get in touch with Loverage and confide in him, for the simple reason he was sure he would not believe him, especially as how he had been acting of late.

After the glazier had been and repaired the window to the front door, Mitchell was still undecided what his next step would be. He decided in the end the best course of action would be to go out for a while, away from the house altogether, he looked at the clock on the wall. "That's it!" He thought. "An evening in the pub, it's early now and there will be hardly any one in there at this time, and I can think clearer away from here!"

The decision made he began to get ready to go out.

CHAPTER 18

Both men stayed in the 'Portcullis' until the time came for them to catch the afternoon transport back to 'Gowendene Manor.'

On their return they went to their respective rooms for a while agreeing to meet in the dining hall when they had dried and freshened up and changed out of their wet clothing.

When Charlie came down to the dining room he could see Choco just inside the room with his hand raised beckoning to him. When he had joined him, Choco told him he was going to go to his room, and walk down with him, but had actually fell asleep on his bed after having a shower and getting dressed, after waking he thought it was later than it actually was, and did not bother, expecting him to be in the dining room already, when he came down and saw he was not there he thought he had probably fallen asleep the same as he had, and was just about to come up to knock on his door.

After sitting down to eat their meals, the two talked while eating, and decided to go to the T.V. room to pass the evening away. Although after they had eaten they stayed in the dining room for a while drinking tea and talking.

"How many rooms has this place got in total?" Charlie enquired as he looked around and saw that although quite a few people had left the room already, there were still quite a number still there talking together, as they were.

"There must be at least thirty or more still in here, and counting those who have already left there must have been at least seventy or eighty here while we were eating."

"Oh! There are about twenty five or so single rooms for short stay people such as ourselves." He looked around the area of the dining room.

"The majority of those who are here now are residents, at least that's what I was told when I came here first by another short stayer like ourselves, he must have left since, because I have not seen him for the last few days. They have joined the main part of the place, a kind of commune way of life, they seem O.K. but don't have much to say to the likes of us, as I have found out since my stay here. It seems most have started off as short term guests and after a while have joined whatever it is here. They don't talk about what they do or believe in, and as long as they don't want to shove some kind of religion down my throat, I'll just as well let them be. I sure don't fancy it myself, although, I would not say no to some of them!" He inclined his head towards a table where Charlie saw four very attractive women were sitting, he estimated to be in the middle twenties. While he looked over towards them, one of the women, a red head, with long flowing, shiny, tresses, dressed in a tight fitting black and white patterned sweater, which showed to the best affect her well formed breasts. Suddenly she had turned her head and looked straight at him. Her eyes seemed to bore right into him. He felt spellbound and could do nothing but look back at her. While she held his gaze her eyes narrowed slightly a smile played around her lips. While at the same time Charlie felt a tingling flush rising from his groin, travelling down his legs, and upwards to his throat, a sensation of heat and excitement surged around his body. He could feel himself becoming sexually aroused in a way he had never experienced before, and could do nothing about. He shifted himself on the chair as he felt the erection of his member was beginning to be caught uncomfortably in the tightness of his jeans, so much so he had to raise himself slightly to adjust it.

The redhead widened her eyes, still with the smile on her lips, then gave a blow towards him, then her tongue ran along the line of her lips just protruding slightly, turning she spoke to her companions at her table. Charlie suspected that she spoke to them about him because, just for an instant they turned and looked his way then back to each other, smiling while talking with what seemed to Charlie an excitement in their manner. Then they all started to rise from their seats to leave the dining room, talking quietly amongst themselves, he noticed she still had a smile on her lips reaching her eyes and was looking directly across towards him with full eye contact, before she got up to follow the others.

"What's the matter with you?" You are as red as a beetroot man!"Choco, knowing nothing of what had just passed between the red head and his friend, was perplexed by his demeanour.

Charlie still with a stunned expression on his face, inhaled deeply before replying. Then told him what had exchanged between the red head and himself except, for the fact he felt it would be still embarrassing for a while, for him to rise from his seat. Choco looked over towards them to see the woman in question disappearing through the doorway into the reception hall. "You lucky shit. You've not been here five minutes, and here you are with the possibility in the offing of scoring with one of the rezzie's, which so far I have convinced myself, was always a none starter event, and to cap that even more, she, looks a real cracker."

As they made their way from the dining room, to the lounge and T.V. room they saw the four woman talking to some of the male residents in the hall, before moving through a door to part of the manor used by the permanent residents, and to which the likes of Choco and Charlie, were not allowed access to.

"I suppose that about puts paid to your chances, with her! It looks from where I am, as if one of the permanent rezzies could be giving her one on a regular basis. Looks like when you get all hot and bothered with the sweats over her again it might have to be got rid of with a hand job!" He started laughing at his remarks. Charlie just grinned at the joke made at his expense.

"Come on pal, let's see if there are any new woman in today, you never know, at least we can entertain ourselves, if there are or not. Least of all, if there are, they would probably talk to us, and not tease as 'yon' redhead seems to have done with you, and leaving you all 'het' up, so to speak."

For the rest of the evening they played a couple of games of pool and then settled down to watch 'The French Connection' on T.V. during which towards the end of the film 'Willie' came around with his trolley of drinking chocolate, and handing them both a mug each he had already poured for them both carried on handing out the same fare for all those in the room before trundling his way with the trolley ect. in the direction of the stairs to the landings, for those who would already have gone to their rooms.

Charlie did not bother with the washrooms for anything but to clean his teeth, he was beginning to feel the effects of the days activity and was also beginning to feel tired and drowsy his head hit the pillow and he was soon asleep.

He did not know what it was, he felt awake, and yet, it seemed as if he was dreaming with his eyes open, all around him was the darkness of the room, but something else also, then he had the distinct feeling there was someone else in the room with him. He peered towards the door, and as he did so his eyes tried to pick out anything, he could see nothing, but more sensed, there was movement there. He strained his eyes more, trying to focus on the area between the bedroom door and himself. Concentrating on the area he saw or sensed movement again, while at the same time he began to feel a tingling over his body, and and feelings of sexual arousal which he could not stop, while time at the same moment he felt this happen, seemed to slow down, but, with a feeling he could not understand making him accept with a dreamlike resignation to the situation as it was happening. Then something brushed lightly against the side of his bed, there seemed to be a resigned calmness within him, he reached out with his hand tentatively as though in slow motion to where he had felt brushing movement, he lay silently his heart throbbing unsure of what to expect, and yet for some unknown reason he felt no sense of fear of immediate danger. Just as he was about to make the effort to rise, with words forming in his mind, he smelt the scent of heavy pungent perfume which seemed to send a tremor through him, sending his senses reeling.

"Who is it? Who's there?" He spoke and tried to sit up.

"Don't ask questions! Just relax and enjoy. The pleasure is for us to enjoy together, now. We met today, and who knows this could be the start of a wonderful relationship which both of us could appreciate, for a long time to come. Skin, soft and cool brushed against him, as he felt the bedcovers being lifted, and then there was shape of someone was above him, hair, long sweet smelling, and soft fell onto his shoulders. Lips full and moist came in contact with his, while at the same time he felt bare breasts brush and and then come into full contact with him on his bare chest, cool and firm as they pressed against his warm body. Her hands travelled over him with light gestured but explicit touches, finding his points of arousal, he began to return the responses, just in the way which had been intended. He felt aroused the same as he had at the table earlier that evening, only many times more so. He knew who it was with him. As she continued with her touching and caressing of him, so he began to explore her with the same deft touches in return, until they were both consumed in a passion of carnal euphoria, giving and receiving pleasure to each other. Then he felt her manoeuvre herself on top of him, felt the wetness of her love juices as she wanted him to enter her as she positioned herself onto his fully erect and throbbing manhood, he heard her moan, and gasp of pleasure as she brought herself down and he entered her. There seemed to be a magnetism, as her legs entwined and locked around his, bringing into play from him actions and feelings he had never in his life experienced before. The passion and ecstasy continued for what seemed forever, then climaxed, only when both felt the need of pleasure given to each other was satisfied, and complete.

Charlie rolled onto his back, feeling the woman next to him, her breathing soft, even, and shallow. Reaching his arm over her he moved onto his side, her hair and body wet with perspiration, she nestled in closer to him, his hand cupped her smooth firm breast while his fingers lightly squeezed her nipple, she muttered something, he could not hear what, as he slipped into deep restful sleep, as all passion with him had been spent.

Slowly he awoke the next morning, to the sounds of footsteps in the hallway out side of his room. As he opened his eyes, from where he lay he squinted as a beam of early morning sunshine shone into his eyes reflected from the glass ash tray on the top of the bedside table.

As he began to move, he smelt the pungent aroma of spent semen, as it wafted up through the bed sheets as he turned over.

With a kind of vagueness the memory of the night before, came back to him. He lay still, his eyes closed thinking, trying to recall every thing he had experienced before falling to sleep, slowly he moved his leg then his arm exploring the area around him, but as felt around him, he found there was no one in the bed with him. He was confused now, unsure if he had imagined or dreamed of the event, or had indeed made love to the redhead the night before.

There was no sign of her having spent the time he thought he could remember so vividly. The bedclothes were not as he remembered them the night before, strewn around, and hanging one sided onto the floor. He was sure that they were, before he drifted off to sleep, after the night of passion, but everything was as usual, hardly disturbed, and as if he had slept as soundly, as he had on his first night of the day before.

He climbed out of bed, stood at the side, the blankets and sheet pulled back, looking at the dark stain in the middle of the bed not sure of what to think in his confusion, over the past night. Was it real? or was what he was looking at the result of a totally realistic, erotic dream, brought about in his sleep state by his subconscious mind due to the escapade with the red head the evening before. He was unsure even now as he began to make the bed tidy again, while at the same time checking to see if he could find any red hair around the pillow area, but even though he looked hard around the bed, and bed clothes nothing could be found to substantiate the presence of the woman in his bed at all.

As he returned from the shower, and on opening the door to his room, he thought for just an instant he smelt just the faintest of whiff of the perfume he had smelt the night before, but just as it registered so, it was gone, he sniffed the room but again, he could smell nothing, and decided immediately it was his imagination and dismissed it as so.

There were about eight people in the dining room when he arrived there, and saw by the clock it was indeed a lot later than he had thought, presuming his new friend had been to breakfast and eaten, then gone on to the sitting room, he helped himself to some breakfast and, hurriedly ate it, deciding to look for Choco when he had finished.

Entering the T.V. room, he saw Choco, standing at the far end of the room in conversation with some one, who seemed to be perturbed about something. He did not recognize him as being one of the residents and, could only assume Choco knew him from somewhere in his past by the way they were talking, and while talking Choco seemed to be trying to calm him down at the same time.

When Charlie went over to them, Choco introduced him as a friend of quite some time. He introduced him as 'Tim Loman' and came from a small town in Wiltshire called Dundlestone, it seemed three years before he had come to the area with some friends and struck up a serious relationship with a girl he had met whilst fruit picking in the area, while staying in a squat locally.

He had been arrested and then convicted, for causing actual bodily harm to a hunt follower, during an anti hunt demonstration. He had received eighteen months imprisonment and had been released after nine months with remission. Both he and his girlfriend had become very close in the two years they had been together. While in prison she had visited him five times, once on the same week as he had started his sentence, and then at the end of each month for the five months. She had also written to him at least once a week, for that time. Every thing seemed fine, and then the letters stopped suddenly for no real apparent reason, that he could see. In the last letter she had sent him she had said she had received the visiting order from him and, would be coming to see him the following weekend. But there were no more letters and, she did not come to visit him when she said she would.

After listening to him, Choco explained to Charlie he had known both Tim and Rene for a long time, in actual fact he told him, he had known them both a fair time, before they had even met each other. He also knew they were devoted to each other, and it was not in her character, to up and disappear for no apparent good reason. Especially as they had worked together, and had a joint bank account, with the last deposit of forty pounds having been made just about the time of her last letter to him. They had been saving together, for almost the same amount of time they had been serious in their relationship which was almost the two years, there had been no withdrawals made except to pay for her fare by train, when she had visited him the times he had mentioned plus a few of withdrawals for ten pounds each, she had used for living expenses which he had know about because she had told him of them when she had visited him last. So understandably Tim was in a bit of a state.

"Where was she living while you were in prison?" Charlie inquired.

"In a squat in Taunton, until it was repossessed, then she had to leave with the others who were there with her."

"So where did she go then?"

"Well I am not sure now, but, but I was told by some one who knew us both she came here, and that's the last I know of her. I know there is something not right about it all, but what! I just don't know."

"Have you enquired at the reception desk about her and if she did stay here?"

"Yes, but they have told me she only came and stayed for two nights, and then left."

"Did she not leave any forwarding address at the reception by any chance?"

They have told me she didn't but that is not so unusual in our situation hardly anyone ever does, things, and plans change, it is very often a waste of time, people hardly ever end up where they originally intended to go."

Choco had listened to the other two as they discussed, Tim's dilemma, and came up with an idea.

"Well it's a queer situation and that's for sure. Why don't we catch the transport into town, we know a lot of people there, and if we go around and make enquiries, and putting the word about we are looking for her, who knows, if she is about she could get in touch with you in some way, or even at some of the watering holes we use, or even better, get in touch with the manor saying where she is, and also, it's only a possibility Tim, but it could be she has been admitted to hospital for some reason, and that at least would explain why she has not used any money in the bank account. What about you Charlie, how do you feel about coming into town with us today and see how we make out."

"I have nothing better to do, and if you think I may be of some help then by all means let's give it a try."

"First place to start I think is the 'Portcullis', I have a few friends there who know about most of the squats around the area, and perhaps they might know where it might be a good idea to start looking if she decided to use one after leaving Gowendene Manor."

All the way into town, Charlie was thinking about his experience or dream of the night before, and was about to bring it up on more than a couple of occasions when the conversation lapsed into silence, but something would be said about Tim's girlfriend, or somewhere else they could consider looking, and he would let it go. Eventually thinking how silly it would seem to the others that, he was uncertain of the event, as to if it actually happened or not, he had to admit to himself it sounded bizarre to say the least, and by the time they had reached Taunton town centre he felt better he had not mentioned anything about it.

CHAPTER 19

Dave Mitchell entered the Harvest moon, and could see immediately there were as he had expected just a small amount of people in the bar area. A young man standing next to the juke box in the corner of the bar a girlfriend at his side selecting a choice of records. At another table were a group of three two women and a man in conversation amid bouts of subdued laughter at some thing they had all obviously found humorous. He walked up to the bar and bought himself a pint of bitter looked around for a short while before making his way to an empty table and sat down.

Within a short time his thoughts turned to the days events, while at the same time he tried to figure out for himself what was that could be happening in his life just recently, nothing seemed to be going right for him. What with the decree absolute, and now the goings on over the feelings he been getting and the voice, it all must mean something, and perhaps cullminating in the situation which had occurred that day. He was sitting down quietly mulling over the situation he had found himself in, and could come up with nothing reasonably tangible to explain what had been happening in his life.

The figure he had seen. Somehow, it had looked familiar, but the manifestation was over so quickly he could not recognize who or even where he had might have recognized them from, or even if some how his mind had been playing tricks on him. True the damage was real enough, but, did he really see, what he thought he had seen within the shimmering blue light, it had happened so quickly and he was at the time still under a considerable amount of stress due to what had been happening to him over the period of time he had been experiencing the strange events leading up to him having to take sick leave. The only over riding thing about the whole matter was now he was convinced he had not been going mad or heading for a complete breakdown. The only thing which now puzzled and worried him was. "Why?" If, as he was beginning to feel he was quite well within himself. "Why were these things happening and, why to him, but no one else around him?" He was thinking things over for quite a while, but in the end found he could not come to any rational conclusion about it all.

Time had passed, the bar had been filling up with customers as the evening had worn on. "Hello Dave! Back again then, it's nice to see you here again."
When he heard a voice he had immediately recognized as belonging to Shephard, he turned to answer the greeting. His thoughts now finished on the of the days events.

He could not think of the mans Christian name, at that moment, and just answered with. "Hello! sit down."

He moved his chair a little way to allow him to sit at the table. Shephard placed his drink on the table saw Mitchell still had over half a pint left in his glass and so did not bother to offer him a refill.
"Have you seen any of the others we were with the last time you were here? His eyes searched the bar as he spoke.
"No not really, to tell the truth I have not really took a lot of notice of anyone as they have come in." Mitchell did a quick take of the room and only then saw it had filled up quite a bit more since he had been there. As he did so the door opened and in walked Jimmy Edwards and his father.
"Here are two of them now"

Later the table he was at filled up with others some he knew from the last time he had been there and also a couple of others who it seemed frequented the pub regularly but were not in there the night he had met Shephard and father and son.

The evening wore on and everyone with him were talking about one subject after another, much the same topics as they did before.

Mitchell after being bought a drink or two thought it was about time he bought a round for those with him, especially as it seemed he had now been accepted as one within the group. He was in the motion of rising, and as he turned noticed that the group of two women, and the lone male he had noticed when he had arrived earlier were sitting and seemed to be interested in some thing in his direction, when they saw him look over towards them they immediately turned away a look of embarrassment on their faces.

While at the same time they seemed to talk in earnest about something, more so aimed at the woman sitting on her own on the opposite side of the table. At one point as he watched he was sure she was about to rise from her seat, but the other two placed their hands on hers and speaking to her while they did so, releasing them when she had settled down after probably deciding not to. "A Triangular problem Mitchell thought to himself, perhaps an affair having been reconciled. "Oh! Well!" He thought. Nothing to do with me, such is life.

"I see you have noticed our Anne and friends, quite an attractive woman is'nt she!"

"What's that you said Cyril?" The father of the potential matlot asked of Shephard.

"About Anne over there. Just said to Dave how she is such an attractive woman natural blond hair as well, not the bottled stuff."

Jimmy Edwards glanced across to where Cyril had indicated with the motioning of his head towards the table with the three seated around. He laughed.

"Oh! You mean Taunton's answer to Doris Stokes, spirits, ghosts, and ghouls, and talking to the dead. Load of codswhallop as far as I am concerned once your dead that's it, all you are is dead meat on a slab until your buried or burnt, and then that's your lot. End of story."

As he finished speaking, Mitchell saw the people in question rise from their table putting on coats, as they made their way to the door to make their exit from the 'Harvest Moon'. As she went through the door the woman Cyril had named seemed to take one quick, but thoughtful glance back towards where Mitchell was sitting.

He picked up the empty glasses from the table to fetch a round of drinks, Jimmy Edwards picked up the rest of the glasses Mitchell could not manage and followed him over to the bar with the intent to help him back with them when they were full.

Mitchell stayed until closing then made his way home accompanied by Cyril Shephard who chatted incessantly until they parted at Mitchells gate with the usual parting words.

Inside Mitchell locked the door and made his way upstairs to the bathroom before retiring for the night, and found his cat Millie curled up, and sound asleep on his bed.

"So you decided to come in after all the old girl, he slid into the bed along side her and, forced her further away from the middle of the bed with a half hearted cry of complaint for being disturbed came from her. Within minutes he was sound asleep.

CHAPTER 20

The three men scoured the town until four o'clock in the afternoon, and had got nowhere. They had gone from one public house to another, which they had known were frequented by by themselves and others of similar life styles. To squats they knew of, and some which were unknown to them but, given the information of their whereabouts by those they had asked information and help of. The only thing they were sure of was that Rene had gone to stay at the manor, but since that time she had not been seen by anyone to who she was known anywhere around the town for quite a while. Where she had gone after the two days stay at the manor they still had no idea! It was as if she had just vanished from the face of the earth.

Then, they all decided, after all the walking around to stop and have a cup of something in a cafe nearby, and went inside. As they sat down with a cup of tea each, Tim saw in a corner were two old friends. A man and a woman, both of them knew Tim and Rene well.

They had obviously come into the place for some refreshments after a while of busking in the town centre. The woman a flute, the man a violin, which was laid across the table in front of them with an attachment which somehow enabled him to play a harmonica while playing the violin. Feeling down and not having any luck in the search for information about her up to now, he still went over to them to ask what they had been asking for the biggest part of the day, if they had seen her at anytime in the last few months. There answer seemed to bring him to life. They told him they had seen her. They remembered seeing her at the railway station, and boarding a train with about five other people, two men and three woman. They were certain it was her, and it was just two months before. They were sure of that because they were waiting for the Paddington to Penzance train. They were at the time on their way to Truro, to the woman's sister's wedding, they were sure of the date because it was the only time they had left Taunton in the last nine months. The time before that they had gone to Weston-super-Mare, and at that time they had travelled by coach, so it could not have been any other time they had seen her.

While they had been talking, Choco had watched his friend become excited, and moved over to where he was, and caught the last part of the conversation. When they had finished, he watched Tim for a while, then seeing what had been said put more of a strain on him, as he now sat, still and quiet in the chair at the table of the other two.

Thanking them for the information, Choco helped Tim to his feet and guided him to the other table where Charlie was sitting.

"Come on Tim, let us see what other information we can find out now that we have got a lead. Now we know at least she is O.K., from what they have told us, also we know now she is not in this town so looking around and asking questions at the moment is now none productive. What we can do is find out where she could have gone on the train, and why."

Tim took a sip of tea but said nothing, he was feeling empty and defeated. He was sure he would have had a message from her if she had gone away for any reason, but after all they had done in the way of searching for her there seemed to be nothing which made sense to him about her going off on a train. He even thought to himself that perhaps the other two who told him they had seen her could have been mistaken and it had not been Rene they had seen, but as he thought that over, he had to admit that if that was so, then they would be back where they had started, no he thought there was only one conclusion and that was for some reason she had decided. She wanted to finish their relationship, and start afresh somewhere else. But still in the back of his mind he was troubled. "Why had she not drawn on any of the money they had saved together because half was hers? Was it a way of saying sorry for finishing the relationship the way she had?"

Charlie made a rollup cigarette and offered it across to Tim, a gesture to him to say that he was involved, and felt for him. But secretly he was thinking to himself, she had probably met someone else and had left with them, or had left to meet them in another town, and did not have the heart to tell him, it happened all the time. At least he had not received a "Dear John" letter while he was inside, that, he imagined could have been even worse. At least he was now on the outside and could perhaps start afresh and do something to take his mind off of the break up.

While Charlie was having those thoughts, Choco was back with the couple Tim knew, and speaking to them.

"Was Rene on the same platform as you or another?"

"No she was on the other side of the platform to us. We were on the down line, she was on the up."

"Did she get on a train before you, or was she still on the platform when you caught the train to Truro?"

"She left something like ten minutes before our train pulled out, I remember it was not very long. I went to the toilet just as her train was pulling out, and ours was just pulling in when I came out of the toilet."

"Are you sure she actually got on the train and was not on the platform seeing someone off?"

"No! She definitely got on the train, from where we were standing we saw them all get into the carriage opposite us and they all sat down in it." The man who had been speaking turned to his companion as if for confirmation of what he had said.

"Yes that's right she was on the train as it pulled out, I even gave a wave to her, although, she did not wave back, but whether she saw me wave or not I don't know. She seemed to be talking a lot with the people she was with, but it was definitely Rene that boarded that train."

"Did you know any of the others with her? Had you seen any of them before?"

The woman thought for a moment, then looked at her companion. "I am not sure, but one of the men looked familiar to me, I can't say where I knew him from, but I do, it was definitely somewhere other than Taunton, but where I cannot remember. It would have been quite a while ago, wherever it was. Perhaps a beach, or in a squat at sometime or more than likely a fair somewhere, but as I have said it must have been some time ago. We have been here for three years, and I cannot remember seeing him around at any of the places we go. If he had we would have seen him."

The man was looking at Choco as his companion had been talking and when she finished, after a moments hesitation spoke. "There was one other thing we noticed. I remember thinking at the time how she had changed in such a short period of time since we had seen her last."

"How do you mean she had changed?"

"Well she was the same Rene but, she was completely different in appearance, by the way she was dressed. She always wore long flowered skirts, with woollen jumpers, Tim knows what I mean, she would always do her own style of embroidery, and when it was cold she would more than likely wear her reefer jacket type coat with the plastic shoulder covers, I mean, she was dressed completely different altogether when we saw her at the station she was wearing a light brown trouser suit, opened with a white ruffled blouse and high healed shoes, not stiletto type but, they were high heal fashion and light tan, as I have said she looked different but it was definitely Rene of that I am positive!"

The two musicians left shortly after Choco had spoken to them, and all three reluctantly agreed there was not much more they could do for the time being, and after drinking their tea they left the cafe and started walking back to the old market place to catch the transport back to the manor house. As they arrived the time was just past ten to five, and as they came to the pickup point so did the transport to take them to the manor.

As they climbed aboard they saw there were three others waiting a little way past the stopping point, with bags and bedrolls, they seemed unsure of what to do, and appeared to be looking at the transport Choco and the others had climbed aboard. "Hey! Driver there are some people with bags and bedrolls a little way behind us. Do you think they want to catch the transport and are not sure what they should do?"

Turning, the driver of the transport van looked behind him to where Choco had just indicated, opened the window and leaned out.

"Are you waiting for the transport to Gowendene Manor?" There was a scuffling of bags, and footsteps hurrying, then the transport lurched to the side as the weight of the people climbed in, when they were all settled, and the driver looked at the clock to see what the time was, there was the sound of more running footsteps, Charlie then saw outside another person come along side, and with panting breath enter the van and seating himself just in front of him, perspiration evident on his face showing he had run a fair distance to catch the transport before it could leave at five, moments later the engine started and they were on their way.

After the usual substantial meal, all three made their way to the T.V./lounge room, to smoke and and talk over the days efforts of trying to find Tim's girlfriend, they talked for a while and came to the conclusion there was nothing more that could be done for the moment, they all seemed disinterested in the television and decided to see if the pool table was free, and if it was to have a game or two. There was no one in the pool room when they walked in and they set about preparing for a game of pool. While setting up to play the game, a man of about twenty six came over to Charlie completely taking him by surprise as he spoke to him.

"I can't say much to you at the moment, but we have to talk. Make out we know each other, and make out we were already going to play a game of pairs, you and myself against your two friends, I will try to explain more as we play, he looked across at Tim. It has to do with your friends girlfriend."

Tim's eyes opened wide in expectation. Moving closer he started to question him.
"What do you know? Have you seen her? Do you know where she is? Come on mate, I have been worried sick over her, if you know anything tell me!"

Choco saw the look of fear appear on the face of the man, and edged his way between Tim and the stranger, bringing out his tobacco tin and offering it out to them all, and using it as an excuse for them all to be close together, and tried to calm Tim and the stranger down, as he saw others in the room looking towards them and obviously wondering what was happening between them.

"Tim, here, have a rollup and, calm down a moment. Who are you, and what's your name?"
"Howard, Tony Howard. I have been staying here for four weeks now, and I heard while I was in the town you have been looking for someone who had stayed here, a friend told me you had been making enquiries, I tried to find you while you were in town today but kept just missing you, calling at every place you had been, and you had always left before I arrived, eventually I decided to catch the transport back here and realized you were already on it, but could not speak to you then." He looked around the room as he put a rollup to his lips, seemed satisfied there seemed no one there who seemed to be interested in them now things had calmed down.

Choco then remembered that he was the late comer who had just managed to catch the transport back that evening just after the three with bedrolls.
"I remember you now, you were the one who had been running when you caught the transport back this evening."

Tony Howard spoke to them as they played a few games of pool, but seemed on edge the whole time he was playing. The gist of what they could understand from him was, that Gowendene Manor was not at all what it seemed to be. He was not sure. He told them, what it was, but there was something phoney about the place and what little he had found out was more than a little formidable, and if they were interested in just what he had found out he would meet them where ever they wished the following day in the town, and tell them all he had found out about the place and those who ran it.

Even though the man seemed in a nervous disposition, he seemed quite genuine, and his fear of talking to them any longer at the manor was obvious to them. They agreed to meet him in the Portcullis bar the following morning. He told them also, he was going to catch the ten o'clock transport back into the town with his belongings and stay at a place he knew of, until he met them there the following day. He also advised them not to talk about anything he had spoken of among themselves, while he had been playing pool with them, while they were still in the manor house.

The next day as they were all sat in the Portcullis bar in a secluded corner each with a drink in their hands, huddled up close together as was the practice of those who usually frequented the place, plumes of cigarette smoke swirling around them, Tony Howard was talking to the others in a low voice, and obviously afraid of being overheard. He started by saying:

Four months before, he had come to Gowendene manor with a friend, they were there for a couple of days when he had telephoned home as had been agreed by his family, just to let them know he was well and to get any news he might be interested in. This particular time he had phoned and was told his father had been admitted to hospital, after what seemed to have been a heart attack, and was at that time in 'Canterbury General hospital'.

Upon being told this, he decided there and then, to make his way to his home town as soon as possible. Deciding to hitch hike and was lucky to the extent that he picked up a lift after having to walk about a mile out of Taunton and on to the motorway as far as Basingstoke, there he managed to catch a lift as far as Chilham, and just a bus ride from Canterbury. The bus dropped him just a few hundred yards from the hospital. In all the total time he had taken from Taunton to the hospital took six hours.

His friend decided to stay on at the manor, suggesting it would be easier for one person to make better time on the road than two. The plan was for Arron, his friend would wait there, and see how things turned out for Howard when he reached Canterbury, in the terms of how ill his father was, and told him he would ring him at his home address the following day, to see that he had arrived safe, and to find out if they were still going to carry on with their plans to travel on down to Cornwall to see the holiday months out there doing their seasonal work, or whatever they could find, so that they would be able at least to enjoy themselves when they had time off.

As events turned out when he arrived in Canterbury, he found his father had been in hospital for five days, before he got the message he was in there. After tests and a few days observation and medication, the staff there had recommended he he return home and carry on, provided he took the medication they prescribed for him, and informed his G.P. of the type and quantity they had been administering while in hospital, and if he started taking things easier, he should be fine with treatment at home.

He had returned two and a half weeks later, his father well out of danger and well enough to cope on his own. The doctor had told him it was a warning in one sense, and that he must slow down and take things a bit easier than he had been doing, because he was not thirty years old any longer but twice that, and his body was letting him know what his mind could not believe.

When he came back to the manor his friend had gone, which even then did not make sense, because just three days before he had spoken to him and he, (his friend) had told him work was still plentiful, and he would wait for him so they could make their way down together.

At first he thought he may have had a chance of a lift down to Cornwall and decided to travel down before him after all, knowing Howard knew of the plans they had discussed together and assumed that when he turned up to find him gone he would make his way to Newquay, knowing, that was where they had decided on staying for the summer. He then made his way to Newquay, and stayed for a few days, hoping he would bump into him in one of the places they had been when there the year before, he asked in the places if he had been there at at anytime, but there had been no sign of him anywhere. He then travelled to a small fishing village they had both worked in in the past catching crabs with an older fisherman they had become friendly with, and earned a wage off of, only to find he had retired the Christmas before, and sold his boat to his sons who were in the fishing industry. They told him he had not been seen at all in the village since they were there before. He took another look around Newquay with no result again. He decided to return to the manor house in the hope there might be a message for him from his friend before returning to Canterbury. When he returned to the manor he had intended just to stay the one night, two at the most and move on the following day. It was just on pure chance he asked again at the reception desk if there was any message from his friend, and what day he had checked out. The receptionist looked at the ledger and gave him the dates he arrived and checked out, he thanked her and then went on up to the room he had been given that night. It was not he said until he had sat down in his room, he realized there was a discrepancy of what he had been told, with what he knew to be true. The date they had told him his friend had left was in fact two days before he had spoken to him on the telephone, when he knew what was happening and was going to wait for him to return to Taunton.

When he realized that fact it hit him like a bomb shell. He stayed on longer in the place to try and see what was going on there, having to go through all the rigmarole of the signing on and the D.H.S.S. business. What he had found out since had quite disturbed him. Since his stay there, there were, he had found some strange things that had been happening there. They were he had to admit in some way small on their own but when added together it showed things had been going on that, unless you looked for them they were not really apparent. But in total are quite disturbing.

"How do you mean when you say strange?" They asked in unison.

"Well if you had stayed here for a month, well less, now you know the things I have told you. You can watch and observe carefully, how some people have suddenly joined the permanent residents, or sect, or whatever it is in that place, with out ever as much as the day before shown not the slightest inclination to do so. Also if you get a chance to speak to them, they seem evasive and, and look at you as if they are not sure who you are. At one time I had spoken to a person the night before, and even arranged to go into town with them the following day and when I have looked for them the next morning to catch the transport, they did not seem to be around anywhere. Then later on in the evening I saw him at dinner and spoke to him he was very evasive and flustered, then someone came up to us, and tells me he has to leave to do some studying. After that I hardly saw the man, until I saw him get on the transport to go into town, and that was the last time I saw him. Then again if you ever manage to get the chance to talk to any of the residents, which is rare, and ask them what they have become residents for, or if it is a kind of religious following, well no matter what you talk about really, before too long there will be someone come with an excuse for them to have to go somewhere or other, then it's "Cheerio! See you again!" With not a bit of what could even be called a genuine expression in their eyes. The next thing is, within a couple of days they are gone, never to be seen in the place again. Since I have been here I have noticed similar things happen with eight people, five men and three woman, and the one thing they have all had in common is that all have all been on their own when they arrive, and all of them had no next of kin. Well! What do you think? In every case I have found when you speak to them all before they become involved with the manor, they are usually friendly as can be, well most of them anyway, like everywhere, there are some who just want their own company and do not have much to say to anyone in the manor or elsewhere. But as soon as they are involved with the manor, their whole personality changes, and they are only interested in mixing with the permanent staff here, does that seem like a strange situation or not?"

Howard after saying his piece just sat there waiting to see if what he had told them had any effect on the three of them.

Charlie and Choco sat in silence, not sure what to say. Both of them were wondering what affect Howard's words were having on their companion. Tim just sat at the table with them, his head held to the side with his hand, while his elbow rested on the table, his eyes tightly closed.

"I'll get us all another drink, while you think and talk over what I have told you. Tony Howard, knowing the effect it was obviously having on Tim, thought it might be better to let them talk among themselves without him there.

"What do you think Choco? Could what he has told us be true?"

"I am unsure what to think to be honest with you. But if the things he has told us are true, and I have no reason to think any other way by the way he has told us and, his nervousness is no act, that, I am sure of. If the things we have just been told, are going on, then more to the point is the question, what is the purpose of it?"

"Did you hear what he said about,.....people with no next of kin and all that jazz.....I'v no next of kin, Rene has no next of kin, except for Tim here, if you think about it, it's a hell of a story, and similar to what we have been finding out when you think about it, the way Rene seems to have disappeared....well...I'm inclined to give him a bit more than just the benefit of the doubt, and say he is straight up front about his theory. It would go a long way towards explaining her disappearance, and coupled with what those two in the cafe told us, about being sure it was Rene they had seen on the platform and boarding a train at the railway station.   Just a final thought,....what did both of you put on your forms as next of kin when you booked into the manor house, and since when did you have to fill in a questionnaire with the questions they wanted answers to in,....well for the want of a better word a doss house, grand style yes, but still a doss house, and like you have said to me when I first met you Choco, it's the best grub you have ever had in any hostel and compares more like a bed and breakfast establishment, right!"

As Charlie finished speaking Howard came back with the drinks from the bar he had bought, and as he placed them on the table in front of them. Tim who had listened intently to what his friends had been discussing, spoke with a voice charged with emotion.

"What can I do if what he says is true, both of you think there is something in what he has told us, can't we go to the police, or someone and tell them what we suspect about the place and those who are running it?"

"I swear that what I have told you is the truth as I have seen it, and as for going to the police, what are you going to say, without absolute proof that crimes are being committed, they would want a bit more than what we could tell them, and who knows perhaps those at the manor have some sort of contingency plan for any kind of suspicions which might be aimed at them, what ever is going on, is well organized, that is definite from what I know of them now."

There was a silence again as each of the men at the table looked at each other hoping something would be said by the other in the sense of what they, should do. One hand reached for a glass of beer on the table and as if a signal had been given three other hands caught hold and lifted filled glasses from the table top, to partake of the amber contents.

Tony Howard took a long drink from his glass, looked at the others with him, shrugged looked around the bar again before he spoke again to them all.

"I don't know exactly what's going on there, but something is and as far as I am concerned I have my belongings with me, and have found a barn on the outskirts of the town to spend tonight in. Tomorrow morning I intend to start early to hitch my way home hopefully I can make it all the way back by tomorrow evening. Then think things out away from here when I feel a little more safer and comfortable in myself. My advice to you is to leave the place as soon as you can, today would not be too soon, that, I am more than sure about.

He stayed for a short while with them, then rose from the table, picked up a duffel, and a large sports bag, walking to the door he turned gave a conciliatory wave of the hand, walked out of the door and was gone from view.

"Well! Now what do you think of it all?" Charlie tried to sound unconcerned but the tremor in his voice belied the fact that he was anything but.

Choco leaned back on the chair he was sat on, balancing it on the two back legs, his feet hooked onto the bottom crosspiece of the table, giving himself control of the balancing act. He took a long drag from his rollup cigarette while his eyes narrowed, as if it enabled him to focus his mind on the question. Slowly he began to blow smoke rings in the air, watching them as the smoke curled inwards over and over, growing larger until they dispersed in long feathery wisps to join the grey haze of the smoke filled room.

"God man, I just don't know what to think, it's one hell of a story for him to have come out with. The guy certainly did not seem to be off his trolley, also, did you notice how, whenever the door opened he would look around to see who had entered, nervous would be a complete understatement, he just could not keep still." Leaning over towards Tim he placed his hand on his shoulder, and with a clear steady, but subdued voice, heavy with purpose he began to try to buck him out of the depression he had fallen into after listening to the information they had been given by Howard.

"As things stand at the moment we need a bit more than was given to us by him. At the moment it is just a second hand theory. What we have to do is find out exactly what it is going on at the manor that has made Howard believe and act in the way he had, when he was telling us all that he knew. See how much of what he has noticed we can confirm as right. Then take it from there. How do you two feel about that to start with?"

"Charlie looked at the other two, who both seemed keen to return to the manor. He was feeling unsure, and did not really like the idea of going back to the place, but at the same time felt obliged to go back with them, not just to show he had the bottle for it but, felt for some reason it was a necessary for them to get to the bottom of whatever there was there going on.

The next morning there seemed to be with them a new feeling within them, which had not been there the day before. A feeling of comradeship and a strength of purpose, although, none of them really had any idea what the purpose was, except it was there.

CHAPTER 21

The next day Dave Mitchell, had finished his breakfast walked down to the local store and had bought a morning newspaper. On his return he had made himself a drink, coffee, it was what he had fancied that morning as a change from his usual tea he had been having. He was sitting in the kitchen at the breakfast bar and had almost finished reading the newspaper, when there was the sound of his door bell ringing, he got up expecting to see someone such as Loverage, or someone else from the station at his door. As he came into the hall from the kitchen, he could see through the replaced glass it was a woman standing side ways on in front of the door, and with the new frosted glass he could not recognize who it was and presumed it was probably some one doing a consumer survey on such things as soap powders or some other such product, as had happened on more than one occasion when he had a day off.

When he opened the door he was quite surprised to see standing on the steps the woman who he had noticed in the pub the night before, who's name he had been told by Jimmy Edwards father was Anne Farr.

"I am sorry to bother you now, and do apologize for my behaviour of yesterday evening in the Harvest Moon. I saw you were embarrassed, I would have spoken to you last night, but because you were in company, and my friends advised me against it, thinking it would most likely be inconvenient for you, for us to intrude. My name is Anne Farr, I have something to speak to you about, which happened last night at the Harvest Moon while you were with your friends and I think it may be of some importance to you. May I come in?"

Now as he looked at her with more attention and a lot closer to her, he saw as one of his companions of the night before had mentioned. She was, very attractive. He could also see she wore hardly any make-up, her hair was a very light and a natural blond colour, closely cropped, and swept forward, giving a small fringe. Bright blue eyes, milky smooth skin, with fine lines around the eyes and mouth, but not too defined, with a complexion usually associated with people of Scandinavian heritage. He judged her to be in her mid thirties.

As he was looking at her he did not speak, but was enjoying what he was looking at so much he began to make her feel a little uncomfortable, and she did a little sideways step, bringing him back to the present, and his failing in courtesy. "I am sorry for staring at you as I have, but you surprised me somewhat I do apologize for my rudeness, please forgive me and please come in."

He moved back from the doorway and drew the door open wider.

"Come in! come in! Again please forgive me for being so rude, it was just you had taken me by surprise, when I saw it was you, I had expected it to be someone else entirely."

As she entered he became curious as to what it was she wanted to speak to him about.

"Something.... something.....happened....at the Harvest Moon?"

He repeated slowly, his brow furrowed, while his mind went back to the night before trying to think of what she could mean, and except for her two companions looking at him, he could not think of anything else, was it he thought, something to do with them.

He ushered her into the sitting room and offered her one of the easy chairs to sit in. "I was about to put the kettle on for a cup of coffee for myself, he lied not knowing what else to say. Would you care for a cup, or tea if you wish, I have both."

"Thank you that would be nice, and coffee will be fine, I take milk and sugar, but just one spoonful please." She replied with a smile, while at the same time making herself comfortable in the easy chair. As she sat there, and while he went into the kitchen 'Millie' decided to put in an appearance, after coming down the stairs to make her way into the sitting room, she walked in as was normal at that time in the morning, as she was just inside the door she stopped, noticing a stranger in the home and sat down on her rear end watching Anne intensely, unsure of her situation with this person she had not expected to see.

"There's a beautiful and large cat here. Is it yours?"

"Oh! That will be Millie. Yes, she is mine I expect she will want feeding. I will see to that while the kettle is boiling."

There was the metallic sound of a dish, and a tin being opened, Millie's ears pricked up and her head turned to the direction of the sounds and then she was off heading towards the kitchen and her dish of food, the stranger in her midst quite forgotten now.

Dave Mitchell walked into the sitting room, a steaming cup of coffee in each hand. "I hope it's not too strong, if it is, you only have to say so and I will put a drop more milk in the cup."

Taking it from him she immediately took a sip, and answered that it was the same as she normally made herself and was fine.

They were both sat opposite each other on the pair of matching easy chairs, Mitchell was the first to break the silence.

"Well now, what was it you wanted to speak to me about."

She sat looking the short distance across from him, a puzzled look upon her face, unsure how she was going to explain herself being there with what she had to say to him, and how he was going to receive it.

"Do you you know who I am or, anything about me?"

"Not much really, just that one of the friends I was with mentioned you were a medium, and your name which was as you have just told me. I think that was about all they said. But what that means exactly I am not too sure and, so as not to offend you I would rather you explain it to me in any way you prefer, if you feel it is necessary I understand. I have heard of people with....shall I say psychic abilities but have never had dealings with them at any time, and have no views one way or another. As he spoke to her he could not help thinking how right Cyril Shepherd was when he had said she was attractive, although he had not used those actual words.

She took a deep breath, her eyes staring at the floor in front of her, she seemed to be trying to focus her thoughts on where, or how she could start. Eventually she lifted her head and looking at him straight in the face began to speak.

"I had last night an experience I have never encountered before, and coming here to see you this morning is something quite, how can I say,..... completely out of character for me."

"So what is it you want to say to me ?" He lifted his cup and took a sip, although he still kept his eyes on her, while waiting for her reply.

Taking the bull by the horns as the saying goes she began:

"While we were both in the Harvest Moon last night, I just happened to glance over in your direction and noticed a spirit form of a departed person. At first I did not pay much attention to them, as I often see them, as they sometimes do return to places they frequented on the earth plain as we say but, as the evening wore on I saw that he, it was a male spirit form was trying to attract your attention but to no avail, it was only then I could see he was in a state of agitation. It was at this point he happened to look across to where I was sitting, and must have realized that I could see him, then within an instant he was standing next to me, and then spoke to me asking if I could hear him as well as see him, to which I answered that I could. Although, the friends who were with me could not. He then told me he had been trying to communicate with you for quite some time, and could not seem to make a breakthrough to you. He then asked me if I would allow him to communicate with me instead and relay to you what he wanted to tell you. At first I was going to come over to your table and speak to you, and explain what had happened, and then ask you if it would be convenient to go to your home and see if I could make contact with him again, and give you a private sitting there. But, my friends advised me against doing so, considering where we were, and as you where all drinking, and could have easily taken offence over being intruded upon over such a strange request, and would probably not have taken me seriously anyway. Eventually it was decided to see if he would be willing to see if contact could be made when my friends and myself returned home later that night, but for some reason contact was not made. Why we had no idea, so we left it at that for the time being. Oh! I have nearly forgotten to tell you, he said you would know of him, and his name was Paul Gage.

Mitchell sat in his chair dumfounded, he could not believe what he had just heard. Up until that moment he had been willing for her to talk of spirits ect., interested up to a point in what she was saying, and in the fact he found her attractive, he also felt a pleasant feeling being in her company but, the significance of what she had just told him shook him to the core!

He placed his cup on the coffee table between them, and was unsure of how to reply, to what she had just told him.

"This Paul Gage, what else did he say to you?"

"He told me he had been a victim of a most horrific murder, and he had been trying to contact you for a while now. Also he asked me to tell you he was responsible and sorry for the incident which occurred in your house a day or so ago, what I think he said,.....I am not sure but it sounded like something to do with a window or door glass breaking, it was he told me through frustration and he overdid what he was trying to do to enable him to show himself to you in the hope you would recognize him and perhaps be able to help him and he in turn could be of possible help to you. Was he a friend? How well did you know him? Since he has been in spirit, he has met others 'over there' and had asked for help and advice as to what he could do to contact you.

After advice and then trying and not getting any success to speak of, others spirit forms had told him that it was probably due to the fact you were of a material nature, and not too well up on the spirituality side of life, possibly because of your 'lifestyle' or daily work influences. I could not answer that, because I know nothing of you except you go to the bar I saw you in, and it was the landlord who had discretely asked the young man who came to the bar before we left where you lived and he told him he did not know exactly but, knew it was somewhere in this location. I knocked on a few doors before I arrived here, asking if they knew of anyone who had a window or door glass replaced in the past few days, the last person I asked pointed to your house from across the road."

Mitchell got up from the chair, walked to the mantelpiece, placing his hand on the edge of it, he turned, not sure now, what to say or how to say it, to the woman, who was sitting still and waiting for him to reply to what she had told him. He picked up from the mantelpiece a small porcelain figure of a woman holding a tabby cat, one of a few lining the mantelpiece, but was only half looking at it, while at the same time running through his mind the curious account of the encounter she told him she had experienced with with the departed victim known as Paul Gage.

"I am a police officer and was working on the case involving the death of Paul Gage, and yes we have very good grounds to suspect his death was murder. I did not know him prior to being involved in the investigation after the finding of his body. Due to circumstances leading up to what you have just told me, I am at the present on sick leave."

He went silent for a little while his eyes looking ahead and past where she sat, and not really seeing anything as his thoughts within his head began to to make sense with what she had spoken to him about, the voice speaking his name, the incident in his home, the smashed glass and light shades, and perhaps the way Millie had been acting recently. He looked at her again, then away, rubbing his forehead with his hand.

"I thought I was going crazy and headed for a complete mental breakdown at one stage. Why was he trying to communicate with me instead of anyone else on the force. Did he say?"

"No! But he never mentioned to me you were a police officer, when he came to me last night in the pub, it was after I arrived home actually. My two friends had gone and I was just about to retire for the night and at first just sensed his presence there, and then he communicated to me in my mind, when I opened up and was in a sensitive enough state for him to communicate more clearly. He seemed to know I belonged to a rescue circle and...."

"Excuse me! A...What..., circle?"

"A rescue circle!! It's....It's for a situation which sometimes happens, a departed person sometimes, through the manner of their passing end up in a kind of,...of..limbo state of awareness, which can cause a kind of panic and confusion to them, and while in this state a number of things may happen that we know of, the most common of which is the spirit becomes what we term as earthbound. During this state of confusion and situations they could be confronted with, they cannot in some cases, understand when they look around and, seem to be, to themselves, not deceased but very much alive, everything looks, and feels, the same as it always did, the body feels as real as when the person was living, which of course it would do, just as water evaporates and changes form while all it's surroundings remain the same, then such is the case with the spirit body intact in every sense, although the essence, consciousness or the state of being remains the same. While in this state of awareness and consciousness, plus the confusion surrounding them they are unaware help in the spirit world is available but they would hold on as long as possible to the surroundings they are familiar with although with out the knowledge they are in fact neither fully in the spirit world or on the earth plain but, as I have said a state of limbo.

That is where a rescue circle comes in or perhaps I should say, are called in, mostly it is through things happening as you yourself have experienced, unnatural occurrences in the home of someone, or a place, as I have already said, a place frequented by the deceased person, of course it can have various results on those who experience such phenomena, from frightening to indifference of the people involved, much depends on the degree and level of the manifestations that occur. It seems by what he has told me that he has gained some knowledge of his state of being now, how so, I am unsure, but enough that he has asked me if I could set up a rescue circle, more so for you than himself, although he will benefit from it in the long run and has asked me if it is possible for me to arrange for you to attend it just once, and perhaps there would be enough power within the circle for you to be able to talk to him through a physical medium, in person for a short while to let you know how he had been murdered and by whom, until you had told me different I was under the impression he had been a friend of yours, and thought it was a situation of him being concerned for your safety and a lot more besides, such was his concern for you to be able to communicate with him, there seemed to be an urgency in his request."

Mitchell had listened attentively to what she had been saying and the seemingly natural and uncomplicated way she had related the things she had been told by Paul Gage, it was as if he had thought she had been telling someone of a conversation she had with a friend in a super market canteen, of an every day event, instead of something so extraordinary.

"He also told me to tell you it goes a lot more deeper than just his death, and it was, at this point the power started to weaken. There were other things happening that you and others should know of......something about souls, but more than that I could not say, because just after that I lost contact with him."

"What on earth does he mean by souls, if that is what he did say!"

Mitchell for a moment began to think he was the subject of a wind up, but dismissed it immediately, when he thought back to what Anne Farr had told him so far, and knew there was no way she could have known what had happened in his house, because he was alone when it had happened, and had told no one what had happened, and as far as the glazier had known it had been the wind slamming the door that had caused the broken window. With that and all the other things she had told him. There could only be one explanation and that was she had been telling the truth ever since she had rung the door bell, and he had opened the door.

"When you mention a circle, What do you actually mean, a seance?"

"Yes of a closed kind, but usually for close friends who are more or less similar in spiritual progression in this life. Occasionally, well on rare occasions really, an outsider is permitted to sit with us but only if permission is granted for them to be there from those in the spirit world. We hold them once a week in a private house with friends as I have said, but sometimes we do hold an open gathering for special reasons, usually they are held for people who have had a traumatic time over a bereavement, and may not have been able to come to terms with the loss for various reasons, the death of a loved one affects people in so many different ways.

He hesitated with his next question, unsure, if he would be making a fool of himself, but as he looked at her he felt sure she would understand, and perhaps pardon him for his ignorance of such matters.

"What happens, do people come along, book an appointment for a seance, say who they want to speak to, then you get on to like an exchange on the other side as you say, tell them who you want to be there at the next meeting, or what?"

She sat in silence, just looking at him for a while, then her eyes seemed to brighten and sparkle, before she burst into laughter. She tried to speak, but could not get hold of herself enough to control her laughter, bursting out every time she tried to answer his question, eventually when she managed to control herself and, apologized for her jocular outburst.

"It's strange really, people come to us from all kinds of ways, from a friend of a friend, to messages from a church meeting, or from other circles, eventually bringing the participants from both worlds together, and for all varieties of reasons. But I don't think I would be wrong in saying the circumstances of our meeting together is in the very least a unique one!"

She saw that she was losing him in the way she was trying to explain the things he wanted to know, and decided to explain to him her part in the proceedings of a circle.

"I am what is known as clairaudiant, and clairvoyant, this means I can see and hear spirits of those departed from this side of life, but mostly I hear them, some are from recent times but also some that have been in spirit for quite a considerable number of years, even perhaps hundreds of years, and they all have various reasons for making themselves known to us in this life, but for the moment it's not necessary to dwell on that point. I am just a receiver, like a radio and, through me those in spirit will talk and, I can hear them and pass on messages to those who cannot hear them, from relatives and friends, who have passed on into the spirit world, most of who will identify themselves to the recipient by personal and private things which only they would have the knowledge of, and pass on messages from life beyond the veil. There are others within most circles who have various 'gifts' of the psychic nature to enhance the performance and knowledge of the circle spiritually, and to better our lives materially as a whole. When I can arrange the evening to attempt the contacting of Paul Gage, the contact could be made in any one of the ways possible to us, through one 'medium' or another, usually through the most accessible at the time. There is also what is called physical mediumship. But that is very rare and a privilege to see and is only used for specific purposes of reassurance and guidance and takes an enormous amount of power to achieve using the whole of a gathering of people and is taken from all of those present, to explain would take more time than I have at present. All of what we do, we do for the purpose of trying to prove to others the truth of survival, and death is just a continuation of life on another plain of existence. Myself and all true mediums, or sensitive's as we prefer to be called have been given various gifts to be instrumental in trying to prove to others the fact that every individual no matter what station in life one is born into or achieves in this life eventually return to the world and form of spirit, and the only thing they can take back with them is their sum amount of spiritual progression to reincarnate in a following life until they eventually become one within the spiritual light on a completely different plain of existence."

Mitchell listened to the woman as she spoke, not really knowing his feelings that he felt towards her, as she seemed to be preaching to him on one hand, but at the same time, it was as if she was describing in a matter of fact way, the way things were, and so absolute was she in the belief in what she was saying to him, he thought of a question he could ask, to see what her answer and explanation would be.

"If what you say is true, why it that we can never remember the time when we were in spirit as you call it, when we return here?"

She looked at him and wondered if she had been going on a little too much with her talking of the subject, not wanting to seem as if she was putting up herself, as a complete authority on what she had been speaking. But, decided, as he had put the question she would try to give him an answer that he would possibly understand her viewpoint and belief, just enough to question what she had told him so far, and then to judge for himself the value of what she had told him.

"Imagine if you can, yourself, above an ocean, and then having to descend down to the bottom to accomplish a specific task of work, and you are the only one with the capability to carry it out.

There are two possibilities in the end. One you fail, or two you succeed. The part of the ocean you have to work in is just within human working depth, if you equip yourself with diving tanks at the start to enable you to carry out the various tasks you have to do, you only have so much air in the tanks to allow you a specific amount of time to do them in, one logical answer could be to carry extra bottles down with you, but this would be, due to the depth you are in and the tasks you have to perform not really feasible, and having to change tanks at such depth would be more than possibly dangerous. The other way would be to don a diving suit with an air line, but again at the depth you are working, and the cumbersome suit you are wearing, and out of your natural environment the tasks become more difficult, you have to return to the surface because of fatigue and return until you have completed your task, and when the task is completed you receive your reward of payment. If you look at life on this earth plain in the same way can you not see a parallel? Our gifts are also for furthering harmony between this world and the next, and tries to show that which ever religion one follows, it makes not one scrap of difference one way or the other, we all have to answer to ourselves, then truth becomes judge and jury, truth about ourselves, we can then see clearly our spiritual efforts on the pathway to our ultimate goal. Something learned or done in one lifetime has repercussions in another, and it is how you deal with the situations that may be repeated to give you the chance to save you from further consequences to hamper your chances for progression to a higher life we should for our own sakes and eventually others, strive to attain."

Mitchell had listened to her talking and was captivated by her voice, and what she had been saying to him. His inner thoughts when brought to the surface began to question his own life and why he had been placed in the position he had now found himself. Was there some thing in what she had just told him, in some ways it made the meaning of life sound so simple and uncomplicated, and yet, in another there was some kind of intuition within him his that perhaps his present situation had been orchestrated in some way that was beyond his present ken.

If that was so then what, he thought, could possibly be the reason, all his life he had never given much thought to religion or matters of life and death, he had just gone along with his life and career in the police force, and doing his job as efficiently as he could. He picked up the mug of coffee he had placed on the table taking a sip he looked at her with a full eye contact as he swallowed the now barely warm drink.

"Why, do you think all this has happened to me. Why should I have become involved in the way I have, and Paul Gage have gone to such effort to contact me the way he has, and almost unhinging my sanity at the same time? Is that a normal scenario of events in your experience?"

"When we do return to this life we have to live to the best of our ability in accordance to spiritual law alongside the material things of this world. Due to our upbringing and other personal internal conflicts and material problems we can lose sight of the reasons we have returned to this side of life, and the more we strive for the material the less we think of the spiritual, then, it seems, it is only at times of stress and self spiritual reflection that we may begin to wonder why we are here. It also seems that the more power or wealth we accumulate the less time we tend to have for those less fortunate than us. There are exceptions of course but in this day and age they are fewer than at any time before, of course there are some who are in a position to help with vast wealth, having had good fortune smile on them who try with gestures of good will do help various causes which are in need, but how many of these people do these things only when it causes no inconvenience to themselves, and is a way to further their image as they would want it to be perceived by others. The one thing available to us, as a.... shall we say measure of our inner self given to us from our life in spirit is conscience, and the free will whether we use it or not, and, something which is not used very much will often be forgotten about, and perhaps even discarded, resulting in a denial that it ever existed, until needed and then only to be found wanting. As can be said true riches are never man made, but given freely from spirit, it is just that man has a destructive urge within himself when conscience and the understanding of it is lacking. There by in some ways gifts of spirit given, can be changed for profit by an individual, or groups of individuals. But that is by the by, the thing now is, are you willing to attend the circle as was suggested?"

Mitchell's mind was reeling over the sermon or talk or what it could be called she had just given, and after thinking it over agreed to take part in, or do, what ever was called for.

"Right that's settled then, when I leave here I will contact my friends and see when it can be arranged. If you give me your telephone number I will call and see if the time and day it can be arranged will be suitable for you."

They spoke for a while longer and then Anne Farr decided she had been there long enough and, would have quite a few things to arrange to do what had been decided on and thought it better for her to leave so as to be able to get on with them, saying goodbye she left Mitchell on the doorstep, very thoughtful, but quite looking forward to seeing her again. His only concern on the matter was he just did not know what to expect of the meeting whenever it was arranged, also the types of people he would meet.

CHAPTER 22

The slip road seemed never ending, but in the distance Tony Howard could now see the entrance to the motorway, plodding on, he kept going the sight of it giving him new energy in his legs. He had walked the two and a half miles that morning after spending a not to cold night in his sleeping bag, on a soft bed of straw in a barn after leaving the others the previous day, and was glad to see the sunrise and be on his way out of the Taunton area, and well away from the manor house.

As he had set out that morning it was cold, but as he had got into his stride his body warmed up from the exertion of walking. There seemed to be a little traffic passing him as he walked, his thumb signalled the want of a lift. He stopped about one hundred and fifty yards from the entrance of the motorway, thinking, if he waited there he would be more likely to get a lift with it being easier for anyone to see him and stop with plenty of time to slow down when they saw him. After a period of about fifteen minutes with a few cars and lorries going past him on the opposite side of the road, as they came off of the junction of the motorway, he was beginning to think that perhaps he had started a little too early. One or two cars and vans went past him without any sign of slowing down, a certain sign they had no intention of stopping. Now that he had stopped walking he began to feel colder, putting his duffel bag and holdal containing his belongings on the ground, he began to walk up and down stamping his feet on the ground as he did so, not wanting them to become as cold as when he had started out for the motorway in the early hours that morning. He had decided on the early start to get out of the cold place he had spent the night, knowing the sooner he started walking the quicker his body would warm up. He looked around at the early dawn sky and saw there was no sign of any rain clouds in sight, and the sun was becoming large and bright in the sky, a contrast of the earlier dawn, although now bright, it did not give off much in the way of warmth as he stood there, he began to rub his hands together, and blew into them wishing he had a pair of gloves with him. He knew there was a clean pair of woollen socks in the holdal and was about to reach down to open it and get them out to put them over his hands, when he saw coming towards him and slowing down a large black Volvo estate car, flashing to indicate it was about to pull in. As it pulled up alongside the kerb next to him the window was electrically opened allowing him to peer inside, as he did so he saw a stunningly attractive woman with dark brown eyes and long black lustrous hair of about forty inside, the woman spoke to him, her voice sounded a little strange, kind of muffled, but he seemed to hear what he was saying well enough.

"How far are you going?"

"I am trying to make it to Canterbury."

"I can take you as far as Ashford. Will that help you?"

"Oh brilliant!" He quickly thought to himself. "I can catch a bus easily from there."

"That would be wonderful, and thanks a lot for stopping."

"My pleasure." The woman replied.

He Picked up his duffel bag and holdal, and went around the bonnet to get into the offered front seat. He had been so happy to see the car stop, and had not even noticed that the car was left hand driven. He could hear a whirring as the window was closing, walked around the front of the car, as he reached for the handle he heard the the tremendously loud sounding blast from a large juggernought's horn which seemed to sound all around him, then he looked at the woman's face in the car which had a cynical grinning expression as the eyes focused on him, just before car and face seemed to dissolve and disappear in front of him. He stood with one hand held out to where the handle had been, the other held his holdal with the duffel bag hung over his shoulder, there was confusion and disbelief, as he heard the loud hissing sound from the vehicle as the air brakes were frantically applied by the driver while almost in the same split seconds the vehicle smashed full on into his body, and the giant wheels crushed his head beneath them turning it into a mass of flattened bloody pulp, and twisting and turning his body into an unnatural position underneath the trailer.

Thankfully he was dead before he hit the ground, from the initial impact from the lorries radiator guard which hair and skin tissue, adhered to, a splash of blood, indicated the area of the terrific force of impact.

The woman Identical to the driver of the black Volvo sat in the car, the real vehicle, and not the mirror image which had been projected so completely by her into the mind of Tony Howard, and had watched the event of the traffic road accident and aftermath, satisfied she had accomplished everything to her own satisfaction, started the quiet purring motor and began to drive away from the scene, unnoticed by other drivers who had seen the accident and had pulled over to assist in any way they could, which for Tony Howard was nothing.

The truckdriver had climbed out of his cab and was leaning in a state of total shock against blood splattered radiator. He turned to the nearest motorist to him, his eyes wide as tears were beginning to fill them, and not seeing the others gathering there who had arrived at the scene to assist. "He walked straight in front of me I couldn't stop, one minute he was at the side of the road, the next he was in front of me, he just walked in front of me in just two or three strides.....I could not stop."

"I know, I saw it happen mate, I saw it happen, it was not your fault, there was nothing you could have done, don't worry I will make a statement to that effect when the police get here. Come on come over here and sit down." The witness to the accident took him gently by the arms and led him away to the grass verge, while another had taken a blanket from his car and placed it around the driver, saying: "Here wrap this around you it will help you, you are in shock about what has happened don't worry."

****

After they had eaten they went to the sitting room to decide what they should do next. They felt uncomfortable as they sat in the room, Charlie suggested for them to catch the transport into town, and make for one of the places they would feel free to talk, and discuss what they had found out the from Tony Howard the day before. The other two agreed with him and soon after made their way to the transport pickup point.

In the same cafe they had used the couple of days before when the two musicians with the instruments were there. Choco picked up the local newspaper, which had been left on the counter from someone earlier, and was casually glancing through it when his eyes caught the headlines of one of the inside pages.

BURGLARY AT PRIESTS HOUSE
AND
PRIESTS DISAPPEARANCE

Reading on he began showing sings of interest in what was written in the paper on the subject, clearly noticed by the other two.

"What's the matter Choco? What is it?

Tim and Charlie leaned over towards him as he placed the paper on the table in front of them. They both scanned the paper but could see nothing to concern them, or their problem in hand.

"The burglary, I know who it was, but the police suspect the priest was probably abducted. Most likely they say, when he came home and disturbed them. But I can not believe that, when they told me about what they had done, they said they had just done the house when there was nobody at home. There was no mention of the priest coming home, and anyway, that is not their style if they had been disturbed they would have had a window or the back door unlocked or open, or some means of escape and have dropped everything there and

124

then, and made their escape without having even been seen to be identified should they be taken in for questioning on suspicion of having done the burglary."

He looked over the table at the other two. "It just does not fit in with what I know about them."

Charlie, said nothing, but was thinking he did not know very much about his friend and, was puzzled as to how he would know so much, if, he were not involved with them in some way.

Whether Choco had seen the look on Charlie's face, or the way he was deep in thought over what he had said, one could not say, but he smiled at him.

"Don't worry old flower, I have never been involved in any of that stuff, although, I have had dealings with some of those who get up to all kinds of things, but mostly to do with petty stuff, such as a little grass now and then when I am flush enough to afford it, or even a loan on either side, sometimes when I might be flush I have loaned money to some of them, and when I have found things hard, I have borrowed from them. But I will have a word with them when I get the chance."

"How did you become friendly with them?" Charlie asked.

Tim was curious in a small way about what they were talking about and, pricked up an ear to listen, although he would be the first to admit he was no saint.

"Can you remember when you met me in the Portcullis?. When you had to sign on and all that rigmaroll, and I waited there for you to come in. Those friends of mine who were sat at the same table as myself when you came in and sat down with me. Well they were among them, don't ask me which two, because I would not tell you. I was introduced to them and most of the others in the place by one of them, after helping him out one night a year or so back when he had been in the unfortunate process of being mugged by three other men from out of town, while I was on my way back to an old abandoned railway carriage for a nights kip. I saw them beating up on him and thought it unfair odds and pitched in to help him out, at the time I thought it was just a case of some one being mugged on his way home. Anyway we saw them off, he was grateful and asked me home to his house for the night when he found I had nowhere permanent to stay. Ended up with a bath and a bed in that order which he told me I needed, met his mother in the morning when she came home in the morning from working as a nursing assistant, in a local old peoples home. When she first saw me, and the way I was dressed, she was not too impressed with her sons new friend, but when she understood the nature of our meeting there was nothing too good for me, as far as she was concerned. Now, whenever I have need of a bath or a bed for the occasional night when I returned to the town there has always been someone I could call on who would see me all right, I could have stayed there instead of the manor but it would be wrong of me just to use her good will without paying something when I could but the only trouble is she would not accept anything from me, and I would feel embarrassed in those circumstances that is why I only see her son when I go to the Portcullis it saves a lot of hustle and does not offend her, because she does not know I am around half the time when I am in the town, and I prefer it that way, and that's about all there is to know really."

"All very interesting but it does not help us with what we are going to do about what we know about the manor does it, or what could have happened to Rene."

Choco's explanation to Charlie about how he knew the thieves connected with the burglary, made him feel better but he did not think it would have made any difference to his friendship with the man no matter how he knew them, he seemed O.K. to him, and had enjoyed being in his company anyway.

After the day spent in the town wandering around and asking discrete questions whenever they could and, finding absolutely nothing of the possible where about's of Tim's Rene, they made their way back to be picked up by the transport.

Later that evening while in the lounge/T.V. room, they were sat around talking and half watching the television, the local news came on with the scene of the accident where Tony Howard had met his death. The commentator, was saying words to the effect that with the evidence gathered, a man, so far unidentified, had committed suicide by walking out in front of a speeding lorry and was killed instantly. The man was believed to be hitch hiking, and the driver was at present in hospital suffering with shock, due to the accident.

It was not the commentary of the incident which first drew Charlie's attention to what was being said, but two broken bags of which the contents had been stuffed roughly back into what remained of them, on the side of the road behind the lorry.

Cautiously he looked around him, to make sure there was no one watching him before he drew the other two's attention to what was being shown on the television.

"Can you see the bags on the ground, where the accident they are showing happened this morning, he whispered to the others. Surely you can't believe what they are saying that it looks as if he committed suicide, or even an accident."

"Don't even look as if you are even mildly interested, I noticed it when the report started. I will get up and go over to the table and get a pack of playing cards, let us just carry on as if we had noticed nothing at all, and are not the least interested in the television, say nothing about anything while we are in this place, who knows if we are being watched in here by anyone. Don't forget we were playing pool with him for a while last night, just act as we did before we knew anything."

Choco got the playing cards and all three played knap with them for the best part of two hours, during which a couple of others asked if they could join in, so as not to seem suspicious they agreed, unsure if the new comers were anything more than they appeared, just guests the same as themselves, the evening passed quietly with no sign apparent of what they knew, or had been told to them by the now deceased Tony Howard. After a long period of playing cards they decided to watch T.V. for a little while, before turning in for the night, and going to their rooms.

Before he turned in for the night Charlie had taken a shower and washed his socks and underpants in the washroom basin and had just finished hanging them on the top of the radiator in his room when he heard the sound of 'Willie's' trolley as he went around the landing, shortly after there was a knock on his door. He opened it and saw as he had expected Willie, holding the usual mug of drinking chocolate out towards him.

"Saw your light was still on and thought perhaps I should knock to see if you were still awake or had fallen asleep with the light on, anyway as you are still up and awake here is some nice sweet chocolate drink for you to go to bed with. Don't forget to bring the mug down with you in the morning, will you."

"Thank's Willie! I thought I had missed you while I was in the shower."

"That's all right! See you!" He turned and was on his way as Charlie closed the door.

The next morning Charlie struggled out of bed stood up and found himself a little unsteady on his feet, walked to the washroom to freshen up, and shave. After shaving he doused himself with cold water to try to get the tiredness he was feeling away. Finishing he went back to his room picked up the mug he had from Willie the night before and went down the stairs to have breakfast.

The others were there already and had saved him a place at the table. They ate and while doing so said very little to each other except for normal everyday breakfast table talk. As they were getting ready to leave the table, Choco and Charlie both saw the redhead Charlie had 'dreamed' about the couple of days before talking to someone near the door way which was out of bounds to them, Charlie with all that was going on since the dream, he had still not told Choco about it. But the thing that interested Choco at that moment was not the woman but the man she was talking to, and he had just come through the residents only door."Bloody monkey Yateman! What the hell is he doing here?" He thought to himself. He stopped looking across to where they were as an idea came into his head, indicated to the others to go on into the sitting room and wait for him, while he walked back into the dining area, on the pretext of getting himself another cup of tea. He then walked over to one of the tables near the door, enabling him to see the two talking. It was not long before the redhead left 'Monkey' then went out of the door towards the reception area. While Monkey Yateman made his way towards the kitchen and serving part of the dining room. Choco got up casually from the table leaving a now empty cup on the table, and walked towards Yateman.

"Morning! You should try the smoked bacon, it's really good this morning."

"Thank you perhaps I will." He replied and walked straight past him.

Choco Joined the others in the sitting room as arranged and motioned them to follow him outside. "If we hurry we can still catch the transport outside." He voiced so that if anyone was watching it would seem a normal statement to make, but the gesture he gave them with his eyes indicated there was more to the statement than just a trip into town.

The journey into the town took the same time as usual but, for Charlie and Tim it seemed a whole lot longer, as they tried to puzzle out what Choco had found out or intended to find out. They sat in their usual cafe they used when the Portcullis was not open and Charlie began to explain to them what the mystery was.

"You saw the guy who was talking to the redhead Charlie? Well! I know him, and know him well, we were best of mates at one time, we lived on the same commune in Wales for two and a half years. This morning I spoke to him and he answered me as if he did not know me from Adam."

Charlie and Tim said nothing but just waited for him to say more or what his point was.

"Don't you see? It looks as if what Tony Howard told us does hold water. Why did he not speak? I mean man, we were close back then, we shared everything together, and the way he was dressed, there has been some kind of radical change in him, eighteen months ago he dressed the same as us, and there he was as large as life with a suit and tie on as well, it all adds up in the direction that we have been told about, things are not what they seem on the surface, just as Howard told us, and I am inclined to believe if I had made myself known then what would have happened? Something similar to what we have been told, would someone have come and given an excuse for him to go elsewhere or something worse if we are suspected to be suspicious of the strange goings on at the manor." While they were in the cafe someone else came in with the local morning paper on them, the three stopped their conversation to be on the safe side and what ever they did talk about was talked in a much lowered tone of voice.

Tim was facing the man and as he opened the newspaper to read inside of it, Tim saw on one side of the sheet the headlines:

HITCH-HIKER KILLED IN ROAD ACCIDENT!

The man was sat too far away to be able to read any more. When the waitress came with a fried breakfast the man placed the paper on the edge of the table and seemed to have lost interest in it, as he began to eat his fry-up with delectation.

"Excuse me sir, could I possibly take a look at your newspaper while you enjoy your breakfast, it won't take a minute it's just that I was hoping for an advertisement in it today and just wanted to see if it's there."

"You can have it I have finished with it I only wanted it for the racing page and there was nothing there I fancied for today, so go ahead and take it." He handed Tim the paper as he dipped a slice of buttered bread into the yolk of a fried egg.

"Thanks a lot, sir." Tim replied.

The paper lay spread out on the table and all three began to read the report of the accident.

A fatal accident took place early yesterday morning, resulting in the death of a pedestrian, presumed to have been a hitchhiker, who died instantly, by being struck by a large road haulage vehicle, the driver of the vehicle was admitted to hospital suffering from shock, and at the time of going to press was still sedated, doctors say they hope perhaps, he will be able to be discharged this morning. An eye witness has told police he saw the victim walk straight out from the side of the road into the oncoming vehicle, and confirms the drivers statement of the accident. A name and address has been found amongst papers found on the deceased, and enquiries are in progress to inform the next of kin, a police spokesman has reason to believe the man came from the county of Kent.

The three friends looked at each other after reading the account of the accident in the newspaper.

Tim was silent for a while, as were the other two, then spoke in a restrained voice. It does not make sense for it to have been suicide, when he left us he seemed glad and relieved to be going home, and I would have said the furthest thing on his mind was suicide. What do you think Choco? Do you think he committed suicide?"

"I just don't know Tim. How can anyone know what is going on in another persons mind? I admit he was jumpy, and seemed on edge most of the time we were with him! Charlie has said, since he talked to us, how he has been suspicious of the manor after hearing what he told us, and of that, I am more than just inclined to agree with, especially having seen Monkey earlier. But as for him wanting to do away with himself, I would have not have thought so."

"The one thing, and the only thing, which makes me think that, perhaps, he was a bit paranoid over the things he has told us is the driver and the witnesses account, when they have both said that he just walked out into the path of the truck Choco."

Charlie had been hoping he would at least get a little support from Tim about what he had said concerning things at the manor, Tim was as confused now as he was before reading the account in the news paper.

Choco reached for his cup to take a sip, as it reached his lips he saw it was now empty.

"I'm for another cup. How about you two?" Charlie agreed and Tim tipped his cup to his lips finishing what he had left and passed it to Choco.

"Here take this fifty pence piece it's all I have left, might as well get another cup out of it, and use what's left towards yours."

When Choco returned with the tea and putting them down in front of his friends, just as the man at the next table got up to go.

"Thanks again for the paper." He said to him, as he walked past their table.

"Your welcome." He replied as he made his way to the door wiping his lips with a tissue as he stepped outside, and out of earshot of the others.

 "I have been thinking, and can not come to any conclusion over the death of Tony Howard as to whether it was suicide or not but, leaving all that aside. Think! In the report of the accident in the paper the witness says, 'he bent down and picked up his bags, then he walked, straight out into the path of the oncoming truck', Right! What I am saying is what kind of person who is intent on committing suicide, calmly picks up his bags when he has suicide on his mind. His mind, it seems to me was orderly in one sense and yet suicidal in another and 'that' does not ring true to me. I really feel there is something wrong with the whole set up of his death, but what that is I really can't say. But I feel it in my water, that some how and, in some way those at the manor are connected with his death, and let's face it we know now for sure, there are strange goings on there exactly as he told us there was." "

"I know what you are saying makes sense Choco, and I for one would not mind in the least just going back and collecting my things and clearing off out of the place once and for all, but the only thing that stops me is for some reason I believe my Rene is in some kind of trouble, and the only lead I have so far is that I know the answer to her disappearance is some way connected with that house some how, and if I did not try to find out all I could so as to be able to help her then I would be failing myself as well as her, there must be more there that we don't know, and since we have been told a lot of what what we know, and what we have found out for ourselves, I am not going to be satisfied until Rene is with me again. So staying there for a while longer and keeping my wits about me is the only thing I can do about it for the time being." When he had finished speaking Tim looked at Charlie and Choco, in his eyes they could see the hope that they would be with him for a while longer in his quest to find Rene, but not wanting to ask them outright, for their help to do so.

Choco immediately agreed to go back with him. Charlie, after a moments hesitation agreed to go along with them, on the understanding it would only be for a couple more days at the most, and also on the understanding that in that time they would not discuss anything to do with what they were trying to find out while they were there, and if in two days they had still found out nothing more than they already knew, then he would be leaving with or without them. Because as he put it the place was beginning to give him the 'jitters' with everything that seemed to be going on there, without them having any idea why. It was only then he told the both of them of the dream or whatever it was he had had concerning the redhead, and how the next morning there seemed to be no acknowledgement from her, that what he had thought, dreamed, or whatever, had taken place with her, and still did not know anything for sure concerning that night, although there were parts of it that remained so vivid and realistic in his mind, he just could not shake off the confusion.

That evening after having dinner they were all much the same, with just general conversation between themselves, but careful and watchful of things going on around them, but few things held their attention for any long period of time. They went from the T.V. room, to the pool room had a couple of games, which their hearts were not really into, then finished up with a half hearted game of cards. They could not concentrate on anything for very long, and decided to turn in for the night.

Tim's room was the first they came to on the landing with Choco's two doors further down the passage. Charlie's room was situated at the far end of the the passage on the opposite side, with the outside passage window situated on the end of the wall at right angles to Charlies door.

Charlie after returning to his room, had been laying on his bed for fifteen minutes or so, deep in thought over that days events, when he was startled out of them, by the sound of Willie knocking on his door and the sound of the urn lid being replaced as Willie had been looking at the amount of beverage left inside. after opening the door and taking the mug of chocolate off of him, with the usual greeting and passing words from him, he walked over and placed it on the bedside table. Then took from his bag toothbrush paste and soap, then went to the washroom. After finishing there he walked back onto the landing and, as he did so, saw Willie at the top of the landing stairs with a small note book, after writing in it for a short time, he then wheeled the trolley into a small anti room opposite the stairs where it was normally kept, closed and locked the door behind him and then went down the stairs, all the time Charlie watched him his back was towards him and he had not realized Charlie had been watching him. Charlie after returning to his room decided as usual to have a smoke while drinking his Chocolate, he got out his tin, and began to make a rollup when he had finished making it he swung his legs and feet off of the floor, turned around to place the pillow against the headboard, so as he could sit up in the bed with his back supported and comfortable while he had a smoke, and drink the hot chocolate, as he turned his body around to firm the pillow his arm caught the mug knocking it off of the table spilling the contents all over the floor, and bedside mat. With a curse, he got off of the bed looking for something he could use to wipe up the spilt liquid. The first thing that came to hand was a dirty tea shirt he had placed over the chair earlier when he had changed after returning from town, taking it he began to wipe the mess up from the floor and mat, wringing it out into the mug which had originally contained it, finishing up with three quarters of the mug full with the liquid. When the floor and mat was as clean as he could get it he began to look for somewhere handy he could quickly dispose of the mug contents. He tried the window and found it would not open, the paint on it fused to the running grooves of the sash window, deciding the only thing to do would be to empty it down the sink or toilet in the wash room, he went out to do so. While there as he emptied down the sink, he saw a door on the opposite side of the building open and six or seven of the residents come out, one of them being the red head. He could see they were talking and laughing together. Then as someone else joined them and the sounds abated, and they then all huddled in a group, and then he saw a torch light coming from the direction of what he remembered to be a small coppice, then those he had seen come through the door were holding torches which they switched on and began to walk in the direction of the first torch light. Charlie then became curious and wondered what the could be up to and thought to follow them, he went back to his room for his denim jacket.

With caution, he went down the stairs and saw there was no one in the reception area, and all seemed quiet. Making his way over to the front door he slipped out unseen, skirted the side of the manor house until he was opposite the area he could see from the wash room window, keeping as far back into the shadows as he could keeping low he managed to get to the area where he saw them walking towards the flashlight in the direction of the coppice. once there he could see flashes of torch light here and there and began walking in that direction, it was not long before he found himself walking on a rough path of sorts, which seemed to be well trodden, the further in the direction he had seen them take the darker and more difficult it became, without any light to see by he kept coming off of the path and getting tangled in brambles. After loosing the path time and time again, he eventually came onto a clearing, and in the distance could see what could only be a window with torch light flashing behind it, using all the caution he could he moved closer and when he was within fifty yards he could make out a large shed type building, the lights went out and then there was darkness all around him, he began to feel uneasy, and decided it might be better to go back to his room and the others and tell them what he had seen.

Getting back to the manor turned out to be as easy as it had been to slip out, the manor was as silent as could be, with not a sign of anyone around, he was worried about getting past the reception area, but there was not even anyone there. He went up the stairs to his room, thought about what he should do, decided there and then, he would go to Choco's room and tell him where he had been and what he had seen.

He knocked softly on Choco's door, but heard no answer, thinking he was asleep he decided to enter and wake him up, presuming he would not mind being woken up to be told that he had just followed the residents making their way to the shed in the middle of and open field in the middle of the night by torch light. Moving close to Choco, Charlie whispered for him to wake up, but he got no response, then talked in his normal voice and still he would not awaken, catching him hold by the shoulders he even shook him but all he did was to give a grunt and lay there on his bed limp. He made his way to Tim's room and received the same response, with him as he had with Choco, and realized then why Willie was always around with the drinking Chocolate, and the reason they always seemed to have such a deep sleep there. They were being drugged!

The next morning Charlie was the first in the dining room and was waiting for Choco and Tim, he felt refreshed and alert, more so than he had at that time in the morning from the first night he had spent there. He remembered how Choco had said he always slept well and had put it down to the country air after he had felt so tired after waking, for the first hour or so since he had been there.

"Just wait." He thought "Until I tell them both how much asleep they were last night." He was in the middle of his breakfast when they both arrived for theirs.

"Morning Choco,.....Tim. Have a good night's sleep."

"Sound! Was Choco's reply, while Tim just nodded.

In between mouthfuls Tim looked across to Choco and Charlie.

"What's on the agenda for today then?" He asked to no one in particular

"Let's take a walk around the grounds and talk."

Choco stopped cutting a slice of toast with beans on, as Charlie spoke.

"Bloody hell Charlie, don't tell me you are getting paranoid already, who the bloody hell is going to be able to listen to us now? Look! The nearest table to us with anyone on is twenty feet away and the radio is on as loud as anything, and we are not talking loud enough for anyone on the next table to hear us."

"Bear with me, both of you, I know something you don't, and will tell you about it when we are outside of this place."

"Choco could tell by the tone of his voice he was serious, which made him agree to what he had asked.

Later that morning, outside and away from the manor Charlie Tim and Choco were sat on a seat in the spacious manor grounds. After he was sure no one could possibly hear what they were saying Charlie filled in the other two on the events he had witnessed the night before, and finished up by telling them they had been drugged at night by the drinking chocolate Willie brought around to them.

After he had finished and answered any questions they asked about what he had told them, he stood waiting, for their views on things as they now stood.

"What shall we do then? Take a look at the shed close up, or what? It is not far the way I followed them last night, but if we went that way we would probably be seen, if there was anyone in the area of these grounds, because there is a lot of cover in the area and we could easily be stumbled on if we were careful or not. The best way would be to go out of the gates and turn the opposite way to where the field the shed is situated in and circle around from behind in the coppice side and keep our eyes peeled when we start to move in the direction of the open field. What do you say?"

He looked at his companions for an answer, and after some more discussion together, they both agreed to his plan and decided they would take a walk in the afternoon after lunch had been served.

CHAPTER 23

After Anne Farr had left, Mitchell decided he would still go out, he was beginning to get a bit bored staying at home with no one to speak to. He thought to himself it might be an idea to drive off into the country for some fresh country air, just for an hour or so, and then call into the Harvest Moon for a drink and chat to who ever might be there.

He had finished washing up the mugs they had used and, as he was putting them away, he felt Millie rubbing against his legs. She seemed a lot better about staying in the house now, content to lay around as she used to. He had noticed this, when he had thought back to the time of the window being smashed, and the broken lamp shades. "Could it be" he wondered. "She could sense there was no harm intended, and that there was to be no more disturbances of that nature again in the house." She walked over to the sitting room door and began to rub herself up and down against it. "What's the matter girl do you want to go out?" He walked over to the door to let her out so she could get out of the cat flap in the front door. But instead she turned in the opposite direction, and headed up the stairs to his bedroom.

"That's it she is back to her old self again." He thought.

After a drive of ten minutes he was parked in a lay by on the top of the 'Quantock' hills quietly enjoying the view, Taunton lay below him, as he gazed out over the valley, memories of the past came flooding back to him, of the times he had come to this very spot in the summers of past years with Gaynor and his then young daughter, Erica.

Where had they gone, those times when everything seemed to be so perfect, with so much hope for the future. As the memories returned so did the sadness and disappointment, it seemed, that his life had handed out to him. In his memories the scene he had before him was bright with lush vegetation of summer, the sky blue and cloudless, while the large birds were gliding above, as the hot currents lifted and carried them over the valley below.

But now, as he looked at the same scene the trees had grown larger, taller, from when in the memory they were just young saplings, with the fresh green leaves. There were just a few leaves on the trees now, most had been shed or had been blown off by the strong winds the Quantock hills were susceptible to, on the twigs he could see some leaves but they were limp with darkened colours of their own species still hanging tenaciously on the twigs, while on the ground they lay wet, dark brown and black, and rotting, as they gave life even in their death, while the parent they came from, conserved the energy it had received from the sunlight warmth and rain of the previous season through them, to awaken in the following spring to begin a new cycle of life.

As he thought of such things, he gave himself a mental shrug. "That's it!" He thought. "It's time for me too, a new year and a new life cycle!" As he drove from there he seemed to come out of a dormant period of his life which through fate had been forced upon him. As he drove, even though the darkening sky announcing the forming of rain clouds and, could see the sparse vegetation around him, he felt the ride and solitude of the hills which had enabled him to think things through had done him more good than he could possibly have envisaged at the start of his journey to the Quantock hills. He looked into the rear view mirror, and there was for the first time in a long while, a long over due unforced smile on his lips.

After returning from the hills, and stopping off for a drink and some lunch at the Harvest Moon, he made his way home, feeling better than he had for as long as he could remember. He was even thinking of starting back to work the following week. It was as he was sat in the lounge the idea occurred to him. Gaynor had made a new life for herself, now it was his turn, he was feeling full of hope for the future now. Which, only a matter of hours before seemed as dark and bleak as the hills he had been on that morning.

Starting in the kitchen, with music playing on the radio interspersed with comments from the local radio disc jockey, he began cleaning the house, sorting out the cupboards, finding things in jars, packets, some which were open that could not be used the contents stale, the use by dates well out of time. Depositing things he had no more use for into black plastic bags to put out for the refuse collectors, as he moved from one room to another he had not realized just how much the house was in need of a clean. The more he did the more lighter his mood became until he found himself singing along with the radio. All the photographs of his ex wife Gaynor, which he had still kept around in the frames ect. he put into a brown paper bag he had found in one of the drawers he had cleared out and put them away in a now practically empty store cupboard. He did not want to dispose of them altogether, because their early years of marriage were happy times, and there were a lot of them, although now, they seemed an age ago and part of another life. All of her things he had seen when he had gone to the wardrobe were taken and consigned to black bags, from shoes to the clothing she had left, even his own favourite black red and white number, and put separate from the bags to be left for the refuge collection, ready to be given to one of the many charity shops in the town, "rather that," he thought than to be just thrown out when some good use could be made of them, everything that was hers went.

When at last he had finished it was late in the afternoon and he had just returned from putting the last black bag out for the refuse collection.

As he came into the house he heard the sound of the telephone ringing. He picked it up and heard the voice of Anne Farr, she explained to him she had spoken to a few friends about what they had discussed, they were willing to hold a circle, and if it was possible perhaps give the spirit of Paul Gage the chance to communicate with him, either through her, or one of the others who would be there. The only problem was, it would only be possible for them all to be together that evening, otherwise they would have to arrange it for a week to ten days later due to previously arranged commitments. So after asking if it would be inconvenient to hold it that night, and him answering her to say he had nothing else on and it would be fine, and for her to go ahead and arrange what ever it was she had to, and asking her where he would have to go, and at what time.

She told him not to worry about anything, and she would come over to his house and pick him up, and could he be ready for seven thirty. When he agreed he would be ready at that time she spoke to someone she was with when she had phoned him then told him she would see him later then put the phone down.

He was delighted when he heard from her he had not expected her to try to arrange things so quickly, and also he was pleased he would be in her company again so soon.

It seemed time stood still, but eventually it was seven thirty and a little later he heard a car pull up outside of his house. He opened the door and saw her as she was about to get out of the car. He put his hand up to let her know he was ready and on his way out, closed and locked his door and walked to her car.

"I am sorry I am a little late, I have been walking a neighbours dog for her, she has had an operation on her foot and cannot do it herself for a while. So I offered to do it for her until she is able, I found myself running late before I took him, but it does not matter too much because they will not start before eight thirty, she had wanted him ready at the time she had told him, so that he could meet the others and get to know them for a while before the circle started.

She was a careful driver but not in the least nervous on the road, and within a short while he felt quite at ease, although it did feel strange to him at first to have a woman in the driving seat beside him.

Twenty minutes later they were pulling up beside a large solitary situated bungalow, some distance past the outskirts of the town at a spur section of rolling hills. Walking through the gate he noticed a combined bird bath and table, on the centre of an oval shaped lawn, which had small shrubs and miniature conifers, in a raised rockery bed garden at one end of the oval shaped lawn. The bath and table were ornamental, made from what he could see of sand and chipping, not having seen anything like it before he presumed it was home made by the owner of the bungalow, as he walked nearer he could see it more clearly and had to admit it was very effective, and added charm to the already neat and precise layout of the garden. As they neared the front door a light came on in the window facing them, then the curtains were being pulled together by a woman of about fifty years of age, looking out she saw them approaching.

"Sean! Anne's outside, can you let her in, while I finish in here?"

A moment later the door opened and they were greeted by quite a large built man of about five ten in height with a silver grey beard, which would have made any eighteenth century sea captain proud to be the owner of. He turned sideways on, in the doorway allowing them room to enter and pass him.

"Come in, Come in Anne!" They entered the hall and then waited until he had closed the door behind them, then followed him along the passage way, Mitchell noticed that as he walked in front of them Sean had a very prominent limp, they carried on walking towards to the far end of the hall.

"Peter and Abigail are on their way and should be here shortly, so... you are Anne's friend, what is his name, Anne?" Half turning in his stride Sean offered his hand to Mitchell.

"Oh! I am sorry Sean, I did intend to introduce David when we had all arrived and, to tell them what I knew, and what we were hoping to achieve tonight if everything goes well as planned."

"Hello David I am Sean, and pleased to meet you. Ah! here we are if you just go into the room there, I will make us all a pot of tea, when Peter and Abigail arrive we will all be here, and then you can get to know the rest of the weirdo's like myself, and Anne. Can you go on in and introduce David to the rest of them in there Anne." He spoke with a broad Belfast accent in a deep loud voice.

"Can I help you with anything Sean after I introduce David to the others?"

"No I'll be fine, everything is ready except for the tea, you just go on into the room with David, I will see to everything, then if you want, you can give me a hand in with the trays and biscuits, when I am ready with the tea."

As he finished speaking Mitchell heard a car engine and saw head lights switch off, through the glass panelled door they had just come through.

"Oh! That must be Peter and Abigail." Sean turned to go back to to front door. "You carry on with what you were going to do, I will let them in."

"Oh! You'r a darling Anne." He answered and with the swaying limp walked into the kitchen. She turned to Mitchell.

"It's his leg, he won't admit it but, it hurts him a lot when the weather is wet or damp. He lost it in the troubles over in Belfast, some years ago. He used to be in the police force over there, so perhaps you both have a lot in common with each other. Although, I have told no one you are in the police force yet, all they know is that you have been getting a spirit from the other side trying to contact you, and it would mean a lot to you if we were successful tonight. I thought it best that way, and that they know nothing of what we both know. That being, the person trying to contact you was a murder victim, before we start tonight except, that it would be most important to us all if everyone who was available would come tonight."

They were all in a large sitting room, cups of tea in their hands, when Anne decided it was time for a formal introduction of David Mitchell to the group of people present.

"Well everyone thank you all for coming tonight at such a short notice, and a special thank you to Sean and Molly, for allowing us the use of their sanctuary this evening ." She put her hand on Mitchell's shoulder.

"Mr David Mitchell." Then the proper introductions began. There were sixteen people there counting himself. The ages ranged from the mid twenties to sixty plus, a mixture of both sexes. Two of them Mitchell recognized as being the ones with Anne Farr at the 'Harvest Moon' that evening, and were the two who had arrived just after them who Anne had answered the door to for Sean, Peter and Abigail Jones.

Anne Farr after a period where Mitchell accompanied her around the room speaking to those present and making himself known to them, although, still not divulging the fact he was a police officer suggested to him perhaps it might be better now to leave the rest for a short while and explain to him what they were going to do that evening. Which was, she told him, they would all go to a room they called a sanctuary, although it could also be called a church room or hall, where it was usually used to conduct church services, healing, development, and rescue circles.

Which, she added was likely to be required that evening. It was agreed they would start the attempt to contact the spirit world at eight thirty as previously arranged. He had been introduced to everyone there, and everyone seemed to be friendly towards him, generating a good ambience in the room.

Mitchell had been told by those there that there was nothing to be concerned about, and he would be in no danger whatsoever, as long as he did what he was told by Anne as the sitting, seance, or whatever he wanted to call the proceedings, and they were emphatic he not leave his seat under any circumstances, unless directed by spirit or anyone who may be under spirit control, and only then on approval of Anne or whoever was in charge of the proceedings. Anne also told him that there was no way of telling what form of communication would be used should any occur.

When anyone addressed him it was always as Mr Mitchell after a while he called every one's attention to himself, then spoke to them saying he would appreciate it if they all dropped the formalities and call him David or Dave which was the name he was most frequently addressed as. "Thank goodness for that." Remarked Sean. "Was it not like being a date in a coconut tree for you old son."

Every one laughed at his remarks, and after that any tense and strained politeness, even though friendly, disappeared immediately and things became the same as if he had known them for years instead of minutes.

At eight twenty five it was suggested they all make their way to the 'Sanctuary'. As they entered, it surprised Mitchell how large the room was, he remembered seeing Molly pulling the curtains across as they arrived, and after going into the other room assumed that the room they used as a sanctuary would be roughly the same size, when in actual fact it was more than double the size from what it appeared from the outside. It was obvious there had been a lot of building work done to extend the original size of the bungalow. He saw at the far end an altar, covered in a green and gold altar cloth, flowers in a vase of different species and colours stood, on tall white porcelain vase holders on each side and, in front of the altar, giving a splendid effect against the dark green curtains which stretched the whole length of the wall. A large polished brass crucifix stood in the middle of the altar in front of a large unopened Bible. In one corner of the room there were Chairs arranged in a circle, obviously taken from the rows of seats which were arranged in the sanctuary facing the altar. A large dark oak armchair with a cushioned seat and back was placed in front of the corner of the room and forming part of the circle. The circle was formed so that a person of the opposite sex was sat on either side of each other, as they took their seats Peter Jones sat on the oak arm chair. His wife on his right and a woman to his left alternating male and female around the circle, on each side of him sat Anne and a woman he had been introduced to as Sally Parsons, who he believed was single and aged about twenty four, she wore a long ankle length and loose fitting colourful dress. Her hair was long thick and jet black, which he believed to be her natural colour. She was adorned with bead necklaces around her neck, and had bangles on her wrists and ankles, and wore Arab style sandals. When he looked around at them all when he had first entered the first room she immediately seemed to be the odd one out with her appearance. His clothes, seemed to conform to with what everyone else there was wearing, and helped him fit in with everyone else as far as he was concerned, although Sally Parsons for some reason was thought highly of and had a wonderful personality, with an amazing sense of humour.

Everyone was now seated, and Dave Mitchell was running through his mind everything that Anne Farr had told him of what the procedure would be. First the lights were switched off leaving the glow from the red low watt bulb, it would take a little time she had told him for his eyes to adjust to the red glow in the room. Then once they were seated he was to remain seated and try if he could to meditate when the music started with his eyes closed. If he found he could not meditate, then just remain in his seat and watch the proceedings, and hope everything would be conducive for a link to be made with the spirit world, through one of those in the circle who would be at that moment the most receptive in what ever form of communication spirit found easiest for them. A prayer was said, and a short while later, soft flute music was heard, and he realized why Sean had placed the remote control on the floor at the side of his seat, with a stereo unit against the wall, the sounds of the music came from over head with the speakers set into the ceiling, which all in all made the effect of the sounds really relaxing. He had drifted along with the sounds of the music relaxed and his mind seemed as if it had been set free he thought of all kinds of things as the music continued, and as it did so, he came to a state of awareness and contentment he had not experienced before, nothing mind shattering but just the fact that he had been able to relax more from the time the music had started, than he had at any time for ages and was enjoying every moment of it, and in this euphoric state he had for the moment forgotten the real reason he had come there that night.

After a period of time, perhaps ten, twenty minutes, or even half an hour, his euphoric state was interrupted by some one breathing deeply, it seemed to be coming directly in front of him, he opened his eyes gradually, unsure really, as to whether he should or not. When they were open and his eyes were adjusted to the red glow of the light, he saw the deep breathing was coming from Peter Jones and, as he looked across he could see his eyes were closed, while at the same time he could feel the temperature in the room begin drop. As he noticed all this the music changed, growing louder and classical. He was not much up on classical music but guessed it would have been composed by some one such as Mozart, Handel, or Chopan, or some such composer, it could be anyone of them he would not have known, such was his knowledge of classical composers or music. The music grew louder and louder and as it did the room temperature dropped lower and lower, while the temperature dropped and he could feel the coldness around him he himself did not actually feel physically cold, in the sense to make him shiver or anything.

Mitchell was unsure at first whether it was a trick of the subdued and red lighting, or an effect of the lighting and the loud music combined, which made him begin to imagine things, but as he stared at Peter Jones he could see clearly there was something taking place. He then began to feel warmer and as he concentrated his gaze on Peter he leaned slightly forward in his chair, he then felt a touch on his arm, with what he was seeing it gave him a jolt.

"Don't be alarmed and don't worry and stay where you are, there is nothing to be concerned about. We were not expecting this tonight but now it is happening we are all privileged this evening, just sit and watch." Anne Farr whispered to him.

He looked around at everyone else in the room and saw they were also watching intently, there was a movement to his right and he saw Sean stretch out his arm with the remote in his hand and as he did so the the sound of the music gradually became softer until it was just about audible, staying that way for a short while longer and then sound of music had gone. In the silence which followed in which everyone could now hear the deep even breathing of Peter Jones. Every one else including himself were now breathing as softly as they could. He although being nervous, and unsure of what was in fact happening, stayed in his seat, while the others there seemed in awe of what they could see happening in front of them, as if, they, were seeing what was happening for the first time, but in actual fact it had been an occurrence in their circle more than a few occasions over a past number of years.

What he could see, he was unsure of, or it's purpose. There was some kind of substance which was coming from the mouth, nose, and stomach area of Peter Jones, it seemed to him to have the appearance of candy floss, and cotton wool, at first flowing and twisting until it resembled flowing muslin cheese cloth, spreading out and falling to the floor soundlessly, then it began to rise forming a kind of blanket of thick smoky formed material.

At this stage of the proceedings, Sean gave a signal of some kind to those sat nearest to Peter. Very slowly and quietly they began to get up out of their chairs and moved away from him, and coming into the centre of the circle while those who formed the rest of it began to do the same, moving themselves and the chairs until there were three rows facing Peter, with Mitchell being seated exactly where he was, with two rows of seats now in front of him, with the first row approximately ten yards from the feet of Peter Jones.

Anne Farr leaned to the side of Mitchell. Who by this time seemed to be frozen to his seat, and astonished at what he could see happening in front of him and then she began to whisper. "Don't worry, what you can see is ectoplasm, just keep watching we are lucky this evening, it is not very often we are privileged in this way without having had to prepare for it with a stage and so on, this was completely unexpected tonight by everyone here, it does sometimes happen like this, but only on very rare, no, extremely rare occasions, and for you to witness something of this nature participating in a sitting for your first time, it's incredible. Look! It's forming shape now! I wonder why there was not any advance information in a previous circle for us to prepare for a physical manifestation tonight as is usual, normally we are told by spirit before hand of such an occurrence planned well in advance, for the preparation side of it it's very unusual, well almost unknown of really.

The material or whatever one could call what Anne had termed ectoplasm began to swirl around and became thicker with every moment passing, but it was not just swirling around as would fog, there was definitely some kind of order about it, and seemed to be forming around and hiding from the sight of everyone there the physical form of Peter, until nothing of him could be seen. The next thing he saw was that the ectoplasm then began to swirl over the floor again a distance of at least six feet of each side of him, and about four feet in front of him and began to form in a more thicker and solid looking material although still obviously ectoplasm, until moments later there was in front of them curtains as would be seen on a stage of a small school theatre stretched from one side of the wall to the other. Then when it was fully formed there was absolute silence in the room, and a comfortable warmth could now be felt by Mitchell, the red light began to go dim, while at the same time the colour of the curtains gradually lost the red reflection they had been given by the light bulb. Then behind the hanging material the starting of a glowing effect began to take place, the colour of the curtains began to change. Not a brilliant light but subtle, seeming to radiate within the material itself, and glowing a pale green and not illuminating anything else other than it's own form, then once everything of the manifestation was complete the red light bulb became it's normal red, and illuminated everyone sitting facing the curtains but not the curtains themselves.

Suddenly the curtains moved, as if by unseen hands, the fabric divided just as if they were stage curtains in a theatre, to reveal standing in the centre of them the figure of a North American Indian dressed in full regalia, standing over six feet in height.

"It's Two Bears Peter's Main Guide and doorkeeper." Anne Farr whispered quietly to Mitchell. "He is here in the form of an Indian, which he was in a past life over two hundred years ago, we have seen him before he is a wonderfully enlightened spirit of the higher realms of the spirit world, just watch and listen to what he has to say to us."

David Mitchell looked on in awe at the manifestation in front of him, his mouth half open and dry, he felt no sense of fear, but at the same time could not believe what he was seeing.

He pinched his arm and ear hard, and felt the pain of each pinch as he did so. Never in his life had he experienced anything of the like before, he then just sat in his seat and watched.

Eventually the Indian guide spoke, his voice deep and clear, as he gave them all a blessing. Then he began to speak to them in the sense of a sermon, but unlike any he had heard before. As he spoke there was within every word a feeling of his love and concern for their well-being.

He also talked to them of the pressures of life and how those in spirit, were doing all that they could to bring harmony between different peoples of the world, and how things were not as they would wish them to be. But while, as he had said there were those in the spirit world were doing all that they could there was at large a menace of the ages which, had now been released back onto the earth plain, from the lower realms of the spirit world, and because of the licence of free will they were powerless to intervene. They, he told them, were gaining in power and influence, with the way the modern world had become through greed, selfishness, and peoples vanity and self importance, this is the food they have fed on for some time. "We have known of these things for quite a long while now, and the only thing we do is to try and instil into such as yourselves, the faith and the belief in the after-life, and give as much in the way of proof as we are allowed, so as to show others that death is but a continuation of life. There are we know amongst you those who doubt or rebuke the things of which I speak, some, through ignorance, many through fear of facing such truths, but when the dawn of truth is revealed to them when they do pass over to this side they are full of remorse, and up until this time they have always had the opportunity to return, for their own sakes, to try to build up a place as you say in 'paradise'.

In some ways you would be right, but, your conception of paradise falls well below the actuality of the state in which it is meant.

All through the ages of life on the earth plain there have been what you in your mortal state have seen as visionaries, and high beings of enlightenment, who have often at times put on the mantle of mortality, to try and guide you in preparation for the coming conflict. As you are living in what is predominantly a Christian state, you must recognize the teachings of an enlightened master, you would know as 'Jesus'."

"He and others have come among you in various forms and personalities, others are Mohamed, and Budda, and there have been many more but they have all spoken the same truth and it is the human failings which have not adhered to the teachings they have freely given in the love they have for you. Which in truth has been corrupted and changed to suit the different causes for individuals and en mass through out history. Promises have been broken causing more conflict with one people against another, the time spoken and warned of is at hand, there are others of all true faiths who give freely of their love to others, in the best way they are able due to circumstances this will be limited, and if you put to mind the recipient of that freely given love, is as important as the giver and remember love has many guises and, the only way it is known is by the genuine feeling given and received. There are others within all faiths no matter where ever the seed was sown have to grow within the same light. But if they only grow within the shadows of that light and are stunted and need help even with all that can be against them help is there, but water without sustenance of food within it is as hollow as words which are not spoken in the true light of love. Reflect on my words and see the true meaning in them."

"There are also we know, those on your plane of existence who hold no orthodox thoughts to any religion, of any beliefs, but because they feel right within their hearts and conscience, that there are things done in your world that they disapprove of, and feel the hurt within themselves that they are not in the position to change matters and have to accept what ever may be done, in the hope that things will change for the betterment of mankind eventually, without the intervention of war or threats of war, but by the eventual evolution of the spirit, so that love of one to another can enter and flower reflecting the true beauty of the real inner spirit and eventually know, that each one of you are but seeds blown to spread over your world from the same plant. For in every soul the seed of life is sown but, without the spark of spiritual awareness to germinate it, it will remain in barren land of it's own making, then wither and be no more."

He seemed to draw himself up to his full height, and looked directly at each of the sitters there, he smiled at them all, then he began to speak as if in authority to convey to them something suggestive, and important to them all.

"There is only one truth and, that truth is within each individual soul, and deep within each soul is the spark of true spirit, which once released in one lifetime will never be extinguished, and in your world today are a lot of beings not willing, or refuse to have the light of spirit into their hearts or souls for reasons of various degrees, from selfishness to power over others, not knowing because of their closed minds to spirit the power they may have achieved was only possible because of the ability they have been given as a gift from spirit and not just to be used for their own ends. They rarely do good for those who are subordinate to them. Once they have obtained a position they may have striven for and have lined their own nests then that is the total sum of their accomplishments, from business to politics all through the ages of time, they receive the same chances and, although they do, they never change, even when placed in a lower station of life they have the ability to rise to prominence, and when successful those who have learned spirituality then go by their inner feeling and then do help those more unfortunate than themselves. As each of those of the light are tempted, so shall all be tempted, to see if they are worthy to enter the kingdom of light forever. We in spirit can see there is sickness in your sphere and, the world as you have known it is dying. The battle of salvation has already begun, the weapons to be used against you can only be defeated by love and faith. Call on us when you are in dire peril and we will answer, but remember, "Your only weapons are love and faith in spirit, use them and you will not succumb."

He then looked directly at Mitchell, then beckoned him.

"Come to me." Mitchell was a little bewildered and unsure what to do, Anne whispered to him. "Go! It's all right because he has asked you."

Slowly he rose from his chair and walked towards the the spirit figure until he was just in front of him, and as he did so he could see that in all respects he was the same as everyone else in the room, and appeared as solid as himself 'Two Bears' spoke, while at the same time he held out his arms.

"Come, Touch me, see that I am not a figment of your imagination!"

Mitchell reached out cautiously and touched him with his fingers on his arms, prodded then he caught hold of his arms and felt the flesh, it felt warm and substantial as he squeezed with his hands, just the same as if it was the arms of anyone there in the room. As he did so he felt an overwhelming sense of joy and peace enter into him. Looking closer he could see the hairs, pores, and veins, the lines on his knuckles, his finger nails, the half moons clear and perfectly formed. He then looked at the face of the Indian, who as he gazed back, smiled at him, his eyes showing deep understanding and immense knowledge.

"Hold out your hand brother!"

Mitchell did as he was bid."

'Two bears' held his hand over Mitchell's and it seemed as if from nowhere, a large crimson orchid dropped onto it, looking as if it had been picked only a few seconds before, with glistening beads of fresh dew on the crimson trumpet.

"This I give you as testament of this night's happening, take it with you, you may keep it in your home for four days, and then it will return to where it has come from. Now return to your seat, because there is someone who wishes to speak to you on an urgent and vital matter." Mitchell returned to his seat, and after he had sat down 'Two Bears' gave them all a blessing, then moved behind the curtains.

Within seconds the curtains parted to reveal another figure the sight of which took Mitchell completely by surprise, even though the original idea was to make contact with him, he had not expected to see who he was now looking at. For there in front of him stood the figure of Paul Gage, although he looked nothing like the figure he had seen at the murder scene. There was not a sign of the injuries which had been inflicted on him as he stood there.

He looked at Mitchell from the centre of the stage.

"You know who I am?"

"Yes Paul. There was a lump in his throat as he answered.

"Good, please listen carefully to what I say there is not much time, because the instrument we are using is growing weak and will be very weak now when I have finished, we do not want to over tax him more than is necessary. I saw you when you came to where my body was found and followed you as much as I could trying to get your attention. I am sorry that you have suffered with my persistence in trying to get your attention. I was concerned that you were going to put yourself and your colleague in danger and possibly a lot of others in jeopardy before you realized what and who you were up against. The people responsible for my death are many and everywhere. I was abducted against my will and locked in a place of darkness for a long period of time, how long I have no idea. The people responsible are evil beyond belief, you must trust no one outside of this room for the time being and by that I mean do anyone.

Before my death I was offered all kinds of temptation to join them and eventually, when they found out I would not accept the things which were offered to me, they put me to death in a terrible and painful way, when it was all over I found myself in a kind of limbo, and could not seem to move from where I was found, but once those young men found me it seemed as if something happened and could move away from the immediate area, as I came back you and your colleague were just arriving, I tried to speak to you then and some of the others that were there but although I could hear everything that was being said, for some reason, you could not hear me. I knew I must have been dead because I could see my lifeless body hanging where it was found. I thank you now, for for telling my wife it was inadvisable for her to view my body and getting it identified by my relative, it was kind and considerate of you.

To join these people I had to renounce my Christian beliefs and accept their way of life and submit myself to their council of ethics which were none existent except for a way of evil indulgences, and to try and bring as many people as possible into the creed of their beliefs. Should I have done as they had asked, they told me, what ever I wished for would be granted. When I refused, they told me what they were going to do to me and I was frightened, I felt completely helpless they returned me to where they had held me for a short while. Then two people came for me and I was taken out to somewhere where I was blindfolded and led down steps there was a hollowness around me, I could tell by the sound of my footsteps it could have been a damp cellar although I had the impression it was somewhere larger than a cellar I was tied down onto a large what I felt could be a large cold table, after they stripped me of any clothing I was wearing they then they left me for a considerable period of time again perhaps two or more hours then I heard the sounds of trampling feet echoing around me, something heavy was placed over my face with the blind fold still in place then there was laughter and talking and then cheering began, and then I had to endure pain so agonizing I know I passed out but, as soon as I came around it began again how long I endured the pain they subjected me to, I really don't know, or how they did it, it seemed to come from within me and felt as if I was being torn from the inside, and no matter how I tried to twist away from it it just kept happening to me, I cried out for Jesus to help me to no avail and then suddenly it was all over and I was in darkness, then there was nothing. Eventually I became aware of something, I do not know what, then I had the sense of being drawn along in a direction, nothing physical you understand but I felt drawn, then there was light and suddenly I saw what I immediately knew to be my body suspended where I was found it seemed as if there was some kind of force that held me there. I tried as I said to move out of the area but could not, then came those who I have told you of and, they began to pour what looked to me like blood, but it was thicker and darker than I had ever seen, they poured it around where I was hanging and though they were speaking as they did so I could not understand any of the words they spoke. Then they left, and I was there until I was found and as soon as that happened I found I could leave the area.

Sean, the Irishman raised his hand to the figure, as if he was at a P.T.A. meeting at a school. "Who are these people you have been talking about who we will have to do some kind of combat against, and how will we know them?"

"If you begin to look for them it will be your undoing, for they will find out you are looking for them, then they will destroy you all, once they find out how much knowledge of them you have.

As for who they are, they are beings and entities who have dwelt in the lower realms of the spirit world, waiting patiently until the time was right for them to return, and to them time has no meaning for once becoming as they are they become timeless in the cycle of things, just as we are spirit, they are spirit but evil without conscience, love, or compassion and do not consider even those they associate with any degree of brotherhood, as they would do unto you so would they do unto each other their whole individual aim is to do as they want, and would use each other to accomplish it in anyway they would deem necessary, but remember that what ever they do to each other no matter what they may inflict there is no release of death for them, to them there is no such thing. Just a return to where they come from until the opportunity for them to return to the earth plain in another form of body. We who are mortal on the earth plain are just the same as them but for us we hope to achieve our goal of spirituality to enable us to rise to the next plain of our existence and as near as we can to attain spiritual perfection. But to them they have achieved their goal of perfection. Their ultimate and only goal left now is to control or destroy all life on earth as you now know it, because they believe it is their inheritance by right right of strength."

He was silent and took the time of the silence to look around at those he was facing, then he spoke again.

There are others who now know of their existence, and we from spirit have been guiding them to you, they have a lot to learn from you but you will also have a lot in your favour from them, contact should be made soon, it has been difficult to accomplish because they are unaware at this moment in time of the evil they have stumbled upon, although when in spirit they have prepared themselves for this life through many past lives to eventually face the perils of this life you will all have to endure and, the first thing they must learn is about themselves, and the attitudes they now hold but, we will be trying to give them understanding eventually of themselves, with your help. The past is the key to yours, theirs, and all of mankind's salvation.

More than that, we are not permitted to say, except the force of evil has everything in their favour to accomplish their complete return which will bring mayhem, and they will have at their disposal the greatest weapons, in man's own weakness to achieve their aims, poverty, greed, and absence of spirituality.

Anything or anyone they cannot control they will destroy, or convert to their cause by promises or possession of bodies as temporary hosts for their eventual return. If they succeed then eventually the world will become a barren waste, and theirs."

He was silent again for a short while, and looked at each person in turn, then asked them to say a prayer for him, as he would for all of them, that they would be successful, and then he wished them well, and that now he had completed his task he would be able to move onto his next realm of advancement. He went behind the curtain as it was seen to open, then he was out of sight of everyone. Then suddenly the curtains began to distort and lose their form, then disintegrated until there was nothing there, except Peter Jones sitting slumped in the armchair, with his eyes closed breathing deep and evenly as if he was asleep.

After a short while his eyes opened and he began to stir, lifted his head as his eyes began to focus on everyone there, his wife Abigail held a glass of water to him and he began to sip from it. The sitting/seance was over.

CHAPTER 24

Dave Mitchell was quiet, his mind could not fully comprehend what he had actually witnessed, even though he was looking at the flower he had been given by "Two Bears", at the home of Sean and Molly Conway, the stem of which he had wrapped in cooking foil as had been suggested, by one of the people he had met there. He had found out Sean and Mollies surname when they had spoken for a short while after the meeting, when Sean was told by Anne he was a serving police officer, and yes he had thought. "They did have a lot in common." He found that out when they began talking together, by the time the evening was over he found he had developed quite a liking for the "Take me as you find me loud, Irishman," in spite of his loud manner there was obviously a lot that was bravado in his manner, hiding quite a different personality when one got to know him better. He left their house with an open invitation to visit them anytime, and that he would be welcome.

"What are you thinking Dave, you look as if you wish tonight had never happened, I hope I have not done wrong in taking you there and introducing you to everyone."

"No, No...it's just that it is so hard for me to take in everything that happened there tonight. The Indian, Paul Gage, and this." He held up the the flower towards her. "How often do you hold those meetings, and things such as have happened tonight occur?" He spoke with a casual voice but inside was still feeling the sensation he had felt while in the midst of the session.

"I suppose it is about six months since anything nearly as significant as tonight has been experienced, by any of us there. Some people have sat in circles for up to ten years and longer, before experiencing anything near to what you have experienced tonight, it was extraordinary to say the least on a first time of attending a meeting, closed or otherwise. There are members in this movement who never do experience what you have witnessed in the whole of their lives, even for as long as fifty or more years as practising Spiritualists. I must say that I for one, think you are very fortunate to have experienced what you have tonight on a first meeting, and have no explanation as to why that should be, as far as I am aware it is unknown of before, and to have been called up to touch the spirit guide of one of the sitters at the same time, with an 'apportation' of a flower as well, well, I just don't know, or understand the true significance of the occasion. I had been sitting in circles for over ten years myself before I even experienced the forming of ectoplasm, and, to tell you the truth I was as surprised as you at what has happened with some one such as yourself present at a meeting for the first time."

"What were you expecting to happen there tonight, other than what did happen?"

"Certainly not a physical manifestation of the magnitude we saw tonight, and that's certain for everyone else who was there." She quickly looked across to him and smiled. "At least now you know a lot more about what I have told you and what you were having some difficulty in accepting, your ears and eyes, as is often said, don't lie."

He looked at the flower in his hand, then straight out of the car windscreen ahead, watching the white lines in the centre of the road as they flashed by in the beams of the head lights, silent and with his personal thoughts of the evening again.

As the car drew up to the front of the entrance to his house, he looked at his watch and saw the time had just turned eleven o'clock.

"Is it too late for you to have a drink in my house, before we say good night."

"I would like to Dave, but I have to be up early in the morning, and it would be too late for me if I stayed, we would only start talking and you know how time goes by when that happens. I am free tomorrow evening though, how about if you have nothing planned and are free come to dinner at my house for the evening. Peter and Abigail are coming, we arranged it a week or so ago, and there is always enough for more people than I invite. Normally I end up putting three or more meals in the deep freeze and have them my self at a later date when I am alone."

He decided there and then to accept her invitation for the following evening, it had been a long time since he had eaten a meal cooked by a woman, and a night with her was something he would welcome, even if there was to be others there with him. At least he hoped they could have a pleasant evening together, and he did enjoy being in her company. He said good night to her after accepting her invitation for the following evening. She had given him her address which was only a couple of streets away from him so his car would not be necessary.

As he sat down in his sitting room, his mind went back to the evening's seance or what ever it was, nothing could get the experience out of his mind. Of standing there in front of the Indian, touching, and feeling him, and then the orchid as it had dropped into his hand the way it had, seemingly from nowhere. He sat with a glass of 'Chivas Regal' sipping the smooth liquid, and savouring the taste as it passed over and under his tongue as he savoured the individual flavour of his favourite whiskey.

Sitting in silent contemplation the evening seemed unreal. The loud ticking of the wall clock seemed to interfere with his train of constructive thinking. He gazed over to the mantle piece, where he had put the flower in a small glass long necked fluted vase he had got out of the cabinet which, contained such glass ware. Thinking at the time it was the first time he had ever seen a flower in it. Having always since they had bought it used it only as an object to fill the glass cabinet with other small items and trinkets.

"What? He was thinking. "Was the meaning to it all." He tried to remember what Paul Gage had said to them all, but because of the way everything had happened, so completely unexpected so to speak, there was not much of what he had said he could recall, 'perhaps' it would all come back to him when it was discussed again. They would probably make it one of the main topics of conversation at the meal table the following evening. He took a final swallow from the glass and found he had already drained it.

Deciding it was about time to turn in for the night he was about to get up from the chair and take the glass out to the kitchen, when he felt movement behind his head which startled him, making him jump quickly out of the armchair, then broke into laughter as he saw it was Millie. She had jumped up onto the back of the armchair to let him know she was there. Probably because she had heard him come in and he had not shouted to see if she was home.

He went to the kitchen washed the glass under the tap, filled up Millie's dish with dried food, and then went to bed.

****

"This is nice." He thought, he had not been invited out for dinner for such a long time, and had been looking forward to the evening all day. "Whatever Anne has prepared for us in the kitchen sure has a nice aroma."

Mitchell looked over towards the kitchen as Anne came through the door holding a large lid covered tureen on a tray and placed it on the table, followed by Abigail who had insisted on helping and had brought out another which was the same size and design as the one Anne had already placed there. While Peter came in with a decorked bottle of wine and placed it on the centre of the table.

"I'll leave it there, to breath for a while, then pour out as we begin to eat, how does that sound Dave?"

"That's fine with me." He replied, his mouth began to water in anticipation of the meal which had been prepared and placed on the table before him. The aroma began to make his stomach rumble, as hunger became more intense, after having no more than a couple of digestive biscuits at lunch time and just a couple of slices of buttered toast at breakfast, afraid he would not do justice to a well prepared meal, and perhaps offend his hostess by not eating much in the evening.

He could see she had gone to a lot of trouble preparing the meal and table before they had arrived. Everything was laid out and arranged, wine glasses, serviettes, willow patterned dinner service, which matched the tureens which matched right down to the serviette rings, and coffee cups.

The meal began with prawn cocktail, served in small porcelain dishes from the same dinner service, followed by Beef Wellington, with old flowery textured roasted potato and minted new potatoes, the veg. consisted of peas with pieces of smoked bacon mixed in, covered with a light buttery sauce, peppered mashed carrot and, swede covered with the same sauce but with added sweetcorn crushed into the sauce, done with the expertise and accomplishment of someone who was a serious hostess when having decided to hold a dinner for friends, putting everything into the preparation and cooking of the meal, to make the evening a success, the third course consisted of caramel torte. All of the evenings fare was prepared and cooked by Anne, even the horseradish sauce which accompanied the main course of the evening, and received appreciative commendations from her guests.

The wine flowed and the evening became more enjoyable and they began to talk of the previous evening.

"You know when I got home, I listened to the tape Sean had recorded and it struck me, what I mean is, it was a similar to an experience we had, Abigail and I that is, had some years ago now, but it still sticks in my mind from time to time. We never really got to the bottom of the mystery it presented us with." Peter looked at his wife. "Do you remember the case I am thinking of Abigail?"

His wife became noticeably uncomfortable as he brought the subject up.

"I don't think I will ever be able to forget it Peter. It will always be to me an episode in our life we could have both done without. Anyway we have had no incidents since the last, and that was quite a few years ago now, but I agree some of the things we were told of by the spirit of Paul Gage did seem to have a familiar ring to them. Except in our case the contactee insisted he was not deceased, and became quite agitated when we tried to explain to him that he being able to contact and speak to us in the way he had was at the time impossible, if he were indeed alive."

Dave Mitchell had listened to what the pair had said and his experience of the night before was as clear then as it was the previous evening, and could not in any way or form have any reason to doubt now anything these people spoke of. His own curiosity was aroused and wanted to know more about what they had been remembering. Anne Spoke to them, before Mitchell could speak.

"What case was that then Peter? I have not heard you speak of it and it has certainly made an impression on Abigail."

Both husband and wife looked at each other.

"As I have said it happened some years ago now." He looked at his watch and saw they had been there for one and a half hours, and as dinner had been eaten, suggested they clear away the table and fill the dish washer with the plates and cutlery and other things to be washed, then sit down in the lounge with a cup of coffee each and he would tell them both about the events leading from the scrawled note from Ken Barber, when they had returned from Christmas shopping those years before.

They were all settled in the lounge as Peter Jones began to tell them of the time from receiving the note from Ken the carpenter.

"The following weekend we had made contact with a spirit person who gave his name as Raymond Steven Hayman, and that he had been a tenant who had lived in the two story apartment some years before, which was at that time leased to Ken's daughter and son-in-law. We gained as much information from him as we could at that time. He had worked, he told us as a 'Core Drilling' operative, he told us quite a few things when we asked him specific questions about himself, which he answered freely and without hesitation. But after an hour or so of communication he told us that if he was deceased as we had been implying since the contact with him. Why! He asked, he could not remember anything about how he had died, and was not fully convinced by us that he was dead, even though we asked him how he could explain, or account for the way he had been communicating with us for the time that he had. He was sure he told us if he had died he would have remembered at least something had it been so.

Anne had been listening intently to Peters account of what had happened and was said at the apartment.

"Sometimes it can happen that a person can pass into spirit without realizing they have done so. When this happens it is usually because of a sudden passing such as an accident, heart attack or brain haemorrhage, or some thing similar. Also there have been incidents where communicators have died as a result of being a casualty on a battle field, and have wandered around seemingly lost for years and do not realize they are deceased. There have been accounts of such things happening during many rescue circles. Could this have been one more such an occasion?"

"That was exactly my reasoning at the time but later investigation of the facts as he had given us only made the matter of his death more confusing."

"How so?"

"Well it was really strange. When I first made contact in the kitchen while I was with ken, everything seemed a straight forward case of making use of the services of a rescue circle, which we did try at the time I am telling you of. The only trouble was, there seemed to be no help from the spirit world while we were holding the rescue circle. Which to those there with us, who at that time had more experience than myself with such matters were totally perplexed. They had never experienced the like of such a situation before and after doing all that they could at the time to help the spirit of Raymond Hayman, and falling well short of a result of any satisfaction, it was decided to see with the information we had received that evening if we could find out anything more about the supposed communicator.

So with that in mind the circle was closed with the promise that we would return in a few days time, when we would have had the opportunity to check up on the identity of him and perhaps find an account of his demise, then with the proof of the event we could confront him with it and hope for a positive result, and with spiritual intervention help him to progress onto the spiritual plane he may have achieved so far."

Dave Mitchell had listened to the conversation and had been taking in everything that had been said.

"How many were in the house when you held this....what do you call it,...a recovery circle?"

The others smiled at him.

"Rescue circle. Is what we call a situation where a spirit of a person may have become earthbound. It can be for all kinds of reasons, unaware of what has happened to them, sometimes it could even be just the fact, that they are aware they have passed over into spirit, and have no wish to leave a place or area where they have enjoyed their happiest times."

"Or a tragedy of some kind, or just to stay near their loved ones they may leave behind on them passing into the spirit world." "There are so many different reasons." Peter had added to what had been said by Anne.

"So....what did you find out about this Raymond? Did he exist or what?"

"Oh! he existed all right. Exactly as he had told us, his statements to us about himself all checked out. But there was nothing we could find out about his death anywhere."

He looked over to his wife, and Dave followed his gaze.

"Go on Peter! You have started, It's best you tell them everything now or they will only keep wondering."

"Do you remember when we first met Anne?"

"Yes. It was at a psychic fair. You were both with an old friend of mine. Clarisa Butland."

"She introduced us, at that time Abigail and I had just become seriously involved with each other. It was towards the end of October of that year." He turned towards his wife smiling. I am sure of the month because it was about three weeks after a coach trip we had with the church to the sea side."

His mind went back to the magical moment as they kissed on the sea shore for the first time, and admitted the feelings they had for each other, and how the relationship grew stronger as time went by culminating in the day they were married and bringing them together as two halves making a complete whole.

Then he remembered what he was talking about and he became serious again and seemed deep in thought, as if remembering something he had forced out of his mind and was reluctant to bring it forward again.

"Clarisa was one of the participants in the rescue circle on both occasions. Do you know where she is now?"

"Well I heard she was in psychiatric hospital somewhere, a nervous breakdown. I was told by someone it escapes me now who told me, it was so long ago, she could be well by now."

"I am afraid she will never get well again according to the psychiatric doctors medical report on her. She it seemed was not suffering from a nervous breakdown disorder, and is now in a secure unit for the mentally insane, with it has been said no chance of ever being released."

"I swear it was all connected with her doing the investigations into the history of Raymond Hayman. As also I am sure was the suicide of Peers Sleeman. He was at the circle also and worked with Clarisa when she was trying to find out what she could about Hayman, they were looking into the matter together." Abigail's words were quietly spoken and showed she did not really relish the fact they were discussing a subject they had left buried for years. It made her shudder at the thought they had somehow unearthed it, and could now come back to haunt her as it had for some months in the past. It felt to her that by discussing it they could somehow evoke another episode as horrific and as frightening as they had the second time they had held the rescue circle in the apartment those four years or so ago, when they got no answers to the so called spirit of Raymond Hayman."

Peter was concerned for her when he saw that she was obviously on edge talking about the incident which had happened it seemed so long before.

"We won't talk about it anymore if it is making you feel uncomfortable Abigail, if you would rather. Peter can tell us about it another time when he is on his own with us."

Abigail got to her feet reached over for the coffee cups they had emptied and placed them on the tray nearby.

"No that's all right Anne, I will just go out and make a refill for each of us. Go on Peter tell them the rest of what we know, and what was similar about what Paul Gage told us last night. Tell it and get it over with, who knows it may become important later on."

"As I have already told you, we came to the decision to hold another circle, to try and help the spirit of Raymond Hayman, everything was progressing well, contact with him had been made and communication in the circle with those in the spirit world was clear. As we seemed to be making progress, we asked him to tell us the last thing he could remember before he found himself in his present state. It was then that things began to go wrong. First he told us it was hot and they had stopped for some lunch where they were drilling. He remembered returning to the site where the work was taking place and standing there after guiding the drill head down into the ground. Then there was silence. The room began to take on a darkness, not in the sense of growing dark, but a feeling of heaviness which at the same time seemed to manifest a...a...presence and to be honest a sense of darkness all of us could feel, and with that a sudden feeling of consternation. All in the room felt it more or less the same time. We heard nothing more from him, then within a short space of time there was an intense coldness in the room and at the same time a feeling of irrational fear seemed to come to us all, suddenly the table we were sat around started knocking and moving, as if there was someone rocking it from side to side violently. Then the next thing was we all saw it rise quickly into the air, then with a tremendously loud crack it split asunder into six or seven pieces. Each piece flew in different directions of the room. One of the sitters received a bad gash in his arm and could not remember it happening or explain it at the time, we all presumed it had happened when a piece of the table had probably hit him. There was total panic among us in the room.

There was one other thing which happened that night. What or who it was we do not know. When we had all scrambled out of the room and looked back through the door way we saw some of the broken bits of the table on the floor but also there was what could only be described as a large dark shadow which was swaying and moving around in there. Then we could all hear voices screaming and shouting, words in language we could not understand but sounding off in an aggressive tone. Then a horrible stench. The smell of which was indescribable."

Abigail came through the door then and had heard the last words Peter had spoken. As she placed the tray of cups on the table. Her husband stopped and held out his hand to her, he could see she was obviously upset by the memory of a time she had always tried to forget, but had always remained there in some dark recess of her mind.

CHAPTER 25

Deciding they would all go ahead with Charlie's plan, all three men walked out of the main gate together, and upon reaching the main road turned in the opposite direction of where Charlie had seen the activities the night before.

Walking for about three quarters of a mile and completely out of sight of the manor, they climbed over a hedge-bank beside the road, then began to circle back towards the coppice where Charlie had followed the torch lights the night before, using them as cover as they made their way towards the shed in the field in the hope of not being seen. Twenty minutes later they came to the edge of the field on which the shed stood. They worked their way around the edge of the field until they were sideways on to the shed and had a more clearer view of the area which surrounded it. They decided to settle down and watch for a while to make sure there was no one else around, before venturing closer. They settled down behind the small bank on the edge of the coppice while they waited, Choco produced a bar of chocolate and offered a piece to the other two, while Charlie opened his tobacco tin to make a smoke, offering the tin over when he had taken what he wanted from it. After the smoke and a chocolate snack, Choco was about to get up from where he had sat down, suggesting there did not appear to be anyone else other than themselves around and perhaps they did not bother with the shed during daylight hours for some reason. As all three got up to their feet there was a sound of a motor vehicle, which seemed to be heading in their direction.

"Get down! Get down!" All three hit the ground together. "There must be a road to the field from the main road but, I cannot see any entrance to the field any where can any of you two?" Tim and Charlie looked around as best they could from where they lay, and all three could see nowhere except for where Charlie had followed the residents into the field in the night, and that was not even remotely near wide enough for a vehicle to travel on." Choco lay in a half raised position his arms supporting the top half of his body to enable to see over the shallow bank they were hiding behind, listening, his mouth wide open, and ears straining to catch any sound.

"It's all right! It's all right, it's coming from the other end of the field, there must be a lane or a track over there. He inched his way forward then raised his head looking in the direction of where the sound was coming from, just enough to see but not enough to be seen himself, the others followed suit, and as they did so, saw reflections of light from the wind screen or side window of a 'Ford transit' van. As they were watching it suddenly stopped, and the engine was switched off.

"Oh shit!" What do you think Choco? Do you think someone knows we are here and they have sent someone after us?"

"I don't know! But get ready to scarper, just in case." As he spoke the sounds of doors opening could be heard, all three were preparing to move back into the tree cover behind them.

Tim and Charlie had already begun to move in the direction of the trees, when Choco stalled them.

"Wait!" He called in a loud whisper.

The other two halted in there tracks and crawled back to Choco's position behind the bank. Voices drifted over towards them, but whoever was speaking were to far away for them to hear what was being said. They lay there, their eyes just above ground level, gruff loud voices sounding angry in tone drifted across on the wind but still they could not understand what was being said. A crashing sound and rustling of shrubbery, as part of the hedge was pulled apart at the side of where the vehicle was parked, and then someone came sprawling through the gap made, followed by two other men. The first man through the hedge was lifted roughly onto his feet by one of the other two, then forced him forward with a hard shove in the back, while the other began to look around the immediate area. Choco an Co. kept watching, sure they could not be seen from their vantage point.

"Look! His hands are tied behind his back. What the fucks going on?" Charlie whispered.

They continued to watch, as the two followed the man who was obviously their prisoner and, as they were mid way from the van and the shed the man decided to make a break for his freedom, while the two with him were talking and laughing together some distance behind him. He turned and started running towards where Choco, Charlie and Tim were hiding and watching, they could see the pain and fear on his face as he made the attempt, and the startled and disbelief on the faces of the two following as he made his escape bid. Charlie was unsure, as were the other two with him over what to do, if the man reached where they were, suddenly he grabbed a broken branch which lay near him, not realizing it was decayed and and as light as balsa wood, all he could think of was he had something in his hand should the other two find them, if the running man reached them. But the man was brought down twenty yards from where they were hidden by one of his pursuers.

All three breathed a sigh of relief, in one sense that the man had not made it, but felt pity for him in another. The man made a futile attempt to kick out at the man who had brought him down, only to receive a kicking from both of them. Eventually he was hauled to his feet and roughly shoved in front of his two captors towards the shed again, while at the same time suffering more blows to the body, as they tried to make him move faster.

Charlie meanwhile, still holding the rotten branch, his knuckles white, as he still gripped it so tightly with the tension he was still feeling over their near discovery.

"Phew! That was close and no mistake!" He muttered quietly to himself.

"What did you plan to do with that? Offer it to them as fire wood!"

Charlie looked to where Choco had indicated, to see the piece of wood he had been holding so tightly in his hand, was now broken when he had raised himself up enough to watch what was happening to the man after he had been caught, and was now just holding just ten inches of the piece of the branch in his hand. Whether it was the nervous tension after the situation, or just the fact that they had not been discovered by the men both could not really say, but both started to snigger at each other. "I don't know what you two find so funny, didn't you see the size of those guys, a sledge hammer would hardly have been able to make a dent in them, especially the tallest of the two."

"Slow him up a bit if you could hit him on the foot though Tim!"

Choco was trying in his own way, and the only way he could think of was to try and make light of the situation now that the crisis of possible discovery was now over. They continued watching and saw the men enter the shed, closing the door behind them.

"What shall we do try to get closer and see what is going on in there?" Tim was feeling they should try something to try to rescue the man they had seen taken into the shed.

"Hold your horses Tim, It might be better to wait things out for a while, and see what develops, and we don't know if there is anyone else about, or likely to turn up, it might make things difficult for whatever we decide if we were seen half way across the field. It might be a better idea if we move out of line of the window, then, after we wait for a while, we could perhaps sneak up close, then look in to see what can be seen inside the shed. They had moved from where they were, to a position so as to be on the blind side of the window. While they were debating how long they should wait before moving in close to see if there was any thing to be seen through the window. They heard and then saw the shed door open, and the two men they had just watched take their prisoner into the shed appeared, followed by five others, two men and three women, one of the men was carrying a briefcase, while a dark headed woman carried what looked to be some kind of large thick ledger.

"Ay! Ay! Charlie there's the redhead 'Ratley' you'v had or have not had. She is a nice bit of cracklin I must admit but, it certainly does look as if she is up to her pretty little neck in what's going on at the manor."

Charlie looked over towards the shed and saw the redhead he had, had, the dream about, although now he knew more about what had been going on at the manor, he was more than sure it had not been a dream but, could not explain to himself, let alone anyone else how he could have functioned sexually and yet be so confused whether it was a dream or not, in a way he was feeling stupid while at the same time angry with the woman if she had actually in some way been able to have had a sexual relation ship with him and had been able to use something, some how, which enabled him to function at the time and, yet leave him in such a confused state he was unsure as to whether he had dreamed it or not. As he looked at the others with her, there was something else which caught his attention.

"Choco!....the guy with the brief case, I know him from some where." He tried to think but he could not remember where he had seen him before but, he was certain it was not at the manor house.

Before he could think any more about the man and where he had seen him, the question he was still asking himself was answered by Choco.

"The D.H.S.S. that's where you would have seen him, because he dealt with me at the same place, I saw him when I made the claim to be able to stay at the manor. Charlie remembered then, he had been the person the woman had taken the forms to and he had signed them at the time for some reason.

"Bloody hell! They seem to be everywhere, perhaps you are right about Tony Howard's death not being an accident, and everything he has told us is just the tip of some kind of fraud scan which has been going, and he was getting a little too close to the truth!"

"Come on Tim! It's more serious than that, and you know it!

"Just the episode with with the guy taken struggling into the shed earlier tells us that, let alone, everything else we have found out which has been going on."

The two large and heavy set men walked ahead of the others towards where the transit van was parked, while the women and men followed them.

"They must be all going away in the van together, and must have left the guy they had tied up in the shed. Let's just wait here a while before we make a move, there could also be someone left in the shed with the guy they had tied up, we have to be careful what ever we do.

A slamming of the van doors was heard and then the sound of the engine starting up, shortly followed by the movement of the vehicle reversing it's way back the way it had come, and away from the three watching pairs of eyes. "Who want's to be the one to take a shufty into the inside of the shed though the window while two of us keep watch?" No one answered Choco's question. "Oh well! I suppose it's down to me, but make sure you keep your eyes peeled while I make my way across to the side of the window."

Choco walked over to the shed as casually as he could, although, his eyes were non-stop looking around him. Reaching the back of the shed without being challenged by anyone, he then moved around to one of the side windows and furtively looked through it into the interior of the shed, but could see nothing of the man or anyone else inside, cautiously he moved to the other side and looked through the other window, but again there was nothing of the man to be seen. He put his hand up motioning for the other two for them to remain where they were. He then quickly made his way to the door and tried the handle, to find it opened easily and and that there was not even a lock of any description there. He quickly stepped inside closing the door as he did so, and stood inside the gloomy interior of the shed, when he had become used to the lack of lighting he could see it was packed with all kinds of farm implements and stores, rolls of barbed wire, cattle salt licks, saws and many more implements used in farming, there was also a large pallet with bags of chemical fertilizer stacked six bags high. But there was not a sign of the man they had seen brought there!

After looking out of the windows to make sure the coast was clear he opened the door and beckoned the others to come over to him.

"Well! Where is he? He was not with the others when they came out of here, was he!" Charlie, had voiced the same thoughts as Choco had when he had first entered the shed, and saw there was no sign of the man they had all seen taken there.

Tim had said very little up until then, but had been thinking all the time while the others were talking.

"Look both of you, we all saw him come in here, and he did not come out with the others as you have said, he can't have just disappeared into thin air, can't walk through walls, and what were those others doing here, in a shed, in a field, and in the middle of nowhere. Those others we saw come from here, they might have been here all night from the time Charlie saw them here last night. There is no way that I can believe they have stayed in a shed all night just waiting to be picked up and taken back to the manor this morning. There is only one conclusion as far as I can see, and that is the shed is a cover in more ways than one." He then pointed his finger downwards at the floor.

"There Has to be a trap door here somewhere, let's just look for where it could be. I suggest we start with that stack of bags there, every thing else here is on shelves, and underneath them are just plain floor boards, and they are all in order as far as I can see in this light. So, I suggest we start looking before someone comes back and finds us here. We won't be any good to the guy if we are caught here and, end up in the same situation as we saw he was in, will we?"

Charlie moved to the stack of bags and began to search on his hands and knees, while the other two kept a watch out of the windows. As he searched for any sign of some kind of exit around them he noticed two thin strips of metal underneath the wooden pallet which were not noticeable until he had got down onto his knees. He got to his feet and caught hold of the side of the stack and gave a push, but it would not budge, moving around to the rear of the stack he tried again, putting his shoulder to it this time and pushed as hard as he could. As he did so it moved with ease in the direction of the door, to reveal below it a large gaping square hole with steps leading down below the floor of the shed. Not expecting the stack to move so easily, Charlie almost went to carry on with another step forward, and just stopped himself in time from falling down the hole, onto the steps. He stood still for a moment to catch his breath, then turned towards the other two, who had heard the stack move and the scrambling of his feet as he had avoided falling down the hole, and were both looking in his direction. "Come over here and take a look at this!" He called to them, stepping back from the stack so as to give them a good look at the stairway leading below the floor boards of the shed. They both gave a last look around out of the windows and then moved to where Charlie was.

"It's light down there, there must be some kind of power source, for electricity to be installed, perhaps a cable from the manor."

"It's not powerful enough to be coming off of a mains power supply, more than likely they have a generator down there somewhere, just large enough to have lighting. What do you think Charlie, are you game for us to go down below, to see what we can find down there?"

Charlie looked at his friend, said nothing but, nodded his agreement to the question. He looked around the shed for a weapon of some kind to use if the need arose for them to protect themselves when they ventured down into what ever lay below them. But could see nothing in the shed appropriate for him to take with him. So he just moved towards the steps in front of Choco. Tim was about to follow him down the steps when Choco held him back.

"Hold on Tim, let's not be rash about this, now we have come this far." Tim stopped giving Choco a questioning look.

"You just asked Charlie if he was game to go and he has agreed what's the matter?"

"What happens if we are all down below and someone comes? We would all be caught like rats in a trap. I think it might be better for one of us to remain here and keep a lookout just in case, and once we are down the steps and if some one does come, you can push the stack over the hole and hide away in here, there are plenty of places for you to hide, that way we would know if we hear anyone coming it will not be you and we will be warned and have time to be prepared to deal with whoever it may be."

"All right! If you want it that way but, should anyone come I just hope it isn't those two we saw earlier, for your sakes, because, you will be well and truly in the shit, if they do."

Choco and Charlie ventured down the steps leaving Tim above, to keep eye out for anyone who may come while they were below. When they reached below they found themselves in the passage way the drillers had found years before. They walked along until they reached the cavern, which was also dimly lit. As they stood in the entrance they immediately saw the stone altar at the far end of it. As they looked they saw movement near it, their hearts missed a beat, until they saw it was the person they had seen brought across the field to the shed. He was against the side near corner of the altar. As they watched they could see he was trying to do something, because of the jerking his body was making in the process. He had not seen or heard them and, it was only as they approached near to him he saw them, and became frustrated at his failed attempt to free himself. His face dripping with perspiration, while a look of defiance towards and at two more of those who he thought were part of the evil people responsible for the situation he was in, and had come with evil intent, he decided that they should not see anything but defiance until the end from him, although inside, he was deeply afraid of their intentions, he thought they had planned for his end.

"So now it's my turn! Go ahead and do your worst, and may the lord see you for what you are, the spawn of evil." "It's all right mate, calm down, we are here to try and get you out of here, stay still while I cut you free."

Charlie kept watch around the cavern hoping there would be no one else around, while Choco produced a penknife.

"Ask him if he is on his own down here." He whispered to his friend.

Choco began cutting the bonds of the man with the knife which was usually used for apples and other uses, the blade was not razor sharp but had a keen enough edge for the job in hand. He managed to cut the priest free quickly, and got him to his feet.

"How are you? Can you walk? We saw the beating you were taking by those who brought you here, did they hit you about any more when they brought you down here?"

The priest could not take everything in at once, so sure was he, when he first saw the two now freeing him, that his time had come, he was initially confused when he saw Choco produce the knife and he had not taken in all that Choco had spoken to him.

"I'll be fine in a little while my legs are numb they tied them up tightly."

"Give them a rub to help the circulation return, we might not have long before someone else arrives. See how well you can walk on them, the sooner we are out of here the better." He put his arm around the man to give a little support while the priest began to take a few steps.

"Charlie give me a hand here, let's see if we can make better progress with him between us.

With the two of them supporting him they made quite a spectacle, and it was reminiscent of some friends helping a friend home after a night out and who was suffering the worse for drink after closing time on a Saturday night.

By the time they had reached half way through the passage to where the steps led up to the shed the priest had begun to walk unaided. They both helped him up the steps and into the shed where Tim was standing near one of the windows still keeping a look out.

"How is he? What was down there? Tim asked as they walked across the floor of the shed, half way across Charlie went back to the pallet of bags and replaced it over the hole.

"Just in case any one comes and happens to look in the shed, the hole will be covered just as it was left, and if they do only come for a look it will give us just a bit extra time to get clear of the area." He spoke as the others wondered why he had gone back.

"We will tell you when we get away from here Tim." Choco answered Tim's question as he peered out of the half opened door.

"Have you noticed anyone around while you have be keeping an eye open up here Tim?"

"No not a bloody soul since you have been gone, but I think we should move away from here as soon as we can."

Moments later after vacating the shed, they were back into the edge of the trees, where they had watched as the priest was brought down and taken to where they had found him.

"Well! What now Choco?" Tim was looking back from where they had come from. "I think it might be wise to go back the way we came and miss the area of the manor all together, and then make our way into the town to the police station, inform them of what we know and then let them deal with whatever it is that has been going on. What do you say, Choco?"

"No! You cannot do that! Father O'Connell seemed to come to life and in doing so was thinking how lucky he was to be free of his captors. "We can't trust anyone, especially the police force they would find out in no time where we were, and we would not have a chance a second time. The people holding me told me they had people everywhere, and after what I have seen and experienced, I am more than inclined to believe them. The first thing we must do is to get away from here as far as we can, as quickly as we can."

Charlie looked at his companions and then at the priest.

"Who are you mate? Why were they holding you? Did you find out about some of the scams they are up to, is it some kind of large scale fraud?"

Choco patted Charlie on the shoulder. "Come on Charlie I'm as curious as you are but the only thing that concerned us was, we saw he was in a bit of bother and felt it right to try and help, he can tell us when we are away from here, and when he is ready.

"That's all right. My name is Father George O'Connell, and as for why they wanted me, that must keep until we are well away from here, and a safe distance from those who were holding me. Once they find me gone they will be looking everywhere, so, I say we should move now to where ever you think might be safe until we figure out what the best course of action might be for us all."

In an hour and half they had travelled a fair distance on the ground, but because of having to detour away from isolated farms and other dwellings, or possible signs of field workers, or anyone else they had seen, they had not covered very much in the sense of distance from where they had rescued the priest. As darkness was approaching they could see in the dusk light, an orange glow of half a dozen street lights in the distance of a small village or hamlet. When they were about half a mile from the village Choco suggested they make for a hay barn nearby to hold up for a while.

The others looked at him puzzled, and wondering what good it would do, saying they were not far enough away from the manor to be out of danger as things were.

"I had an idea when we first saw the lights in the village, and have been looking for somewhere to hold up for a short while, and the barn over there is quite isolated, with not much chance of anyone seeing you. Eventually we will have to go onto the road, anyone seeing us all together would remember it. We can't take any chances of being seen at all. Do you agree?" There was a murmur of agreement, but still the puzzled looks persisted.

"I am going on ahead to the village, there must be a pay phone there, and when I find it, I will see if I can get a friend to come and pick us up as soon as possible. That way there will be less chance of us being seen at all, and that is all to our good, once we are clear away from here, we can then discuss what to do next.

Once they were all inside the barn he left to walk to the village.

CHAPTER 26

"Hello, Mrs Bradley? It's Choco! Is 'Dixie' there?"

"Choco! How are you? I thought you had left the area, until Dixie told me he had seen you around. What is it do you want a bath, or a bed for the night? Which ever, you are always welcome, you know that!"

"No I am fine, thanks Mrs Bradley it's just that I was hoping Dixie might be home, and would be willing to do me a favour." "Well yes, he is home but he is still in bed, he was working all night, doing some work out of town some where in a factory.

Apparently they can only work there at night, something to do with the security at the place, anyway he should be getting up now I will see if he is awake, just hold on I will be as quick as I can, and that's enough of the Mrs Bradley business, I have told you before it's Pearl to you."

A few minutes later a sleepy sounding voice answered the phone. "Hello!....Choco?....What's up?.....What time is it?"

Dixie Bradley yawned down the line, and scratched at his crotch while standing in his underpants.

"Dixie! Don't be so disgusting, and put some clothes on, some one might see you through the window."

Mindful of what his mother said to him Dixie reached over and casually drew the curtains to hide himself.

"A favour if you can manage it Dixie."

"Yeah! What's that then?"

"You sound lousy! Are you all right to drive?"

"I'll be O.K. in a minute or so, had along night, that's all. I have a mouth like a vultures crotch, but other wise I am fine. Where do you want to go, and will I need a full tank?"

"No, and it's not that I want to go anywhere, it's just that I want to be picked up, with some friends, and it is not too far away from you. I will explain more when I see you. Will you do it for me?"

"Yeah! 'Course' I will. When do you want to be picked up and where?

Choco looked at the number on the telephone and saw at the same time the name of the village. "I am in a village called Stelam-Fen-Fitzbourne, Do you know it?"

"What the friggin hell are you doing out there it's out in the back of beyond, if you wait a while you will see the London to Plymouth stagecoach pass by on it's annual run, the passengers won't say much because they will probably be dead of starvation they don't have a buffet on board. So....when do you want to be picked up?"

"An hour ago!"

"You in bother, or what?"

"You could say that, and add some! Be as quick as you can."

"O.K. I'll just have to put some kicks and a shirt on and I will be on my way, stay near the telephone booth if you can and I will see you there."

"I will be waiting in the bus shelter, it's just past it and I will be able to see you coming."

"Be about fifteen to twenty five minutes, you just wait there."

The phone went dead, Choco walked to the shelter and waited.

"Wonder what will come first Dixie, a bus or the stage coach." He smiled to himself, "Stage coach, trust Dixie ever a character."

Choco waited in the shelter keeping a low profile hoping there would not be a bus along before Dixie arrived. Now and again a car or other some such vehicle passed by as it passed he would casually turn away from the drivers view, and lean out as if he was waiting for a bus to come from the opposite direction.

It was while waiting for Dixie, Choco's mind began to think of the problem of where to go when the transport with his friend arrived. "We will cross that bridge when we come to it." He thought to himself.

Dixie saw Choco as soon as he had stepped into view from behind the bus shelter. Climbing into the cab of the van Choco could see that his friend had really had a night of it, his eyes were full of sleep and blood shot red.

"If we can drive on and just pick up my friends and then we can take it from there. They drove on until they came to a lay-by which was near to the barn where the others had hidden themselves.

"You wait here, while I go and get the others waiting for us."

Choco then got out of the vehicle and launched himself over a hedge and then headed in the direction of the barn. Time he thought was of the essence now to get as far away as they could from the manor. They had no idea of how much time they had left until the man they had rescued was discovered missing.

Charlie was the first to see Choco approach the barn while he was standing just inside of it keeping an eye out for anyone who might be around.

"Any luck with the transport? He asked of his returning friend, to which Choco nodded in the affirmative.

"It's parked in a lay by a short distance away. Is everything all right here? How is the guy we took from the shed is he O.K. and feeling any better than when I left here?"

"He seems to be coping quite well now. Wait until you hear what he has been telling us. We don't know the half of it according to what he has been telling us. We could be up to way past our eyebrows and sinking faster than the Titanic with ice cubes as ballast. There is a lot going on, and I think Tim is getting scared shit-less for what could have happened to Rene, he is over with Father George, that's his name by the way. Father George O'Connell. He is Roman Catholic priest, and just see if you can guess where you have heard of him before. Abductions,.... and all that stuff,....ring a bell with you or anything."

"Bloody hell! Tell me you are joking, you won't believe who I have down the lay by waiting to give us a lift away from the area."

"You don't mean....No never, not Dixie!" They looked at each other, not really sure what the other was thinking. Then, simultaneously burst out laughing, at the total coincidence of the situation, a priest who had been kidnapped, then burgled, being rescued by the same person who had done the burglary.

"What happens when he finds out about who the priest is."

"Well I suspect Dixie will freak out but the priest would not understand why if he is around when that happens."

"Well where do you want to go now Choco?" Dixie inquired, looking back at the other passengers in the rear view mirror as they scrambled into the back of the vehicle. He recognized Charlie from the day he had seen Choco at the Portcullis, and wondered what the heck they could have been up to for them to be in such a hurry to and panic to get into town or wherever they wanted him to drive them. He also wondered where they had got the old guy they had to help into the back of his van, and what his connection was to whatever it was they were having a problem with. He did look familiar, or his face did, maybe he thought to himself it was one of the other two's father, then dismissed his thoughts thinking, whatever, it was no concern of his.

"Drive on to the main Taunton road for now, we need time before we decide where to go. Charlie keep an eye out of the back window for any of the bad guys, just as a precaution that we are on our own now." Choco finished speaking while at the same time was running the facts of their situation through his mind.

"Don't know perhaps it would make sense to go to the police station and tell them what we know and then leave it in their court so to speak." He was thinking aloud to himself but Tim heard him.

"I don't think that would be wise Choco." He remarked.

"According to what the Father has told us, it seems that these people have contacts every where, and the police station I should think would be one of the prime places to have them. I think the best bet would be to find somewhere neutral and think over what to do about what we now know about the manor and the going's on there."

"Where's a place around here we can call neutral? We cannot go to the the priest's place, it would be a certainty it would be the first place they would look for him."

Father O'Connell looked across at Choco, and gave a nod of agreement.

"Can anyone come up with anywhere we can go where we can discuss the situation we are in in relative safety." Choco sighed. "We need a house or at least somewhere that is not known to have any obvious connection with us."

Dixie had been listening to the conversation going on around him, and the more he had listened the more confused he was becoming.

"Are you going to put me in the picture about what's going on or not Choco? Seems to me I should be at least told what you lot are into. Is it drugs? Have you been tea leafing, and come unstuck. Is there some dealer after you for ripping him off over a deal with him, and now he is after you all because of it? Come on at least let me know something!"

Choco looked over the seat to those sitting behind him, not knowing what he should tell him. "What do you think? Should I tell him what we know and what the problem is? Or for his own sake it might be best he was kept in the dark about everything and just drop us off wherever it is we decide to go?"

The others just looked at him not really knowing what to say, after being told by the priest of the things that had happened to him, plus what they had found out for themselves they more or less thought it might be better in his own interest he be kept in the dark, and to just drop them off when the time came and to get on back to what ever he was doing before Choco's telephone call asking him to come and pick them up.

"I wish I could tell you what we are up against Dixie, but I don't think any of us knows for sure, except we all agree it's pretty heavy shit, and we could have possibly bitten off a bit more than we can chew, it may be best that you stay out of it as much as we can let you, for your sake and your mother's. We have to find somewhere that can give us breathing space to think what we can do next about the situation we are in, I think that's about all you need to know as I have said for your own safety." He turned to the others and asked if they agreed with him, to which he was answered with murmurs of approval.

"Well that's it then." He replied.

After a short while they started to reach the outskirts of Taunton. Then, after reaching the brow of a hill, Dixie pulled into a lay-by every one looked towards the front of the van towards him, as he switched the engine off. He straightened himself up, gripped his hands tightly on the steering wheel, arms straight and forwards, and was silent.

"What's up 'Dix'. Is there something the matter with the motor?" He turned to them all, saying. "We are almost in Taunton now, and you have been saying you needed somewhere safe for a while. I know of somewhere but whether it will be any good for your purpose I just don't know. It's a caravan, well really I should say a mobile home, a six birth, no electricity though, but no one knows of it except myself and a couple of girl friends I have taken there, on a couple of occasions. I bought it about three and a half years ago, it's on it's own site in a dead end secluded lane about twenty minutes from here. I sometimes like a bit of peace and quiet, or want somewhere to take a girlfriend for a night. You are welcome to use it until you sort out whatever it is you have to. There is water, tea, coffee, sugar and a tin of powdered milk but, if you do, you will need food ect. and candles, you can cook there because there is a gas cooker with a full bottle of gas. Well what do you say? It's up to you."

It took no time at all for the others to agree to his offer. Father O'Connell looked at the men around him, then spoke to them.

"Why you have done what you have for me I don't know, but I will be eternally grateful, but must tell you how much I thank you, and may God be with us for I am sure we will have need of his love help and protection."

After agreeing to Dixies offer they drove to a garage and purchased a small amount of food, candles and a two gallon plastic container for water, filling it up a the garage fore court using money loaned to them from Dixie, due to their own lack of it.

The caravan was in a perfect location for their needs. It was as Dixie had told them. Situated at the bottom of a lane with with a high growing hedge row and was not possible to be seen from any other position other than coming down the lane it's self, and then only when one came right down to where it was situated, due to the fact of it was tucked into a corner of where at one time it had turned at right angles to carry on in another direction but had for sometime been filled in, leaving a large high bank behind it.

"Well there it is!" Dixie spoke, his voice tinged with pride.

"I have painted it and and treated the roof, not a leak anywhere, and I have not seen a soul around here and, that's over three years now. Well what do you think?"

"I think it's brilliant, but let's get inside, put the kettle if there is one there and brew up some tea or coffee, and talk about what we are going to do while we drink, have a smoke or whatever."

"Aye! That's the ticket". Piped in Tim at Charlie's suggestion. He had been the quietest all through the journey in the van on their way there, and was now trying to get himself motivated and out of the distressed state he was in worrying over the situation Rene might be in.

"I will leave you now to do what ever you need to, and will be back here in about an hour or so, after I have taken care of a bit of business in the town. The key to unlock the cover so that you can turn the gas on is on a hook above the sink in there."

That said, Dixie turned and walked to his van and drove away, his hand out of the window with a parting wave to them as they watched. He was very soon out of sight, and the sound of the motor became muffled from the hedge-row each side of the lane as he made the sharp turn and away from them.

The inside of the caravan was quite tidy, and not the usual mess, quite often associated with a bachelor's pad. There was a small area that did for a dining room in the day time with a portion of room dividing wall that came down making a double bed. Four more were made available from converting bench seats in the sitting room at the opposite end of the caravan, giving six sleeping places in all. Which they were all sat on, sipping tea, while, except for the priest smoking 'rollups'.

"Well what do we do next? Charlie's words broke the silence.

"and, what, do we actually know about the people at the manor house. I know according to what Father George has told us they are dangerous, that much we do know."

"I still don't know the whole of it so will someone fill me in with what I don't know." Choco while speaking had really been addressing his words to the priest, who was sat on the opposite bench to him.

Father O'Connell turned towards them all and let out a sigh.

"If Satan has children, then those who abducted me are them. I was told by someone who came and spoke to me, that originally the reason for my abduction was that I was to be sacrificed and then my body was to be used to defile ground somewhere which had been consecrated in the past, and which they would then use for their own purposes to further their own ends. What exactly they meant by that I have no means of knowing, except it bode ill for all who would be in discord with their beliefs and practices. My death would also be used to test in some way the powers they indicated to me they had acquired since they returned to this world. But because there was someone who was becoming a potential problem while trying to trace a friend who had gone missing, they used him instead, in what way or how I really don't know. Someone within their ranks, then suggested to them that perhaps if I could be persuaded to join them, and renounce my beliefs, and then with my help they would be in a position to further their aims and if I could be used to obtain for them people they could use for the many purposes they would require them for, willing or not, and in return I would have anything I wanted, such as power and position and, as they put it, wealth beyond my wildest dreams. I had until then been trussed up and, had not eaten for the time I had been abducted, which I estimated to have been a period of at least five days. I was left in the room where there was in front of me a table laden with food and drink, to eat and drink my fill, and was told while doing so think over the option of joining them or death. I thought about what was told me when I was left alone, and reasoned that if I said I was willing to join them it might give me the chance to escape and warn the church authorities that they were doing these things, and then perhaps they would be able to do something about them, but later found out and realized just how naive I was about them and the power they really had access to. As soon as I had voiced my decision, untruthfully of course, they seemed to know immediately what I really planned and practically told me word perfect what I was thinking at the time. I now know that these people are really evil incarnate. I really do not know, if they can be stopped."

He then began to tell them the full account of what he knew and had seen, and ended his account of his capture and rescue saying, he was not now really sure about what he should do for the best. Except to pray for the world's population, and that we find an answer to them through prayer, the love of God for the salvation of souls.

Charlie spoke up then saying. "We have 'one' thing in our favour."

"With so much against us, with from what we have just heard from Father George here, tell us what you think that is, so that we can at least have a crack at them what, or who ever they are." Choco invited.

"Well look! We only found Father O'Connell by pure accident, after I saw those people last night and followed them to the shed. We had no idea what we would find in the shed, and certainly not steps leading down to the cavern where we found Father O'Connell when we rescued him from out of their clutches. No one has seen us going to, or coming from the shed, as far as they would be concerned he has managed to escape under his own steam and without help from anyone. So there is nothing to tie us in with his escape. Well what do you think?"

Father O'Connell looked across to them.

"It sounds good, very good, except for one detail. I was tied up what about the ropes when they examine them they will see they have been cut and, they know that I had no knife on me when they left me there."

"I just knew my scavenging and tidy ways would do me credit one day." Choco reached into his pocket and brought out the ropes he had cut to release the priest.

"Waters under the bridge as they say. What do we do now then, we are involved in things which up until a moment ago we thought we had no control over. But now it seems we have an edge that stands in our favour. They can know nothing of our involvement with Father George." Choco had decided that addressing the priest as 'Father O'Connell' all the time seemed to take away some kind of uniqueness of the situation they were in, away, and alienated the priest from the rest of them, when in actual fact they were all equally involved in the situation they found themselves. "He should be safe here with us while we figure out what to do next." He then turned to them and asked. "Any suggestions."

"We have to go back to the manor!"

"We what? Choco could not believe what he had heard Tim say.

"I know you are concerned and worried sick over Rene Tim, but, to go back now after knowing what we know, that, is surely madness."

"No wait! Hear me out! It's not just because of Rene, although, that is just as important to me. It's just because, they know nothing of the fact we know what they have been doing, and our involvement with Father George, we have to go back, or they might become suspicious, especially when we have all left what belongings we do have there. With Father George gone from where he was being held, added to the fact we have been asking questions there over Rene's stay at the place, there, and in the town. Also we don't know for sure if anyone had seen us with Tony Howard, before he left to make his way home, and don't forget we played pool with him the night before we met him in the town. I think Tony was the one used as a sacrifice instead of Father George, think about it, it all fits, as to how they did it I don't know, but I think they were responsible in some way." Tim got up from the bench seat, and walked to the teapot on the table and began to pour himself another cup. There's still tea in the pot if anyone wants some." He then looked around to see if anyone would comment on what he had just said.

After a short discussion on what Tim had just spoken of and the agreement that what he had said made sense, the decision was made to go back to the manor, but mindful of the danger they would be in should they make any mistakes while there.

Charlie was not sure about the situation of going back but agreed in the end to the others and himself it was right and made sense that they should do so. Saying when they left the manor the following morning they were going to leave the area so as to make their departure from the manor seem as normal as possible.

"What time is it now." Choco asked, eyes looked towards the kitchen area at the wall clock. Someone answered that it was just coming up to eleven o'clock.

"Dixie should be back shortly, which should give us enough time to get back to town to catch the transport and return to the manor, they always have a different driver every time they go into town so they probably won't know whether we caught it or not this morning."

Father O'Connell not relishing to be left on his own for so long, asked why they were going back there at lunch time instead of catching the evening transport, surely it would be better to spend as less a time there as possible. Charlie and Tim were inclined to agree with him and said as much. Choco then explained his reasons, being, the less time they were away from the manor the less likely any suspicion would fall on them with having any thing to do with Father George having escaped. The others then could see the logic in his decision, and agreed to return there as he suggested.

Dixie returned as promised, and brought with him a couple of sleeping bags and some blankets, saying he knew how cold it could get there in the night sometimes and he had them spare in his room at home. When told they wanted dropping off in the town he just accepted it, saying he did not understand what was going on, one minute they were telling him they needed somewhere to hide and lay low for a while and the next they were going to go off galavanting around town where they could be seen by all and sundry, but if that was what they wanted, then he would take them there.

They were dropped off in one of the back streets, which was only a short distance from the Portcullis, and pickup point.

That evening, after the evening meal they went to the lounge as usual and watched television as usual, but with no real interest. They were feeling the tension of the days events, and decided to play a few games at the pool table, trying to lift their spirits which was proving quite difficult. There were more than one or two times they became paranoid over small incidents such as someone might be innocently looking over towards their direction which had no bearing on their situation, but the tension the were feeling in the place began to affect them more as the night wore on. Eventually Choco suggested it might be as well for them to go to their rooms for the night, until they met for breakfast in the morning.

As they made their way to the door to leave the lounge Willie the old guy appeared with the urn of drinking chocolate, giving a mug to everyone he came to. Charlie told them to take it from him but not to drink because of the night before when he had tried to wake them up unsuccessfully, and that he believed the drink was drugged.

Charlie was at the stage of just midway of awake and asleep, when he heard the sound of the door to his room open. He lay there still, his eyes open as a shadow past in front of his window, his heart began to thump, feeling like a heavy weight knocking in his chest fit to burst through his rib cage. He felt paralysed with fear, and lay there as if he had been set in cement, and unable to move. After what seemed an eternity a voice he immediately recognized as Tim's whispered for him to get dressed and come to Choco's room as quickly and as quietly as he could.

The relief he felt as he realized it was Tim flooded through him he was about to curse Tim but his senses returned reminding him where he was, and how precarious a situation they were in. Choco's room was in darkness, as he entered Choco whispered.

"Don't switch on the light, come over here and take a look at this!"

"What is it?" He could see the both of them standing back from, but looking out of the window. Moving closer he came level to where they stood, and looking out of the window he could see at least a dozen or more torch lights their beams pointing this way and that. Heading in the direction of the woods he had seen the others going to the night before.

"OH! OH! I think the shits hit the fan, and I think it's going to spread far and wide by the morning. It's just as well we are leaving here tomorrow."

"This is nothing Charlie, you should have been here a few minutes ago. I remembered what the the priest said about twelve o'clock or after, and I thought I would have a look out the window about then and was just about to give up and get into bed when I saw a light coming from the direction of the woods and the path you told us about. Some one came out across the yard there and met whoever was coming with the torch, they both went inside the manor and the next thing I know is there are loads of them down there all running around like headless chickens. Until that was some guy came there and started to give orders like a bloody general at the battle of 'Waterloo'. Those two guys we saw who were taking Father George into the hut were there and were told off by him in no uncertain terms, and let me tell you they seemed shit scared of him, and that is no mean feat, you saw the size of them both, either he he is an expert in the art of Karate, or has four 'Shredded Wheat' for breakfast and with his main meal of the day, or that power the priest has been talking about is real high octane stuff."

"How can you make a joke of all this Choco, I just don't understand how you can stay so calm in the light of what we know, and what we know is probably no more than the tip of the iceberg."

"Well now! The thing is I always say, if a bit of humour gets attention and you can still laugh when everything seems against you, then it can give you an edge should the need arise to bounce back. What say you Tim?."

They all continued to watch until the excitement of the moment had passed, moved away from the window had a smoke together talking in whispers, before going back to their own rooms for the rest of the night, although by then they did not want to sleep but more or less waited for morning to arrive. When it did they met together carrying their belongings in the canteen, and later caught the first transport into the town and waited for Dixie to pick them up as had been arranged the day before.

CHAPTER 27

Dave Mitchell was silent as was Anne Farr, they sat thinking through in their minds the account of the evening they had just been told of.

"It must have been horrific."

"It was Anne but that was only the beginning, things began to happen to us one by one after that night."

"How many of you were in the circle that night?"

"There were nine of us altogether the second time. Of that nine, one is in a mental institution, two have committed suicide, one has left the area, and two have just vanished to where, or when they went we don't have a clue. It seems they just packed up and left where they lived overnight three years ago. We have not heard a word from either of them since, which we could never figure out as we were all close friends."

"That's six plus plus yourselves. That leaves one more where is that person now?"

"Remember I told you one of us was injured, and believed the injury was caused by the broken table. Well some how or other it had become infected even though he had gone to hospital, had it been stitched and he had a tetanus injection. When he returned to hospital four days later they found the wound open and the stitches had come away with the dressing, having come away from the skin. It seemed as if the flesh had been eaten away and was painful to the touch, with it seemed just a minimum of swelling.   Being puzzled by what they saw the medical staff took swabs for testing.

The result was that there had been a release of some kind of exotoxins from the strain of bacteria similar to clostridium tetani, but it was in some way it had mutated and instead of attacking the muscular part of the body attacked the flesh. The symptoms seemed to visually accelerate when the bandage covering was removed they tried to stop it with a jelly cream but no matter what they did they could not stop the spread of the infection, and as time went on they could see a rapid breakdown of the cellular structure of the arm, the pain became so great that they had to heavily sedate him while they tried everything they could think of to halt the deterioration. They tried all kinds of antibiotics, but it was to no avail. It spread with astonishing speed to the rest of his body and was pronounced dead within a week of being admitted to hospital.

We could learn nothing more about his death, than he had been placed into an isolation ward for unknown or undiagnosed diseases for close monitoring. The information we did get was from someone we knew and was on the ward at the time. It was relayed in confidence because the person on the ward knew he was a close friend of his and knew he was a close friend of ours, we in turn kept the information to our selves.

But the most strangest thing of all was what we were told by this friend. After he had died his flesh and muscle left on the outside of his body after a day in the cold morgue, seemed to have been eaten away until there was nothing left down to the bone, which lay perfectly intact, until it was touched, then it just disintegrated into powder. A greyish white powder, while at the same time leaving all the internal organs intact and fresh."

Dave Mitchell's ears pricked up when he heard the description of the body crumbling away into powder when touched. his mind went back to the body discovered in the field at Blunders Farm, Loverage and himself went to, and had examined with the Bridgwater Police. The description was identical to what Peter had just described. "Why" he thought to himself "was there no information of the death of circumstances of the deterioration of the two bodies. As far as he was aware their case had been unique and had not been experienced before. Something, he thought should have been known of the unusual similarities between the two. Why was that connection not made? Where was the post mortem report on the first victim, and why had it not shown up on any computer data, when the second body was found."

"What's the matter Dave?" Anne could see there was something on his mind.

Her voice brought him immediately out of his thoughts, and he looked at his companions at the table, still a little taken back from what he had just heard.

"The circumstances Peter has just described of the person who died in hospital....the bones crumbling to powdery dust when touched. I experienced a similar case a few days ago. As far as I knew it was the one and only case known of, at least that was what we were led to believe. Now I hear from Peter that he has heard of a similar thing happened to someone a few years ago. No matter how I look at it, it just does not make any sense."

"What was the conclusion of how it happened in your case? Was there any sign of a wound on your body when found?"

"It was impossible to tell when we saw it, there were all kinds of theories. From aliens in U.F.O's to some kind of biological warfare germ which had escaped from a research laboratory, but whatever was suggested there was nothing that had credence or held water. When the body was found it was impossible to make any sense of it's condition, just a skeleton with all the internal organs in perfect condition, and the identity of who ever it was is still unknown."

Mitchell reached for the coffee cup and took a drink from it, they had been talking for quite some while and the coffee was just luke warm, but he emptied what was in the cup anyway. "You said earlier that what was said by Paul Gage last night, was in some way similar to what was said by this Raymond you had contacted. What exactly did you mean?"

"Well what I meant was how both men were restricted to certain areas and how only when someone entered the area were they able to leave there. It seemed to me there may be a particular reason why that should be. I also feel that it could not be due to the trauma of the way they had died. There has to be another reason, and I feel the reason is somehow tied up to whatever these people we have been told of, use the sacrifice of their victims for. Although I can't understand why one saw himself hanging and knew he was dead, while the other was so sure he was not deceased and could not see himself. He actually told us he had no memory of his death occurring. Have you any views on it Anne?" "Before I answer that, I think there is one thing I must ask you Peter. When all the things were happening to the others in the circle with you when you had contacted Raymond Hayman, was there anything happening to you and Abigail, did the husband and wife attend the rescue circle or not, and did they live in the the apartment after that night? Or was there any indication that the spirit form Raymond Hayman was still there after what had happened?"

"They returned later that evening as we were leaving, saw the state of the place, the table broken, and as we were still coming to terms with what had happened. I suppose we must have looked still a little more than shocked and frightened. They decided there and then that there was no way were they going to stay there another night. Apparently they had some one go and remove all of their belongings the following day without apparently no problems. Since that day we had not heard of any more disturbances there and I have passed the apartment block many times since and there is someone living in the apartment where the rescue circle was attempted. I have spoken to the father of the couple and he has said since they have moved they have not had any more disturbances of that nature since and are well and happy together.

"As to your question of whether we experienced anything similar to what the others had, well the answer to that question is that we did, and to the extent it almost split our marriage up altogether. Abigail became depressed and no matter what we did her depression would not go away. I became irritable over the least thing and began to fall out with close friends, frequently over the smallest of things, I became extremely argumentive. In fact my whole personality changed but I could not see it my self. Then one night I was in a really bad mood over a job of work I had done for a friend and completed, and which he had agreed to pay me in cash because I had agreed to do it at a large discount for him. My friend had not had time to go to the bank that day as he had agreed to, he had apologized and told me he would go to the cash dispenser and draw out as much as he could that evening, and as soon as the bank was open the following morning and draw the rest and bring it around to me at my house.

There was no reason for it, I just went berserk, grabbing him by the collar and pinning him against the wall of my house. I know now it was ridiculous but at the time it was as if I had no control over my actions, and was about to hit him with my fist. Suddenly everything went blank and felt for just an instant a blow on my fore head, I fell to the ground. The next thing I can remember is seeing myself on the ground. I watched for a while. There seemed to be something going on with my body, then I could see something dark coming away from the area of my fore head like a darkish wispy, or vapour like form is the only way I could describe it, it was only for a fleeting moment but I know I did see it. Then a voice I now know was 'Two Bears' said you will be well now, and then, in what seemed an instant I felt as if I was waking from a sleep, and my friend was helping me from off of the ground. From then on I felt like my old self again.

On my return home Abigail was her old self as well, the only conclusion I have been able to come to over that period of our marriage is that we were under some kind of psychic attack that started the night of the breaking table. From who or why we both had no idea. But somehow Two Bears was able to intervene and had stopped it, why it had taken him so long I can't say but thank God he did, because who knows what would have happened if he had not bless him.

From what we have now heard, and what we know so far it seems there has been a lot more going on than we could possibly imagined. Since that day we have had nothing similar happen." "Could what was said to us all last night be connected in some way to what happened to Abigail and you Peter, and the friends you were in the rescue circle with. Could it be part of what we were warned of last night by Two Bears and Paul Gage. Perhaps Paul Gage's description of the people now at large were aware of you at that time because of the assistance you were trying to give him, and that was the reason you were all attacked in the way you were. Also when you think that way what else has been going on we are not aware of, it is beginning to make me shudder just thinking about it."

As Anne finished speaking Mitchell's thoughts went back to the list of missing people Loverage and himself had discovered, and realized only then he was in the middle of something bigger than he ever imagined, or was ever to imagine in a whole lifetime. He was about to mention this fact to them when he suddenly decided not to, and would speak to Anne about it when they were on their own, so as not to worry Abigail unduly.

A short while later Peter suggested they call for a taxi to take them home asking Mitchell if he would like lift which he declined, saying it was not far to his house and he would welcome the walk home. But secretly to himself he hoped for a short while on his own with Anne.

CHAPTER 28

"Where do we go from here? Charlie remarked as they climbed into Dixie's van after waiting for him to turn up for them."

"I stayed with the old guy last night, and when I opened the door I frightened the shit out of him, seems he thought I was someone else. Mind you, it can be a bit scary out there at night on your own until you get used to it. He was just about to settle down for the night when I arrived. He looked knackered and all in when I picked you all up out in the sticks. He is all right though, but seemed a bit concerned over what happened to him, he didn't want to tell me a lot, said you might not like him to tell me too much about whatever is going on, all he said was somebody had it in for him, is all. He didn't seem able to settle down to sleep last night but I helped him out with a glass or two of whisky and man can't he knock them back. Then again I suppose the way he was when I picked you up, he could well have done with them. Not a bad bloke though, he he woke me up with a cup of tea first thing this morning."

"So he did not speak much to you then Dixie?"

"No, like I said, he seemed knackered and all in." Dixie's eyes were all around each side of the van as he was pulling out of the side of the road where he had pulled in to pick them up, his voice spoke casually and in a matter of fact way, as if he had made the statement just for something to say as he picked them up."

"To be straight with you guys, there is only one thing on my mind at the moment, now we are away from the manor, and that is to see if I can find out what has happened to Rene, once I have stowed my gear in the caravan." Answered Tim to Charlie's earlier question.

"O.K. Tim, I understand your feelings on that subject, but first I suggest we all go back to the caravan now and see what we can come up with in the way of giving you some sort of angle on where to look. From what those two buskers in the cafe told us, and at the same time it will be better for us to be able to talk freely again." Choco turned towards Dixie then.

"Are you going to stay at the caravan tonight with us or going home?"

"I will stay for a while with you until mid afternoon. I usually take the old dear and her friend to bingo, and bring them back home when it is finished, I do it every week on this day, it's their one night a week out, and they look forward to it. I will come out to you tomorrow afternoon, what with all the pissballing around you have had in the last day or so it may be better for you all to get some rest and relax for the rest of the day anyway, what do you think? Also I did a bit of shopping before I picked you up, should be enough in the boxes in the back there to last you for a week or two with no problems, came to over sixty notes, you can pay me thirty five for it when you get some cash together, that's the best I can do for you, cash is a bit tight again now, or I would have let you have it for nothing."

"Oh! that's great Dix. That will be a load off of our minds. What sort of stuff did you get for us? You are probably right a rest will do us all a lot of good. So! You got on all right with Father George last night, that's something else then."

Choco had a glint in his eye when he had asked the question, and Charlie felt a gentle dig in the ribs.

He started to pull out into the road and joined the flow of traffic.

Charlie leaned over to Choco.

"I still don't think he realizes who he was drinking with, and on such friendly terms with last night yet, do you?"

Choco grinned and lit his cigarette.

"Are you, going to tell him?"

"Why should I. Father George has already been through enough, and Dixie has got on so well with him, who knows, perhaps some good may come out of the friendship eventually. How would he feel if he found out he had been burgled, as well as kidnapped, and the burglar was none other than his new found drinking partner. Better let things drop for now and, and wait for the penny to drop natural, be a shame to spoil a friendship so soon after it has been made don't you think?"

Choco gave a sidelong glance towards his friend as he was driving, and had a tongue in cheek grin over the situation he found so comical.

"Well you lot, if you take a box of groceries each that's in the back there, and carry them from here, and as I said you should have plenty to last you for a while."

Each grabbed hold of a cardboard box containing the things Dixie had got from the super market earlier, and began to carry them up the lane towards the caravan. While walking Charlie became puzzled by some of the items he saw he was carrying, in his box, there were jars of baby food a pack of disposable nappies, and also a pack of sanitary towels with various other things he could not understand him having bought for them. He mentioned the fact to Choco as they walked along, Choco stopped in mid stride, and took a closer look at what he had in his box. Dixie saw both of them holding the items they had found, and casually made a casual kind of apology to them both. But excusing himself by saying it was the only shopping receipt he could find with enough variety of items they would need, and he did not have enough time to look around for others as time was getting on by the time he had left before he had to pick them up.

"Dixie! I don't believe it!....You didn't?"

"Didn't what?"

"What do you mean! Didn't what? Didn't half inch this stuff from the supermarket!"

"Don't be soft, of course I did! You don't think I had enough money on me to pay for it all, did you? I drew out fifty notes from from the hole in the wall yesterday, and had almost used that when I put twenty notes worth of petrol in the tank, and then there was the stuff we bought yesterday, the fifty was almost gone by the time I went to the supermarket. It seemed to me you were all up the creek without a paddle, I thought at you would at least not go hungry, perhaps if that Father George friend of yours says grace or blesses it, it would make it all right for you and your conscience, or if you feel so bad about it, then dump it and go hungry, as they sometimes say on game shows the choice is yours."

Choco saw the look on Charlie's face, who was dumfounded by what had been said by Dixie.

"Come on Charlie, there's a bit more for us to worry about than a bit of shoplifting, and as they say, needs must.

On reaching the caravan they could smell and see wood smoke coming from the chimney of the caravan.

"Well it looks like Father George has a fire going in the caravan, at least we can get warm in a moment or two, first job is to put the kettle on, what say you Tim."

Charlie looked over to Choco wondering again how he managed to keep light hearted, so much of the time, it seemed to him there was nothing that got him uptight, or that he took life or the situation they were in serious at all.

But that was just the impression Choco wanted to convey to the others who were with him, inside he was feeling anything but flippant over their situation, his own common sense, and some thing else, a feeling within himself, he could not explain at the time from when they had seen the priest taken to the shed, and decided to try to find out what was going on, even then there was the nagging feeling they were about to become participants in something they might be sorry for, and later wish they had not become involved in, but as the way things now stood they had picked up a hand that had been dealt to them, now they would it seemed have to play it through to the end, whatever that might be.

"How did things go last night for you? No problems I hope?"

"No problems Father, well not for us, though we saw there was for those at the manor, it seems you were missed about midnight or there abouts, and there were people running around everywhere looking for you, we could see them from the window of the room I was in. It seemed there was hell to pay." Choco having spoken of the events they had witnessed the night before, brought a light chuckle of laughter from Charlie and Tim, while Dixie looked on not understanding what it was they had found so funny, not having heard the priest describe to the others those at the manor as as the spawn of Satan.

After Dixie had left they sorted out the groceries, putting them away in the cupboards around the kitchen area of the caravan. Tim volunteered to get on with preparing a meal for that evening. Father George volunteered to help, although, he explained he would be no help in cooking, but could peel potatoes and open tins, or anything which might be of assistance to him.

Meanwhile Choco suggested it might be a good idea if Charlie and himself went for a walk around to see, exactly where, they were situated, in relation to the area around them, in case they had to move out of the area on foot sharpish at night, they would have some idea where to go.

They scrambled up the bank of the hedge row which hid the caravan from sight, and on reaching the top found they were in a field with enough height to be able to see part of the road they had travelled on before turning off into the lane, curving away from them about six hundred yards from where they were standing, before disappearing out of sight. They moved along in the opposite direction and away from the lane, and saw the lane was situated at the bottom of a small valley, between two small gorse shrub, bramble, and tree covered hills, mostly Elm, with some copper beech, dotted here and there. Towards the far end of the valley high on the opposite hill stood a large old gnarled oak tree, older than any of the others they could see, it seemed to be standing proud, as if it was a sentinel, and there to watch and protect the entrance to the valley, and had done so for centuries.

They decided to climb to the top of the hill from the field they were on, to see if they could get a better view of the surrounding area. On reaching the top they had quite a view of the whole of the valley and roads around them, and could also see how well the caravan really was hidden from sight, and isolated from anywhere, the nearest farmhouse they could see, was quite a distance from where they stood. Satisfied of their position and the fact they had a clear idea now of the area around them, they began to make their way in the general direction of where they knew the lane to be and caravan was situated, skirting around the base of the hill they had been on, through the gorse and brambles on tracks made by deer rabbits and other animals found in the locality. As they did so Charlie called Choco's attention to a plume of smoke he had spotted behind a stone built wall farther and lower down from where they were standing, in a small area of dead ground they had not realized was there, and had it not been for the smoke Charlie had seen they would have missed completely.

"Must be a house down there, we must remember it's there and make sure we are not seen as we walk back to the caravan. But we must bear it in mind, there must be a small road leading off of the one we used to get to the lane where the caravan is, it probably carries on and passes it after the lane turnoff. Maybe we should take a walk along the roadway tomorrow just to make sure we know what's there it's getting too late, and by the time we return, I expect Tim will have something ready to eat for us.

As they finished skirting the bottom of the hill and near part of the lane where the caravan was situated, the wind began to pick up and it began to rain. They quickened their step to get back as soon as they could before it became heavy and they became soaked. As they drew closer to the hedge, behind which the caravan was situated they could smell the aroma of food cooking.

"Seems as if we are having onions with whatever it is he is cooking tonight Choco."

"I don't care what it is, as long as it's hot and tasty, and not taste like nick food, because that's where Tim learned to cook, in the prison kitchens. He said he enjoyed cooking so much he had been thinking of getting a job as a cook when he came out of prison and had set up home with Rene, or so he was telling me when he suggested he didn't mind doing the cooking for us earlier."

He looked across and began laughing, as Charlie again made a face of disbelief.

"Come on lighten up man, he is as good as gold, and I would stake my life on him at anytime to back me up if, things ever became unpleasant."

As they stepped into the caravan they were greeted with a smile and a chuckle from the priest, it was good to see there was something that could make the priest laugh after the ordeal he had gone through the days before they had rescued him, he was quietly laughing so much, they were curious what it was that was amusing him so.

"What is it?" Charlie whispered to him.

"It's stew." He then nodded towards the kitchen and moved aside to let them see inside where Tim was busy with the evening meal.

There was Tim, standing with a cup of tea in one hand and a two pronged hazel stick he must have cut earlier, stirring the stew in an enamel washing up bowl which had been in the sink when they had left earlier. He turned around and saw the look of wonder on their faces.

"It's the only thing I could find big enough to cook a stew in for us all, there is only a kettle and a small milk saucepan here."

There were just enough plates, to be able to serve everyone a good portion of stew, which they were all ready for. Then after they had eaten they sat and listened to the radio Dixie had left them.

As the night wore on it had been decided to go into town the following afternoon when Dixie arrived, to see if they could find the buskers and try to find out the destination of the train Rene was boarding, or at least the direction.

The sun had risen, the rain had stopped during the night, there was a light mist surrounding the caravan. The hollow sounding pt'dump, of water droplets could be heard on the roof of the caravan falling from the branches overhead. A side window was opened, and the cold damp air began to permeate the inside of the caravan.

"I've made some tea, and there is some toast made, come and help yourselves, first come first served, if it is all gone by the time any of you get here then you will have to make your own." Choco's voice broke the silence of the caravan, eventually covers were pulled back, the sounds of stretching and yawning could be heard, some one broke wind.

"Bloody hell Tim was that you? You dirty sod, first thing in the morning and before breakfast. Oops! Sorry Father I forgot you were here" Charlie apologised.

"That's all right but I am afraid it was me it slipped out when I was'nt looking, and Tim's stew caught me on the hop, but it was a good stew wasn't it!"

Tim looked across to Charlie and winked.

"I suppose if we did have to rescue a priest we were lucky to get one with a sense of humour, the next time I won't put any baked beans in the stew and save on gas, how does that sound Father.

"Loud and clear my son!" Was the reply from the priest.

Father George smiled quietly to himself, and thinking it was strange he had been rescued by these so called dropouts of society, perhaps they were the best choice available to him, but as things had turned out, they were in his estimation more than perfect, a better choice would have been very difficult to find. He was beginning to enjoy being with them, and their sense of humour. But just what Mrs. Willard would have made of them he could not imagine for a moment. Since he had known them it seemed there was not one of them who was the individual overall leader as such, but they all seemed to pitch in with ideas to help each other, which now seemed included him as well, with a bond which seemed to grow with every passing hour he was in their company.

At the back of his mind was the worrying feeling of concern for them with the knowledge he had of those at the manor who the had spoken so often of. He had more or less accepted that it was some where below, in the manor house he had been held, and he just knew some how that the capabilities he had been told of by James Coulter were not just idle boasting, and by their part in his rescue they had placed themselves in the same mortal danger as himself. Other than leaving them, which he had already suggested, and to which they would not hear of, he did not know what he could do to help them if the matter of danger came to a head. Also where could he start, he had no real idea, but there was he knew a real danger to them all while he was with them.

＊＊＊＊＊＊＊＊＊＊＊＊＊＊＊＊＊＊

At the same time that morning things were being organized back at the manor house to locate and eliminate the escaped priest at the first opportunity.

James Caulter was stood at a table looking looking at the details of an O.S. map. While standing next to him was a man, elderly with grey hair, beads of perspiration covered his forehead and face, while in his hand held out over the map and dangling from his fingers was what seemed a darkened smoked coloured crystal quartz, swaying back and forth from a silver chain, while looped between his little and third finger was a small piece of material cut from Father George's dog collar, while his left hand fingers were guiding and pushing a twelve inch wooden ruler laying flat on the map, as it came to an area the crystal pendulum stopped swaying and began to gyrate, the man marked the line of latitude and turned the ruler and repeated the procedure in the longitude direction until it began to gyrate again, looking closely at the map and studying the place where the the the lines crossed he made a mark. He looked at Caulter, and then breathed a sigh of relief.

"Here right at this spot on the map, that is where the priest is now." Acting as a dog would pleasing it's master. He then looked around at the others who were present, now confident in himself and sure he had fulfilled the task which was required of him.

Caulter moved him aside, and looked at the marked area of the map, and did a quick calculation.

"How could he have managed to travel that far, and not be seen and reported to me by any of our people? It looks as if he may be travelling down this lane. If that is so which direction is he going, and where is he heading for?

He stood thinking for a while then gave the elderly man a pat on the back on the back.

"You have done well, if what you say is true."

"It's true, I can vouch for my skills, they have never been wrong when I get a result, it's as I have said he is there Mr Caulter."

The fear when being questioned by Caulter seemed to have returned, he had never met the man before, but had been informed by those who had, of the things he was capable of with those who had not pleased him, or had let him down over something in the past, he expected results from anyone he summoned before him to do a task he required, and who so ever failed him in what he wanted them to do, was met with a swift and final judgement from him, and his wrath knew no bounds, he would not accept failure of any task he had given someone to carry out.

"Wait for an hour, but keep dowsing intermittently, we must see which way he is heading." He then turned to another of the onlookers there.

"Be ready in an an hour to have our people in place to follow at a distance when we know which way he is headed. I will go now to get in touch with the people who will deal with the priest once and for all, and return in an hour." He turned on his heels and was gone from the room, his wife following him close behind.

****

It was midmorning and they were sat around the caravan talking over what they would have to do that day. Tim had agreed to stay with Father George, while Choco and Charlie went back into town, to see if there was any noticeable activity due to the disappearance of the priest, and to look for the buskers they had spoken to when they were told they had seen Rene boarding the train.

Tim had wanted to go with them, but was eventually persuaded by Choco and the others he would be more use to them staying with the priest, and preparing a hot meal for them when they returned using the excuse he was the only one of them who could cook with any degree of competence and that the stew he had cooked for them was better than any of them could have possibly done. With that said it seemed to satisfy him. But as they were on their way to Dixie and the waiting van, he stood in the doorway of the caravan and called them back.

"I am an idiot, here you are about to go into the town with hardly any money to your names and here I am with plenty in the bank I have saved with Rene. Here! Take my cash card and here's my Pin number." He handed the card and his pin number on a piece of paper.

"We are all in this together what ever it is, and you are going into town to try to see what you can find out for me about Rene, and wherever she is, she would I know want me to do it. So draw out a couple of hundred notes, so we have at least have some readies in case we need it."

Choco was about to refuse, but could see the logic in what Tim had said, and reached up and took the offered items from him. "Thanks Tim, it will certainly be a help to have a bit of money on us, and believe me when I say we will do the best we can to find out where she is for you. Have that meal ready for us for when we return, if she can be found don't worry mate we will find her or at least get some idea where she could be."   With that said they went to the waiting van.

After parking in the multi story car park in the centre of the town, they made their way to the cash point out side of Tim's bank and drew the money. Then they made their way to the area in the town where they had seen the buskers on the previous visits to the town. They first came across a girl of about seventeen or eighteen, her hair was brown, and with the thick matted look, and styled with dreadlocks with silver rings and coloured ribbons interwoven in them. A medium sized 'collie cross' dog, curled up at her feet, while she played a flute. There was a felt, wide brimmed hat with a few coins scattered inside of it a couple of feet away in front of her. They could see there were a few other buskers around but no sign of the two they were looking for. The girl and dog eyed them a little suspiciously, she stopped playing and reached over to her hat and retrieved the few coins it contained, putting them in her pocket.

Choco saw her actions, moved nearer, and putting his hand into his pocket with drew a small amount of loose change he had there, and handed them to her. Her attitude changed immediately, she smiled at him.

"Thanks. I'm sorry for what I did just now, but two days ago I was ripped off with a few pounds I had been given, and it was hard work to get it in the first place. I didn't want to take the risk of the same thing happening again today." She rubbed the neck of the dog affectionately. "We don't want another cold night without anything to eat again tonight do we Bo Baggins." The dog squealed at the attention, and excitedly nuzzled her neck, a wet tongue then slapped her cheek.

"All right! All right boy, enough, don't get carried away now." Her laughter made the dog lick her even more until she was able to steady him down with her hands on his shiny black coat pushing him gently down and away from her.

"We are looking for a couple of friends of ours they have been busking around Taunton for a while now, I wonder if you know them? The man plays a violin and harmonica, the woman a flute the same as you.

"Oh! You must mean Tina and Flyn, they were here until about ten minutes ago, they are friends of mine as well, they have to gone to a cafe now for a break and a bite to eat. They are probably in 'Black and Whites', the cafe down there, off of the main street, they are always in there about this time of day."

"Ah! I know were it is they were in there the last time we saw them."

Choco thanked the girl, and they then made their way to the cafe hoping they would still be there, if that was where they had gone.

Luck was with them when they arrived, they immediately saw them through the window, all three went in, Charlie walked to the counter for Coffee, while Choco and Dixie went to the table where the two were sitting.

The couple told them the time of their train they caught that day, and told them Rene had left no more than five minutes before them. With that information they decided to make their way to the railway station and see what train left five or so minutes before the buskers train that day, and find out it's destination.

As they made their way to the railway station along the main road to the booking and enquiries office, Charlie saw coming in the opposite direction to which they were walking, the bus tranport vehicle from the manor turn into the the the waiting area car park of the station. As it turned he saw there were people in side of it he tried to count them but they had turned too quickly, and were around the corner before he could do so.

Charlie was about to say what he had spotted, and had given Choco a nudge on the arm before he spoke.

"Yes I know keep walking." Choco had spoken before Charlie had the chance to tell him what he had seen.

"Let's get onto a platform other than the one they get on and watch which train they catch, it may give us a clue to what we want to find out for Tim.

They hurried around to the platform with the canteen on it and waited inside, to watch the others when they arrived. Moments after they had sat down the others arrived and stood on the platform opposite them on the other side of the station. "My God! Look who it is Charlie, your red head is there, with a suitcase as well. Where do you think she is off to, it seems to me to be a repeat of what the two buskers saw, and look there are the two others who were sat at the table with her when, you became all worked up over her the other day."

Ten minutes later a train pulled in, there was a bustle of movement as the three watching saw the women and two men accompanying them climbed aboard, moments later the train pulled out of the station, as the three men came out of the canteen they saw the end carriage of the train going up the line growing smaller and the noise of the diesel engine deminished as it moved faster, and then out of sight.

"What do you make of that old mate?"

"I don't know but it could answer some of the questions of why some people at the manor disappear Choco, but the question is where do they disappear to?"

Just then a porter came on to the station platform.

"The train which just pulled out on the far platform, can you tell us what train it was porter?"

The man stopped and looked at the three men, as if he had been asked for a hand out by the three scruffy dressed men in front of him, although, Dixie was not dressed as untidy as his companions.

The porter seemed to go blank for a moment.

"Train." He looked in the direction Choco had indicated. Then as if the penny had just dropped. "Oh! the train which has just left platform one, ah now! That would have been the eleven thirty eight express to Birmingham, calling at Bristol Templemeads only."

"Thank you, is there another train any time about two thirty?"

"Yes....that would be the...two twenty three, but it is a slower train calling at most stations past Bristol, to Birmingham."

Choco gave the impression he was trying to work out a problem in his mind.

"What about penzance, would I be able to catch a train at about the same time say about two thirty five or there abouts?"

"I am afraid not sir the nearest time to that would be the three thirty five, over an hour later, the one before that would be the one ten."

"Are you sure about that porter? My friend was sure he caught one about two thirty two months ago."

The porter thought again. "Yes he might well have that would have been the two twenty nine, but that train only runs from May the first, to the last Sunday in August, it a special service for the holiday season."

With the answer he was given, Choco thanked the porter, and then the three made their way out of the station.

"Well what next, we still don't know for sure where they have gone, no but we have narrowed it down to Bristol or Birmingham, that at least is something we can tell Tim when we get back. Then he will have to make his mind up when we tell him what we know, what ever he decides, I would rather we all remain together and try to fight this thing whatever it is. But if he does decide he want's to go to Birmingham or Bristol, then who are we to stop him. Anyone fancy a drink in the Portcullis before we go back to the caravan." There was a total agreement to his question.

170

CHAPTER 29

James Caulter had returned to the room and had been told by the dowser that the priest had not moved out of the location of the lane for over an hour and a half. He thought quietly to himself for a while, then moved away from the table, turning to the others who were in the room he spoke quietly to himself, but audible enough for the others to hear him.

"I think he is holding up there until night fall."

Then he spoke with a voice loud and clear, as if he had come to a decision to act as soon as possible.

"We will not need anyone there after all, we will deal with the priest from here."

He turned to one of those in the room nearest him.

"I want four fire maidens in the chamber in half an hour with Jackson, go and arrange it now."

Those left in the room, with the exception of the dowser, took on an expression of glee and excitement at his words.

Caulter returned to the map, and remarked to those left in the room.

"The nearest house, to where he is, is almost a mile away from him, and he probably doesn't know it's there."

****

Father George had finished peeling potatoes, carrots and cabbage while Tim was finishing preparing the stuffed chicken to put it in the oven to cook.

"What shall I do next Tim?" He asked wiping his hands on a towel.

"Well there is not a lot you can do for a while, the veg. is ready leave the cabbage soaking in the salt water in the bowl for now. Why not put the kettle on for a brew, I think we have earned it don't you."

"I'll put it on, and while its boiling go down the lane and gather some fire wood for the stove so we can have plenty of fuel for heating tonight it was quite cold in here last night when the fire went out, and I noticed there was a pile of sawn up branches that should not be too difficult to be carried back here. I thought about it this morning when I was out for my walk."

"That will be fine Father, you do that and when the kettle boils I will make the brew, then come to give you a hand with what you gather. I saw a sack under the caravan, perhaps if you can put the small stuff in there for kindling and I will carry a few of the larger branches back for chopping because there is also an axe near the sack, is that all right with you?"

"That's fine!" With that the priest filled the kettle putting it on the lighted stove, then went out of the caravan and into the lane, a moment or to later he was out of sight of Tim, and the caravan.

****

In the chamber the man known as William Jackson, lay spread eagled on top of the stone altar, with his arms spread wide, four woman held his feet and hands tightly clasped in one of their own hands, in line with each corner of the altar, while the free hands poised near the large candles near them. Their manner and expressions completely absorbed in what they were doing, their eyes closed, while their minds were in tune with Jackson's.

Jackson while his body was laid on the altar, his inner self was in the lane, he moved as if gliding up the lane walking but in a way where he felt no resistance, when he espied the priest a short distance in front of him, he came to a stop, and manoeuvred himself until he was standing behind the priest, he watched as he straightened up from pulling a tree branch into the centre of the lane. He began to walk towards the sack some fifteen feet from him, although because of the concentration required the sack was unseen by Jackson, his complete attention was focused on his quarry, he came close to him and placed his unseen hands on the back and stomach of the priest, he then telepathically gave a command to the four women he was in position and ready. The women then placed their hands on the flaming candles at there sides, absorbing and sending the heat and energy from them, while at the same time multiplying it many times over into a tremendous force as they relayed it to Jackson, to be released into the priest simultaneously, they kept on giving until it was all over with the priest, it had taken just seconds to reduce him to the charred corpse, which lay smouldering on the ground, with the stench of burnt flesh and bone being trapped in the confines of the lane. Not until then did they release their hold on Jackson, who soon returned to his body jubilantly pleased with his task accomplished.

****

Father George was bending forward and finished putting a few more twigs in the sack, he had almost filled it, he straightened up and lifted it feeling the weight, and decided it was near enough full and not too heavy for him to carry, he put the sack on the ground. He walked away towards the side of the lane where he had seen a large sawn off tree branch which he pulled into the middle of the lane ready for Tim to carry when he arrived, and deciding that when the branch was chopped into small lengths there would be enough to keep the caravan warm until the next morning. As he walked back to the sack he felt a sharp searing pain in his stomach, so intense it made him cry out, he fell to the ground crying out in agony, he lay there unable to move, and as he looked down and pressed the area where the pain was with his hands, he felt a burning sensation, then saw where he had felt the pain flames spreading all over the centre of his body, he heard a crackling and hissing. He could not believe what he was seeing. He attempted to beat himself, but it was to no avail he felt as he beat the area aflame it was not his clothing on fire but himself, the flames leaped around him consuming his body and all the while he was conscious of a terrible pain as they licked around him like animated and hissing cobras of fire, until he felt his strength leaving him and could do no more but suffer the excruciating pain until he passed out and was mercifully dead. His body or what was left of it, a blackened charred object on the ground. It had taken just a matter of seconds, but to the priest it felt close to an eternity.

****

Had Jackson looked around him from where he had dealt with the priest, instead of returning immediately to his physical body on the altar, he would have seen Tim standing just a few yards away, in the bend of the lane, having arrived to help the priest with the fire wood.

He had been about to call to father O'Connell that he had arrived, at the very moment the women had released the energy that entered into the body of Father George, as it had entered into the priest, he could see a kind of silhouette of Jacksons form, shimmering in a red and yellow brilliance. He saw it, but could not under stand what it was he was seeing, but instinctively knew it was frightening, evil, and dangerous. A moment later he had seen the priest burst into flames, he watched helpless and frightened, then as the priest lay there charred and smoking, he took to his heels in panic as fast as he could, back the way he had come, with the vision of Father O'Connell in flames, and screaming in agony, in his mind's eye.

Before reaching the caravan he saw a gap in the hedge and scrambled up over it into the field Charlie and Choco had gone into and continued to run blindly in the direction away from the road, but towards the valley between the hills and then across the slope which led to the dead ground the others had seen the day before. Down the slope of the dead ground it levelled out, and still he kept running, panic still within him then suddenly he was confronted with a stone wall of about five six in height, he kept running towards it and as he came to it he jumped and scaled it with ease, swinging his legs over and letting himself drop to the other side, as he let go he realized too late the wall was over twelve feet high on the opposite side from where he had climbed, looking down he saw a wheelbarrow full of soil and someone in the act of wheeling it away, he landed on top of it, as he did so, it broke his fall but tipped onto it's side, while the person holding it went sprawling the opposite way against the wall with a loud shout.

****

Sean Conway had promised his wife molly, he would finish moving the rest of the soil he had left in a pile behind the back of the house, after digging out a small fish pond he had built on a grass area there, he had admitted to himself she was right, and that when it rained, or when ever he went into the garden shed for his tools, he would invariably drag some of the soil into the house and make the kitchen floor dirty again, it had been there for well over a week now and molly was becoming more irritated with the mess he was dragging in on his feet, eventually after having to take his shoes off every time he came through the back door he reasoned it would be better in the long run, and to have peace and quiet reign in the house again, by moving the mess away at the first opportunity.

His false leg had been giving him gip for the last half hour, as he had shovelled and brushed the pile away, with the last load now ready to be taken around to the side of the house, and spread evenly over the vegetable patch ready to be dug in with compost when the spring arrived in the following year.

As he began to wheel it away the handles were wrenched from his hands, a dark heavy shaped form fell onto and tipped the barrow sideways, as he heard a howl from whoever it was. The force of the weight twisting the barrow out of his hands and making him lose his balance, he fell against the wall numbing his elbow and momentarily winding him as well.

He was confused at first, then seeing the person responsible for him laying on the ground, sat groaning and holding his ankle in his hands. He struggled to his feet with the intention of having a go at the idiot who had jumped over his wall like some kind of wild maniac.

"What the hell are you playing at, jumping over peoples walls like some kind of nutter?" He bellowed.

"Who are you? Where do you come from? I have not seen you around here before! Where do you live?" By now he was flushed red with the anger he was feeling, his elbow now coming back to life and throbbing, the stump of his leg felt sore and he was feeling in a real bad mood now with this scruffy individual before him.

He moved closer, and as he did so saw there seemed to be something else wrong with the man besides the ankle injury. Puzzled he put his hand on his shoulder.

"How badly are you hurt?"

"Get away! Don't touch me! Leave me alone! Tim yelled at him. Then began sobbing, babbling and rocking to and fro on his haunches.

As Sean was puzzling about what to do, his wife appeared behind them both in the kitchen doorway, wondering what all the fuss was about when she had heard Sean's voice raised in anger. Seeing Tim on the ground and and her husband standing over him.

"Sean what have you done to him." She cried aloud.

"Nothing! He just came over the wall, almost on top of me.

Tipping the wheelbarrow over and sending me flying into the wall." He gave his elbow a rub as he spoke.

Molly came over to where they were. "What is he saying?"

"I don't know, sounds a load of jibberish to me. Do you think he is wrong in the head perhaps?"

"How bad are you hurt? Can you stand on your feet young man?"

Tim remained there shaking and sobbing uncontrollable.

"Sean, Put the kettle on, and make him a cup of tea, put a couple of spoonfulls of sugar in the cup."

"What!....What do you mean a cup of tea woman? The mans an idjit, he could have killed me coming over the wall like he did, and now, you want me to make him a cup of tea!"

Molly turned on him.

"What's the matter with, you Sean! Can't you see there is something wrong here? The mans a bundle of nerves and can hardly catch his breath. He looks about all in. It seems to me he is in some kind of shock. You just go on in and make the tea, while I see if I can get to the bottom of whatever the matter is here, and don't forget the sugar, it's good for shock, and I am almost sure that could be part of his trouble."

She turned her attention back to Tim, her voice seemed to calm him down some what, he tried to speak but could not get the words out. She caught hold of him gently by the arm. "Come on, let's see if you can stand on your feet I will hold your arms."

Gradually with a bit more coaxing Tim was on his feet, and then she helped him walk into the kitchen and onto a chair, while Sean was pouring water into a china teapot. She stood for a while, unsure of what to do, then her years of nursing skills came back to her, kneeling down in front of him she undid his laces of his boot on his injured ankle, then carefully took his boot and sock off. She saw it was swollen but probably only sprained, filling a bowl with cold water and some ice cubes from the freezer compartment of the refrigerator she lifted the foot into it.

"Let your foot soak soak in there for a while. It will help with the swelling, and to bring the bruising out sooner. I don't think there is any damage other that a sprain. See if you can move your toes."

Tim Did so, although, as he did his mind was still on the terrible sight he was a witness too, such a short time before. "There that's a good sign to start with, at least there is nothing broken. now what has happened to get you in such a state to want to jump over walls as you did?"

Sean came over to them with a cup of tea and handed it to molly.

"Did you put plenty of sugar in the cup Sean?" She asked as she handed it to Tim. "Here now drink this and then we will see if you can tell us what caused you to come over the wall in such a reckless manner."

His hands were shaking as he took the cup from her, he was still in shock, steadying his hand she raised the cup to his lips.

"Come on now drink, it will help calm you down, and then perhaps we can get to the bottom of what's bothering you.

Sean meanwhile, had calmed down and stood next to his wife, and held out a cup to her, until she took it from him. They both stood looking at Tim as if they were waiting for a patient to recover from a coma.

After a couple of swallows Tim seemed to regain a degree of composure, although the shaking had still not gone completely. He emptied the cup as if it was some kind of elixir, which allowed him for the first time since the experience in the lane, to focus his mind on the present and the people he was with. The meeting of them, and the event of coming over the wall was just beginning to sink in, he tried to apologize to Sean, but his mind went back to why he had been running in such a blind panic. He shuddered as everything seemed to come in focus, and the reality of the situation was brought home to him. He thought of his friends for the first time since the death of the priest. As he did he went to stand up, the pain as he put his weight onto his foot, let him know perhaps he had better wait a while with these people, and ask one of them to go and wait at the entrance of the lane to warn them of what had happened there.

All these things went through his mind but he had still a little confusion around him he had forgotten those with him did not know of the experience he had there. Then Sean's voice broke in through his thoughts and confusion.

"Were you running from someone? Was there someone chasing you?" Sean asked.

"Yes. No. I don't know. It was horrible, I was frightened......Father George......he's...he's dead It happened......I saw it...it was something, there was something there.....there was...,something there, but I don't know what it was, he just burned, went into flames. I watched, there was nothing, nothing I could do, I was afraid.

He looked at Molly, a dazed look on his face, with tears falling unashamedly down his face.

Molly turned to her husband, handed him her cup, gestured to the hobb of the cooker where the kettle he had refilled was boiling away.

"Top up the teapot before the kettle boils dry."

Bending down she took the cup from Tim.

"I'll get you a refill, you look as if you could do with it.
Just sit there and try calming yourself down some more, while I fetch you some more tea."

Upon reaching her husband, he gave her a look of curiosity, and widened his eyes, and for a fraction of a second looked at the ceiling, as if to convey to her, he understood nothing of what Tim had said.

"What is he about, fire, and someone called Father George being dead." She whispered. She picked up the refilled cup from the kitchen table, then returned to Tim.

"Here you are, I have put sugar in it again, it seems to have done you good the first time. Now what is your name? What do we call you, and who is Father George you have mentioned? has there been and accident somewhere? Is that it. Is that what has happened. Has this friend of yours been killed in a road accident?"

After about three quarters of an hour Molly and Sean had pieced together what had actually happened to Tim, in between spasms of emotion and frustration of not being able to get them to understand what it was he was trying to convey to them. At first it was unclear and sounded so preposterous, but after questioning Tim at length came to the conclusion he was not unbalanced and something unusual and horrific had taken place, and Tim had witnessed it at close quarters. Causing him to have been in the state he was in when he had come over the wall, and fell onto the wheelbarrow.

Sean was looking at the way Tim was dressed and was puzzled.

"What were you and a priest doing out in the middle of the countryside without transport of any kind?"

When he had mentioned transport, Tim's eyes noticeably widened, as the memory of the thought he had earlier came back to him.

"My God the others, the others. I must warn them not to go back there."

"Others? What others and go back where?"

"The caravan!"

"Caravan? What Caravan, and who are these others you are talking about?"

"The friends who I was with, when we rescued Father George."

CHAPTER 30

"Rescued? You said rescued." A sudden thought had come into Seans mind.

"You have said his name was Father George. Father George what? What was his surname?"

"O'Connell! Father George O'Connell!"

"Oh God! Mary, Mother, of Jesus. The Priest is none other than the priest the papers and television have been on about the last few days or so. What has been going on? Those friends of yours, where are they now, and the caravan you spoke of where is it?"

Tim became worried then, the memory of the manor and everything else these people did not know about, how much he should tell them he did not know, or even if he had said too much for their own good.

"My friends they must be told what has happened to Father George. He looked at the clock.

"I have to get to the entrance of the lane where the caravan and the body of father George is."

"Where is this lane and what time are your friends arriving there?"

"There is no set time, but they will be back soon if they not already there. I should have had dinner ready for about four o'clock, that is any time about now."

By this time Sean and Molly were becoming totally confused and apprehensive of the things they had been hearing, they both looked at each other, and both remembered the evening of the seance with David Mitchell and Anne Farr. Was this something, they were wondering to themselves, something to do with what was said that evening by Two Bears and Paul Gage, and contact being made by others soon. With the circumstances of their meeting it seemed a good pointer to that fact, and the fact the two disappearances in connections with clergy, added to their conviction that it might be. Husband and wife discussed their thoughts with each other quietly, and away from Tim, they came to the conclusion that it was more than just an accidental meeting, and that in some way Tim had been pushed in their direction, after the scene he had witnessed of the burning priest.

"What should we do Sean?" Molly looked at her husband her eyes showing concern over the conclusion they had come to, hoping for him to come up some way of diminishing her fears she was having over the situation.

He thought for a few moments, and tried to think of the best action to take. Then with a false bravado to try and allay any fears Molly was beginning to have, he spoke quietly to her, after thinking and deciding he should take a look in the lane himself.

Moving back to Tim he placed his hand on his shoulder.

"Will you be all right to come back with me to where you say the lane is and show me where the priest is, or is your ankle not up to it? You say your friends are due back there at around four o'clock. It's three forty five now, perhaps it might be better if we were there when they arrived, don't you think?"

"It will be O.K. to walk on, but even so, there is no way I am going back in the lane again."

"How about if I drive you to the entrance, and then you point me in the direction and tell me how far up into the lane he is? Will you agree to that?"

"As long as I don't have to go in the lane, that's fine."

He turned to molly. "Will you be all right here if I drive him to meet his friends, to and see the situation for my self?"

"I'll be fine, but take care, and wait for his friends before you go into the lane. Don't go in there alone. You never know what you could be up against."

"Don't worry woman, but I have to take a look see." He replied.

Sean had driven about half way to where the lane entrance was, when he suddenly jambed on the brakes, as he remembered something which had come back to him said the night of the spirit contact, about them not being on their own, or something to that effect. Anyway he was going back for Molly. Tim was taken by surprise at the sudden braking and asked what the matter was. "I have just remembered something and have to go back and pick my wife up." He replied.

Molly was in the doorway as they returned.

"I have just been on the telephone to Anne, and told her what has happened. She said she would be over with her policeman friend Dave. They should be here in about fifteen to twenty minutes time."

Sean explained to her why he had returned. Agreeing with what he said about her being left in the house on her own. She wrote a note to Anne explaining the whereabouts of the lane and, in case they would rather wait until they returned she had left the door key in the usual hiding place, saying if she wanted she could use it and then wait inside her house for them to return.

Sean parked his car a little way off of the road in the side and in the entrance to the lane, so as to allow traffic to pass while theirs was hidden until one came into the lane it's self, but they could still see if any traffic was coming from both directions on the main road through the trees. Contrary to his original plan he decided to wait for Tim's friends to arrive or Anne and Dave Mitchell should they decide not to bother going into the house and make their way to the lane.

It was not very long after they had arrived at the lane and waited, when they heard, and then saw Dixie's van pull into the lane entrance.

As soon as he saw the others pull into the lane Tim had got out of the car and although limping and still in pain, made his way to them as they pulled up nearby, waving his arms at them as he did so. Sean had got out at almost the same time and was walking just behind him and made the scene slightly comical walking with a limp on the opposite side to what Tim was, both walked towards the others in the van.

"Oh God what's up with Tim, and who the bloody hell is that with him, there's someone in the car as well, looks like a woman from here. What's going on? Could that be Rene?"

"It's definitely not Rene Charlie, but he seems all in a bit of a panic for some reason. I don't recognize the woman or the man for that matter. Take it easy and be careful just in case they are something to do with those at the manor in some way."

As they watched Tim and Sean come closer to them, they saw Molly get out of the car and come towards them. Choco gave Tim a questioning look towards Sean.

"It's all right they are friends and have helped me, I jumped over their garden wall after Father George,....Oh God Father George....Father George he's dead Choco, he's...dead...Burnt."

"What do you mean, dead, burnt?"

"He's dead Choco, burnt, he just seemed to burst into flames. There was something there with him when it happened, I saw it, whatever it was I don't know, but there was something with him when it happened. It scared the shit out of me and I ran. Then I met these two after jumping over their wall and falling on the wheelbarrow he was holding, that's how I hurt my ankle. They are all right and helped me out at the time although Sean that's the womans husband, he was pissed off with me at first, but they turned out to be sound people in the end."

Those in the van talked to Sean and Molly about what Tim had told them had happened to the priest, but were still puzzled and unsure as to what had actually happened to the priest. Choco tuned to Charlie wearing a puzzled expression, then back to the husband and wife.

"Have you been down the lane and seen where Tim says it happened?"

"No he said he was scared to go back down the lane and suggested we wait for you to return. I was going to take a look as soon as we arrived not long ago but heard you coming and decided to wait and meet you. Perhaps we should all go together now and take a look."

Choco looked at Tim, who he could see seemed still in a bad way and a little distant, as if his mind still had not accepted what he had witnessed earlier.

"How far up the lane did it happen Tim?"

"About a third of the way up, in the middle of the lane, you cant miss him. Don't ask me to come with you, I don't want to go back up there ever again." He remembered the chicken he had put in the oven to cook.

"When you are up there turn the oven off in the caravan, I put the chicken in to cook, it's probably

177

burnt to a crisp by now anyway, just fetch my belongings from the caravan, I will wait here."

When Dixie had parked the van, Molly suggested she stay with Tim, remembering why Sean had come back for her, even though she was unsure how these people she had just met could be some way involved in what they had been told was about to happen, but at the same time she was sure they were, because of the way they had met. What was it Paul Gage had told them? They were being guided towards them and they would know them by the manner of their meeting. As she looked at the young man standing next to her, the way he was dressed and the way he lived, she could not imagine, and a little taken aback that he could be one of those the spirit of Paul Gage had spoken of, and would be coming in contact with as things began to happen, could this, she thought, be the start of what they had been told of, and were these men the ones they had been told of who had been prepared in earlier lives for this....whatever it was they were be involved in.

The four arrived at the spot described by Tim, saw the remains while they were a little distance away. As they moved closer they were all affected, the smell of burnt flesh permeated around, as a cold breeze changed direction and blew towards them, all were physically affected either with weakness in the legs or the feeling of wanting to vomit. But to the three friends there was a tremendous feeling of loss, and sadness, coupled with anger, as they all came to the conclusion that whatever it was that had happened to the priest it would have been instigated in some way from those at the manor.

"What could they have done to make something like this happen, it's as if no one can escape them, no matter what they do."

"I don't know for sure Charlie, I have heard of things like this happening to people but have never experienced anything like it first hand."

"Spontaneous combustion! Human, Spontaneous Combustion, that's what it's called. It's something to do with the build up of body gasses and then somehow igniting for one reason or another, no one knows exactly how it occurs." Sean added.

A silence then prevailed between them no one sure of what to say next. The three friends and their new acquaintance stood viewing the remains of what only a couple of hours before was a human being with feelings, and a personality they had all started to grow fond of. To all of them, the confines of the lane began to take on a cold and, dismal barren, feeling, as if the quiet and stillness was in some way an epitaph for the friend they could see laying on the ground before them. The trees seemed to be arched making a canopy and bending over with them in sympathy, of those mourning the loss of a friend in such a grotesque manner, a droplet of water hit the side of Charlie's cheek as a slight drizzle rain began to penetrate the overhanging branches, and the skies above became darkened with rain clouds changing the light within the lane, the place began to take on a cold emptiness which made all of them feel the need to leave there.

The oven was switched off, they locked the caravan door bringing Tim's things with them. They walked silently past the remains of Father George, Dixie stopped to cover him with a blanket he had brought from his caravan, nothing was said as he did so but, the appreciation of what he had done on his own back was recognized, by looks and gestures as he rejoined them.

As they arrived back at the entrance to the lane, they saw Dave Mitchell had arrived with Anne Farr and were at that moment standing talking to Molly, they saw Sean and the others coming and as they did something was said, and they began walking towards them. Choco and the others stayed back.

"Is it true Sean?" There was a look of concern on both their faces.

"Yes I am afraid so Anne! So! What do we do now Anne? We have to think carefully. I think, the priest's friends are the ones we were told of at the time of the seance.

"Oh Shit! It's D.S. Mitchell, what the fuck is he doing here, what have you been up to Choco, who is that with him, another plain clothes peeler. Bloody hell he's seen me now, you haven't anything in your bags you shouldn't have, have you, no 'wonder weed' or anything hooky, he will probably want to search the lot of us, thank god my vans clean, and where I wonder is ''let's go Loverage'' if one is around the other's not far away. Oh! shit I could have done with out this."

"Calm down Dixie! Calm down, they are probably here because of Father George, remember he's in the lane back there."

Mitchell had seen Dixie's van parked in the lane when he had arrived, and was puzzled as to why it was there, and moments later saw him accompanied by the others as they came into view."I think we have pulled a bit of a gaff bringing our policeman freind with you Anne, it might prove a little problem how he came to be here. We will have to inform the authorities I know, but it might be better if he was not involved in any way with the discovery of Father George, perhaps it may be better to go back to my house and discuss what we should do next."

Thirty minutes later they were at Seans house, there was an uneasyness about the situation with Dixie, he could fathom out there was something going on which he still was not privy to, and seemed to be getting a little peeved off about, moving alongside Choco and Charlie, he got their attention.

"What's going on Choco?" He whispered. "What did that geezer mean when he said about keeping quiet about Mitchell not being involved in what we know happened in the lane, and now he has just said they are going to phone the law and tell them he found the body while he had gone out for a walk. Come on Choco fill me in, it's no good saying it's better for me not to get involved anymore, my caravan in the lane where the priest is, now makes, me involved and when the fuzz come here, what do I say when they ask me if I know who he is and, what he was doing out here? I have gone along with you up to now, not asking questions about what you have been up to, but now I think perhaps I better know what has been going on for the sake of all of you, or I might drop you in the shit unintentionally."

"Hold on Dixie, we will fill you in later. I just want to hear what they are saying, there is something strange going on and I am not sure now, myself, what it is, let's just wait and see if we can find out what is going on with them first!"

All four friends were standing together when Anne Farr and Dave Mitchell approached them. Mitchell gave Dixie a look of recognition, but nothing more, and stood a little to the side and slightly behind Anne.

"Sean has told us a little of what your friend has said happened, to Father O'Connell and a little of what you spoke of concerning Gowendene manor would, you mind very much if we spoke to you about what you have told Sean, and perhaps anything else you can remember about the manor, before and after you you rescued him?"

"Will we need a brief with us when you interview us?" Dixie Spoke before any of the others could reply. I don't think the lady means an interview Dixie, a talk with us is what I think, the lady means? Am I right?" Choco spoke to Anne although, his eyes were on Mitchell, as were Dixie's.

Mitchell laughed, a look of amusement filled his eyes.

"It's a change Dixie, but we are not interested in anything you might, or might not, have done, and the lady has nothing to do with me or 'Let's go' Loverage in the way of our occupations, we are just friends."

"Yes that's right, Dave and I are friends. It's just the fact that the experience you have had recently, may have a bearing on something we have been told a little about. With what Sean has told us he has already heard from,....is it Tim?" She looked at Tim a smile on her face waiting for the answer to the question she really already knew, but had asked so as to get a rapport going and, then perhaps an insight into what else they might know.

"If we tell you of our experiences of the last few days, then perhaps you will feel the same inclination to let us know what it is, that you find so interesting about us, something about you were expecting something like, meeting up with others, I think, were the words used earlier by Sean, the man we saw Tim with when we arrived."

"Of course that would only be right, especially as I expect it will turn out that it is you, and your friends who we were told of."

"What were you actually told of about us and, was it us specifically, do you know us or anything about us, if so how, and

"I'll tell you what! How about, if we all leave here, and go to my home so as we can get to know each other and leave, Sean so as he can get in contact with Taunton police station when we are gone. It might be also a good thing if you are not here when the police do arrive."

"What about him, he is a police man isn't he. Why are you so keen to get him away from here before getting the police from Taunton here?"

"There are a lot of things we must discuss, among them, that will be one more we will explain to you, but for now what do you say, will you leave here now, and follow me to my home."

Choco looked at his friends, a questioning look upon his face.

"I will, what about you three." They agreed they would go with him.

An hour and a half later, Choco and the others had spoken to Anne and, Mitchell of their experiences from the time of beginning the search for Rene, and then of them speaking to Tony Howard, to the rescue of Father George.

Anne listened to every thing, and by the time they had finished telling her their account of the past few days, was, convinced that Sean and Molly had been right on their suspicions as to who, they, believed they were. None other than those they had been told of at the seance.

To her at the time it seemed inconceivable that it could be them, purely by their dress and way of life, and that they seemed so unlikely to be the type of people who would have any knowledge of the things they would need to assist them in in the task that had been told they would have before them, at the seance on the evening Mitchell had attended.

Anne Farr her mind working overtime, decided the information she had gained from Choco and friends, was far too important to be able to keep to her self, and accepted it could have far greater consequences due to the length of time it had been going on. She knew she needed help from someone else, who she was sure would possibly have a lot more understanding of the situation than she could envisage at that moment.

"Choco, I have been thinking. What you have experienced and have told us, I know is very important. But I don't think I have the ability on my own to understand what to do next for the best for all of us. Would you mind it if I got in touch with some friends I know and, will you all tell them what you have told me, I would not ask unless I was sure of the impending danger we might all be in, because of what is happening."

"What about telling us what we want to know?"

"I think when you understand the significance of what you have told us, you will understand that it might be better for you to hear what you require from someone far more qualified to give you the answers than myself. Will you stay here, until I can arrange a meeting of friends later this evening, you can stay and have some refreshment here while I try to arrange it. What do you say?"

All four friends agreed to her request, but not without a little nervous apprehension.

CHAPTER 31

The friends Anne had contacted had agreed to meet at her house that evening. The lounge was large enough for everyone, some sat on the floor, in chairs, armchairs, and a large sofa, without being too cramped.

Introductions were made, and Anne had run through the events which had happened so far to those concerned on both sides.

To Choco and Co. the new arrivals were an assorted lot. Charlie and those with him were taking a look as each person arrived. Their ages ranged from mid twenties to the mid sixties both male and female, eventually he counted nineteen new persons in all excluding Anne Farr and Mitchell. Charlie noticed as he glanced towards the door as the people arrived a woman who looked vaguely familiar, a woman of about twenty three to twenty five, wearing an orange and black dress with a large multi coloured flower pattern, long ear rings hung from her half hidden ears, her hair, shiny, and jet black hung down past her shoulders to the middle of her back, it seemed to sparkle as she moved, she was speaking to two people with her, a slim but not thin figure, then she began to move away from the two she had been speaking to. As she spoke to those she past, he saw her ear rings were crescent shaped and silver, she also wore other jewellery, around her neck hung a gold necklace of chain links, with what looked from where he was standing a medallion depicting a sun burst it's rays projecting outwards, on her fingers were rings, and around her ankles he could see thin silver bangles above the Asian styled sandles she wore. He vaguely recognized her but where he had seen her before he could not remember, but it would have been somewhere around the town he felt sure. As she walked around he watched her, her eyes had a natural sparkle about them, showing her to have a lively sense of humour. Later he would find she had quite a lot in common with him, all though, at this time he could not have the vaguest idea in which way they would manifest themselves, or under what circumstances. When Anne had finished speaking there was a silence in the room, then those that were on chairs began to fidget unsure after hearing Anne's account of what she knew so far, what there was planned next for the evening or what they were really there for. Then there was a sound of someone moving and coughing as they rose to their feet from one of the armchairs. He was a large framed man, and could have been a double for Richard Griffiths the actor of stage and television fame.

He walked around until he was facing everyone in the room then, taking off his glasses he began to clean them, with a handkerchief he had taken from his jacket pocket. Looking first at Anne, and then to the others in the room, his eyes squinting while he cleaned them, until he had put them back on.

The fidgeting, and the low sounds of whispered comments made concerning the information given to them by Anne, ceased at the same time.

"I can understand now the urgency and reason for this meeting, although, had it not been for her persistence, and had it been anyone else other than Anne, who, while insisting for me to attend while not giving me, or, as I would expect any of us the reason she had wanted us here, in truth I feel I would have had more than likely declined the invitation. But as most of you here who know her, will understand her perseverance for anything she feels so strongly about, so here I am."

He looked briefly at a note pad he had been writing notes in, while Anne had addressed everyone there when they had finished arriving.

"As I have already stated, I can understand now her urgency in forming this meeting, but what escapes me is, if the things we have been told of are true, why has knowledge of the people you have come into contact with only just coming to light now, when supposedly things have been happening for quite some time, years in fact, is what we are led to believe. I am not for one minute doubting the things told by those of you who have come into contact with the elements of the people in question, but if what you say is true. Is it possible there are events taking place now that could be a kind of vanguard, of something which has been fore told would be eventually happening, of which we have been warned of for centuries?"

He had spoken the words in such a manner of casualness, that he had taken everyone there by surprise, and when the penny eventually dropped, they realized immediately what he had implied by his words. Everyone there was held spell bound and silent by his statement, when he had finished.

Charlie looked at his friends, who also had as much of a look of puzzlement on their faces as did he. Although he had just met the man before him, an instinctive feeling came over him that there was more to him than appeared at first sight.

"I can see and understand that most of you here are on the same level of spirituality by the feeling of combined harmony emanating around this room. There is also a similarity in all of your individual auras, not identical but quite similar. If I am right and I pray to god I am not, then we maybe the spearhead of a battle mankind will experience only once, and with only one chance of winning it, it will, I feel not be fought with a series of battles to end the war but, one final battle for all of us, with each individual together, although, each of you with an independent mind of faith, and belief, but together in harmony and united while fighting to survive it, will not make the task insurmountable. I also think there may be just one avenue open for us to enable to win it. So I feel we should go over again and make notes of what we know, to try and find out who, what, and where they are, and what it is they are actually up to."

He waited for a moment to let his comments sink in to those in the room, before continuing. "The reason I feel strongly that we should go through everything again, is because I believe it will be immensely important for us to know and to be able to understand what we are actually up against and in that sense at least, we may be able to defend ourselves against what ever means they can use against us when the time comes. I have heard, from Anne, as you all did of the things they have managed to achieve against those who have fallen foul of them, some of you will understand the power of good, and have always reasoned that good will always triumph over evil, it usually does but, at times it depends on in who's hands that power is and how adept they will be with it's use."

Choco and the others put down on paper everything which had happened with them, including the things which Father O'Connell had told them, and compared notes with each other, just to make sure that everything was covered and nothing was missed or forgotten.

When everyone had finished writing down everything they could recall, the papers were handed back to the Richard Griffiths look-a-like, who then went into the adjacent sitting room to read and compare them. Everyone from Choco to David Mitchell gave an account of their experiences. Tea coffee and refreshments were brought out of the kitchen, and placed on the table in the lounge for everyone to help themselves.

After a period of about half an hour the man came back into the lounge took a cup of tea as it was offered him, then sat in the chair he had used earlier.

Choco and the others had made their way across the room to where Anne and Mitchell were sitting, as he came up to them while the man who had taken the papers with the accounts they had written had sat down he spoke to them.

"Who is he?"

Before she could answer.

"That's just what I have been wondering!" Mitchell interrupted.

"That gentlemen, is Marcus De Clare, I have heard, from some source or other that he, or someone for him has traced his ancestry back to Gilbert De Clare, and that was back in the thirteenth century. He is also an accomplished psychic and medium, and extremely well respected in the field of psychic phenomenon. He is also well known name in Spiritualist circles, and a walking encyclopaedia in the local history of the South West of England to boot. He can be trusted on anything he says, and could possibly be one of the best assets at our disposal, that, was one over riding aspect of why I was so insistent he should be here tonight."

As she finished speaking every one's attention was focused on Marcus De Clare.

Seeing that he had everyone's attention again he took a momentary look at the notes he had written, then began to speak.

"I only wish that what I have to say was not necessary, but I believe after having read everything you have written of your experiences at Gowendene Manor, and other things since, it would only be right for me to reluctantly convey the conclusion of what I have read, and try to explain to you what I believe to be happening, and has been happening unknown to the world at large for quite some time, and hope we have discovered it in time."

The fidgeting started again, but was short lived as he then continued to speak.

"The fact of the matter is, as I see it, and truly believe is that if we try to fight these people, as we are now, we will be coming in conflict with forces so evil, we would not last very long at all. Also, we would be fighting not just to win but for the survival of our very souls, and any steps we take to do combat with them, we not only place ourselves but every creature and soul of Gods creation in jeopardy. In other words, entities of the lower realms of spirit have at last breached the the living world as we know it, with the help of misguided and power hungry beings from the past who had been banished to the lower plains influencing those in power in the present, who have with patience and stealth built up a network of evil, unknown to anyone other than themselves until now. I believe they are now working towards world domination and are almost ready to attempt to bring all the evil power they posses to bear to achieve that end. In other words what I am saying is the start of what prophets have spoken of for centuries, and what is told to us in the Bible and other holy manuscripts, of all religions, it seems, is now upon us.

If we take just a small part of what can be seen in the world today, such as wars, famine, and natural disasters, which in most part are due to mans greed and evil, which we are only now beginning to see the result of, after the selfish and unthinking concern for every thing which has been put in our care and has been neglected and used to the detriment of the balance of the ecology of our whole environment, which will eventually aid the evil to bring about the environment they wish and desire.

Everything we have been told by prophets and wise souls, who, for their concern for us, have left the higher realms of the spirit world and donned a human mantle to try and warn us of the impending dangers we all face. But while doing so have kept faith in what they know of the forms of life eternal, and tried to tell us of these things, also, they came to tell us if we strayed from the path of righteousness, there was still the chance of spiritual progression open to us all to enter the world of spirit and love, love, not of our present understanding, but of the interpretation of what is really meant by spiritual love, which encompasses all understanding of all things.

In other words, such as, accepting the things as being wrong for far too long, but out of their hands, things such as injustice, wars, brought about by the power bestowed on leaders who have brushed aside the oaths and promises they have made when in the race to be elected, to line their own nests, and then have paid little heed to what has been going on around them in the lives of ordinary citizens, until they speak out and rebel against systems of corruption and apathy, they feel they want no part of, then they are seen as trouble makers, ridiculed or imprisoned or worse, but always remember these people have the strength to fight with words rather than arms of destruction, and with some inner strength they might not understand at the time, of their misfortune, which comes from sometime in a past life where the understanding of spiritual progression has been revealed to them, and manifests itself unconsciously in that present life, and whereby they have no fear of death itself and are allowed to speak from the heart to spread the word of individual conscience.

We have for some considerable time now been experiencing on a world wide scale famines, and natural disasters, which have been mostly due to how the world in essence has been neglected in various ways, mostly to extract wealth for the few to enjoy a higher standard of living, who bear no thought for the consequences of their acts. These things mankind have had their eyes closed to for such a long time. There are few who seem to care, for the starving, and the lost souls, who in their lives are experiencing the ills and evils in today's life. All for the benefit of those in control of their situation. To expect that things will end up well for them without any effort on any one's part is just a state of wishful thinking."

The room remained quiet, as everyone in there had listened intently to what had been said by Marcus De Clare, when he had revealed his conclusions on what felt had been happening. With most of them there knowing his reputation within the circles he was known to have attended for years, as a guest sitter in both closed and, open, which he had helped and advised with, in the past. It was taken for granted by them all that every word he had just spoken to them was as important to them as was the air they needed to breath.

Charlie, Choco, and Co. had just sat and listened to what had been said and although there were things he spoke of that they did not understand they were all of the same opinion that what had been said far outweighed any conclusions they had come to about the experiences they had encountered since they had become close friends. Charlie watched his friend as he took from a piece of silver foil it was wrapped in, a chunk of chocolate, and bit down on it just as Marcus De Clare began speaking again.

"All of you have gifts of spirit, and this I feel very strongly will be the only means of defence and the only way we may be able defeat them, although, we must not under estimate or, over estimate their abilities. They I am sure, will have weak spots where or what ever they may be we must try to find out. As for our ability to find any Achilles heel that they have, perhaps chance will play a part, or intuition, or even given away by them somehow, whatever, we must be ready, and able when the time comes to have some form of protection, and the tools, with which to defeat them.

For some reason I feel it is perhaps a possibility that, we had before we were born into this present life, a specific task or purpose, for us all to be here at this time. What that purpose is, for some reason must remain unknown to us, at this time. There may have been some kind of agreement with us when we were living on our spirit plain while in the spirit world. Also those in spirit on the higher realms would have known of what was happening in the lower realms, and the more I have thought about it in this way, the more convinced I am in what I have told you. Can the reason be that we are all together at this time, could it be we have all accepted the challenge, in some way, before we were born into this life, why us, I have no idea, but I am sure there is a purpose, and a way to triumph against the lower realms, I just hope we will be competent enough as a force to even do battle with them when the time comes, for who knows what might happen if we are not."

Choco the whole time had listened to what he had said and had forgotten the chocolate he had put in his mouth and bitten down on the once, and then left the two halves at either side of his mouth beside the side of his cheeks and the bottom of his gums. The chocolate had melted and lay as a thick sweet liquid, he worked his tongue until the liquid was at the back of his throat and with one long slow gulp swallowed it.

Marcus de Clare rose from his chair, looked at Choco and those with him.

"Even those we have just met I feel are here because they should be, perhaps if Anne would be willing to take them under her wing so to speak, we may find out what gifts they have, or as the case may be, may have, but need to be developed. In any event perhaps we can at least find out why they should be part of what has been discovered about those from the lower realms of spirit.

He then stood up in front of everyone in the room, still looking the imposing figure he had been since he first began to speak to them. He stood quietly his mind racing, trying to be sure there was not anything else he could think of they should know of the conclusions he had come to, deciding that there was not much more he could say to them about what he had already spoken about. Eventually he did begin to speak again.

"They do it seems have powers, and to be honest it does seem quite daunting to me that we might have to go up against them.

If that scenario does happen then we must be prepared to see it through to the end, no matter what." There was another short pause before he continued again.

"We cannot for the moment even contemplate becoming involved with them for to do so would I feel have disastrous consequences for all of us. What I feel and suggest is we need two things.

Time, and information, information such as how big a problem they are, and as near as we can discover how large, and how organized they are. Time! As much as we can get, so that we can prepare ourselves to be capable and effective enough shock them, when they do find out we know of them, and as I have said once we show our hand to them in any way we must be prepared to see it through all the way. We cannot as I have already said try to stop them with the means we have at our disposal now, for to do so would as I have said prove foolhardy and result in defeat for us without even accomplishing anything. So I suggest we form a developing circle with all of us for at least two nights a week and see what with the help of spirit we are capable of to help ourselves in anyway, such as concentrating on improving, and   perfecting any gifts we may have and perhaps obtain new ones, to help us. As he said the last sentence he looked at Choco and the others.

As the evening drew to a close, Anne Farr came over to Choco and the others while they were preparing to leave and together as a group. She was accompanied by Mitchell and as she talked to them he listened to what she was saying.

"Would you all be prepared to do what Marcus has said, and to sit in a developing circle and give it a try just for a while to see if there is anything you are capable of doing to help? It would mean meeting at Sean's house perhaps six nights a week for approximately six or seven weeks before we would know anything for sure if as as Marcus has said we have that long. We might be able as well, to find out why, as Marcus has said, why it is you have become involved, because as it was already told us by spirit that we would meet, and for the life of me I am curious as well, no disrespects to you but, I cannot see at the moment why it should have been, as our backgrounds and way of life are so completely different, but there has to be more to things than us just meeting as we have." Turning she spoke to Mitchell.

"The same invitation goes for you as well David, would you be free for a couple of hours a night from, shall we say tomorrow night from seven thirty, then perhaps after a little while we may be able to shed a little light as to why we are all here together, what do you all say, with the circumstances as they are?"

Choco agreed and when he did the others followed suit, although Tim was still a little unsure at first, but eventually agreed. Mitchell was it seemed in full agreement, and it was decided they would all meet the following evening as arranged.

CHAPTER 32

Marcus De Clare came to Sean and Molly's house every evening they held the circle. Which had been going on for six weeks, with no sign that anything was known about what they were doing, or they were even known of by those at the manor, which to all was a welcome relief.

Choco and the others had returned to the caravan, Tim returned with them after a lot of convincing from the others that when they had returned, there seemed nothing to be afraid of there. No signs of anything untoward or harmful against them had happened, resulting in him leaving Molly and Sean's house where he had been staying temporarily, at their suggestion when they saw initially how adamant he was that he was not going back there, and did not want to see him sleeping rough in an old pill box as he was going to do. After the time he had been staying back at the caravan he seemed now, to hold no fear at staying there anymore which seemed to make things back to normal, as far as they possible could be, after the the death of Father George.

Choco and Co. sat in with the rest of the group of people to try to see if there was any evidence for them being able to find out if they indeed did have gifts of any kind. But after the six weeks had passed they started to become disillusioned with the possibility of them being able to achieve anything of the paranormal nature. But such was the feeling that they should be there, by the others, and that they must be something to do with what was happening, also, they still believed they were the one's who had been spoken of the weeks before at the seance. They agreed to continue sitting with the others there. Even David Mitchell had found he he was able to achieve things of a paranormal nature, from clairvoyance to a higher perception of intuition, with one thing after another.

As it happened, they had all met at Sean and Molly's, Marcus was there as usual to see if he could be of help to them in any way, while at the same time he could not disguise the fact that there was something on his mind which was obviously troubling him. After finishing the usual hour of meditation, and then the time spent trying to boost their performance on their different psychic abilities two hours had passed. As someone went to the kitchen to make drinks for them all before finishing for the night before making their ways home, he seemed as he sat down into a chair to have come to a decision, and asked for their attention for a moment or two before they finished for the night.

He began telling them that he would like them all to meet at his home on the coming Saturday, and it was imperative that they all did so for their own safety, and it would only be for a hour and a half at at the most. He felt, he told them, that things might be coming to a head shortly, and there was a fact that he had found out, also some more information about those at the manor and bit more besides. There had also been quite a lot of activity going on that he was unaware of until just that very day. Although at the present time he was as sure as he possibly could be that, the fact that they knew about things going on at the manor was still unknown by those living there, and if they left matters as they had done up until then they should be all right for the time being.

Every one there agreed to meet at his house as he had asked.

****

After arriving back at the caravan the topic of conversation was of the statement Marcus had made, about something he had found out.
"What do you, think it could be Charlie?"
"I haven't a clue and just dwelling on it will only make us on edge, it cannot be something detrimental to us for the time being, or he would have told us of it there, and then, when we were all together."
Choco thought for a moment.

"Or, it could be that he did'nt want to tell us because, he was afraid it might frighten the shit out of us all, what with all the talk about gifts, psychic attacks, and power they have. I reckon we have as much chance of developing any gifts of any kind, as the Pope has, of becoming pregnant. If it comes down to it I think we will just have to use what ever we can lay our hands on, a bit of four by two would cause a bit of a headache on anyone gifts, or no gifts, and I think in the end that is what it might have to come to, what do you say Tim?"

"A lump of wood, or even an iron bar would not have been any use to father George, remember!"

"Yea! That's true, how the hell did they do that. Do you have any ideas of your own about it?"

"To tell the truth I don't like even thinking about it, and as for how it was done? Another of these gifts they keep talking about, and while we are talking about gifts and developing, there is nothing that I have seen, to give me any confidence, so far with those we have been sitting with for the last six weeks, clairvoyance, healing, and that guy that can move a bloody magnet by concentration and looking at it, that's going to be a good weapon of defence that is! What is he going to do, make them lose their way when they do eventually find out about us all and come to get us.""?

After a few days they had followed Sean and Molly, as they had suggested the reason being, that they had no idea where Marcus lived. Eventually they arrived at his house which was about four miles from the outskirts of Taunton on the old A38 road to Wellington. The house, a large Georgian property standing alone on a hill just a little way off of the main road they had been driving on. The entrance was gained by driving up through a lane with a high banked wall on either side, topped with a well trimmed laurel hedge, until the lane opened up and led to a wide tarmacadamed car park which covered a large expanse of ground wider than the length of the building which was surrounded with Douglas firs interspersed with Beech and Lime trees.

As they grouped around the two vehicles that they had come in, they could see there was already approximately twenty or more other vehicles there, having arrived before them. Dixie broke the silence.

"I wonder if all the drivers came here alone, or if there were other passengers with them, because if there were, it would mean that there are a lot more people here tonight than we have ever been together with at any time before, when we have met with those we have got to know in the group.

A flight of flag stoned steps illuminated by out side lights attached to the wall of the house, led up to the front of the building, which had been cut into a deep sloping earth bank, miniature conifers in concrete tubs lined each side of the steps spaced about four feet apart, and having the appearance of small soldiers with pointed hats stationed ceremoniously in the dusk light, waiting for some kind of official dignity's visit. Reaching the top of the steps an area the length of the house and thirty yards wide was again flag stoned with a large pond sunk in the middle, surrounded again by various tubs with shrubs in which placed strategically, tended to break up effectively the large expanse of open area of the patio. Each end of the area was flanked by a natural sand stoned wall reaching each end the of the sides of the house, and reminiscent of Greek styled architecture.

As they entered the house they saw right away that Dixie's comments earlier, were well founded. There were indeed, more people there than they had met at any time before. At a quick count Choco could see there were at least fifty people there. "What the hell is going on here? Why are all these people here? So much for keeping things to ourselves, as that Marcus guy has been saying to us.

"Choco muttered to whoever was closest to him, which happened to be Dixie.

"It gets curiouser, and curiouser, as Alice said!" Was his reply.

Someone spoke, but they could not hear the words, but after they had been spoken there was a movement towards a large pair of double doors. Choco and the others began to follow others as they moved towards them. Going through them they found themselves inside a large sitting room, come library. They saw immediately the furniture had been moved around into the shape of a horse shoe, so that wherever anyone sat they could see a table and three chairs set at the open end of the horse shoe. Every one seemed to know every one else there by what Choco and the others could see as greetings were exchanged between one and another inside the room, but as they entered, there was just a cursory acknowledgement to them, with a slight puzzlement as to who they were. Choco could see the curiosity in them, by the expressions some had on their faces, and also heard one or two quietly asking others they knew, if they knew them or why they were there.

"Seems we are more like intruders here, than part of the gathering of friends." He muttered to Charlie.

"I just knew we should have called in at the caravan to pick up our Sunday best, one never knows who one could meet at these gatherings, don't you know." Charlie then made motions of flicking dust off of his torn and faded denim Jacket.

They watched as the other people were in parties of three four, and five close together in conversation, and they all began to feel a little conspicuous in the present company they found themselves.

Charlie sat down as did those with him, and took a sweeping look around the room, to see how many in actual fact he could remember seeing before at the other meetings they had been to.

He could not notice any one missing from the last meeting when they had been asked to come that evening by Marcus. As he did so he saw the young woman he had first seen at the home of Anne, still adorned with the jewellery she had worn there with a similar mode of clothing she always wore. She waved to some one while she was in the doorway, and mimed something to them above the sounds of conversation. He looked to see who she had been miming her words to and saw Peter and Abigail Jones motion for her to join them in an empty seat which they more than likely had saved for her when she arrived, a few more people had arrived by now, and he estimated there must have been over sixty or more now in the room.

After a period of ten minutes or so of entering the room, he saw Marcus leave the side of the room where he had been speaking to two elderly people, a man and woman he estimated might well be in the late sixties or early seventies. He moved from there with the two following him, to the table and chairs where the the two sat down while Marcus spoke to them for a little while, then rose to his feet, and as he did so the hum of conversation began to die down, until there was complete silence.

He opened a buff coloured folder he had been carrying in his hand and took from it some sheafs of paper with writing upon them, took a short glance at the top few pages, spoke again with the man sitting next to him, the man answered while at the same time nodding his head, as if Marcus wanted something he had been told, or had read in the papers verified, before he spoke to everyone there.

"Good evening everyone! I am so glad and relieved that you are all here. I know there are some among you who have had to cancel previous engagements to be here this evening, I apologize for any inconvenience this may have caused you, but I felt I had no other choice than to have you all meet here as soon as was possible, and advise you all, to relay everything we speak of to the few who found it impossible to be here.

The first thing I have to tell you there is a chance that the secrecy of our existence may have been compromised through no fault of ours, it is not certain at the moment, but we will have to take steps against such an event should it be so. But we will deal with those facts later. Because of various facts which had come to light since, the terrible death of Father George O'Connell, and when we were first warned of the people at the manor, and the experiences of our new found friends who had stayed there. Also since other facts we had found out, initially from the papers about the experiences of some among you here now, we had taken steps to try to find out as much information as we could since we first met together at Anne's house, and at this time others besides myself have made discrete enquiries and steps which at the time we assumed would be in reasonable safety of not being found out. But it seems we may have seriously misjudged the ability of our adversaries, to such an extent I fear some of us may have paid the price of over confidence dearly. He then remained silent, to see how his words would effect those before him. Noticing immediately there was a hush and then the sounds of whispering among them.

A voice spoke up from somewhere in the room, loud enough to be heard, but unsure in it's tone to be judged as confident as the speaker asked.

"What are you saying Marcus, that we have all been compromised in some way, or that there is suspicion of our existence being known of, by those at the Manor."

Marcus refrained to answer immediately to the question he was asked, instead he spoke to the elderly gentleman next to him, nodded then replied.

"Some of you know Mr Ivor Ramanouski, but for the benefit of those of you who do not, let me tell you that he is a good friend of myself, and has been for longer than I can remember, in the last six weeks with the help of his wife Alice, he has been in touch by mail and other means to various friends of groups, all over the world who are as like minded as our selves, and who until now were as in the dark as much as us until, we were told. I contacted him as soon as I had found out about Father O'Connell's death, and arranged to see him that night with his wife Alice. We discussed at length what we had spoken and written notes of together, and surmised that it might be possible that if what's being happening in this country could also be happening in others. He suggested that if he contacted people he knew, and asked that if it was possible, to see if there were anymore places such as we have now found out about here, there just might be similar things happening in other countries. At first there was complete disbelief at what was told them, until they made discrete enquiries, and with the knowledge of our experiences, they found similar situations as we have found here, from disappearances of clergy, to the setting up of 'Gowendene manor' type establishments for the homeless, in towns and cities from the U.S.A. to Canada. If as it is suspected, from north America cities right through the majority of major cities in Latin America, proof of this is not absolute, but from what we have been able to learn from the friends of Ivor and Alice in the time since they have done investigations in North America it seems by small clues and with what we know of the way they tend to work there is a increasingly likelihood that they are a lot more than just active there. If that is so, then I am sure they are well established in Europe, and more than ever sure there has to be a strong possibility they have at least gained footholds in the Near and Far East by now. In other words I feel they have it seems accomplished the first part of the aims they had in mind..... To have a foot hold in every part of the globe......North, East, South, and West. Which in turn will make any defence against them immense."

It was then he turned once more to Ivor Ramanouski saying:

"I will let Ivor tell you in his own words, so to give you the information, and in more detail than I can, because he knows the people over there, and I do not."

Ivor Ramanouski stood up a head of silver white hair, thick waves at the sides of his head shorter on the top the standing remnants of a long over due crew cut, while about his collar the hair protruded in length covering his starched white shirt, giving an unaccustomed look to his otherwise near perfect tailored appearance. He stood there in front of those present, fiddled with his watch strap on his wrist, looked at his watch face, but not really looking to see what the time was or, at the second hand moving. He was thinking as he looked up. Where should he start, should he tell everyone there what he had discovered or hold back on most of what he knew to be the problems they all faced or were likely to face if, or when they started happening. Suddenly his mind was made up for him.

"Don't hold anything back Ivor, if you do it may cause problems for some one here later on, better they know it all so as they will know what they will be up against." Marcus had noticed the hesitation in his friend, and tried to give him the boost he felt he needed. Ivor took a deep and silent breath, then began to speak.

"I have experienced many things in my life, but, this has to be one of the most tortuous, and disheartening I have ever had.

I have numerous friends in the United States, and other parts of the world, I spoke to some of them in confidence and have written letters to others about what has been discovered here. They in turn have confided in other close friends of theirs, explained what I had told them of our problems over here, and enlisted the help of close friends and relatives who have the same beliefs as us. It seemed that wherever they went, and after a while of making discrete enquiries, the same things that had been going on here were happening to a varied degree over there, or starting to occur, with startling similarities. Perhaps not in such an advanced stage as we have experienced, but, they are happening, and I feel it will only be a short space of time before those on the American continent will be in much the same fear and jeopardy as we are now experiencing. At first it was met with disbelief, but as things began to emerge as being similar to what we have knowledge of here, it turned to utter astonishment. Since then the friends I have made over quite a number of years, after understanding the extent and nature of the problem, theirs and ours, have pledged their support to us and suggest if possible, we pool our knowledge about what ever we find out, and they have offered to help us in any way they can. I accepted and offered the same to them on your behalf. Because I feel that whatever we find out from now on should be made available to them as they are willing to do the same."

He waited a moment to see if there was any dissent to his latest statement, there was none so he continued.

"When I had first told them of Gowendene Manor and the use it had been put to, someone suggested the idea that the same thing could be happening over there, or anywhere those from the manor had infiltrated or had sent people. Enquiries were made with the utmost secrecy, so as to try and keep any knowledge they might find out, should they do so, to them selves. Eventually there was at first a suspicion that there were similar events occurring there, as we have found. But it now seems on a much larger scale than at first thought. There are it seems, many places offering refuge to the homeless and down and out people of all ages. The first place they had investigated, which they began to get suspicions that it was being used in a similar way as what has been going on here, was a small town ten miles or so from Quebec in Canada. It was almost a carbon copy of what has been happening here in Taunton, but the place was not so isolated, and we have photographs of some of the people who stay there and some who visit there every so often, at least about once a fortnight male and female, and as you will see there seems to be far more business people visiting there than usually associate with places, such as they are. They have been seen to come and go quite frequently, so I think each place varies in importance, and why that should be so we do not yet know."

At this point he stopped, then bent down to the side of his chair and picked up an attachá case placing it on the table he opened it and removed from it a large A4 size envelope, then took from it two square plastic bags, which every one there could see contained photographs he took photographs from one of the bags and laid them on the table and then did the same with the other bag. Walking around to the front of the table he handed one of those sitting in the front of the horse shoe, the photographs he had taken from the first bag.

"These are some of the photographs we have taken of the various occupants of the house in Canada, as you will see they look to be the usual people one would expect to find living in such a refuge, plus some people who work there on as I have said a regular basis, but others who are more likely to be business men, and by the way they dress and the vehicles they use are extremely well heeled. As I said earlier why they visit we do not know but they do seem out of character for the place. He then pulled out the photographs from the other bag and handed them to the person he had given the first batch to, to pass around to the others there. When you look at the second lot of photographs you will see some of the same business men as were seen in the first lot of photographs, the difference is that they were taken at different hostels in different, cities, states, and even countries. Also, like here, my friends have discovered that people have gone missing. Some bodies of the missing have been found dead, also killed by unexplained means. There have also been quite a number of persons of different religious persuasion, Christian, Muslim, Hindu, and others of lesser known beliefs, all those found have met their ends in an identical manner as those which have come to light here. Such as different forms of mutilation, spontaneous human combustion, but there did not seem to be any answer to what has been happening from any of the governments of the countries concerned, except a kind of enigma as to how these things were happening.

Since our friends had known what we had been experiencing, they decided together not to stand by without getting anymore information from the authorities of their country they but would try through unorthodox means the information the authorities, they thought, were sitting on, and not willing to release to the public at large. Since then we have been able to gather from various sources, with a large amount of inside help from friends who are now in the know, of what we understand to be happening, and there seems to be a complete clamp down on information by the authorities of the countries concerned. Since there was obviously something happening in the highest echelons of power the only conclusion they could come to was that some how they have gained positions and control in all aspects of government, in most of the countries we know they are active in. Absolute connections have been made with the things that concern us, in as much as we can be sure of, in, Trinidad, Belize, and Jamaica, with just a suspicion of a few other countries in the Caribbean. Take this with what we already know of things happening in the U.S.A. and Canada, we can see that things are a lot more wide spread than we could ever have imagined when things first came to our notice."

He then looked towards Marcus, and his eyes indicated a secret pre arranged message to him, understanding what was meant, Marcus got to his feet as Ivor sat down. A serious look on his face, similar to when he had first spoken to them all at Anne's house when they had all met and come together as a group. He stood still his mind seemed to focus on whatever it was that both men knew and which was unknown to the others in the room except Alice. Who was at that moment staring ahead, her eyes not focused on anything in particular, but conscious of what was about to be revealed to every one else there. Marcus as was his usual manner, reached over the table and picked up the glass of water he had filled while Ivor had been speaking and sipped from the glass. After clearing his throat he began to speak.

"Ivor has told us already that his friends have managed to get photographs of......some some of the people at the other places known to have connections with the group we know of here. As he had said some of them are regular visitors to all the hostels that have been watched. We have no idea what they are engaged in while away from the hostels they visit with such regularity, but feel they must hold some kind of high position within the, shall we call it for now the International Organization Of Evil, and in some way part of the co-ordination of the whole network. Ivor and Alice, after receiving calls from various friends from the States, and Canada concerning what they had discovered decided, two weeks ago to go over and see for themselves the situation, and see if they could be any assistance to them for a short while. He returned home last Wednesday, but now since his return, he has received some bad and disturbing news from Canada, to be precise.......it seems they had been able to follow and report on some of the individuals, mostly to airports, and had even managed to find out some of the destinations of the individuals they had been following. Things seemed to be going well and then some how or other, and for reasons we have not been able to ascertain, the sending in of reports came to an abrupt end with also the disappearance in three of the groups of people who had been following three different individuals, they seem to have disappeared without trace. The rest of those who were in the same groups of churches, cannot understand what has happened to them. In total there have been nine of the members who have disappeared without trace. The friends of Ivor contacted him on Thursday to ask if anyone here had tried at anytime to follow any of those we know to be connected with the manor, to which he replied that he did not think so, it was only then that they told him about the missing members within their church groups. It seems each group of friends chose to join forces to follow three people they had seen visit the premises on a regular basis, deciding on which individuals it would be they then worked in threes each three doing stints of eight hours each, following him around the clock. Things seemed to be going well for a few days and then those who had been watching had disappeared, along with the other six making nine altogether who live in Canada. Since receiving that the telephone call he has tried to contact his friend on no less than seven occasions but to no avail, once or twice he could understand, but not seven times. He is to say the least more than a little concerned about his safety, and also relieved they had told him they would keep everything they might fine out in their heads and not on paper, or computer.

So......in a few words I am afraid some how or other, unless when I try later to contact them again and am successful, we must assume the worse has happened to them, and presume it is more than likely he would have been under interrogation, and possibly during it from what we know at this end, he would have probably cracked due to the methods they would have employed."

Marcus then addressed everyone there to say it might be as well to have a break, and while they were doing so there were a few of them there he would like to speak to in another room so as to discuss with them some facts about the situation they might find themselves in, calling out three or four names Anne's and Peter Jones among them, he told the rest there to relax smoke if they wanted, but was sorry there were no refreshments for them due to the fact he had been expecting so many that evening, and would not have the time to prepare any for them, but the urn he used for boiling large amounts of water was hot and in the kitchen along with coffee milk and sugar and disposable plastic cups, so they could help themselves to coffee or tea if they wanted.

After a period of about three quarters of an hour Marcus and the others returned to the room, and he made his way to the table with Ivor to join Alice, who had remained there while they had left the room. Still standing while Ivor and Alice remained sitting he looked around and when he saw he had everyone's attention be began speaking to them.

"After hearing what Ivor has told us, I feel we must fear the worst has happened to them, just what the worst could be heaven only knows. But there is one thing for sure, we at least know what ever we may have to do, we must be prepared to work quickly when the occasion arises."

There was a sense of cautious realization that there was indeed now something that the whole room had to accept, and that was the possibility that the people they had been trying prepare to do battle with could now know of their existence, and at the same time there was a resigned feeling that it had to be, with each of them there having to accept they would all have to be classed as expendable for the safety of everyone else in the room, knowing the end would only be acceptable if they emerged victorious over the evil they had now come to accept was within their midst.

Marcus then continued speaking, while everyone's thoughts were still on what had been said and what there was they could do about it, and not having any clear answers, they looked and listened to him, in the hope he might have some answers to their private thoughts.

"As I have already said, we must fear the worse has happened to those Ivor has told us of, and in effect they have given us a warning, in the results of complacency. We will now have to think hard before anything is done from now on, and we must be able somehow to be able to keep in touch and inform each other of anything that might be construed as being suspicious or out of the ordinary, or anything which might have a bearing on something connected with the manor house no matter how insignificant it might seem. What to do now?....I for one am unsure, but, I have a very strong suspicion the answer lays in the way and reason we have all come together at this time. I just hope it will make it's self known soon and in time. There is little doubt in my mind that things could be well on the boil for us and the sooner we can come up with a decision on what we should be doing next the better. What I would like you all to do if you will, is for everyone to meet back here in one weeks time, that is one week from today.

He then called Anne over to him and began speaking to her, while doing so he glanced once or twice towards Choco and the others with him. When he had finished speaking to Anne she looked at him her face had a look of uncertainty upon it, as if she was debating a possibility of something she was unsure of. Moments later she was on her way over towards where Choco and the others were preparing to leave.

"Marcus has asked me to ask you if you would remain behind with your friends for about half an hour or so, he want's to speak to you about something he thinks may be of use to everyone, and perhaps find out how we all fit together in this thing. Do you mind staying for a while after everyone has gone?"

All four agreed to Marcus's request.

CHAPTER 33

While Anne had been speaking to Choco, Marcus was speaking to the rest of those there, who were getting ready to leave his home, and asked a few people to stay behind. He then named them, those he had named seemed to be leaders of various circle's. He then turned and indicated for Choco and the others to come over to him. As they made their way towards him they saw Anne Farr doing the same, after speaking to Dave Mitchell, who, as she left him, sat down on a chair nearby.

As she reached the table, so did Choco and the others.

"I am so glad you have decided to stay for a while longer it might be so very important for us all."

"Why did he want us to stay behind. Do you know?" Charlie asked. While wondering if Marcus was going to tell them they did not seem to be progressing with the developing circle in any direction, and perhaps with the time left it might be better to find out how best they could contribute to what ever was going to happen and be of use to them in other ways, and they might as well call it a day, and not to bother going to the circle anymore. Then all of a sudden a picture of one of the photographs came into his mind. Something or someone in it.

"What was it? WHAT WAS IT," he had noticed? He had not really been looking at them, seeing as they were taken in a foreign country and except for what had been said about those known over there, he did not have much interest to take a good look at them.

"Anne the photographs! The photographs, where are they?" She was taken back for a moment not really understanding what he was talking about, and every one was moving around the room leaving.

"Photographs?"

"The photographs Ivor handed around earlier!"

"Ivor, oh! Yes I see.....I think he has them all back. Why did you recognize some one in them?."

"I Don't know for sure, but there is something. What! I am not sure about, but can you see if I can look at them again."

"Something, wrong Anne?" Marcus had been a few steps away from them and had caught part of the conversation.

"No Marcus, it's just that Charlie has asked if he could look at the photographs again, are Ivor and Alice still here?"

"Yes, they are waiting in the other room for us. Come on in with us now, anyway, he can look at them there, while I speak to the others before I speak to all of you." Charlie, Choco, Tim, and Dixie, gave each other puzzled looks as they followed him and Anne to the other room.

"What's the 'crack' going to be now Charlie, think they might be calling it a day with us all?"

"Don't know Choco, I was thinking along the same lines a moment ago."

"What's, the to do, with the photo's Charlie?"

"I wish I knew,....I wish I knew. But there is something at the back of my mind about them, but I am not sure what."

As they stood waiting for Marcus to finish talking to the others there, Anne had been over to Ivor and asked if they could borrow the photographs, to look at again. He gave her them and she walked back to Charlie.

"Here you are Charlie, which pack did you want, or do you want both of them?"

"Just the pack with the businessmen in, that's them. He took a bag out of her hands, and then took them out of the envelope they were in, leafing through them he stopped.

"That's the one." He held one of the snaps in his hand while he passed the others to Choco to hold. Looking at it he saw the picture of what looked like part of a park, a wall in the distance with a couple of young women pushing prams along a path together.

Then his eyes went to the subjects of the photograph, there were two men and a woman walking almost line abreast, he looked at it, at the figures of the two men and woman, one of the men's face was almost hidden as the woman's long lengths of hair was being blown forward and almost obscuring the whole head except for the hair, blond, short styled, and parted. He looked at the photograph. "What was it? What had registered, with out him actually realizing it until later, after the first time I saw it.?" He was thinking. He kept looking but there was nothing that would come to him.

"Well what is it Charlie, do you know one of them in the photo or not?" Choco asked, while looking at the photograph himself.

"Charlie continued to look, at the woman closely, and then the man nearest in the snap, no there was nothing which would come to mind, he looked at the far figure of the man who's face was obscured, and felt drawn to him. "What was it there is something, but what, he looked at the man, his coat,..shirt,.... tie,.....the tie,....the tie, that was it, it's the tie, he looked again to be absolutely sure. Yes it's the same, and the hair, I know him Choco. I know him, and so do you!"

"Know who?"

"Know who that is, on the far side of the photograph."

"Far side? How can we know him, and how could you tell who he is from that photo?"

"The tie and tie pin, look at them, where have you see them before."

"What do you mean where have I seen them before, how the bloody hell do you expect me to know that. To me, it's a tie, and pin and that's all."

"Well, Choco my old fruit, you have seen it before, and the guy. Remember, when we first saw Father George when, he was being taken to the shed, and afterwards when the other two came out, there were others with them, do you remember?" He pointed to the snap again that is the guy we saw coming out of the shed, the same guy who works in the D.S.S. office and who I saw when I filled in the doc's there to stay at Gowendene Manor. I can tell by the tie and pin, it's the college tie of the local public school he must have went there and has always worn it to work, habit, pride, or necessity, who knows or cares, I know who he is and that must count for something, and great deal of luck for us."

"Are you sure it's the same tie and pin, the pin looks pretty small, for you to identify."

"Not when I have seen them every day for for about six months, the school is right next to where I was squatting the first year I went on the road, after leaving the holiday complex, at Minehead. I don't know how it will help us but we can tell Marcus when he finishes talking to that lot."

Marcus had spoken to the people he had wanted to, and then they had joined their friends out in the carpark, then started on their ways home.

Anne Farr was the last person he spoke to and the conversation he was having with her was much more lengthy than with the others, during which he beckoned to Alice and Ivor to join him. There was it seemed to those watching, and glancing at each other with very deep and puzzled expressions on their faces, as though, there was some kind of decision being made, and eventually it seemed as if something had been decided. They stood there unsure of themselves and feeling out of place, standing in the corner of the room. Then Anne left the other three and made her way over to them. Each of them had his own thoughts on what was being spoken about them, Charlie wondered if because of the fact they did not seem to be able to contribute anything in the way of some kind of psychic ability they were going to be asked if they wanted out of the situation in case they might jeopardize the rest there. But in actual fact what they had been discussing was the exact opposite.

On reaching them she began to speak to Choco, while the rest listened in.

"The thing is." She began.

"Marcus and the rest of us have been puzzled, over the way we have all come together at this time, and he says he knows instinctively that all of you are in some way part of what is going on now, but he cannot understand in what way it could be, you do not seem able to develop any thing in the psychic field which could be of help to us all. Tim jumping over Sean's wall after witnessing what he did, which drew us eventually all together, he can not put down to pure coincidence, he feels that in some way we were guided to meet together when we did. He feels there is a lot more to you than just to be here, and has given a lot of thought to the matter. He has told me to ask you first if you feel happy with being part of what is going on, and if you are he would like you to speak to him and Ivor over something he has thought might give us some answers, and perhaps in which direction to go, it's only a suggestion and he would not be offended if you did not want to participate in what he wants to suggest to you.

"Come on! Let us all go into the sitting room it is smaller and more comfortable for us to talk over what I want to suggest we try with you. Ivor and Alice walked over to them as they began to move towards the room. When they were all settled Marcus told them he knew they all smoked, so if they wanted to they could smoke in the room and it might help relax them.

"As Anne has told you we are puzzled why you have been led to us in the way you have, I have thought and thought over everything I can think of and can not get any answer, and yet, I know I am right in believing you are part of what ever we will have to do in the future against those we know of.

"What I feel I should do, don't ask me the reasons because I really don't know of any, it's just an impression I have been getting since I have been thinking things over about all of you, and in the last day or so, for some reason I am convinced it is the only thing to do. Have you ever heard of hypnotic regression therapy?"

"Something to do with adults getting rid of hang ups, by confronting something which happened in childhood, and seeing a shrink and all that kind of thing. Is that it?"

"What does he think we all have hang ups, or what?" Choco thought as Charlie had answered Marcus.

"Well yes it is in a way but, not quite in the way I mean it, what I am suggesting is, perhaps it might answer a few questions we would like the answers to by using a form of deep hypnosis."

"Will it hurt, and will I feel O.K. when you have finished?" Dixie asked.

"No if anything you will probably feel highly enlightened full of energy, and wide awake. Dixie's eyes gazed questioningly at Choco.

"He means, like stoned, on wonder weed."

"Oh Yea!" He replied a with a grin which reached his eyes.

All four agreed to co-operate with what Marcus suggested.

Choco lay relaxed in the armchair, his eyes were closed and he could hear the voice of Ivor strong and clear, and was listening to everything that was being said, he could not fight what he was being told to do. His body felt restless and tense at first but finally, following the instructions he was given by Ivor, he began to feel relaxed and felt safe warm and comfortable. He was for quite awhile still aware that he was in the chair at Sean's house. But as the instructions from Ivor continued, he seemed to drift deeper and deeper and felt in his mind that all thought of where he was unimportant, all he wanted was to enjoy the feeling he had at that moment, he heard Ivor tell him how heavy his arms were, and then asked him to try and raise one of them, after he had told him it would be impossible for him to do so, he tried, but it just would not move no matter how he tried to concentrate on doing so, he was then told by Ivor to raise them and it would be all right for him to do so, he tried again and he raised it to shoulder height, then when he had done so he was instructed make it rigid and outstretched, and told at the same time he would not be able to lower it again until told he could. Then Ivor's voice seemed to be fading but Choco did not seem to care. Then all he knew was a feeling of complete peace, and his thoughts seemed to disappear, as his consciousness became void and he was in a deep hypnotic state of subconscious awareness, then he could hear a voice speaking to him which seemed to sound all around him, asking questions which for some reason he could not abstain from answering.

Ivor was almost satisfied he had Choco in a state of hypnosis deep enough so he could work with him, but wanted just a little more testing to see. In a gentle voice he asked him to raise his arm again to shoulder height once more and hold it rigid again, and hold it until he was told he could return it to where it was. Choco did so, and after it was held out straight and rigid for some four minutes with out dropping or muscular quivering in any way, Ivor was satisfied he would now be responsive to what he would ask him, and told him he could then lower it again. He then nodded to Sean who with, Marcus, Anne, Molly and Alice had been watching the the whole procedure closely as they had on numerous occasions before. As soon as Ivor had signalled he was ready Sean switched the stationary placed vidio recorder on ready to record what ever was said.

"What is your name and how old are you."

"Arthur Bartholamew Taplow, and I am thirty five years of age."

"Arthur. Do you mind if I call you Arthur?"

"No, don't mind."

"Arthur I want you to go back in time if you will. Will you try for me?"

"Back in time! Yes?"

"Yes Arthur back in time."

"All right back in time!"

"I want you to go back to the time of your twenty first birthday, can you try to do that for me?"

"My birthday twenty sixth of June, my birthday." That's right today is the twenty sixth of June and it is your twenty first birthday."

"My birthday today, twenty one today, twenty sixth of June my birthday."

"That's right It's the twenty sixth of June today and it is your twenty first birthday, and the time is eight o'clock in the evening where are you, and who are you with?" Pause.

"Ponti, Weavers arms, Weavers Arms, Ponti."

"Is that a public house?"

"Yes, Weavers Arms public house, Ponti."

Ivor looked at the others.

"What does he mean 'Ponty' is that someone's name."

"Who is Ponti? What do you mean when you say Ponti?"

Marcus suddenly started smiling, quietly moved over to Ivor.

"Never mind asking any more, I think by Ponti he means Pontifract, it's a town in Yorkshire."

"So Arthur you are in the Weavers Arms in Pontifract, who are you with?"

"Wendy, Simon, Luke, Kath, and a few others oh! God and Pete, he's in the toilet now with Arran, being sick, he can't take the booze, never could, he passes out every time we go out, have to get Taxi for him again tonight."

"I see, now listen to me Arthur, what I want you to do now is go back further in time, go back to the first day you went to school, to, the very first day you went to school. Can you do that?"

Suddenly Choco started to give the impression of being stressed. His arm up in the air his body twisted and shook.

"Done lee me mam, I dode wanna do stool, wanna say ome a yoo, I's do pees if ooh leff me Mam, dode lee me, no no nowww ah mam!"

Tears formed in and around his eyes, and the language of a frightened child came from his lips on the first day of his school life, his legs seemed all limp, such as a child would be when dragging them, not wanting to walk. This continued for a little longer the others listening to him then Ivor spoke again.

"All right, all right, Arthur. Now listen to me I Want you to go back to as far in the past as you can remember, think back to your very first memory, try Arthur, your very first memory.

There was a pause, followed by silence then, Choco began to make facial movements his eyes looking at something unseen by the others there.

That's right Arthur, that's right. Now what I would really like you to do is go farther and deeper, back farther and deeper back, back, deeper and deeper, I want you to go back to where you feel you want to be in another life in the past, before you came into this life, back, back, farther before you were born into your present life.

He could hear the voice but now all thought of association with who it belonged to was gone, all he could hear was the voice and he felt an overriding compulsion to answer and obey, he could not resist.

Pause

"Where are you Arthur? What can you see?"

"Blue, I don't know, it's all blue."

"What do you mean Arthur all blue? What's all blue?"

"I don't know! It's just all blue, and it's moving, I am moving everything moves, like the sky, moves like the sky."

Pause.

"Different now lots of colour, going every way at once, a tunnel, in a tunnel, moving in a tunnel, nice, nice beautiful colour every where, I am here but can't see me, I am here, and I am every where, Oh! wonderful, wonderful."

They all watched and listened, but a long period of silence followed his last words to them. Ivor spoke to him a few times, but Choco remained silent, but they could all see his eyes moving under his closed eyelids, he gave a small almost imperceptible jerk, just a sight jerk of his body, they all saw it.

"Who are you, what is your name?"

"Barabbas! I am called Barabbas. My name is Barabbas!"

Ivor was stunned and lost for words. He looked across to Marcus and the others a look of incredulity on his face, and saw much the same expressions on their faces.

"Ask him where he is!" Marcus said his voice caught in his throat as he spoke.

"Where are you? What place are you in?" Ivor asked."

"Nazareth, the city of Nazareth!"

"Why are you here?"

"I have work here, and friends to meet."

"Who are your friends? What are their names? Do I know them?"

"I know not, But I do not know you, so they do not, until the time comes, if it comes, and one of them tells me you are a friend then shall I know you as a friend. You could also be in the pay of the broad swords and wish to know something of me and my friends." They continued to ask more questions, and details of life when he was supposedly living, names people places, until the time came when Choco began to become a little stressed and the communication was brought to a close very brusque and suddenly with the words:

"I must pass by you now. Goodbye."

"Is he all right Ivor?"

"Yes! yes, he's coming back, he is all right. Arthur when I snap my fingers you will fully awake."

"How do you feel Choco?"

"I'm fine, never felt better. How did it go, and do you think it will do any good for us?"

"What can you remember Choco, can you remember anything?"

"Yes I can remember when I had my twenty first, and when I first started school, it was like it was happening for real all over again and I knew what was going to happen a split second before it did it was really weird but at the time and even now it it was enjoyable, and I feel so relaxed. That was it then,... nothing else you can remember?"

"No, it was such a nice experience, I would do it again."

****

Dixie lay in the armchair which had been occupied by Choco a little while earlier, his eyes closed, he looked as if he was sound asleep, his breathing was even, his head slumped slightly to the side, his mouth slightly parted.

Ivor was still mindful of the experience they had, had, with Choco, and only just managing to come to terms with what had been a completely unexpected result of the hypnotic regression session. They had tried to ask more questions but it seemed that for one reason or another once Choco had said he must go to meet friends they could get no more communication from him, they had decided not to tell him of who he had claimed to be when he had gone so deep into the hypnotic trance state believing there could be a reason why at that time he could remember nothing of what had taken place and recorded on the video camera.

They had asked many questions and were given the answers, some which could be verified, and some that could not. But they had all thought the facts he came out with, were so precise and accurate on the lives of those living in the 'Holy land' nearly two thousand years before. The usual things which were in the scripture's that most people would have known of today, he hardly knew anything of, but he knew the names of persons who were prominent in a local district of Jerusalem, and Nazereth, that they thought only someone living at the time, or someone who had done a lifetime of research and study on would have known. When asked specific questions, if he knew them he would answer without any hesitation what ever, but when asked things most people would have known answers to to-day he became puzzled and confused at what they were asking, and to those listening to events Choco described about the life he was in, was more than convincing to them.

Dixie gave the same responses except for particular events in his life, but his, last earliest memory was at the age of two. Ivor then asked him to go back to the time before his present life, that part of the procedure was almost the same as Choco's the colour episode ect. Then they saw the slight jerk they had witnessed before with Choco. When they asked where he was and who he was, his answer was a little low in tone and and unintelligible.

"Can you speak up, we cannot hear you very well, what did you say your name was?"

Dixie seemed confused and did not at first seem able to understand what was going on, but eventually began to speak clearly.

"Ephramire, my name is Ephramire. Who are you, am I dead now?"

The others were not prepared for what he had said to them, and were much the same as they were, when Choco had first spoken to them telling them who, he was.

"Do not be afraid Ephramire, I am a friend, can you tell us where you are?"

"You know where I am. Can you not talk to me? If you are here can you not help us, take the pain away? He was supposed to do great things but he does nothing!"

"Who is, he?"

"Can you not see. Him! The 'Nazarine' If it was not for him we would not be here today, they took us this morning, so they could hang him with us and poke fun at him and say: Look! A king among thieves, 'see how they hang well, together.' Is this what I have come to, as a side show to a king of nowhere. Me Ephramire, of the city of Tarsus. See! My mother comes to witness my death would that I could have spared them this they were no part of my misdeeds, and behold them they also suffer through me. With my dying breath I spit and curse them all. See! it grows dark, death comes for me, the Nazarine told us it would not come, but he lied, I go cold in the darkness, and some how it welcomes me, they will do as they wish with me for I am no more."

Dixie had had returned to his present time, and upon questioning him about the session he had just had, he could remember only the same things about his present life, the same as Choco, and nothing of the life deep in the past. They decided then that they would tell no one of what had taken place while they had been under regression. So sure were they that for some reason Choco and possibly the others when regressed would remember nothing of what had or would be said when the other two went under regression Hypnosis. That night Choco and Dixie had very little sleep, they had it seemed not been able to relax, and eventually the light of dawn filtered through the canopy of branches above the caravan, and decided for them it was time to rise, and that day everything seemed overshadowed some how as if there was someone watching their every move, and no matter how they tried they just could not shake it. During one part of the day they became very irritable with themselves, but it passed and then towards evening, they seemed to be back to their old selves, laughing and joking with the others there.

****

The following day saw Charlie and Tim at Sean's house, and after briefing them on what the procedure was they began on Tim the same as they had with the other two the day before.

Tim was well under hypnosis and after the usual procedure to move him back in time they began asking of the time before his birth before the present time he was in.

"Where are you? What can you see? Is there any one with you?"

The questioning began.

"Trees bushes, flowers, some people are walking from me,....they used to be friends, but now they hate me for what I have done, I must go now for it is done, what I have done I am now ashamed, I have betrayed him he knew what I was going to do, and he still let me do it why, why, why did he let it happen, he knew they were coming for him why did he not flee he could have. He told the others that I was going to betray him. Why did I do it, he was a friend and helped me in the beginning, I was loyal to him but I was also jealous. Can you not see the temptation was great for I was only a man, it was not just the money but the things they had promised me, and I was afraid of them they told me they would arrest him at some time and if I did not do as they said they would come for me after they had arrested him.

They knew him not for who he is, and hated him for what he was. They have the power of life or death and he has said he will take unto himself their conscience for what they do in his fathers name, and yet they see nothing except for their own gratification in what they do, they believe that their power is absolute. He has forgiven me for what I have done, but I cannot forgive myself."

Ivor his throat dry asked in a husky voice asked: "Who are you, what is your name?" Although he knew the answer before it came.

"My name? My name is Judas, Judas Iscariot, do you know me?"

Three out of four whispered Ivor, what do you make of it Marcus? What does it all mean? Also why are they all connected in that one and same time in history which also seems to tie in with what is happening now?"

"I don't know, it is all, very interesting, but the thing I don't understand is why they cannot remember anything about the time they were regressed to, it is the first time that I have known that to happen, at regression sessions how about you Ivor?"

"Yes it is true but I feel for some reason they have had to go really deep into hypnosis to bring back memories which are so important to this incarnation, and feel that is why you have been so intuitive and insistent, that the way through could only have come through deep regressive hypnosis.

"If the memory is so important to them for this incarnation why is it only through hypnosis that it was retrieved, and even then they can remember nothing of it so far."

"Do not have the answer to that, but if you think of the things we have been putting down to coincidences concerning things which have happened then add what we have heard so far then the thing which have been happening come out of zone of coincidences and into something much more profound. Perhaps when we regress Charlie, then perhaps we might be a little more inclined to make a few more assumptions."

****

"Where are you?"

"In the house of Aulus Viteliuse!"

"Who is he, and why are you there?

"I have been summoned, and he is in favour with Tiberious Claudius Nero, it bids ill for me."

Marcus looked across to where Alice was in control of the video camera, a frown on his forehead. This was a bit different to what he had expected, he whispered to Ivor.

"Ask him who he is, what his name is?"

Ivor just waved his hand indicating he was just about to.

"What is your name, what should I call you?"

"My name is Pontius Pilot I am, procurator of Judea and Samaria, entrusted to me by Rome."

Ivor seemed to become a little excited to a large degree, he knew something of the Roman period of that time, and was anxious to know what became of the man who had given Jesus to the priests of Judea.

"Oh! I see, now I would like you to come forward by two years."

He waited a little while.

"Where are you now?"

"Rome."

"Where, in Rome?"

"In the home of Casius Drusus a good friend, we are waiting for someone, they should be here soon."

"Who are you waiting for?"

"Marcus Flavious, we cannot go without him, only he knows the way!"

"Where are you going?"

"To the meeting in the catacombs. Ah! I hear them coming, come we must go to join them, they are late, Casius is with them already, that is good, things must be well!"

CHAPTER 34

"What do you think about what we have seen and heard tonight?"

Marcus had addressed those who were still with him, shortly after Choco and the others had left to return to the caravan.

"I think there is one thing we can learn from tonight and that is they were undoubtedly connected with what we are in the middle of, but I am at the same time, still a little confused." Sean was in the middle of putting some coal and a couple of logs on the fire which had become a little low on fuel, and giving it a poke in the embers to try to get it going again.

"In what way are you confused Sean?"

"Well, I was not really sure whether regressing them would help in any way, but when they were, and turns out completely different from anything I would have expected."

"What I mean is, would any of us have expected them to have been the personalities from history who have always been condemned as being the 'no goods' in the crucifixion era, and if we go along with what they say is right and true, and by the way they answered every question we asked without any hesitation, it seems more than likely to me are completely genuine in who they have said they were. The other puzzler for us is why couldn't they remember who they were when they had come out of the hypnotic regression?"

"Another thing, if we now accept the regression as a fact as to who they were, how in blazes could it be a help to us now. When it seems even they have no idea who they were, nearly two thousand years ago!"

Anne had listened to what had been said by Sean, and was thoughtful, for a while then spoke to them all.

"Perhaps we are thinking too much, and while doing so have confused the issue somewhat. We are looking at things with the way we are now, being human, and in the material world, we cannot even begin to think 'why' the reason is, that they should have been born in this time, and remember we were told by spirit that there were others who were going to join us when the time was right, it might sound silly, but when you think about it, as Sean has said they were all together and in a period of history where they have been detested since that time. Even now when I heard them say who they had been, I was appalled, and that is the emphasis we are putting on the fact, and in doing so maybe clouding our sense of judgement. What do we know of ourselves, they have come together at this time, and they were also connected together when the crucifixion happened, who is to say that we were not also connected in some way in the same era, and perhaps the same maybe said of us, if it was so. Perhaps we could be some one from that time we would not like think or admit to our own selves, the thought of being, and could have been detested the same as they have through the course of history albeit we were not such prominent citizens of the period in question, but could also have done as bad then, and since that time have made spiritual recompense to allow us to find the spiritual path we now follow. There were more than enough people persecuting Jesus, than those we know of from the scripture's."

Marcus and the others had listened to what she had said, and had to admit she might have had a point in the theories she had put to them.

"I have had a thought perhaps along parallel lines as your thinking Anne. Some people hold the view that we are born in life sometimes with a purpose to fulfil, I might be a bit mind boggled, but thinking of terms as you have just spoken of, what if, shall we say for instance, just as we have been advised by spirit at the seance, and in other ways, of what was going to be happening. A short time ago we were forewarned of the events which it seems are now upon us. There is evidence written in the Bible that Jesus also knew what was going to happen to him. What if while in spirit a pact had been made whereby Judas had agreed to be the one who would betray his master, and remember it was not just the betrayal of Christ he would have had to agree to, but to be the scorn of hate for nearly two thousand years, think what that may have done to him in the intervening years, to be despised and hated, and all the time what he did had to be done to ensure that the teachings of Jesus, and the manner of his death was the fulfilment of the prophesies which had been handed down from the time of Moses. While at the time, Jesus, was hated by the very people who he had been, as he had said, sent down to earth as the 'Messia', just as they had been told would happen."

"That he would come on earth as the son of God, this was told to them in their own prophesies, and when the time did come they could not accept his words and teachings mostly because it would mean they would have to lose the importance and standing they held before he started preaching to the masses who had begun to listen to him, and could see his words were the truth."

"The heads of the Jewish church would see what would happen to their position if he became accepted for who he had claimed he was. In those days there was only one answer they could have for such a man, and by them doing what they did allowed the prophesies to be fulfilled, and if we think back to that time, and of what we are experiencing now, Choco, Charlie, Dixie and Tim, would have no more idea today what might have been agreed by them while in spirit than, shall we say Judas did at the time he betrayed his master!"

After he had finished speaking Marcus looked at his watch, and remarked he had an appointment early the following morning, and suggested they might do well to finish for the evening. Think about what had been discussed when they were on their own, to see if anything else might come to mind, which might also have a bearing on the situation they had before them.

****

Choco and the others went from Sean's house back to the caravan and for a short time after discussing with each other, the events of the nights regression, and how they would have liked to have seen each other talking about their earlier life when they had been children, instead of waiting in the room next to where the regression was taking place.

They had all accepted the reason given them by Marcus and the others there that, if they had, it might have influenced who ever was to follow the first regression to then subconsciously influence the following person to be regressed with the same kind of answers. They had accepted the decision with no argument, but had asked if they could watch the video recordings at a later date, just for amusement. It was not long before they retired.

****

Choco found himself standing high up on the side of a cliff face looking down into a road which passed along in front of him.

It seemed to be getting dusk as the shadows were long and drawn out reaching the opposite side of the pass he was looking into. He had no idea how he had come to be there or why, as he continued to look he could see movement near the entrance of the pass as a column of about forty people all men were walking three and four abreast, as they came closer he could see there was tiredness in their gait, they continued until they were almost below him, and then began to make their way upwards and to the side of the cliff face into a small recess with a rock overhang above it. As the first of the men arrived, they began to put down bags and weapons they had been carrying underneath the over hang. He became unsure of where he was, or what it was he was a witness to. It was as if he was watching some kind of play being acted out. The men were all dressed in Arab dress, and seemed to be worn out. A group of four then stood alone talking to one other who seemed to be the leader who was pointing in different directions, while still talking to those with him.

The four then went to where the bags had been put and took from them something wrapped in what seemed to be a large leaf of some kind. The four he had been speaking to then went in

202

different directions, one of which was towards where he was standing, as the man came closer he saw he was carrying a bow, and some arrows in a leather quiver across his back. He passed and continued on up the small trackway that wound it's way up the cliff face until he reached the top. Then he seemed to be trying to work out which way he should go from there. Choco followed him, and while he did so the man turned and looked in the direction he was standing, but did not seem to be able to see him. Choco then started to become puzzled and confused over the situation he found himself in. The man then seemed to make up his mind over something, and made his way towards a spur of the cliff and sat down watching, while he undid the leaf to reveal food, which Choco could see was bread, meat, and what looked to be dates, the man began to eat, and later reached inside of his clothes and pulled out a small leather bulbous drinking bottle lifting it to his lips he began to drink.

Choco then decided he would leave the man and go down to where the others where who he could see were making camp for the night. As he drew close to them he could see some were busy sharpening weapons while others were cooking food around an open fire, others were carrying water from an open ground well, near the cliff over hang. He waited to see what they were talking about, they were speaking in a way which sounded strange to his ears but found he could understand what they were saying, much of the conversation seemed to revolve around the soldiers of Rome and about someone they referred to as Cais, and the legion, it did not make a lot of sense to him except that they were either going to meet this Cais, or were trying to get away from him.

Whatever, it was clear to him they intended to spend the night where they were.

He watched as everything seemed to settle down for the night, and saw some others join the man he had been watching, and they too seemed to settle down for the night, or two did while the others it seemed were keeping watch out for those below to sleep in safety.

He just continued to watch and listen to the men in intermittent conversation, and as he did so the time he watched seemed to pass with unbelievable speed, because the next thing was it had gone from darkness to the early glow of dawn.

He was watching those below him from the vantage point he had first seen them when they had come into the pass, when he saw someone hurrying down the slope of the opposite side of where he was standing, until he reached those sleeping, then he was rousing those around the embers of the fire which had been burning most of the night.

As they were woken up there were hurried actions of panic and the person who had talked to the four before they went in the directions he had indicated began to shout orders to those around him, and they then began to get into some semblance of order, lining up after retrieving the weapons from where they had stored them before settling down the night before. As he watched he saw the others who had been watching, come down from the other respective vantage points and join the group of about twenty who started, while others were grouped around the person who seemed to have taken charge of the events which seemed to be about to unfold in front of him. While this was happening there was a lot of shouting going on and pointing in different directions. The man who it seemed was in charge of those around him spoke to those who had returned from lookout points, and Choco could make out they were concerned about something they had seen coming towards them from two directions on the road leading to the pass they were in. The leader seemed to make a swift decision on deciding what to do, and as he did so a runner came towards him pointing and shouting towards the direction the pass road led to.

As he did so Choco looked in the directions indicated, and could see columns of Roman legionares entering the the pass from both ends at the same time. The sun glinting on the gold eagle of the Roman empire, held aloft as they marched in step in four abreast, within a short space of time one of the columns saw the men they had obviously been following and stopped. The commander of them then gave orders to a subordinate, who then spoke to a soldier who was carrying a large horn, who then gave three long blasts with it. The next thing the column manoeuvred it's self into an extended line four ranks deep so as it was facing those trapped in the middle of the pass and waited.

Within a few minutes later there was the sound of three blasts of a horn from the other end of the pass from the other column of soldiers, who were as of yet still not within sight of those in between. Those Choco had been watching then began to withdraw to the higher ground area of the cliff overhang they had spent the night under, and around, and began to take up a defensive position in and around it. Archers, about ten in number took the highest position while those with hand weapons began to take up a position under the overhang, spears ready to be picked up placed nearby. The two Roman forces converged on the area below them numbering about one hundred strong. The centurion in charge decided to send a mediator to speak to those they were about to do battle with, with what could only be for terms of surrender.

There was a short exchange of words, ending with the mediates returning to their respective sides. Then one section of the Roman force began to fire arrows towards the position of the defenders while another section advanced shields held high, up the incline towards the rock overhang. Two other sections meanwhile had started moving to their flanks, each side of the incline, the leader of the arab force deployed some of his men to try to cover them, but in doing so weakened his frontal defence hoping his archers could inflict damage enough to delay or even halt the frontal advance, but it was to no avail the Roman force continued their advance, using their archers accuracy to great effect as they concentrated their fire on the small force of archers above them, and soon the accuracy began to take it's toll on the smaller force's, casualties mounted depleting the defending archers, who had been having little effect against the larger force confronting them. In a short space of time the advancing force was upon the first of the defenders, who against such a large force were giving good account of themselves even to the point of halting the advance, but this was short lived even when those who had left the frontal defence to try and stop the flanking movement happening returned to assist them. In the end the overwhelming force and professionalism of the Roman legionares began to turn the conflict in their favour, but even so with the ferocious attitude and anger towards their foe, and the knowledge of what would happen to them should they be taken prisoner spurred the defenders on with blind fury. There could be as he watched the final act of the bloody scene before him only one conclusion of the end, with just about one dozen left against the professionals of the Roman force. Choco then suddenly felt drawn to the leader, who, while surrounded was giving a good account of himself with the few others who were wounded, and bloody, but standing and still doing battle along side him. The feeling was instantaneous, similar to a really cold shiver, then a hot flush seemed to throb and then pulse through him, and he was facing a legionare who arm raised held his sword aloft, he felt his arm thrusting forward and saw gripped in his hand a heavy wooden handled sword, blood spattered as was the hand holding it, felt the slight resistance as it penetrated the area of the centre of the throat of the man before him. At that instant he could see a look of disbelief and shock in his eyes as he withdrew it. He half turned, and as he did so, he felt a blow in the left hand side of his back, a tremor and then a numbness went through him, and all of the energy seemed to quickly drain from him, he felt himself falling his throat gurgled as frothy blood came from his mouth, he looked up skywards, to see another soldier his arm raised holding a sword and coming down quickly towards his head, he felt just for an instant the blade as it penetrated his skull, and then there was a redness all around him and then darkness descended. Then the feeling he had experienced the moments before returned, then light returned and he was looking down on the scene of the body of the man he had been watching, and had then become. Saw the blood running freely and surrounding the prone form on the ground the face seem relaxed and except for the blood matted black hair seemed peaceful.

He continued watching and saw all around the Roman legionares turning bodies over so as they were face upwards. Then one of them came to where he lay and he heard the words "We have them all now here lies the one known as Barrabas, it has been a long and hard trail we followed but it is over now and we are victorious."

He knew then what he had experienced was, himself in another lifetime, and in that instant the life he had lived in that time became clear as the memories seemed to return, and then he saw before him within a period which could only be termed as instantaneous other lives he had lived up until the present, and somehow he felt the spiritual knowledge of them which had been forgotten, and all that was left was a feeling he could not shake about what the intervening lives he had lived had given him, some kind of inner feelings he knew that were there to call upon in some instinctive corner of his being, but was puzzled as to why he should have experienced such an event and the knowledge of who he had been, the memories of that lifetime leading up to the final battle, of how he had become a Christian, but in his own way, not really accepting the total commitment of the christian teaching but adhered to such as suited him, with his hatred of the Roman authorities of that time. Then his thoughts were interupted.

He heard the sounds of coughing and awoke in the caravan, as Tim was drinking a cup of water, and the others were just stirring from sleep. They all began to arise from their beds, but the silence within the caravan seemed heavy with no one inclined to speak except Tim to say he had put the kettle on.

CHAPTER 35

As Tim found himself watching the man confusion over took him. He could make no sense of what was going on in front of him, as he watched the man pacing up and down back and forth, how long he had been watching he had no real idea, or, how he came to be in the place where he was watching. He looked around, the scene before him was arid, and the man seemed some how familiar to him, but he could not really understand how this was so. He was quite tall bare headed, his long hair hanging loosely down almost to his shoulders and greasy looking, probably due to the heat and stress he could see he was obviously in, he was dressed in the clothes one usually associated with the middle east.

Patches of scrub and course looking grass where dotted around in clumps, on rough stony ground, trees, with dark green, round shiny leaves were around here and there, what type they were he had no idea.

Tim continued to watch the man and found himself moving closer and closer to him, it seemed that he had no option, and as if there was a kind of attracting force drawing him closer to him. As he did so he could see there were tears in his eyes and running down his cheeks, he also saw at the same time he was talking to himself, while his head was bent over and his eyes, though tear filled, were looking at the ground.

The man was obviously distraught about something, he lifted his head, and then began to walk towards one of the trees which was nearby, as he came close to it he stood still, and began to look around him he seemed to look right through Tim as there was no sign he could see him, as he had looked his eyes were on the same level as Tim's eyes, although they seemed to be focused on something in the far distance, but not really seeing any thing, he seemed to be in a dreamlike state, was how, the only way he could describe the mans posture. Tim turned to see for himself the reason, if any, made the man face and stare in the direction, in such a dreamlike manner. As he did, there came a feeling within him of confusion, shame, and guilt he could not understand. In the distance he saw a hill with two wooden crosses with figures hanging from them. He tried to shrug off the feelings, and fear he was getting but to no avail, it seemed as if he was trapped in the situation and surroundings he was in, all these feelings happened in the instant of turning, but what he saw brought home to him memories his mind at first just could not cope with, leaving him for an instant in a vortex of confusion. When he seemed to find himself again, he felt frightened, and apprehensive, but above all could not accept the experience totally as being relevant to himself, and as if there was some kind of block had been lifted to give him an insight into who this man was he had been watching.

He then saw the man walk to the tree as if he had come to a decision, then began to search around his clothes, pulling out of them a leather, bag purse, tied at the top with a leather thong, which he pulled and opened, then partially tipping the contents which he knew to be silver coins into the palm of his hands, and then as if in anger, he threw the bag and contents away from him.

Tim watched as the contents of the bag flew out and scattered, glinting in the sunlight, over rough stony ground, leaving the bag flattened and empty.

The next thing he observed was, the man bent down and picked up a length of rough twined rope, unravelling it he made a loop and placed it over his head and after tightening it around his neck climbed the tree, tied the loose end around a stout thick branch ten feet or so from the ground.

Tim felt completely helpless and wanted to stop the individual doing what he could see his intention was, and that in itself was frustrating to him the scene rolled on, leaving Tim an unwilling witness.

The man sat on the branch his feet dangling, looked around for a moment then launched himself off of the branch.

In that same moment, Tim felt the sensation of a jerk, tried to understand what was happening to him, as he felt the sensation of choking, and felt a tearing in the vicinity of his neck and throat, his eyes felt as if they were bursting, then his tongue felt three times its normal size, while at the same time he was gasping for breath. It seemed to him every part of his body was paralysed, except for his arms and legs, his arms as they reached upwards, to his throat as the cause of his pain seemed to be coming from there, his legs kicked downwards, and tried to stretch in length to find ground to stop the weight of his body causing more pain to his neck. He tried take in air, and though his brain told him what he must do, his body could not function to carry out the signals transmitted from his conscious mind. In that precise moment he knew he had in some way been watching himself, and the person who earlier seemed familiar to him, was in fact himself, as he was in an earlier lifetime.

As this realization dawned on him the memories he had experienced earlier and then almost immediately forgotten returned and became crystal clear. He could remember the betrayal, who the person was that he had betrayed, and the friends he had lost due to the betrayal, the reasons, he could remember, but he felt there was more, more to it than he could at that time have understood, and that his earthy feelings could take.

Then he began to drift, the pain and discomfort he had experienced in the former life began to fade away, he seemed some how to be moving away from the tree, although at the same time as he looked back there was the body he had once been the consciousness and driving force of, hanging limp, with just a spasmodic tremor as the last vestige of the life force was drained from it. He seemed then to move as if some how he was caught in a torrent of euphoria and relief, relief now of full understanding, and understanding his previous lives now redeemed by his final voluntary despicable act of atonement. Which he now knew the past two thousand years of mankind's detestation of his memory was part of, was now over. But some how, in some part of his subconscious memory there was more, and the lid of that part of him had now been slightly lifted, not enough to give him the full understanding of the events he had just experienced, but enough to enable him to in his present state of being to understand he had learned much more of spirit in the past than he at present understood in his current lifetime, and felt he must now endeavour to try and rediscover the knowledge and reason why he had endured the experience he had just had.

CHAPTER 36

Dixie looked around, and could see around him the walls within the passage where he was standing, were large and grey blocks of stone. He listened, there seemed to be voices coming from somewhere ahead of him, some high pitched, and some of low moaning. The height of of the passage where he was walking was only about two feet past the top of his head. Fire brands were placed every so often each side of the passage, giving a subdued orange yellow glow to the walls. As he walked he could see dry stains of darkened blood on the floor and, walls, drips splashes, and smudges. As if someone had been dragged along injured in some way. He was feeling a little confused about where he was, although the place had a ring of familiarity to him, but he could not understand why.

He carried on walking, filled with curiosity and a little fear, he did not like what he had seen up until now, a loud voice bellowed somewhere to his front. There was a heart rendering scream, which died away amongst speech which he could barely hear amid other groans and and shouting coming from the direction in which he was walking. As he rounded a corner, he could see ahead of him a torch lighted area, more torches and light than he had seen up until then, which illuminated the area with a yellow orange glow. Then he noticed another source adding to the brightness and why it was so light. The area had bars across the passage sealing off an area of about twenty square metres. A red hot brazier stood almost central of the open area, red and orange flickering flames rising from the outer edge while at the centre red hot coals burned and changed colour while they did so. The intensity of the hear could be seen by the number of red hot implements used to inflict on various parts of the human anatomy, pain through torture, glowed within it, some flat, round, and others shaped for various other horrific purposes when in use.

He walked forwards, and as he did so he heard the clang of an iron grill somewhere beyond the open area, with the brazier, and could hear words being spoken, there was also the sounds of chains rattling, and then the shuffling of feet, then he saw four men come into view from an entrance which, until the flickering of flames from a hand held torch of reeds held aloft by one of the four, who was dressed in a loose fitting garment reaching his ankles, and covered by a leather apron, a large thick belt in which was tucked a short leather whip behind his back. A large iron ring was hanging on his side upon which could be seen a bunch of keys. Behind him, he could see two men were in chains which were fastened around their wrists and ankles, by wide iron manacles, their dress, consisted of nothing more than a loin cloth around the midriff. Dirty and dishevelled and looking as though they had already suffered at the hands of those who were escorting them into the open area where he was now standing, by flagellation and other means of punishment evident by the cuts and bruising on their bodies, probably he thought, for crimes of one kind or another. They walked past him, their heads down and eyes fixed in a glazed state on the floor in front of them. As they passed within just a few feet of him, there was no sign that any of them could see him, or even noticed he was so near to them. He followed them from a distance, until they came to an upward sloping passage which led off of the one in which they had been walking. Then the one in front who was escorting them took from his belt the bunch of keys and selected one of them, which looked to be the largest of them, and opened a large heavy iron grill door so as they could enter the sloping passage, then stood back and shoved the two prisoners ahead of him.

Shortly after they were out in bright sunlight, and facing a pile of prepared and stacked timber, of various lengths and thickness. The two guards then pushed their prisoners forwards, towards two heavy lengths of timber, which seemed to have been already selected and and put aside, told the men to pick up one length each and to move on ahead in the direction they indicated by pushing them forward in front of them.

Walking along behind them Dixie turned and looked at the building where he had just followed them out of, and could see it looked more like a fortress which had been purposely built for holding people in. The outside was a sheer wall and here and there at different heights and levels of floors there were small slit window apertures, with solid square twisted iron bars set into the walls.

They walked down narrow streets, where people were talking and, and shop owners were selling their wares, flat loaves of bread could be seen stacked in front of a shop or two on tables as they went past them, fruit and vegetables on stalls, people were mingling, and some were greeting friends they saw only on occasions such as shopping, and haggling over the prices of the wares on offer. The smell of fish became predominant as they entered a particular part of the street. Some there, glanced at the two men struggling to carry the heavy timbers upon their shoulders, but did not seem too interested in them, it seemed to Dixie it was a common occurrence in that vicinity, and they seemed not to pay too much heed to what was happening other than doing business for the day.

Eventually they had travelled out of the confines of the town and had made their way towards a hill he could see in front and in the direction they were heading. Perspiration dripped from the two prisoners faces and bodies, their bare feet were cut and sore as they walked on the stony surface of the track they were on, still heading towards the hill.

As they came closer to it, he could see crowds of people heading towards it ahead of them, and eventually as they reached the summit all around them were stalls being set up. Water carriers were around carrying leather water sacks with earthen ware bowls, to be filled from the sack's contents, to be sold to the crowd around them. The two men as they passed them swallowed and licked their dried cracked lips, perhaps, in the hope, that there would be one of the carriers there who would at least let them drink some, even though they would have nothing to pay them with.

Dixie followed but still it seemed that no one saw him, he went ahead of the men carrying the lengths of timber, looking at the faces in the crowd around him as, they seemed to be interested in things and people around them rather than what he was a witness to. But as he was looking casually around at the scene before him he felt drawn to two faces which for some reason he felt were familiar to him. Why he had no idea, they were a man and woman he estimated were in their late fifties or early sixties. They also looked right through him, and as they did so he had a tremor and an inner feeling of guilt as he watched them. It was then he noticed the woman was being comforted by the man with her, and there were tears in her eyes. He stopped to watch them, drawn, for some unknown reason, to the pair of them, a little while later the two men carrying the lengths of timber came level with them, one of which looked towards them and spoke briefly to them as he passed, as he did so the woman broke down completely as the tears fell streaming down the cheeks of her lined face. The man with her put his arms around her in a lost attempt to comfort her, as she continued to sob uncontrollable on his chest, his hands moved over her head in an attempt to comfort her as best he could, a look of pure anguish on both of them.

He turned away from them both and then began to follow the prisoners in chains again, as they came to an area where there was a strong scaffold type of structure erected. The men dropped the heavy timbers which they had carried until they were near the point of exhaustion, onto the ground, then, dropping themselves onto the ground afterwards. While they were sitting, the manacles and chains were removed.

Dixie watched, the two men in the leather aprons, as they proceeded to take the timber, lifted again by the two prisoners, over to where there were two other longer lengths all ready laying on the ground, nailing them together with eight inch long heavy nails horizontally. As he continued watching, the two prisoners were then made to lie down arms along the cross sections, their fore arms were lashed to the wooden cross sections with ropes. Then their hands were nailed to the cross sections, as this was happening Dixie felt compulsorily drawn closer, and closer towards one of the prisoners as he lay there. The two who had escorted the prisoners from where he had first seen them, then began to lash the calf of each leg together with a leather strap to the upright section. The feet were just resting on an angled block of wood which was nailed to the bottom of the long upright. Using the same length nail as they had fastened the cross section together, they began nailing the men's feet to the block. As they did so Dixie felt a tremor again within his body and heard and felt for what seemed an instant, confusion, a rushing and reeling of his senses. The next thing he knew, he was on the cross looking up at the sky, feeling in his hands, arms legs and feet excruciating pain, and then knew instantly, why he had been observing and drawn to one of the two chained prisoners.

Time as he lay on the ground seemed to go slowly, he could hear the men who had nailed him to the cross talking. The language they were speaking seemed strange, although, he understood every word they spoke. His eyes were watering with sweat, and tears combined, making them sting, he wanted so much to rub them, but knew in the position he was in it was impossible. Somehow his present consciousness and the conscience of the prisoner seemed to blend into one, and each for a minuscule moment had the knowledge of the other. With each life running parallel with the other. There was an understanding and humility which came with the blending before Dixie was once more in substance wholly the earlier incarnation. What he was feeling to those who had done this to him could not be put into words. His ribs felt stretched his stomach felt taught, and elongated, pain racked through his whole body.

Then above his head he felt someone move the wooden timber slightly, then the sounds of friction as a rope was threaded under and around the top of it, then the grunt of satisfaction as the task was completed. Then more movement as he felt himself being lifted a foot or more, then the cross he was attached to tilted slightly and stopped, he turned his head, and through blurred and sweat distorted eyes saw a rope looped and then tightened, near the position of his hands. Laughter broke out over something that was said, by whoever was tying it, then the same happened at the other side of him. Moments later he felt himself rising, and as he did so the pain increased in his arms and legs, every part of his body ached, he cried out in pain, but his cries fell on deaf ears, to his plight. No one seemed bothered over his predicament or cared, they were there to watch him being crucified and die. Suddenly the cross he was nailed to wobbled, and then there was a jolt and he felt himself fall for a moment, then after the increased pain he realized the bottom of the cross had been raised and then fallen into a hole which had been dug to receive the base of the cross, then there was almost immediately a bump behind him, as the cross was supported by a horizontal which ran behind the upright timber. The sounds of earth being rammed and packed into the hole in the ground, vibrated up through the wood he was pinioned to. Then everything was still, and he was left hanging there.

A while later there was around and below him, shouts of derision, and jeers, accompanied by the sounds of hammering, then he saw between himself and, his accomplice who had with him committed crimes he was now being punished for, and had been crucified with, the man they called, the Nazerine, and king of the Jews. He noticed as he hung there in the same plight as himself and his friend, an attitude and composure of complete resignation to his plight. His eyes looked at him full of love tears and compassion towards him, and said something in the order about forgiving those who were doing this to him. For his plight (Dixie's), all he could do was smile, and told him not to fear for he would not really die that day.

Then he heard the name 'Ephrimire' being called, and as the name was called, instantaneously, more memories of who he was, and every facet of the life he was reliving came flooding back to him, and with it, he immediately recognized the voice of the caller below him, as his father. He strained his head to look below him, to where the voice had come from, and there, were the couple Dixie had seen as he had watched the two prisoners carry their timber cross pieces, of the crucifix. He could see them both, his mother with his fathers arms around her. He then felt remorse, anger, and the futility of his way of life, which had brought him to the end he was now suffering so painfully. As he looked below towards them he tried to speak to his parents, but through the dry throat and parched lips no sound would come except for a hoarse whisper, he cried out with frustration and strained his body increasing the pain to try and some how punish himself for the misery he could now see etched in his parent's faces, when he could not answer their call to him.

Time passed and darkness of the day was just about falling, he seemed to be drifting in and out of consciousness, fire brands were lit and the orange glow from them as he opened his eyes seem to bring an unreal and emptiness within him, he looked one more time towards where his parents had been the last time he had seen them, but they were not there. He had no idea that as he had been hanging there, and had not been moving they had assumed he had passed on.

There was later a voice which spoke to him, he heard questions being put to him, and felt they were asking questions which seemed stupid to him, but he answered them anyway amid the pain and anger he was feeling.

Gradually in time it was night time and darkness had fallen there were only a few around below him, but most of them were there to see the end of the Nazerine, some were his friends but the majority were not. The pain, and anger he had held within him subsided. He found himself slipping out of the physical feeling and pain he had been experiencing. Later he found himself a little way above his human form hanging on the cross.

In the light from the torches held by people below him, the body of the Nazerine was being taken down and then wrapped in a cloth, they then took it away to a waiting cart, and then down and away towards the direction of the outer limits of the town.

He watched everything as it unfolded in front and below him, looking at the same time if he could see his parents but they were not there.

Then he saw the two who had accompanied him to where he was to meet his fate, one of which climbed a ladder, wrenched his hands away from the timber cross piece, then released the leather straps and ropes which had secured his arms and legs to enable them to take the strain of the bodies weight, and after they had done so, he watched as his lifeless body fell onto the rough ground below.

He also watched later, as they transported the two bodies of his friend and himself, in a cart out into the desert, and then after chopping them into pieces, threw them out of the cart onto the desert ground to be consumed by wild animals and, carrion of the desert skies to feed upon.

Then everything seemed to become light with a misty haze and he felt himself move into the centre of it, while at the same time felt a feeling of welcome, a feeling as if one had returned home after a long and tiresome journey away..........

****

Charlie could see ahead of him lights in the distance as he came over another hill, he had no idea where he was, or where he had been heading. All he knew for sure was, that for some reason he was going in a direction that felt right to him. All around him was in semi darkness, the only light which he had available to him to enable him to walk in the direction he had, was due to the half moon above him in the night sky.

There was a purpose in his step, but he had no idea as yet what that purpose could be. All he knew was it felt right that he should be where he was. A while later he saw the reflection of the moonlight on water below him and a little to the left of him. The path he walked on seemed well worn and wide. As it had been ever since he had found himself walking on it. A donkey brayed on the opposite side of the hill towards where he could see the moons reflection on the water, causing the silence of the night as he continued to walk to be broken. Then, the lower down the hill he went, more noises of cattle could be heard, the braying of the donkey was joined by the sounds of goats, and sheep, as he began to get closer to them, he could hear the jingle from small bells around the necks of the goats. He saw then clearly in the moonlight, they were accompanied by a young shepherd boy of around ten or so in age tending them. The boy was dressed in a long thick woollen woven garment and was sat on the ground on a blanket. A fire of dried oxen dung burned in front of him, giving off a pungent dried and burning grass odour, mixed a sweeter smell coming from some herbal smelling small dry twigs under it which the boy had used as kindling. When he had come to where the boy was sitting he spoke to him, but there was no response. Then

211

the idea that the boy might be deaf occurred to him, he reached down to touch him on the shoulder, as he did so there was still no response, but, also as he had touched him his fingers just seemed to penetrate through his clothing without any feeling whatsoever. This he could not understand, he stood back not sure now at all what was happening to him or, what his purpose for being there was.

He then walked over to where the cattle were, tried to touch feel the sheep and goats and found the same thing happened as happened with the young shepherd boy. It was a situation which perplexed and annoyed him, and to which he could not come up with a rational explanation to himself about. He felt and then rubbed his arms, they were solid and felt as they always had. "What did it all mean?" He asked of himself. He had passed the boy a little while ago by now, and was still walking when he saw a distance ahead of him lights, that could only mean there was some kind of a town or village ahead, and then something within himself seemed to be drawing him to it. There was the silence as he walked along, and then another point about his situation hit him. The silence it's self. "Why was it as he walked he made no sound and could not hear his own footfalls on the rough ground, even when he purposely scuffed his feet, he still did not make any sound?"

A little later he had entered the area of the lights, and what he now knew to be a city, and by the buildings around him could see it was quite an important one. He found himself walking aimlessly around watching others go past him, some in company, others on their own, some were hurrying as if they were trying to get to their destinations as soon as they were able, then there were others who just seemed to walk at a leisurely pace as if they had nowhere particular to go. All were wearing clothes of an ancient Roman era, he looked at his own dress to see he was still wearing the clothing he always wore, denim jacket and jeans. Again he asked himself. "What has happened to me? What am doing here, and why?"

He passed an inner city wall, and then through a large gateway leading onto a large and wide street, he entered and as he did so he noticed a group of people come onto it from a turning in front of him, they walked away from him going in the same direction as he was walking. He watched them from a few yards behind, and saw that there were three men and, three women.

He became interested in them, mostly due to the stealthy way in which they were conducting themselves, furtive looks and talking in whispers, when they did speak to each other. All seemed to be well dressed, and wearing clothing much the same as he had seen by everyone he had seen since entering the city, but covered with a hood attached wrap around cloak, of a soft looking but thick material.

He followed them for quite a while, going deeper and deeper into narrower streets, until they arrived at a dwelling, which had small amounts of light shafts coming from small cracks in window boards which had been pulled together. They stood out side for a few moments, as if waiting to make sure they had not been followed. One of their number left them, and walked a little way back towards where they had come from, stood for a while listening and looking around the open area behind him. Where Charlie was standing, he could have put out his hand and touched him. He noticed too that the man was perspiring heavily and seemed nervous. Deciding that everything seemed well he returned to those he had left, one of who then walked ahead of the others to a dwelling, nearby, knocked on the door the knocks sounding like they would have been a coded signal, known to those inside. The door was quickly opened, and as soon as it was the six hurried inside, as quickly as they could and quickly closed the door behind them.

Charlie followed them inside, there was a lot of hugging and greeting going on, as he entered behind the last person going into the house.

"Is everyone here?" One of those who Charlie had followed asked of a person who was already in the house when they had arrived. He was an elderly man with white hair and a full white beard, wearing a drab grey one piece robe, and who had been the person who had opened the door to let them in.

"Everyone except Cassius, he has gone on ahead to take the 'old one' to wait for us in the home of Pollinius, his home is quite near the catacombs, and Cassius thought the journey here might be too much for him, we must hurry, and leave here soon, if we are to catch the tide."

"How many managed to get here safely?"

"All together we are thirty, we are to take half in each boat, and payment is to be made as soon as we board them.

"Good! Then it might be wise for us to make our way to meet the others, it could be, we have been missed by now, and there could be a search under way as we speak. Come Drusarian, let's get ourselves away now!"

Charlie as he listened to what was being spoken he could tell there was an urgency in the voice of the one who had come with the five others.

"It is a small distance to travel now, it would be better to go in groups of five or six to avoid any suspicion when we enter the catacombs.

"How many of the Christians are willing to come with me as a rear guard should it become necessary?"

"There are eight who are willing, and I feel they would give a good account of themselves should the need arise. Not including the old one, but with Cassius, Pollinius, and you and myself will make eleven in total."

"Good that will be enough I hope, and the preparations in the catacombs, are they completed now?"

"All ready as far as we can go, without bringing everything down upon us, before time that is. It will not take long to complete everything should we be discovered, and where the planned fall-in there will only be a matter of a few hundred paces before we will be free to board the boats waiting to take us away. Then once we make the fall-in no one would be sure where we have gone, or in which direction until it is too late and we should be well away by then."

Once the word to leave was given, there was a lot of hurried action as the people in the house began to pick up their belongings in bags which they could carry comfortably, of their possession's which contained mostly goods of value, gold and money. They began to file out of the house from the back entrance in the suggested groups, after two individuals had gone out before them, one of which returned to take the first group.

Charlie himself now was curious as to what was going on and who the people were. Some he could see were citizens of the Roman Empire, while others there, by their dress were obviously the Christians mentioned when he had entered the house. He followed the first group of people to leave and enter a small courtyard just outside the back door of the house. He then watched as they all walked behind a wall in the back of the courtyard to where steps led down into the ground which were revealed by the removal of a large plinth, which, before it's removal contained a statue covering the steps. He waited outside until the last of the people had left the house, the two men who had left the house before the others and had removed the plinth and statue replaced both before making their way on foot to the boats by another rout, thinking two of them would not look out of place walking together to where the boats were moored.

Charlie had followed the last group as they had entered the tunnel, and the silence which was evident in the house was now thought to be unnecessary, and there was a buzz of conversation now which Charlie listened to with mounting interest, and now beginning to enjoy his position as an unseen eaves dropper, although, he was still puzzled, and could not account for his situation of being there.

The tunnel which they had first entered and travelled along connected a few hundred metres on with a larger and higher passageway which they illuminated with reedstems which had been soaked in olive oil then bound in thick material which burned consistently from the time it was lit, and gave off quite a lot of light to enable them to travel at ease.

They had been travelling for about fifteen minutes when there was the sounds of a commotion ahead of them, everyone stopped. Then Charlie saw running towards them the two men who had stayed behind to cover the steps with the plinth. As they came up to them they were a short time trying to catch their breath, eventually they started to speak to the person who had asked the door keeper questions when they had first arrived at the house earlier.

"There are people back at the house, they were arriving as we had left they did not see us, but there were soldiers and priests from the city with them, we could hear them breaking the door down from where we were hiding, I fear they have found out you have been helping in the escape of our fellow Christians, we only made our escape in time, others, are as we speak, only a short distance from the outer wall entrance to the catacombs, we came by way of the entrance you will use to get to the sea shore."

"How many are there at the outer wall entrance?"

"Twenty soldiers, and about the same number of priests, and their followers!"

"We must hurry now, and get to where we have made preparations for if such circumstances should happen. Thank goodness for planning. Have you seen Pollinius and those with him? Do you know if they have made it to their part of the catacomb and are waiting there for us?"

"They must be there by now. The junction to this tunnel from the outer wall is just ahead we must get past it as soon as possible. They will not take too long to reach there, once they start on their way towards us."

They had just passed the section mentioned by one of the two who had stayed behind in the house when there was the faint sound of running footsteps heard behind them and coming from the direction of the junction mentioned.

After running themselves they reached the point in the tunnel where the preparations had been made and others were waiting for them. The leader of the group who had spoken to the two who had stayed behind took control of the situation.

"We must make sure we can delay those on our heels long enough for the elderly and the women to reach the exit near the sea shore to be able to get safely to the boats to take us away from here." As he finished speaking one of those who had been waiting for them in the catacombs, came up to him.

"There is a sharp bend in the tunnel a little further on, perhaps it might be better for us to reach there and make things difficult for them to catch up with us, we delay them long enough to finish knocking the roof supports down completely, with just enough time for those who delay them to get through before they collapse completely. What do you say Pontious?"

"It seems a good idea, but I will remain behind with the eight volunteers. Drusarian must go with the women and the others, but remember, the safety of the old one is paramount, he must not be taken no matter what else happens, tell Drusarian he must be taken to safety, and he must tell this to Pollinius.

With that the leader drew the men who had offered to stay behind as a rear guard, four of the eight began to hide in recesses made to contain the bodies of the dead, laying flat, hidden from view with daggers drawn. Four others then stood a little way in front of them in the centre of the wide tunnel, with slings filled with large lead shot as ammunition. As the others left there was darkness all around them, as they waited listening to the footsteps growing louder and closer.

Behind them where they waited they could hear the sounds of banging and hammering as the roof supports were being destroyed for the planned roof collapse. Then there was a flickering on the walls accompanied by heavy footsteps as the torches of their pursuers started to light up the darkness behind the bend of the tunnel. As they came into view the rear guard were in darkness while those carrying the torches, and those with them were easy to be seen. The four in the passage, with the slings swinging above their heads, released their missiles and hit their targets as they rounded the bend, two leading with torches fell to the ground hit in the head and did not move once they were on the floor. Those following behind were confused, and did not understand what had happened, then another fell and another, the sling men were good with the weapons they used. One of the following party bent down to pick up one of the torches from the ground and as he did so was hit in the side of the head by one of the missiles and feel onto the lighted torch as he did so catching his clothing on fire, but there was no movement from him as he lay dead on the ground, the four slingmen fell back. As they did so those behind the fallen men could see what had happened to them and they began to fall back themselves and parted to allow the soldiers through them to engage the slingmen, who were moving farther back along the tunnel, and drawing them on. As they came level to where the leader and the four Christians were hiding, who had allowed them to go a little way past them not knowing they were there. As they did so and with surprise on their side they fell on them from behind with daggers flashing, and mortally wounding those they fell upon once their presence was known they ran in the direction of the slingmen along each side of the passage way, allowing the slingmen room to use their slings again upon the group as they came past the fallen inside the tunnel.

Just then there was heard in the direction they were to run to a rumble, and a crashing sound, then some one gave a long blast on a horn. All of the defenders knew what it meant and began to run as fast as they could in the direction of the immanent fall-in. They arrived there to find that half the roof had now collapsed into the tunnel, and there was just about enough room left for them to climb through before the rest of the room caved in.

"Hurry! Hurry!" They could hear those the other side of the collapsed roof shouting to them.

"It will not stay up for much longer!"

They all but the leader and one others made it to the other side as the roof finally collapsed all together.

It was only then as he felt the roof collapse on him, and felt the physical pain, did he realize why he was there, and who he had been. As his spirit left the body of the man he once was, he could see just below him, the feet sticking out and just visible a crushed torn bleeding, and twisted arm.

"But what did it all mean he asked himself?"

He awoke in the caravan feeling strange and a little disturbed over what he had, had revealed to him in such a strange way while he had slept.

CHAPTER 37

Ivor Ramanouski and his wife Alice had travelled into town to do some shopping for themselves and Marcus, after, on his request for them to stay at his home, if it was possible, so as to enable them to work together without having the inconvenience of being so far away from himself and the others, and seeing as it would cause them very little problem to do so they agreed, and were just in town to pick up groceries ect.

They had done most of the shopping in the supermarket, and had taken their shopping out to the car park and locked their purchases in the car boot, and had decided then they would have some refreshments in the supermarket cafeteria before making their way back to Marcus's home.

As they came out of the car park they saw straight in front of them a cafe, and decided instead to make use of it, rather than returning back into the supermarket.

Stepping through the door they could see it was not too crowded, and had a nice clean hygienic appearance. Alice sat down next to the window just inside of the door which gave a nice view of the busy high street, while Ivor went up to the counter for tea and toasted buns for them both.

They had sat down for no more than five minutes when the door opened, and a man and woman entered, as they passed the table where Ivor and Alice were sitting the woman stumbled, and as she did so her hand came in contact with Ivor in the area between his left ear and shoulder halfway up on the side of his neck. As it happened Ivor felt the fingers of the woman ice cold on his neck, it made him jump, and and his hand automatically went to the spot she had touched and gave it a rub.

The woman with the aid of her companion stood up, and apologized profusely, whilst at the same time, hoped she had not caused him to spill his drink on his clothing.

Ivor assured her there was nothing to worry about and that it had been an accident, and could have happened to anyone.

The woman and her companion gave a smile and apologized once more then moved to a table on the far side of the cafe, after going to the counter for drinks. They sat down and were in conversation for about ten minutes or so before leaving the cafe smiling and nodding to Ivor and Alice as they went past them on their way out.

Ivor and Alice then left themselves, about ten minutes or so later. After they had been back at Ivor's home for an hour or so Alice remarked to Ivor about a red looking rash about the size of a fifty pence piece on his neck, below his ear lobe, and how she had not noticed it before, it also seemed to be weeping around the edges, she got up from the table to take a closer look at it. Marcus leaned over from where he was sitting to take a look, and after doing so suggested they should bathe it and apply some anti septic he had in the bathroom cupboard, to be on the safe side against the spread of infection. When that was done they all agreed to go to Anne's house later that evening after they had all eaten dinner, to discus what they should do to take steps on what to do for the benefit and safety of all of them in the coming weeks.

They had eaten dinner, and while doing so noticed the rash had worsened and had spread almost down the whole of one side of his neck, and Ivor had at the same time said how it was giving him a pain and sore burning sensation.

****

Choco and Charlie meanwhile were standing outside of the caravan, every one had decided for the day to do what ever they wanted too, the two friends had decided to take a walk around the fields around the caravan and call in on Sean for a chat and perhaps a drink. Dixie and Tim had decided to go into the town to do some shopping, and drop some washing off at Dixie's mother's house for her to wash and to reasure her that he (Dixie) was well and was staying with some friends for a few days, and for her not to worry. Looking out of the window she could see Tim in the van, and because of the way he looked and was dressed was not to happy about his choice of friends until Dixie told her he was a good friend of Choco's. "Does he want a bath while he is waiting for you. He looks as if he could do with one! His clothes could do with a washing while he is at it. Haven't you anything you could let him have to wear, he looks awful the way he is sat there, and what are people going to say when they see you with him?"

"Oh come off it mum, he's all right! A good friend and we could do with a few more like him about now!"

His mother looked at him, a questioning look, as if to say.

"What do you mean by that?" Dixie realized then that perhaps he had opened his mouth a little more wider than he should have.

"Oh! it's all right mum, stop fretting over me all the time, I just meant to say I could do with a bit more help with a bit of work I have on at the moment, that's all!"

"What about Choco? I am sure he would help you if you asked him!"

"He is already helping me, but still we could all do with a little more help is all." He thought it best to leave the matter there, not wanting to worry her unduly, with what he knew might be in front of them, with those he had been told of, and knew of what they were capable of. "Better she is kept in the dark than know anything at all." He thought to himself.

Choco and Charlie were walking along the field next to the lane and heading in the general direction of Sean's home, the air was fresh and weather quite pleasant for the time of year.

Coming to the field which dropped down towards the wall surrounding Sean's house they decided to sit down on a fallen wind blown tree trunk, the tree was dead but it was a comfortable and dry spot to sit on. Choco got out his tobacco tin to make himself a rollup and offered the same to his companion. It was at this time he he decided to talk to him in a round about way of the dream or whatever it was that had happened to him the couple of days before.

"How have you been sleeping lately Charlie?" He asked casualy.

"Not too bad really considering what we know has been going on." He replied.

"Any dreams, at all?"

There was an underlying statement to his question, in his tone, which Charlie immediately picked up on, he looked at his friend.

Each was silent, although, both had wanted to tell 'some one' of the dream or whatever it was they had experienced because, of the content and realism of it. It seemed to them both as the words had been uttered the time was right for each to share with the other the content and conclusions of the dream, each of them had that night while asleep. Every one there that morning on waking had, known, the others there had experienced something similar that night while asleep, but did not really know for sure, how to bring the subject up because of the way it had seemed so personal, and not really wanting to admit to each other who they now believed they had been in the former life portrayed in the 'dream' so vividly, and knowing there was an important reason for it, it just remained for them know what the reason could be, and perhaps talking to each other might well in some way reveal that reason to them all.

Choco then thought without hesitation he would come straight out with it, and did so, giving Charlie a complete account of his experience that night. Even to the fact of saying who he believed he was that night, and adding, he did not think it was a dream in the usual sense, and volunteered he did not only think it was an experience of an earlier life deep in the past, but knew that it was without having any doubts about saying so at all.

Once Choco had opened up, it was as if a weight Charlie had been carrying was lifted from his shoulders, for as soon as Choco had finished his account then Charlie told of his experience in his sleep state. After he had finished there was a moments silence before Charlie spoke:

"What made you bring it up at this moment?"

"I don't know exactly, it just sort of came to me that this might be about the right time, and you have been acting the same as the other two. The silence, the surreptitious looks, I was pretty sure of the reasons, because I was the same."

"If I am, who I think I was, and you say you know who you were in times past, then who do you think the other two were in the past, and would they have had the lives they were in, in the dreams they had, connected in the same time period of history as us?"

"Well, that I don't know, but what if when they return we put the question to them point blank, and see, if they match up with us in the same time zone of history, and take things from there. I am still a bit puzzled though about something."

"What is that then?"

"When we were all regressed that time, why was none of what we have 'dreamed' about come out then, if, as it seems, it was so important, and relevant some how, to the situation as we find ourselves, in now?"

Both friends then decided not to continue their walk to Sean's house, but to retrace their steps back to the caravan so as they might be able to talk longer on what they had admitted to each other, and to try and come up with answers which might fit the situation of all of them, and how, and in what way they were connected to the others they had so recently met and were friends with.

The others had arrived back at the caravan later that afternoon, had dinner and sat around the radio listening to the news until it had finished. Charlie looked across the room at Choco and with a nod of his head prompted Choco to reach over to the table and switch the radio off. After which he looked at the other two and asked as casually as if he had been asking them for the time.

"What were the dreams you two had the other night, if you tell us yours, we will tell you ours! How does that sound.?"

Dixie and Tim sat on their seats, and looked into the eyes of the other two there and could see them smiling.

"Shit man! If you knew about it since then why did'nt one of you say something before now." Dixie spoke with a certain element of relief in his voice.

Later after they had related to each other the accounts of their dreams, and were questioning the reasons for it. There came around them all, an uncomfortable feeling while in the caravan, which none of them could explain, the suddenness of it gave a feeling of woe to all of them, there was some thing wrong, and they all sensed the same thing spontaneously, that it had something to do with Marcus, and that they must get in touch with him somehow right away.

"Sean! Sean's house we have to get there, he has a telephone, we can use it to telephone Marcus and find out what the problem is.

They all agreed without any discussion that there was indeed a problem. It just seemed to them all that it was so, and were acting on that fact, as one. Later they would come to realize that in fact it was a gift they had already used, without even realizing it. They were in fact working in unison with the same objective, the welfare and intuition of danger for one of their own. Combining the power they had and, until that time had no knowledge they possesed individually, to make them first aware there was a crisis, then identified without any prior knowledge the possibility there was danger in the direction they had all sensed the danger lay, and for who.

Within minutes they were at Sean's house, they knocked at the door rang the bell and, but it seemed to take ages for Sean to answer the door. He had been drilling holes in the kitchen wall to put up a kitchen cabinet after altering the kitchen slightly, before he started to redecorate, the walls and retile the floor, but eventually he had answered the door and could see at once they seemed worried and anxious.

Choco was the first to speak.

"Phone Marcus, we think there is something wrong at his house or something wrong with him, or even both. Phone him Sean! Now!"

"Marcus?....How do you mean something wrong, what do you think the matter is?"

"We don't know but we do know there is something going on, that is why we came here for you to phone him to see if we are right, which some how we are all sure we are, and he is in danger of some kind."

Sean looked at the four of them on his doorstep, he was to say the least a little confused. But could see that all of them had an urgency about them he had never seen before, at any time, or with anyone.

"Come in, Come in. Molly the men from the lane are here you had better come down after you finish bathing, they say there is something wrong at Marcus's house, I am going to see if I can talk to him on the telephone."

"I will be down as soon as I dress!" She replied with a shout down the stairs.

Sean dialed Marcus's number and the phone kept ringing for quite a while but no one answered.

"He only telephoned me this morning and everything seemed all right with him then, while Ivor and Alice had gone into town to do some shopping. He said they were going over to Anne's later?" At Anne's? You can Phone her and see if they are there. But I feel you will be wasting your time I feel what ever it is, it is at Marcus's home." Charlie spoke to Sean with conviction, but Sean still decided to phone Anne just to be sure.

Choco turned to Dixie. "Go out to the van and turn it around ready to go in the direction towards Marcus's place. I think it is a matter of urgency we are on our way as soon as we can, but we will see what Anne has to say, before we start on our way."

Sean had managed to telephone and talk to Anne.

"Yes Sean! Marcus had agreed to come to my house this evening but he has not turned up yet, I have been a little worried over the fact that if he is home that he has not answered me, and he is well over an hour late. I do hope he has not had an accident of any kind on his way over to me."

Sean then told her what Choco and the others had been saying to him. She then told him she would make her way along to Marcus's house and that if they left now they should arrive at the entrance about the same time, and agreed with Sean that if she did arrive before them, then she would be wise to wait for them to arrive, before going any farther.

"Put your foot down Dixie, we want to get there before Anne in case she is tempted to go on into Marcus's without us, and perhaps put herself in danger. What danger I don't know, but the more I think about it the more I am concerned for the well being of Marcus and those staying with him. I get the same feeling I had when I knew Marcus was not with her."

Sean and the others had piled into the van so as they were all together, Molly was sat in the back of the van with her husband, after hastily putting some clothes on when told of the men's suspicion, that they felt all was not well at Marcus's house. Sean was very quiet and, kept looking at the others with him, wondering what had happened to them, since he had last seen them before their visit to him earlier. A change had taken place in them in some way. But he could not put his finger on exactly what it was, except that as he was sitting in the van with them there seemed to be a very highly charged sense of energy within the four. An energy and vibrancy he had never experienced before, coupled with what he could only define as a sense of concealed calmness, confidence, and commitment in what they were possibly be about to be confronted with, even though they had no idea what that could be, but he felt good that they were there.

When they arrived at the driveway they saw Anne had arrived just before them and was standing at the side of her car, as she saw them arrive she walked towards them.

"Have you seen anyone about since you arrived?" Choco enquired of her.

"No, but I only arrived a matter of minutes before you."

"I think it was wise for you to wait until we arrived, god knows what we are going to find in there!"

Choco to all intents and purpose seemed to take charge of the situation.

"It might be best if Anne and Sean walk up to the house along the driveway, if there is anyone around they would have heard the van and your car arriving and stopping at the end of the drive. If you keep to the centre of the drive, and there is someone in the shrubbery they will have to show themselves, to challenge you. Meanwhile if Charlie and myself go into the shrubbery and quietly creep our way up the left hand side, and Tim and Dixie keep to the right we can be ready for anything that comes at us, I hope." He whispered, the last two words.

"What if there is someone there and they jump out on Anne and Sean." Tim whispered.

"Clobber them, and we will talk after, just take no chances." Was the quick reply.

They walked all the way to the house along the drive. There had been no challenge, and the house was in darkness, and not a sign that there was anyone home. The out side lights which were always switched on as darkness came had not been switched on, and not a glimmer of a light in any room that they could see. Sean and Anne walked to the side of the outside veranda on in the house at all, but I just know Marcus is in there." Tim commented as he towards where the light switch was located, and turned the lights on, as they came on so the others appeared coming from each side of the drive.

"What do you think Anne, is anyone home there or not? I am not sure if they are or not myself. Sean spoke as the others came to them.

"We have been around the back of the house and there are no lights." Reached them.

"There is only one thing we can do Tim. We knock on the door and take it from there, see what we come up with.

They had knocked and knocked loudly on the door, using the heavy bulls head ornamental knocker, it's sound thumped solidly on the door.

"What are we to do asked Anne to no one in particular."

"Try the door handle and see if it is open." Charlie answered. She reached down and pushed the handle, there was the click as the door opened.

Cautiously they filed into the front hallway of the house, Sean reached to the side and switch the interior hall lights on, the brightness stunned them for an instant but they soon got used to the glow of them.

Dixie was the first person to hear the sound of voices, and motioned to the others to be quiet to see if he could tell which way room they were coming from. As they walked farther along the hall they all heard the sounds were coming from the large sitting room they were in the last time they were there. Choco moved quietly along towards the door and put his ear against the key hole and listened. Then looked through it. "There is no light on in there but I can hear Marcus's voice, but cannot under stand what he is saying."

"Are you sure it's Marcus you can hear?" Choco asked him.

"Sure as eggs, are eggs, and he is talking to someone, it sounds like a woman's voice answering him." He replied in a whisper.

"When I open the door, I will switch the light on in there, then when I have, you three come straight in behind me and be ready to go for any one we don't know. Is that all right with you?" The three friends nodded.

Choco then caught hold of the door handle and opened the door quickly moving inside and switched the sitting room lights on.

As the door flew open, a stench met their nostrils of what seemed to be rotting and putrefying flesh, as Choco switched the lights on he retched at the same time as were the others, who had followed behind him. Such was the sight which met their eyes as the lights went on, they just stood looking in disbelief. Marcus was sat in a chair, or the person they knew as Marcus, but he was in a terrible state, his face covered in sores and what looked to be blood blisters with puss oozing from most of them, his eyes were covered and he could not see making him blind and completely helpless. All of his bare extremities showed the same degree of running sores with red and purple looking, puss filled blisters.

As he heard the door open and the rush of footsteps come into the room, his voice cried out. "Who is it who are you?" "Oh God Marcus! What has happened to you? Where are Ivor and Alice? It's Anne!"

"Over here Anne, I am Over here!" A voice came from the far end of the room near a curtained window that had a view onto the outside back garden. The curtain had been pulled down and was hanging to one side, the other side curtain had been pulled off of it's tracking, leaving the top half of the rail bare on one side, and below that was the spread out curtain covering the top half of a body on the floor beneath the window. Alice was sitting on the floor near it in the same condition as Marcus.

Charlie rushed over towards Alice, following Anne's lead, but before they got to her, they heard Marcus shout out to the others not to touch him, or Alice, because it seemed that what ever they had was highly infectious, and deadly. Charlie then saw the body of Ivor partially covered with the curtain, stopping him dead in his tracks at the words of Marcus. Turning to Choco and the others he shouted for someone to get sheets and blankets so as to be able to move them both near the fire for warmth, and try to make them as comfortable as they could without touching them, and to put the rest of the lights on in the room so as to give them more light, so they could do what ever was possible for them. He then began to walk over towards Ivor, to see how he was. As he got close Anne shook her head at him, and spoke in a low voice.

"It's no use Charlie, Ivor has gone!"

"If you are not careful you could all end up the same way as us, it might be better if you leave us and save yourselves." The words came from Alice, as she had heard Anne tell Charlie of the demise of Ivor.

As all this was happening Tim was still standing in the doorway to the sitting room. At first he felt and saw the total confusion within the room as the door was opened, and then everything seemed to proceed in slow motion to him, and he felt completely detached from the scene in front of him. He saw the lights of the room go on, but even though the lights from the ceiling, and walls were on, and the room should have been well illuminated. In the room he could see swirling, in shades of dark brown a kind of underlying wispy fog like effect. As he watched the others in the room it was becoming gradually darker by the minute. He could see it, but could not understand what it was he was seeing. Then suddenly all action in the room slowed even more, and eventually everyone there seemed to have frozen, and was still, he looked towards the grandfather clock which was facing him and the pendulum had stopped in mid swing, and there was silence all around him.

Then he felt within him a trembling, not a physical thing, but a kind of vibration which seemed to come from deep within him which some how gave a freedom within his mind, an opening of a visual aperture, it seemed to him strange at first and then it had a familiarity to it, as if it was something he had experienced before. Then suddenly, things, times and events started to become clear to him. Times feelings and experiences which he had learned somehow, but also, of a potential within himself and he knew now was the time to draw on them. He then began to see in his minds eye, periods in time, and an understanding of the lives he had lived from before and after the crucifixion, he saw the gradual changes in these lives from his first spiritual awakening to the present time, he saw the progression and the relapses, within his own progress, of each life, the shame guilt and later the elation as his spiritual growth had evolved over countless centuries and even from the beginning of time itself.

Watching, and in an instant, re-educating himself in all he had learnt in his many past lives. Then his minds eye began to focus on one period of a life he had lived, and he immediately recognized himself remembered, and relived that life in the twinkling of an eye, of learning and accomplishments he had attained, they immediately came back to him and he knew himself now, HE WAS ARMED NOW WITH THE KNOWLEDGE, AND CAPABILITY, and knew what he must do.

Tim moved forward into the room, but as he did so, it was not the Tim the others had come to know, it was a much more knowledgeable figure in appearance and bearing who had lived in the mountains of Tibet several centuries before, who had the knowledge of life and it's meaning. As he walked towards Marcus his face was transfigured, older looking, and with oriental features with a light and an energy within him manifested in his eyes and emanating around the room and which was perceived by those within it.

He opened up his mind and in doing so drew to him part of the forces of life and energy from the atoms of every living organism around him, he became part and in tune with them taking, and prepared to give freely from them and himself until he felt he was ready to proceed with what he had to do.

The others in the room just watched in awe, as he leaned down and touched first Marcus and, then Alice, he walked over to Ivor, stopped, looked down on him, said some words then moved away a sadness of understanding in his eyes. After he had left Marcus and Alice there was a change beginning to appear in the condition of their affliction, the sores and blisters began to disappear, the puss seemed to just evaporate, and by the time he had reached Ivor, they had been healed completely.

After he had finished with Ivor there were no outward signs as to how he had met his death, he turned and walked to Alice.

"It was to late for me to help one of you but worry not for him for he is well, and will reap the love he has given freely many times over with those who are dear to him who are in spirit for it was his time and now he has gained a little more within life's mantle to aid him in paradise. The others will be well, but we must leave you now and divide from each other, to allow the progress to continue in this world. Let your spirit be willing and keep faith with those who love you in spirit, and you will not fail in your quest of everlasting life."

Anne, tears welling in her eyes, and standing a little distance away from where 'Tim' was standing just managed to answer, "Bless you friend." So relieved was she for the safety and healing of Marcus and Alice from the terrible plight that had taken their friend from them.

Shortly after they were all standing around the confused figure of Tim and, explaining what had happened and his part in the drama as it had unfolded. He was confused in one way but mostly over the way it had happened, he could remember everything which had taken place except for after he had actually walked into the room to heal Marcus and Alice, the memories of past lives the different personalities he had been in his various lives, even the the name he had when he had been the oriental priest in Tibet, but that name he had kept to himself.

They could not fully understand exactly what had happened to Ivor and the other two but, after talking with them and were told of the incident in the cafe when the woman put her fingers on the neck of Ivor, and the resulting rash which had appeared, they knew right away it was down to those at the manor who were responsible for his death. Marcus also deduced they knew a lot more about them than he would have wanted them to know. It was obviously the woman who had singled them out in the cafe, probably after following them, they had waited for the opportunity to some how infect him with a plague like disease, but far more virulent than anything known of, and probably no medical treatment was available for the treatment of it.

Marcus and Alice were well, and there were no visible signs of the sores and blisters which had been evident a short while before. Later, Ivor's death would be registered as a heart attack which in it's self saved a lot of questions which would undoubtedly have been asked.

CHAPTER 38

"We have been cautious up until now while we were under the impression that those at the manor house had been unaware of what we know of them. Well unfortunately, it seems now that the cat is out of the bag, and we have paid dearly for it. We now know at the very least they have a certain amount of information that we are on to them and, what they stand for, also, they will know that we are not completely defenceless against them, just by the fact that Ivor was the only one to succumb to the infectious disease they had infected him with. They must have assumed that when they had infected him with the virus, it was so virulent it would have spread to the rest of us, which except for Tims intervention, I feel it might well have. But in doing so sadly Ivor has lost his life, for us to be warned of their knowledge of our existence. What or how much they know about us, even to how many we are, is a mystery at the moment, but at least we have now been warned, by an opening shot across our bows so to speak."

Marcus had been addressing everyone who had been at the meeting when they had first become aware of the people at the manor house.

Since then they had accomplished more in the way of defending themselves than they could have envisaged in the beginning. Everyone there had been told of the way Ivor had met his end, and there was sympathy for Alice from everyone in the room. To which she had responded by saying she was grateful for the feeling of them all, but it helped that at least Marcus and herself had been spared to fight in what ever capacity they could against the evil that had made her a widow.

Time had passed since then, and Choco and the others had spoken to Marcus of the (realistic dreams) they had experienced. After which Marcus produced and had let them listen to the tapes they had made while they were under hypnosis, explaining he had not wanted to let them hear them until such time as he thought circumstances warranted, so they could not be influenced in any way by them, and and had waited until such time as he thought would be appropriate, with the death of Ivor and then Tim's intervention in the saving of his life and that of Alice, coupled with what they had told him of their own dreams he had decided immediately, that time had arrived. He further more, told them, he did not understand even now why they were amongst them, but felt more certain than ever, that they would be responsible in no small measure for the defeat, if at all possible, of those at the manor house, and who he felt would be pitting their all against them, from this time on.

"I feel the time has come to see if it is possible for us to dish out to them something to show we have some power on our side, rather than sit back and let them do whatever they want to us. Somehow I feel we will have to take the bull by the horns to find out as much as we can about any weaknesses they might have that we may be able to exploit, and to at least stop the evil from spreading any more than it has already."

"How are we going to achieve that?" Someone in the room excaimed.

"We know practically nothing about them, or, how many of them there are, and we cannot possibly go confronting them in their own territory, they would know who we were within a minute of us arriving, and would have as much chance of leaving as a fly stuck to fly paper and then covered with super glue."

Marcus looked at the speaker, saw that it was one of the people he had known for quite a time and was the leader of one of the developing circles he had visited on numerous occasions in the past.

"Yes what you say is true. There are a lot of you here tonight, some of you knew each other before our first meeting together, and some did not until you were introduced, and have since then become good friends. But, what you do know is that all of you have abilities, some to a lesser degree than others, but, in the last few months you have all improved on those that you have, and perhaps combining one with the other we should at least have a workable and effective force at our disposal, and perhaps now would be the time to bring whatever we do have in our favour to the fore.

The first thing I would suggest, is that we must find one of them who is vulnerable in some way, and perhaps even be in a position, that we could gain information from them that will be of help to us in finding any weak points they may have, and if at all possible, try to rescue them from being controlled by possession, and bring them into the light, because I have reason to believe that everything about the possession of the individuals we know of, is not quite what it seems, all of them it would seem have been deeply possessed by those from the lower realms, and they have no control over their minds and bodies and the actions that are performed by who ever controls them. It could also mean that there is a good chance we could exorcise who, or what ever is possessing them. Which again could give us even more information about what to do against them. That is why I feel we must some how capture one of them and exorcise them and in doing so perhaps learn as much as we can what their main objective is to bring about whatever is their final goal."

Choco then stood up, and as he did so all the eyes in the room were upon him.

"I think the part of them turning from what they are, towards our way of thinking, on the evidence of what we have seen so far. If you are right about the possession bit, and in the hope you are right in your supposition, I for one will have a go at whatever you suggest. I have an idea of someone who we perhaps could get at, but how to do it I am not sure. The person I am thinking of is not at the manor all the time, and they seem to have some clout within the organization it's self, and in that sense have quite a few answers to some of the questions we would like to know. But how it could be done, I am not sure at the present time, perhaps with a discussion a way could be found."

Marcus listened to what Choco had said, thought to himself that there might be some credence in what he had suggested.

"I will speak to you later about what you have spoken of and see what we are able to come up with, with as less risk to ourselves as possible. Also I think it would be wise that with whatever we may come up with should only be talked about by those who are to take part, that way should anything go wrong it might not be so detremental to the rest of us.

Later that same evening saw Choco and some others talking over a plan they had come up with. Which was to kidnap the person they had seen near the entrance of the shed when they had rescued Father George, and Charlie had recognized in the photograph, and who worked at the offices of the D.H.S.S., when he had made the claim to enable him to stay at the manor. Marcus agreed the idea they had come up with was good, but the method they hoped to use was to say the least a little unsafe for their health.

They were planning on snatching him from the office when he left, taking the chance they would not be seen as they tried to accomplish the task. But with the location of the office and the distance involved to walk to the carpark, and the use in the area by other pedestrians at the time of day he left the office would probably jeopardize any attempt they made, with them falling at the very least, foul of the law, and there would be he was sure more than him leaving the offices at that time.

Marcus was also against another idea they came up with, of following him from the office to see if they could establish a routine he followed, which would enable them to kidnap him without any witnesses to the event. But remembering how others had tried this tack before abroad, and had not been seen again he thought it was too risky, but at the same time he had a thought along the same lines to carry out the surveillance, but altering the method of doing so slightly.

The others were puzzled by his words, but he told them he would have a word with someone who may be able to help them with less risk attached to any of them.

Charlie then suggested that they make a start as soon as possible as it seemed for the moment time was running against them.

****

Sally Parsons had watched the man who had been pointed out to her the day before, she looked at her watch then and saw it was just coming up to four o'clock in the afternoon.

It was now three thirty in the afternoon of the following day and she had been told what was wanted of her from Marcus, and was getting herself ready to be able to follow the man who had been identified to her. She lay on her bed at home, using her own method of relaxing techniques, was in the final stage of leaving her physical body. Using her mind she began to take control of her astral body, and manoeuvred her form out of her physical body, until she was standing up in her bedroom she thought and concentrated on the location of where she wanted to be, some where near the entrance of the D.H.S.S. offices to wait and watch for him to leave the building from a good vantage point, after being told of the concern Marcus had of the disappearances of those they had been informed of in the United States.

Around her bedside Charlie, Choco, Tim, and Anne watched as she seemed to go to sleep, and stayed that way for the best part of two hours.

After a period of about ten minutes or so those watching her except for Charlie left, her bedside and crept out of the bedroom with one of them returning to poke their head through the door to check everything was all right, and progressing satisfactorily. While keeping vigil on her, they noticed that the only thing they could see was a small movement of her eyes beneath her eyelids, to those there she looked to be sound asleep on her back with no other movement of her body at all. On more than one occasion Choco and the others had looked into the room and could not see any evidence that she was breathing, so still was her body, except for the very slight rise and fall of her breast area.

Sally had reached the area she had decided to watch from for the man to come out of the building. She waited for long after the time she had seen him come out the day before. Time passed and she began to wonder if he was actually in the building, she had seen others leave at the same time as they had the day before, but he had not appeared. Time continued to pass and as she continued to watch the building seemed to be empty, except for the small number of office cleaners that had arrived and entered the building. She eventually decided to enter the building herself to see if she could locate him within it, just to make sure she was not wasting her time waiting, when he was not even in the building.

She moved into the building, moved is the only way one could describe it, it was more of a thought process than physical movement, regulating the speed to what ever she wished it to be, by thought alone. Moving down the corridors of the building she could see that most of the offices, and large rooms she looked in were empty, and mostly any of the activity which was going on was being done by cleaners. She moved up the building floor by floor and could see mostly the same as she had seen on the first floor, then after a while she had reached the top floor of the building, and had about decided the man was not in the building, when she looked into a small office off of the passage way and saw Seers sitting at a desk, in front of a computer monitoring screen. She watched for a little while from the doorway, while he was waiting for a printout from a printer attached to it. The printing finished he picked up numerous sheets which he had printed off and placed them into a folder, which he then placed into an attachå case. She continued to watch as he retrieved the disc from the machine, then taking from the drawer of the desk he was sitting at, a long stainless steel box which he put the disc into, along with a number of others already there, locking the box after he did so then placed it back into the drawer. As he picked up the attachå and got to his feet to leave the room. Sally moved back away from the door and in the opposite direction of the passage to where he would be walking to leave the building, as he came through the door he turned away from her, checking as he did so the case he was holding was securely locked with the catches fastened, and began to walk away from her in the direction of the stairway. Then he suddenly stopped, waited for a short while, then slowly turned and looked back in the direction he had just come from, looking to the left and right of him, the case hanging limp by two fingers in his right hand and at the side of his leg, while at the same time a look of concentration was on his face, looking all the while in the general direction of where Sally Parsons was standing, although, there was no actual sign he could see her but by his expression it was a sense to him of feeling, and nature he had not experienced before, and was puzzled by it. He started to walk back in the direction he had just come from, with deep furrows on his brow as he seemed to concentrate on the immediate area around him. Just then a door opened behind him and slammed shut as a cleaner who had been in one of the offices, and had finished cleaning there was moving into the room he had just vacated, momentarily he lost concentration, in that moment Sally, her mind reeling at the situation which had developed so quickly, willed herself onto the floor below, and then out of the building altogether, and some distance from the entrance, to wait for him to appear as he left the building.

The situation which had developed while in the building, made her realize to follow the target was not going to be so easy and cut and dried as she had at first believed, and was now aware that she should take the task of following him a very serious matter. She decided it might wise to watch him leave while at a safe distance, and to do the same when she followed him to wherever it was he was living, and hope that whatever it was that had made him sense either her presence or, what ever it was that perhaps gave him some kind of intuition there was some thing not quite as it should be in the passage as he had left his room.

"Did he?" She thought! "Have some kind of inkling that she was there." It puzzled and, worried her, to quite a degree.

Some five minutes later she saw him come out of the exit and walk to a car parked outside of the entrance of the building and which was facing away from her, a woman was sitting at the wheel and had obviously been waiting for him.

She had noticed the car pull up there just as she had returned to her present position but had paid little attention to it, or the occupant in the driving seat. The woman spoke to him as he opened the door, he answered, patting the case as he did so. She watched as they drove by her seemingly deep in conversation and seemed unaware of her presence as they drove by.

Following the car from a distance did not prove a problem for her, and within a short space of time he was pulling up outside of a house, about three quarters of a mile from where the man had been picked up.

Sally Parsons watched as the man got out of the car to open the garage attached to the house, the woman drove the car in, the man lowered the door from inside and then she saw the woman, who Sally presumed was the mans wife, leave by a side door of the garage followed by the man, both entered the house by the front door.

****

Marcus had listened to what Sally Parsons had to say of the incident at the offices, and where the man lived, and the fact she believed him to be married. He was, more than a little concerned when she had told him that she felt the man had somehow sensed her presence in the passage of the offices, but more than relieved that no harm had come to her. "Perhaps?" He thought.

"After she moved away from him, he might have dismissed it as something he had imagined momentarily.

Choco had heard what was said to Marcus and every one else there, and voiced an opinion to the fact, that because they knew that they could do things they had already proved was possible for them to do, it may in some way be turned to their own advantage.

Marcus was puzzled by his statement, and asked him in what way he had meant.

"Well, think about it? The way everyone seems to talk of these people. We all talk as if they are not human, and cannot be harmed. Think about what Sally has just told us about the man, she followed! She told us he might have sensed her there, but the main thing about the encounter, if that is what we can call it! Was, as she has said, he, seemed concerned, and if we use that train of thought. What was he concerned about? Was it the fact he had sensed something? Or could it be that he had been taken aback, that it was possible for him to be watched in that way? Don't forget up until now they have always believed the cards were all stacked in their favour, and they have no evidence of what we might be capable of, any more than any of us do at the moment.

Also there is a possibility he may have been thinking, he was being watched by one of his own for some reason unknown to him, and nothing to do with us. Remember Sally said he seemed to sense something amiss and not that he had actually sensed who or what it was he had sensed there with him. What do you think? Could that at least be possible, and we could be worrying about what happened there unduly?"

Marcus gave this some thought for a while, and agreed it was possible he was right and, even if that was so, what should be their next move.

"Easy! Let's go and get him as soon as we can, the longer we leave it the more time he has to think about what he might have sensed while he was in the passage of where he works. How to go about it should be the next question!"

All of them came up with all manner of ways, but Charlie's idea seemed to have become the most viable, except for the violence which might have to be done to accomplish the capture of the man, plus the fact his wife would have to be taken as well at the same time. The plan was to abduct him and his wife from their house, by knocking on the door forcing their way in and overpowering them, drastic but as they thought it over it seemed to be the only way to them, because except for the offices where he worked and the times he would visit the manor they felt there would not be any other better opportunities available to them. Marcus was not happy in any way with the idea, because he had been against any violence of any kind from the start of the discussions about the abduction.

Choco was a little annoyed by this attitude, with the possible circumstances they faced from those at the manor.

"Come on now Marcus! How can we accomplish the thing if we are not prepared to use at least the minimum of force necessary. Let's face it, they did not let that stop them, and to my way of thinking, it's about time we started to dish out a bit of what they do for once, instead of being on the receiving end of things from them.

Remember how Father O'Connell was taken and the treatment he received. Did they have any qualms about how they treated him, and eventually what his fate was to be at their hands? As for the problem of his wife, well if she is there, then so be it, there's room in the van for her as well, and perhaps in the long run there might be a chance to free her from whatever you say you feel has happened to the both of them, possessed and all that stuff."

Everyone there could see Choco was anxious, and wanted to make the move to take on those at the manor now as soon as possible.

Tim had been listening to what was being said and was thoughtful over an idea he had since Charlie's suggestion of getting them from their house, and had while thinking had come up with an idea in his head he thought might work, and gain them access to the home with the minimum of fuss and commotion. But it would involve someone he was not sure would co-operate, he broached the subject as soon as Choco had finished having his say.

"Can I say something?" He spoke before any one could comment on what Choco had said.

"What if we could use the police to gain entrance, and perhaps the others could get in straight behind them, once entry has been gained. We have someone with us who has a warrant card they could use on some pretext or other to gain entrance, haven't we? We are all supposed to be on the same side, and against the same thing, or am I wrong?"

"That's true but will he go for it?" Charlie question hung in the air for a while.

Choco inclined his head to those around him. "Can we get hold of him, put it to him and see what he says? We kept him out of being involved with the finding of Father O'Connell. Which would leave him free from any suspicion as to whatever happens to this guy we need to talk to....Right?

As it happened, the abduction of the man and wife went better than it was possible for them to imagine.

They had planned to go about the task in a similar way to what Tim had suggested. Mitchell had immediately agreed to go along with what was suggested, and to gain access to the house using his warrant card. But as it turned out it was not necessary, due to the fact Dixie, Charlie, and Tim had gone up to the house from the side entrance and had noticed the side door to the garage was ajar. All four slipped in after telling Mitchell to make an excuse to get the man (or both) into the garage on the pretext that there had been a series of break-ins of garages and and that the culprits had been apprehended, giving information their garage as one of those where goods had been taken from. Michell had knocked on the door, it was answered by the husband, holding the attaché case Sally Parsons had seen him with. The wife was behind him buttoning up her coat. Obviously they were on their way out as he had knocked at the door. He thought quickly, so as not to delay their departure any longer than necessary. He held up his warrant card. "Detective Sergeant Mitchell, C.I.D.! Sorry to trouble you sir. There have been a series of burglaries from garages in the area today, and we have arrested the suspects and one of the garages they admit to taking goods from is yours, would you like to check to see if the items we have on the list of goods recovered are indeed from your garage." He held in his hand a sheet of paper, purporting to be a list of recovered items.

"Would you mind just checking, to see if there are any items missing I have a list here of what we have recovered, it won't take a moment. I can see you were on your way out and will not hold you up any more than is necessary."

The man, taken by surprise became flustered for a moment, until his wife came to the side of him and then seemed to regain some composure.

"It's the police dear, asking if we would check our garage to see if there is anything missing, apparently there has been a burglary and the policeman says we might have had some things stolen from us from the garage."

"Have you noticed anyone loitering around the area by any chance sir, I thought I would ask, just in case it was possible you might be able to identify the culprits we have in custody, it all adds to the evidence should you have seen them."

"Oh! I see." He seemed to think for a moment or two.

"I don't think we will be able to help you in any way there Sergeant, we have only been back from work an hour or so, and we have both been out all day. I work at the local D.H.S.S. offices, and my wife works at a charity hostel for the homeless. So I am afraid we will not be much help to you."

Both, husband and wife, came out of the house locked the front door and made their way to the garage, Mitchell followed behind them, and was relieved the doorstep conversation was over so quickly, as they made their way to the front of the garage.

The four inside the garage had heard the conversation the couple had, had, with Mitchell, and in doing so knew they were on their way into the garage and had quickly taken up positions, to be hidden when the couple entered.

There was the sound of footsteps and then the garage door was raised, Tim and Choco stood behind the sides of the raised door, while Charlie and Dixie crouched down at the back of the garage behind the boot of the car. The man and woman entered the garage together, the man holding the attaché in one hand with the car keys were in his other, while the woman followed Holding her hand bag and shopping bag in the other. They walked towards each side of the car doors, when suddenly they both seemed to sense the presence of the four in the garage with them, but it was too late, Choco and Tim pounced. Choco on deciding what they had intended, had definite ideas of how he would accomplish the task with as less a chance of messing up as possible. In his hand he held a sock filled with sand, and as he came up behind the man, and as the man had stopped he hit him just behind the left ear, while Tim caught him as he fell unconscious towards the ground. The woman was taken back as Dixie and Charlie rose from behind the boot of the car, quickly moving towards her, she was unable to turn away from the 'pepper spray' Dixie had sprayed into her eyes, then both men had grabbed her whipping her hands down and behind her back looping both of her wrists together with plastic ratchet ties, which were normally used for tieing young saplings to wooden supports. Both were trussed up the same way and bundled into their car, Tim meanwhile had picked the car keys up off of the ground opened the door and had got into the drivers seat next to Choco, started the motor and drove out of the garage. Charlie and the others remaining closed the garage door and made their way to where Dixie had parked his transit van a little way away from the house and followed Choco and Tim, it had taken barely more than a few minutes from the time the husband and wife had entered the garage.

The man began to regain consciousness, just as they were pulling out of Taunton onto the wellington road, he was confused, gagged with plastic sealing tape, then as his senses returned he became enraged. He struggled to sit up in the back of his car, as he did so Choco pushed him down and made him lay low, and to one side of the seat and told him to sit still. He struggled again his temper flaring, then he saw the futility of struggling in the situation he found himself in, turned and looked at his spouse, and saw she was in the same situation as himself trussed and gagged, and saw the irritation in her eyes due to the mace spray.

As they pulled into Marcus's drive, they saw the headlights of Dixie's van pulling in behind them.

The door to Marcus's house was open and they could see Marcus, Sean, Molly, and Peter and Abigail standing there.

"How did it go?" Someone asked as they reached the door.

"Sweet as a nut!" Was the reply from Choco. While looks and relief appeared on their faces showed that they had not been as comfortable about the task as they had all tried to give each other.

CHAPTER 39

They were both led quickly to chairs and made to sit in them, nothing was said at all to them until Marcus arrived, accompanied by Alice, Anne, and others, Molly and Sean among them. The two abductee's were in considerable discomfort but otherwise they were uninjured except for sore wrists where they had been secured by the plastic tying tape, and the man also had a swelling behind his ear. Before Marcus had a chance to speak to them, Alice moved him to one side with a slight pull on his arm indicating she wanted to speak to him back in the hallway, where they had just come from. With a puzzled frown he followed her. In the hall he could see she was both excited, and irate. "Those two are the ones we saw in the cafe when Ivor became infected with that rash he died from." The words were spat out with venom. "Are you sure?" He asked in whisper."Of course I am. Do you think I could forget their faces. Ever?" "If that's the case, I think we will handle the questioning without them realizing that we know that they were some way responsible for the death of Ivor, and the terrible thing that happened to us. That way we may be able judge the best way to put questions to them, and see if we can try to realize when they are lying or not. They walked back into the room feeling a little confident, Marcus had all kinds of questions going through his head he would like the answers to. But knew just a fraction might be enough to find out a little of their weaknesses for them to exploit. "If in deed there are any." He thought with a nervous tremor about him. He walked up to the man first, and was about to ask him if he knew why he had been taken, and brought to his home. Then saw the man was just sitting in the chair, and appeared to be not in the least concerned that he had been taken and brought to the house. The woman with him was much the same although she was sitting eyes closed and seemingly relaxed in her chair. "What do you think think you will accomplish by bringing us here?" There was a mocking tone in his voice as he spoke. "Also!" Marcus thought. "There is not the slightest hint of fear in him as, he speaks." Choco, Charlie, Tim, Dixie, and Dave Mitchell, had waited for Marcus to enter the study, listened for a little while as Marcus began to question the man sitting before him, after which they had gone to another room. Marcus suggested they did so, until such time as they were called, so as not to give anything away should the two captives sensed there could be more to the four, than they seemed to know at the present time. It was a precaution as well, due to the reaction he had got from the two, since he had spoken to them, but he had not told them that, just that there was a fresh pot of tea made for them in the other room, and for them to go and help themselves. Which left, Alice, Sean and Molly and the few others with them."Why don't we dispense with these bonds, and talk face to face, Marcus De Clare. We thought you would have been eliminated with the two of your friends, it surprises me that you are still alive, you must live a charmed life, but never mind we can put that right before we leave here, and make sure of no mistakes on our part. We do detest situations, of when we find we have only managed to do half a job, now be a good man and cut these bonds from us and then we can get down to the nitty gritty shall we say. All the time the man had been talking his spouse had been sitting the same as she had when he had first entered the room, her eyes closed, with her hands tied behind her, not speaking and not moving. Marcus listened to him talk, and as he did the confidence and reasoning he had initially, when he had entered the room seemed to fade. Moving towards the man, he turned to Alice and asked her to fetch the sharp letter knife from on top of the table behind her. She turned, not thinking that anything was not as it should be. Sean, Molly, and the others with him seemed to take what was said as normal. As Alice did so, Marcus for just an instant, thought of what he was about to do somewhere, in the back of his mind, he tried to rebel against it, but there was in his will, torpor, and a sense of weakening, he could not seem to function defiantly against what he had been told to do, and found himself helpless, and could not go against the instructions he was being given by the man. Receiving the Knife from Alice he began cutting the bonds which held the man and woman's hands together, the man then moved to his wife and gently touched her on the forehead, and as he did so she slowly opened her eyes, and smiled at him, but not the kind of smile the others there would not have understood so lethargic were they about the situation. She then closed her eyes and sat again as she had since she had entered the room. Sean and Molly watched the proceedings calmly, as if they were two bystanders watching something with only half an interest to what was going on in front of them, much the same as the others there. "Ah! Now, that's better Marcus De Clare, it seems your friends pulled the plastic thongs a little too tight, look how deep they have bitten into my wrists." "I am sorry." Was all that Marcus could utter, an uncontrollable feeling of fear began to overtake him, and no matter how he tried he could not stop it happening. "Now be a good chap again, and send someone to bring the rest of your friends in here now. It seems a more appropriate time for us all now to become introduced to each other, and see what we can come up with to enhance this gathering of friends in our honour, we must see if we can give, you something, for us to remember of our visit to your abode. Turning to Sean, while there was a small pocket of fight left within Marcus's mind, which he tried to bring to the fore, to battle with this control the man had over what was happening to them all in the room, but it was to no avail, the more he tried the weaker his resolve became. He finally submitted to it. "Sean ask the others to come in here for a moment, will you?" "Yes that will be fine, a moment will be enough. Now you can go and sit down with your friends and watch the proceedings, who knows it might be very educational for you, although your education on the matter will I think be short lived." He looked over towards his wife who was now back in the same position as she had been before he had touched her on the forehead, eyes closed quiet and motionless, and not seeming to be part of anything that was going on, but in actual fact was the source of the power which had been allowing the man to take control of their situation, from captives, to captors.

Anne had been in conversation with Mitchell, asking how things had gone with the abduction. Choco and the others thinking there was something of a personal nature going on with them, had moved a little distance away from them, to allow them if they wished to speak in private, and were in deep conversation themselves over the easiness of the capture and the transporting of the two to the house of Marcus. "Marcus has asked me to tell you he would like to see you in the other room." Sean stood in the doorway, delivered the message, and then turned to return to the other room without saying anything more to them, which was quite unlike his normal self. They stopped their conversations, and then began to make their way to the sitting room. Anne and Dave were the first to arrive, they entered the room and were suprised to see every one there sitting down except for the male prisoner, who was at that moment standing in the centre of the room untied and walking free. "Do come in, we must introduce ourselves more formally, my name is, well, I am known for now by the name of leonard Seers, he pointed his hand over towards where his wife was sitting, and forgive my wife for not introducing herself but I feel I should do the honour for her, my wife Dorine. But not to worry about her too much, she is busy at the moment working on, shall we say your behalf. Dave Mitchell and Anne Farr had entered the room, and almost immediately they were aware of an oppressive and and overwhelming sense of fear, in what way she had felt it, she could not begin to understand. She could not understand at first, but as she looked at the woman, she could not help but to see what was a vortex of power, giving off feelings of absolute terror and fear within the room which was engulfing all that came within a short distance of her. But she saw right away that it was feeding in some way on all the people who were in the room and with the power it was gaining from them it was growing in strength, and taking all thoughts of resistance to it, away from them, and deplete those it was affecting until there was no will of their own and were ending up totally subservient to it's power alone. "No!" She thought. "It is not using it's power, they are, using it in some way, and then directing it at us. She tried to back out of the room but could not even move her legs off of the floor and had seemed to become paralysed, with fear, and the fear began to grow with every passing second, her body began to shake involuntarily, she tried to concentrate, to ask help from spirit, for help against this evil, but even her mind was beyond any semblance of thinking coherently her thoughts becoming jumbled. Moving her eyes with all the concentration she could muster within her confused mind, she in a micro second of time, saw Dave Mitchell in much the same condition she knew herself to be in only he was knelt down on both knees cowering against a wall, afraid to look elsewhere, it had registered, and was then forgotten, such was the dilemma she was now in. It was as soon as they came in sight of the open doorway, and a few yards behind Mitchell and Anne, that they had the first inkling that there was something wrong inside the room. The four all stopped walking and there was a period of hesitation, they could all see there was a darkness to them, which surrounded the doorway where Mitchell and And Anne had entered, as they looked they all saw the man they had captured and brought to the house, standing in the centre of the room, with Marcus and the others sitting in chairs and obviously in great stress. As they were about to walk into the room, Charlie held his hand across the doorway, indicating they should stay where they were. Charlie had seen everything well before the others had, because of the conversation they were having among themselves, and the because of the fact they thought they were as in control of the situation as they had been, when they left the room earlier. He could not say how he knew there was great danger in the room they had been about to enter but something, some primeval instinct, seemed to warn him of the fact. While at the same time he seemed to know what he had to do, and again he did not understand it, but some how the knowledge was not just in him but seemed part of him. Seers standing there looked full of confidence, as the four friends stood out side the room. "Come in and join us, you seemed so impatient to get us here and have gone to all the trouble of sitting us down and making our stay with you so comfortable. Come in and let us do the same for you, it will give me great pleasure to get to know you all. Charlie walked straight into the room, ignoring Seers, and began to walk directly towards his spouse, and as he did the dark gloom of the room seemed to increase the nearer he came to her, while at the same time, he could hear voices which seemed to penetrate his mind, shouting all manner of abuse at him. Some of the language he could not understand but the meaning was obvious to him, to try and draw him closer and to the centre of them and then to possess his mind, until he became another subject of their will, and to live in torment without any way of escape. He stood still, and tried to clear his mind of the torment they were inflicting on it. There was something he could do but what was it, what was it? Then above, and clearer than all the voices screaming in his head was a calm and medium pitched voice. "Return outside you came in unprepared, return outside! Then you will know!"

As he turned his legs began to feel as though they were wading through thick treacle and he began to struggle, he had to fight them in his mind, in his mind. Eventually he made it out of the doors into the arms of his waiting friends. As he did so he knew what he did not have with him and it was the only weapon to use against the evil in the room. "What was it? What was it? " Some how he had to go into himself, know himself, and remember what it was he had, had in the dream, of the night of dreams. The answer he just knew was there. He needed help and if he asked for it he knew it would come, how? He was unsure but come it must, if he was to have any chance of saving his friends in the room. Why he thought was the man so confident that he held all the aces, as this thought came to him he gradually felt the tension and fear he felt over his friends seemed to leave him, his friends outside the room with him seemed to become distant from him and yet there was a part of them that would not separate, it was then he realized what the answer was and the reason he had been able to get out of the room and not succumb to the evil power within it which had been trying to possess him there. It was their love for him and their trust in spirit, that they all now held, that was the answer. As the fact came to him he knew it was not for the first time, he knew, a tremendous feeling of well-being and such an increase of love and understood reborn feelings began to flow into him and from him. He knew then he was going back into the room now and there would be no fear with him at all, for he knew beyond all doubt he would not be walking in alone and completely defenceless, as he almost had before, he only had to ask for help from the realm of light and it would be there, as it always had been, and always would be, it was the trust, love, and faith, he had within him which would attract the like of which he would need, and which he knew nothing could stand against. It had been with him from the time of his earliest form of life, before the time he had volunteered to sacrifice his own name and the life he had chosen into the history of the despised. He had made an agreement then, and that agreement would still hold sure. Because it was not just showing him the faith he had in spirit but he had been shown the absolute proof of life everlasting, and he also understood, the evil within the room was stagnant and none progressive, and must be stopped no matter what the cost could be to his present life. He turned around and said a small prayer for help, and in that instant he knew why he had first walked to the woman, and not the man, it was she who was the channel for the evil, while he directed it for them both, each was protection for the other. As he walked through the doorway, the others stood in the doorway and watched. He felt a warmth flood through him and as it did so he seemed to become swathed in light, and as he moved forward the light went before him with each step he took, as he went the darkness began to retreat back towards the woman, as he looked at her he could see the entity that had possessed her began to show itself, and he also knew that the thing at one time would have been human but, what he could see now was nothing more than a degenerate thing of evil, which could not hide itself from his vision. He could then see the look of rage which was manifesting itself in defiance for what he stood for. It tried to reach out to harm him, but seemed to burn as it entered the aura of light which was surrounding him. It spat and yelled abuse at him, shrieked that it would kill it's host, who it possessed. Charlie felt what to him seemed an infusion of power, which gave him direction and, some inner instinct of knowledge, of what he had to do, while at the same time he felt he had someone within himself who in some way was guiding and allowing him to absorb the power of light which was surrounding and protecting him. "Leave now, and go to the realm appointed for you!" His voice boomed out, confident and strong. "Leave now, or be written out of the book of life forever!" "You cannot win, I will be back, we are many, and we will rule here no matter what you do, there are too many who will succumb to our will, we are legion, I will find another to do my will, this world shall be ours, it is, almost, now. With that last statement the entity was gone from the woman, he then turned his attention to the man and as he did so saw that the entity which had possessed him was in the process of leaving his body also. His face contorted and his body shook caused by the exit of the entity which had taken his living body over. While this was happening those in the room were taken aback for a while, and then moved to the woman trying to reassure her that they were friends and, both of them were now safe. Leonard Seers and his wife made an almost instant return to their own consciousness within their own bodies, it was obvious they were confused and could not understand what had happened to them, for a few moments they just looked around their surroundings, and people in the room with them their eyes going from one person to another, questions formed in their minds, where were they? What had happened to them? Strangers surrounding them did not help them to come to any, positive conclusions. "How are you feeling? Don't worry you are among friends, just sit there, until you feel less confused." Anne spoke to them in a clear but soft friendly voice, while at the same time pressing her hand on the man's shoulder preventing him from rising out of his chair. Moments later it seemed that their memory of what had happened to them, and of the events prior to them becoming possessed by the two entities, who, only moments before controlled every aspect of their bodies, and had replaced their personalities with their own, to be used for their own evil purpose. While in the state of possession until the moment of release, they had been in total spiritual torment, with as they had believed not the slightest chance of ever being released from. The spiritual suffering, of misery and despair they had endured while they were in the state of being possessed, was still in their memory making them unsure if what they were experiencing now was in fact reality, or just another aspect of the internal torment they had experienced, and would be placed back into the state of purgatory moments later. Of the two the wife seemed to be in a worse state of mind than her husband. They could see around them the unfamiliar walls and furniture of the room, along with unfamiliar faces of people who seemed friendly towards them, but as they saw these things they were still afraid that there would be some part of their ordeal that was not fully over and reluctant to accept the ordeal they had gone through as completely in the past and they were now safe. Questions formed in their minds as to how they came to be where they were, and how those around them had become involved with what ever had happened to them. Also where they were. Choco could see the way their minds had been working, and of the confusion of the situation they found themselves in, and proceeded to calm their fears as best he could, assuring them every thing was now well and they were among friends. After they realized that everything was as they had been told, and that no harm would come to them, they began to ask questions of those around them, who except for small pieces of information they were able to answer of their earlier plight, they could answer very little. It was then suggested that after a cup of sweet tea they should try tell them all they could about the events leading up to the situation they had just been released from. Well any that there possible to answer that was. "What was the last thing you can remember, before you awoke here?" Marcus had moved over near the couple to ask questions, which, the answers to, might in some way help them in the near future . Anne came into the room with two cups of tea for the husband and wife, she smiled as she handed each of them a cup of hot sweet tea. "Here now drink this, take your time if you want, but if you can try to talk to us while you drink it, it is of the utmost importance that you tell us everything you can remember." "I can't say exactly what actually happened but I can remember it was over a period of time." He took a sip from the cup, and then looked over towards his wife as if to wait for her to verify what he had just said. She returned his gaze, and, there seemed to be a hesitancy, before she spoke, then as if she had then focused her mind on what it was she wanted to say, she began to speak. "I am sure it was sometime after we had attended a party given by one of our friends, who was at that time working in the council engineering dept., at least that was the period when things started to happen that we could not explain. Even as I think back to that time everything seems a little vague, and out of focus. But, I am sure that whatever it was happened to us stems back to that period of time." She looked towards her husband as she finished speaking, and holding her hand out towards him, the look in her eyes, and that simple action, told the others there, she had not by any means come to terms with her experience. He put his arm around her shoulder, pulled her gently towards him, nothing was said, but as he handed the empty cup to Anne the meaning was clear to her, by the relief shown on his face. "What time of the year was the party held?" Marcus had become intrigued by the little the woman had said, and was curious about in what way the possession of the man and wife had been accomplished. "Why it was just before Christmas the twenty second of December. I had just been promoted towards the end of November, and it was just after that I received the invitation for both of us to the party. I had met Phil Grainham at the 'Conservative Party Sporting Club'. I had been a member there for about three to four years, prior to meeting him. It was not long after the meeting we were invited to the party. By Phil and his wife, as their guests. "How long have you worked in the D.H.S.S. Taunton office?" "I was transferred from Bridgwater to Taunton in eighty five, so that makes it five years now." Marcus looked at the others there, and indicated for them to remain quiet, and say nothing. "What!" He then asked. "What, year is it now." Seers looked at Marcus, and with a hesitancy in his voice answered. "Nineteen ninety?" Marcus, his eyes fixed on the husband and wife sitting in the chairs in front of him had wondered to himself, just how long before, the complete possession of the two had occurred, and was more than surprised the length of time, the two entities had possession of their bodies, and also, what they had achieved in that time for the benefit of those in control at the manor, and, what his roll was, besides working as an official at the claims office of the D.H.S.S.. What had he been doing travelling to America, and other countries he had been seen in. "I am sorry to be the one to tell you that the year is now nineteen ninety four. So you see Mr Seers, you have both been under control for almost five years. It's now the later half of the month of October." Seers was obviously taken back at the information he had just been given, and was flustering, to say something, anything. But, he could not put into words, the feeling of disbelief, at the words he had just heard. His wife looked at him wide eyed, then thoughts began to come into her head. Thoughts, and memories, of when they had both become unwell, and how they were touchy with each other over things that seemed to provoke them both into rows, and at times periods of violence towards each other, which, they had not participated in all the time they had been married, before the party they had attended with Phil Grainham. There was now something which came to mind, a memory, a distorted memory, which as she began to think on started to become clearer. As she concentrated on she could remember fragments of a series of situations, which as she thought about, she started to become cold, which caused a tremor to travel through her body. She remembered drinking and talking at the party, her husband always by her side. She remembered laughter, conversations with others there. Some were good friends, and others she had met that evening for the first time. There were furtive looks from some there, when they had first arrived which she had dismissed as the night had gone on, as being due to them not really knowing anyone, other than the Grainham's and a few close friends, which had, at the time, made her feel a little uncomfortable. She remembered travelling in a car driven by someone other than her husband, he was laying against the side of a car door, his head against the back seat headrest unconscious. Then walking as if in a semi dream, through a passage way, being held up and assisted by someone, as she thought about it, it seemed as if she had, had a little too much to drink, although, as she now reflected on that night she was sure he had not had more than three glasses the whole night. Then suddenly, it came all back to her, as if someone had opened a door facing her, with with a abrupt movement, revealing a light filled room, displaying all the contents it held, before her. It had been triggered by the memory of seeing her husband draped over the shoulders of a very large man, of over six feet in height. She could remember as she was stumbling along the passage, trying to reach over to touch him, but some how her arms would not function, but hung down by her sides limp dangling freely. They, she then remembered, came to inside a cave or room with walls of solid rock, although, the memories she was having seemed to be fuzzy and disjointed in some way. Then later she remembered, they were taken outside of the room to another close by and made to stand in front of it while it was opened as it did so she recalled a feeling of fear, and hostility towards them, with her husband holding her close to him. Then she felt them both being propelled forwards into the facing room. Then there was nothing, she had no memory of anything after that, about where she was or had been until now. The only thing she could now recall, was waking up in her home, the day after the party. It was after that she remembered that her husbands personality, along with her own changed completely. Marcus and the others had listened to Leonard Seers as he began to talk about what he could remember. While his wife had been remembering everything she could recall, to herself. With a little coaxing, and questions being asked on particular points, Marcus was pretty sure they had found out a lot more information from him than he had really expected, from the time before he had been possessed, which was important. "These names he has given us Marcus, do they mean anything to you, and how many are there all together?" Anne was wanting to know how much information they had gained since the episode that had happened in the sitting room the night before. Choco broke into the conversation asking if he should take the Seers to where they had parked their car after getting them both to Marcus's house. "No." Was Marcus's reply. "I want them to have some time on their own for a short while longer, while I discus an idea I have, with David. He is in the other room at the moment waiting for me, can you ask everyone to come in there as quickly as possible." "Mr and Mrs Seers have given us fifteen names that may be of interest to us. All of which are not unknown to us, and I may say without fear of contradiction, they almost all hold some position of importance in there own right. If even half of them are connected to those at the manor, they could use their position in various ways with a certain amount of effect against us. I feel we must act quickly, if the names we have are going to be any good for our cause. Further more; It has occurred to me that since last night the Seer's could be in considerable danger, now that they are with us, with the entities who had control of them are defeated. They would now almost certainly be missed by the others. Perhaps there could even be some kind of communication between them in such cases as the one we dealt with. Who knows? Also, they would have been warned again as we have come off better once more against them." Marcus then began to explain to those there of the idea he had and what he had in mind to see if it could be carried out. "If it is possible, and with the help of David with his position in the police force, and Leonard Seers, if he would be willing to participate in what I have in mind, perhaps we might be able to gain some inside knowledge of the workings of those at the manor and, perhaps even other groups who are active in this country. Mitchell And Choco had agreed to participate in the plan Marcus had put together, with the agreed help of Leonard Seers and his wife. He explained the plan was not without certain amount of danger. All three were to go to the office where Seers had worked in the pretext of investigating a fraud of some kind. Sally Parsons had told him of the stainless steel box which she had seen Seers put a computer disc into, when he had been possessed by the entity. Marcus was convinced that there could be information on the disc she had seen him use, and more than likely on the others that it had been placed in the box with, giving them access to material that would probably have quite a lot of information on who else may be being used in the same way as Seers and his wife had, by those at the manor. The idea was to go in with Seers collect the box under the guise of what the discs contained was, evidence of a fraud. The only trouble for Mitchell was the fact that he had to keep his actions hidden from Loverage, not wanting him to know anything at all about what had been going on, so he could use Choco with him in the roll of a police officer, and it made him feel a little safer in knowing he had one of the four friends with him. Choco meanwhile had borrowed some of Mitchell's clothing to help in his appearance as a police officer. Should anything be said about his hair style he would say he was normally working under cover as a drugs squad officer, should any comment be made about his hair, he would say he was only with Mitchell because there was a connection between the fraud Mitchell was investigating and a drug dealing operation he had been in the middle of when the suspicion of the fraud came to light. As it happened there was no comment made at all when the three made their way to the office from the side of the building, some heads turned but that was about all. The office staff greeted as he led the other two to his office. They entered and then shut the door behind them. Leonard Seers, when they were inside, looked at the other two with a puzzled expression. "What are we looking for?" "Anything to do with Gowendene manor, that would be the best place to start." "Right, let's start here!" He moved to a filing cabinet and opened the drawers. Mitchell began to thumb through the foldered contents. Gowendene manor, Gowendene manor, 'G' 'G' 'G' Goddard, Gollet, come on,...Gowendene, Gommet, Gowendene,...Gowendene, ...Gowendene manor,... Gowendene manor...Here we are Gowendene manor." Mitchell pulled a buff colour folder from the cabinet with Gowendene manor written in large bold black letters, made from a marking pen. Then placed it into a large polythene bag. Choco was with Seers as he opened the drawers of his desk, and saw right away the stainless steel box Sally Parsons had told Marcus of. "That's it, put it into the bag with the folder, Dave has found. Is there any more with reference to Gowendene manor on in any of the other drawers there." He asked of Seers. "No, seems that there is just the box here. "Anything else in the cabinet Dave?" "Not that I can see." "Well that must be everything then, come on, lets get the hell out of here while the going is good. Just shut and lock everything, and we can be on our way. Bring the keys you have on the key ring with us." A quick search as they were leaving the office, revealed nothing more to them pertaining to the manor. They walked casually through the administration part of the office with hardly a glance from any of those there, who seemed to be working on forms and word processors, oblivious of anything else going on around them. Passing through the office they came outside into the stair well, and started down the stairs, towards the buildings exit. As they did so they passed on the stairs three women, 'Bag ladies', and as they passed Choco and the other two, he felt a coldness, and a feeling of depression, such as he had never felt before, he looked back and watched for a few seconds as the three women trudged slowly up the stairs and through the doorway they had just left by, and out of his vision. As they were leaving the exit they heard a loud banging, and then there was the sound of footsteps running down the stairs in their direction. They stopped and watched from the car park as the doors burst open with the sounds of voices shouting as people began to hurriedly vacate the building spilling out onto the street a few yards from where they stood. Choco went back to where they were all exiting the building, and asked a man with a child of about eight years of age with him, what was happening and why every one seemed to be panicking. "It was madness. Three women came into the room where we were all waiting to be interviewed by the D.H.S.S. officers, one of them walked over to the door just as someone's name was called. When the door was opened she just pushed the person aside and went through the door into the office administration part of the building, and began laughing and shouting at everyone in sight, as did the other two in the waiting room area. While at the same time they took from the bags they were carrying two gallon cans of petrol and began to empty them all over themselves and the floor and walls. They were splashing it everywhere, and laughing as if they were crazy as they did so. The one who had gone into the administration room came back out and threw a lighted box of matches into the office she had come from, I was sure what was coming next and grabbed my boy and ran out of the place as fast as I could. I had got myself onto the stairway and on my way down when the doors behind me opened and there was a frantic scrambling of the others behind us as we ran down the stairs. Then there was a whoosh and I could hear the screams amid the laughter of the three women, of those who had not managed to get out of there. It was horrible, terrifying, I cannot believe what they did in there. As he finished speaking Choco heard the fire alarm sound, and as it did so, the emergency exit flew open, as office staff, and others, who had managed to get out of the other part of the building made their escape. Mitchell shouted to Choco to come back to the car park and get into the car before the fire service and police arrived, so as not to be seen there, by any of the uniformed as they arrived.

CHAPTER 40

When they arrived back at Marcus's home and gave him the box of discs and the folder, he asked how it had gone, and if there had been any hitches. They told him everything went like clockwork, and mentioned to him of the burning of the offices, and the part the bag ladies had in it.

"They were obviously from the manor, and with what they had done showed that what we now have in our possession is probably very important to those at the manor house. We had only come out of the building moments before the place was on fire. It's probably completely gutted, from the fire in the area where they threw the petrol around. As we drove away we could hear the windows exploding with the heat from inside the building."

"Were there any casualties besides the women who started the fire?" Marcus asked.

"The number of people in the room as we left the office where we got the box and folder must have been at least thirty or more, and then there were the office staff there as well. When we left, we could see only about twenty or so who escaped and were in the area outside the building, so, sadly it seems, there would have been quite a few casualties. There was nothing we could do about the situation, and we left shortly after, before the police and fire service arrived."

Choco had listened to the conversation between Mitchell and Marcus.

"At least with the place having burned so ferociously, they must be assuming the discs and any evidence against them, must have been destroyed in the fire. They were slow to act for once, probably because they did not know we knew so much about their inside connection at the D.H.S.S.. What we have to do now is to see what we have got on the discs and in the folder that might be of help to us. I don't think they would have bothered to have burned the building if they had not thought the discs and anything else there which they felt might have caused problems for them."

One and a half hours later, everyone in the room with Marcus were dumfounded by what had been revealed on the discs by Marcus using his own word processor.

He had got into the data base section and one of the names who had come to light, was Tim's girlfriend's name 'Rene'. According to the information revealed she had stayed at the manor for five weeks and was now down as moved to Canterbury in Kent. But the thing that worried Tim was that next to her name in brackets was the name, Mary Kearns, D/B/Burning 1587. Samuel Smythe, Accuser died 1606.

"What does all this mean?" Asked Tim, of Marcus.

"Look at the top of the printout, about six or seven names down."

Charlie put his arm around his friends shoulder, and when Tim looked at what he was told of he saw the name Leonard Joseph Seers. (James Stepps) Taunton. Executed. H.D.Q. 1560. Accuser Benjamin Hallows.

Marcus had gone through the list he had shown to the others and other things which were revealed to him from just one of the discs, and had said it was just pure chance he had chosen the one they had looked at with the names which meant some thing to them. "To me what the list conveys is; The first name is the person born and living in our time, the second name I believe is the name of the person who has possessed the body of the first, with the date and manner of death in the time they had lived before, with the name of the person who had accused them of the crime of heresy.

There was quite a period of time when everyone was in deep conversation about what they might be able to achieve now, since they had the information on the discs, of the people who had been possessed, and the towns or cities they were to be found in, with Tim one of the most eager to do something with the knowledge they now had.

"There is a situation I think you should all come and see. While we have been all talking about what we have found out and accomplished, it seems we have had a visit from something at the manor." Sean after speaking looked towards Leonard Seers, and by the expression on his face everyone could tell it was him he was concerned for, he made his way towards him. Then as he spoke to him, the face of Seers seemed to drain of all colour, turning to a shade of pale white. With a faltering voice, he asked what was wrong, and then began to visibly shake.

"It's Doreen, isn't it! What's the matter with her?" He started to leave the room and as he was about to pass Dixie, Sean indicated to him not to let him leave, who caught hold of him as he did so. Sean reached him and held on to his arm as he tried to continue his way out of the room. He faced him unsure of how he could say what he wanted to, but somehow the words came.

"It's too late for you to do anything for her I'm afraid, too late for anyone to do anything."

Sean looked towards Marcus.

"Can someone get him a brandy or, something strong to drink. It seems you were right when you said to us that nobody should be left on their own. Anne will you stay with him while we see what we should do next?" He motioned discreetly for the others there to follow him. When they arrived at the room where she had been resting, after her husband returned that morning, and had gone to the sitting room to see the results of just what they had achieved with the information on the discs. There was a terrible odour that came from under the door. He saw the reactions of the others with him as came towards the door.

"Yes I smelt it myself, that's how I came to open the door earlier, it's not pretty in there, and there was nothing I could have done for her, nothing anyone could have done, when I found her."

As they moved closer to the bed they could see there was no chance for her to be anything, but, deceased, and any chance of recognizing her for who she had been was impossible. Her face it seemed had been eaten away. By what they could not conceive. There was not one part of her face that had not been affected from the top of her head, her hair had come away and lay all over the pillow in clumps, eyeless sockets, the deep red and brown of raw meat with globules of watery blood over the surface, and even as they looked it seemed whatever had happened, was still in effect happening as they watched. The flesh over the rest of her body as they looked was in actual fact visibly moving as it was being consumed at a very rapid rate, every one there felt a sickening feeling in the pit of their stomach. Such was the sight before them.

"Oh my God, how could this happen without anyone hearing anything, I would have expected anyone to die in this way would have been in agony, and screaming in pain. What could have attacked her to do something like this."

"It has the look of that flesh eating disease that the papers were on about a couple or more years ago, which started in the hospitals, can you remember it Marcus. Apparently it was rife at one stage, and there was a big out cry about it at the time."

"I know what you mean Choco, but I cannot believe it could be the same thing to do this much to her in the few hours she had been up here sleeping."

"What are we going to say to Seers about her condition, I have only said that she was dead remember, nothing about how she had died? He is bound to eventually want to come up and see her, he does not know about what they are capable of, and to come up and see what has become of her.....I feel so sorry for him, what can we say?"

"I will speak to him and try to break the news of her condition as gently as I can, and advise him that it might be better for him not to see her as she is. But if he still insists on seeing her then some one must go with him, and that, I would not welcome personally. I think that is all, that can be done for him, under the present circumstances."

Marcus then covered Doreen Seers over with a clean sheet, and leaving her on the bed was as much as he could do for her, other than to say a prayer for her soul. Then everyone there made their way down to the sitting room where Anne and Seers were. No one could look at him directly in the eyes such was the feeling of sorrow and pity for him.

Marcus then suggested he went into his study to see what else there was on the other discs they had, and asked that perhaps as they had seen what had happened to Doreen Seers Mitchell would accompany him in there while he did so.

Later there was a knock on the front door which Dixie had answered, to find Sally Parsons and six other people, two men and four women with her, he recognized from earlier meetings. "Hello! Dinsly isn't it? I have brought every one I could get in touch with and left a message for those I could not. They should be here before very long. I told them Marcus wanted us all here as soon as possible, as he said it was urgent and important we should all be here before eight o'clock this evening. My, it's beginning to get quite cold out here, and there's a fog beginning to come down now, as well."

"Come in, and the names Dixie, not whatever it was you said." He smiled and held the door open for her and the others to enter.

When they had gone into the sitting room and met the others, they were told about the discs and what had happened at the D.H.S.S. offices.

While Marcus and Mitchell had gone into the study Choco, Anne, and Sean. Had spoken to Seers about his wife and had done their best to comfort him, and had explained to him as best they could all they knew of the people at the manor, and what they had been up against since the knowledge of them had come to light.

They had left him then, in the corner with Alice with him as company, just to keep an eye on him, seeing how distraught he had become since the incident with the resulting death of his wife.

It was two hours later when Marcus returned to the sitting room, and at first seemed surprised to see so many people had turned up since he had left to go into his study. He remembered then how he had earlier telephoned Sally, asking if she could arrange for as many as could be got in touch with to come to his house, feeling once they found out what was on the discs should be disclosed to them all as soon as possible. As they came to the centre of the room all talking ceased. His first question to Choco, and Sean, was how Leanard Seers was now taking the loss of his wife, and was there any thing more that could be done to comfort him. They told him he seemed to be adjusting himself as best he could over his loss, and how they had decided to leave him quietly with Alice to talk to, when ever he felt able. It was also, just a safety precaution seeing as how they had been able to attack and kill his wife while she was alone. Marcus then decided the time might be about right for him to inform those there what he had learned from the tapes, now in their possession.

"It's nice to see you all here, an unexpected pleasure to see you here especially after such short notice, and will save me having to get in touch with you all again to tell you the things we have now found out since yesterday. No doubt you will have been told of the terrible thing which has resulted in the loss of Doreen, the wife of Leonard Seers who, thankfully, has been most instrumental in the acquisition of the information I am about to relay to all of you, and for that alone we are deeply in his debt. I know you will all agree with me when I say you all understand by now, Mr and Mrs Seers, were not responsible for any of the things they have done while under the control of those who had possessed them. Even as I speak I see the person who is trying to give comfort to him is none other than Alice, who's own husband was one of the victims we know of who they were used to pursue and kill, when they were under control.

Well now back to the matters in hand, and before us. In the next few days we hope to be able to strike back at the evil which has taken control of so many innocent victims to do their will, and eventually we hope to release them from the horrors of the existence they are experiencing, due to the evil that controls them. But I must also inform you that what, we have perceived to to be a lot of knowledge of them before we were in possession of the discs, was in fact, just a scratch of the surface of what the reality of their actual influence on world affairs are, and I feel it is fair to say we may well have a long and bitter battle with them, and must not take anything for granted. They are sly, evil, and with no conscience. With total world domination as their ultimate goal, and to lose against them would be totally unthinkable for the consequences of mankind. We must be prepared and willing to give everything we have if we are to stand any chance to defeat this evil we now face. Should situations turn on us and move in their favour, then we must at least leave as much of our mark and efforts as we possibly can, so that others may come behind our failure, with at the very least, all of the knowledge we have gained, in their possession when they do so."

He then asked to speak to some of them there in his study, and named, among them; Sean and Molly, Anne Farr, Peter and Abigail Jones, Sally Parsons, Dave Mitchell, Choco, Charlie, Tim and Dixie. They all followed the others named into the Marcus's study, all of them except for Mitchell, had no real idea what it was he wanted to speak to them of, except that it was something to do with what he had found on the discs. Which had more than worried both Marcus and Mitchell, when they had realized one of the main functions of Gowendene Manor was of a nature they had not realized in their wildest dreams. Everyone had filed in and had filled the small room as best they could with a good view of Marcus who was sitting at his desk while Mitchell stood beside him.

Marcus was sitting down at his desk facing them all. The room had taken on an atmosphere of tense expectation, and a nervous excitement. The silence of which, was broken by his voice. "From what we have been able to make out with the information on the discs. We have discovered there has been a lot more than we could have possibly imagined been taking place for the last ten years or so." He looked up at all of them there for a moment, wondering to himself what their reaction would be when he informed them just what else had been going on at the manor besides abductions, and the possessing, of the victims who stayed there, and others they had found uses for in the furtherance of their ultimate goal.

"In England, Ireland, Scotland, and Wales, we have the names of twenty nine establishments which are importantly connected with the functions of 'Gowendene Manor' and it seems they play as much an important a roll to one another, in other words I do not think that the manor we know of here, is any less, or more important, than any others of the establishments we have found out about.

But to put it in a context that we all might understand, shall we say, a building such as the manor is the same as one room in a house, all are part of the same building but, the difference is that there are distances between each room in miles, rather than inches. While all the time one room knows what is going on in the other. While at the same time to anyone without the information we have, would assume there was no connection at all between any two places. It would also seem a logical conclusion, to assume that all the establishments around the world would have the same kind of link with any other world wide, exactly the same as we have already mentioned in this country, when the links were established world wide, as we know they are, the situation to us will be somewhere, as a comparable, the same as having a mansion the size and area, of shall we say the city of Bristol, and that as you will see is a heck of a size mansion, which alone shows us what we are going to have to face, and full on, with very little in our corner physically or materially to call upon. Enlistment of more people other than we have at the moment would be difficult, and could put us in a more precarious position than we are at the moment. Simply because, we cannot take the chance of having to tell others of what we know, because if we did, then there would be more of a chance that any strategy, or method of action we may intend to take, could become known by whoever we intend to try and defeat."

There were numerous voices trying to speak at once, and asking questions of Marcus. Marcus held up his hands to them, and then pointed to one of those Mitchell recognized as being one of the close friends of Sean, he had met on the first occasion he went to the house where they held the seance when he had met and touched the solidly spirit formed, "Two Bears."

"Do we know if the other places are the same as what we have found out about the manor here, or do they have other functions?" "We just don't know anything about them for sure at the moment. But that is one of the reasons I have asked all of you to see me. We have the names of the places, and where they are. Names of people much the same as I have already told you earlier. Names of people who are alive today with names, and dates of death of some who were alive in another life back in history, more than that I feel we must find out for ourselves, from the information we have discovered on the discs in our possession."

241

CHAPTER 41

Five days had now passed since the meeting held at the house of Marcus. The four friends had returned now to the caravan.

Tim was feeling a lot better now about being there than he had when they had first returned, after he had witnessed the death of Father George O'Connell.

"What do think, and how do you feel about coming with me then Dixie? We know where she is, and it would only take a day to be there and back."

"We don't know enough about the place she has gone to, the routine there, or who is in charge of the place or, anything that would help us to be able to get her free from there. Also if she is possessed like the others were, it is more than likely she would resist us trying to take her away from there anyway, and she would have a lot in her favour with those there to be able to really put up a resistance against just two of us!" His eyes caught Charlie's as he finished the last sentence to Tim.

"I just can't stay here and do nothing, you heard what Marcus said when we were last at his house, and he told us what the people who were possessed by those entities would be going through. 'Absolute fear and horror'! Those were his words, and just from the small amount we have heard from Leonard Seers more than bears out what he told us."

Choco and Charlie had both been listening to their two friends talking, and had to agree with what Dixie had been saying to Tim about not knowing enough about the place that Rene was staying in. Choco had been having thoughts along the same lines himself, and had talked over a few ideas he had been toying with, to Charlie, before Tim had spoken to Dixie about travelling to Kent.

"Tim, we all know just how you must be feeling about the plight of Rene, and how much you want to go to her aid. But think! If Dixie drove you up to where she is, or, we presume she still is. How are you going to accomplish even a small amount of what you hope to, without any knowledge of why she has gone there in the first place. Also think about what you would be able to do when you got there, except to watch the place for a few hours before having to return here, and then it could only be at a safe distance, remember what we were told happened to the others when they tried to get close to them. They followed them, then they they were never seen again. No Tim I really think we must put the rescue of Rene on hold until we find out a little more about where she is staying."

"Oh yes, and how do we do that, if we don't go there, and see what we can find out about the place ourselves?"

"We can see Marcus, and see what he thinks of an idea I have, that could possibly help you Tim, and the rest of us with little risk attached. We have to find out what is going on in the other places we have found out about. Then again, they are more than likely just other Hostels for the homeless, the same as the manor we have here, but the one thing we have to do is find out for sure what they are, and what function they serve."

****

"How do you feel about giving it a try Sally? Are you comfortable about doing this, remembering what happened to you when you did the same with Leonard when he was possessed, and he reacted the way he did?"

"I think I will be fine. As you have said I don't have to enter the building, just watch the place from a safe distance."

"Who did you have in mind to accompany you when you go Choco?"

"For some reason I think it might be as well for all four of us to go together, so as we can take it in stints to sleep, when Sally does her bit, I think there should be two of us watching over her at all times just to be safe. But what about where we are to stay, these friends of yours in Canterbury, what have you told them to let them agree to putting us up there for a couple of days, or three?"

"Only that you are good friends and needed somewhere to stay while you were visiting the City on an important assignment for me, which needed a high level of concentration, and that you needed somewhere quiet at short notice, where you would not be disturbed."

"When I first suggested we ask if we could use Sally, I was thinking more along the lines of whether it was possible she could have done her *stuff* from here, and not for anyone to have to travel all the way to Kent."

"I am afraid for the purpose in hand it would not really have been practical to have tried the method of surveillance from so far away without the knowledge of the surrounding area."

They eventually arrived in the town of Canterbury after a few stops on the way in cafe's. The weather had been rain almost all the way there, and had only seemed to cease as they had entered the out skirts of the city. Passing through the centre they found they had taken the wrong direction to where they should have been heading for.

"The sign said Bekesbourne is the way we have just come from. That's where Four acres cottage is, it's on the way before we get there."

"O.K. O.K., anyone can make a wrong turn, can't they? I already saw the sign before you said anything, we will have to go on before I can find some where to turn the van around!"

Sally Parsons had been in the company of the four, for a few hours now, and they never seemed to let anything get them down, from the weather to the fact of going all the way from Taunton to Canterbury, not knowing what they might encounter if things for some reason went wrong. Although, she had convinced herself there would not be much danger to them if she just did what Marcus had asked, and keep her distance from the place.

They had been travelling on a 'B' road for about fifteen minutes and had passed a cross road described to them by Marcus.

"There's a layby ahead of us, now look for the bridge on the opposite side of the road. It's supposed to be just a hundred yards or so on, and the cottage is just past it."

"There is the bridge and that could be the cottage, start to slow down Dixie, in case we have to swing off of the road to get to it." Charlie was looking at the sketch drawing Marcus had done for them.

"Yes it looks by what Marcus has drawn here, there could be a small drive there."

"Four Acres Cottage! That's it all right, we are here, pull in, pull in Dixie, but don't block the entrance there may be someone in there will want to get out in one or other of the two cars which are already parked here." Choco was giving the place a good scrutiny as he came along the front of the cottage.

As they climbed out of the van, they saw they were on the side of a rough stone and hard packed earth, drive-in, which ran at right angles to the cottage. As they stood out side of a low wall with a rustic gate, the small door to the cottage opened. A tall man with brown, parted, sun bleached long hair, and aged about the mid thirties appeared, followed, closely behind by a woman near the same age. Her black hair tinged with silver flecks tied in a bunch each side of her head by bright red ribbon, there was a smile upon her lips, as if about to welcome some old friends she had not seen for ages. A two piece tweed suit with a white frilled collar, seemed to match the jacket, trousers, and a prominently green tartan sports shirt, with a dark red tie which was flapping each side of him with every step he took towards them, making a heavy thud on the ground from his leather soled brogue shoes.

"Hello! The names Giles, Giles Ambrose Poulder-Haigh, my wife Penny. Marcus told us of your coming, and how many there were of you. We have replenished the refrigerator, there is also plenty in the chest freezer, it's next to the refrigerator, you will see it there, and you must help yourself to whatever you want. Marcus has asked us to give you as much privacy as we can, for the two or three days you need for what ever experiment it is you are trying to do for him, or, with him. Well I am sure you know what I mean.

Now, these are the keys to our cottage, we will be away for, well, at least three days anyway. So, make yourselves at home. We are going to take the opportunity to visit my parents in Anglesea, be a treat for us both. If you leave before we are back, just pop the keys into the Post office, I have already told them you are staying here, but also told them you are friends of ours looking after the cottage while we are away. I have not cancelled 'The Times' newspaper, but when you finish with it keep the copies and just put them in the rack I will read them when we return. Who is Sally, and who is Mr. Chocklo?"

"I'm Choco!"

"I'm Sally."

"Good, Good, now, Choco?"

"That's it old son,....Choco."

"Well Choco, Marcus, has told me to tell you, he says under no circumstances must any of you take any risks with what you are about to do, and to ask you, Sally, to make sure you write down everything you think may have significance in direction, on the experiment, as soon as you are able. He said, I was to say exactly that, and you would know his meaning." He handed Choco the keys told them all to go right on in and to make as if the place was there's. Wished them well, adding they were on their way to catch the train in Canterbury which would be leaving there in thirty minutes time, and since they had now arrived at the cottage, and would have plenty of time left in the day to settle in, they would be on their way. He also said should the need arise, they could make use of his wife's car the Renault 6 parked in the drive, but if they did they would have to put in some fuel because it was running low, the keys are on the key hook in the hall.

Walking into the cottage they could feel the heat from the central heating system. A welcome contrast to the cold and dampness they had felt outside. Stepping inside, Penny Poulder-Haigh's influence on the dwelling was obvious, different shades of orange pastel colours in emulsion paint, with an emphasis on the colour pink with fabrics and furnishings, which had been arranged in an orderly and neat fashion. Glassware, Georgian silver, of all kinds of items accompanying medals through three centuries of war, paintings, of modern, and the Victorian era adorned the walls, and in glass cases, which were situated in various strategic positions around the room.

Dixie's immediate interest was caught by a particular painting as he entered the room.

"Bloody hell Choco! Have you seen this, I think it's real, the real M'coy!" He went closer and gazed intently at the frame and picture within it.

"It is, it's the real thing, how much do you reckon it's worth Charlie? I think it's a genuine Salvador Dali!" Charlie had followed him over to it when he had seen his interest in the painting. "To you Dixie, it could cost anything upwards of ten years of your time. Don't you think after two thousand years it might be about time to quit and, call it a day." Choco was grinning as he spoke and while the others laughed, Dixie's attention had moved to other places of interest to him, such as the silver and glass in the cabinets.

It was quite late in the evening when things had settled down and they were eventually discussing the reason they had come to the area.

"Will it be the same procedure as when you went tripping before or whatever it is you call it Sally." Charlie asked.

"Yes exactly the same, but we must find out where the place is and see it, so as I will know the directions to get there when I 'trip' as you say." Her smile towards him as she answered, was at the same time saying, look out for me when I am working." Don't you fret girl, we will be as alert to anything untoward or harmful to you, with more attention than a cat sizing up a mouse with the intention of a quick catch. Just, you, take no chances. with your part of the proceedings, that's all."

Tim as usual had been delegated head cook and bottle washer for their stay there, and had found in the refrigerator eggs, bacon, and sausages which he promptly started to prepare for them all. Three quarters of an hour later they had eaten and were in the middle of discussing the first move to find out the whereabouts of the place they wanted to observe. They had on the table left by the Polder-Haigh's a street map of the city of Canterbury.

"What was the name of the road, the place was on Charlie? Was it Tower Bell Road, or Bell Tower Road, and what was the name of the place called?"

"Hang on, I have it written down on the paper Marcus gave us, with the directions of how to get here."

He searched through his pockets and pulled out, the by now, crumpled sheet of paper with the drawing and directions they had earlier used to find Four Acres Cottage. He unfolded and spread it out on the table smoothing the surface of the paper flat with his hands, on the now cups and plates filled table, nearly knocking over one of the cups containing an almost full measure of coffee.

Sally saw what had almost happened, and got up from the table collecting the dishes not in use any more, and took them out into the kitchen. Tim saw what she was doing and decided it was time he started to wash the dishes and cooking utensils and clean up the kitchen area anyway, and went out into the kitchen behind her to start doing the chore. He washed while she wiped the dishes, and then they both put them away chatting friendly to each other about the forth coming task, Rene's involvement, and possible chance of rescue, as they did so.

"Here we are, the place is called Kalleshin House, and it's on the corner of Bell Tower Road, and Pictmount Way. That should not be to difficult for us to find. The Cathedral is nearby."

"What do we do for sleeping arrangements, I have just looked around and there are three bedrooms, one is the main one normally occupied by the owners of the cottage, and two I suppose are for guests with two single beds in each. I suggest that Sally has the double in the main bedroom, while we use the single beds. What do you say we have had a long day and travelling here has made me a bit on the tired side. Perhaps with every thing now sorted, we should think about having an early night, and start first thing in the morning. We can go and see where the place we want is and then take it from there. What do you all think of that idea?" There were murmurs of agreement to what Choco had suggested, and shortly after they made their ways to the bedrooms to sleep the night away.

CHAPTER 42

"We should have waited a little longer before starting out, the place is choc-a-block with traffic, must be the rush hour when everyone is on their way to work, and the roadworks back aways have done little to ease the situation. Anyway Dixie how's the car handling, a bit better than the van for driving in all this traffic. Yeah?" Charlie arching his back stretched his arms upwards, touching the roof of the vehicle as he spoke.

"Isso..kay, I s'pose." Dixie replied, while trying to light a rollup he had quickly made while he was stationary, and waiting for another set of roadworks traffic lights to change.

"Sodding councils are all the same where ever you are, they always make roadworks priority at the worst times of the day. Why don't they let the main traffic through, and start working when the rush hour is over? All they are doing here, is white lining, and that they could do at night when there is hardly any traffic around."

"Bell Tower Square, we have just passed Bell Tower Square that must be the cathedral tower I can see a little way over there, we must be near to where we want to get to. Everyone keep their eyes peeled we must be near either Pictmount Way or Tower Bell Road."

"Pictmount Way, turn left now Dixie, we must be at the far end, and Kalleshin House, must be, at the end of here, if this road leads on to Bell Tower road, we must have gone wrong at the first traffic lights earlier. There! Look, there, before the end of this road, that looks as if it could be a side entrance to that large building inside that laurel hedge."

They drove past a low stone wall overhung by a hedge of laurel trees, an entrance which was closed by a wooden gate with an ornamental arch made of the same kind of stone as the wall. A white board covered the top of the arch with the name 'Kalleshin House' (Tradesmen's Entrance only) in black bold lettering.

"You're right Charlie swing a right when we reach the end of this road Dixie, then we can see the front entrance of the place, there might be the same type of sign they had at Gowndene Manor, you know, Hostel for the homeless and all that crap."

As they neared the end of the road they saw a young woman pushing a pram turn the corner towards them on the side of which the house stood. As they stopped to turn Choco had a peculiar sensation as they turned the corner, the woman stopped and, then looked over towards them for a moment, then seemed to shrug for an instant as they drove on around towards the front and the entrance of the building. The wall continuing around alongside the pavement, was still low but, free of any trees or shrubs. A large expanse of green lawn, with women pushing prams around on it, or sitting with them in a shelter, and facing the sun, as it began to break through the morning cloud covered sky.

"Move it Dixie, carry on driving, and don't stop!" Choco shouted to his friend from the back seat of the car. As he accelerated along the road, Charlie saw the sign above them across the main gate entrance:

'KALLESHIN HOUSE'
(PRIVATE MATERNITY HOSPITAL)

"Holy, shit! Did you see that you lot? Did you see what that place is? What in hells name else, are they capable of? They must be possessing mothers, and their children here. I should have realized it when I had a feeling come over me, when the woman passed us pushing a pram, while we were waiting to turn out into the main road towards the front of the place."

Everyone was more than a little disturbed, about what they had seen in the grounds of the maternity hospital, and the first thing they wanted to do was to telephone Marcus and tell him of the scene they had witnessed on returning to the cottage.

"I don't think it would be wise before I take a closer look at the place Choco, and just to say that

246

the place is just a maternity hospital, could be, a long way short of what else could be going on there. Remember what you all found out about Gowndene Manor, when you started watching for things that your friend had told you to look for, the same could apply there. It could also be used for more than a Maternity hospital. I think we should wait a little while, until I can see, what there may be to see, other than it just being a maternity hospital."

They all agreed to wait until Sally had given the place a little more time observing what might be going on there, and she had suggested, it might as well start that afternoon.

"Now remember what Marcus has told us all about being careful and not to taking chances. Are you sure you know your way there? We made a lot of mistakes trying to find the place remember."

"Yes it was easy once we found it, and the way back here was straight forward, once we turned off from the second set of traffic lights, it's a straight road, and I will be fine. Tim, it's just a thought, but do you have a photograph of Rene I could have a look at, who knows perhaps I might see her there, and if I don't know what she looks like I would not realize it."

Tim found the one he always had with him, and carried in his wallet, and showed it to her. It was just a close up head and shoulders photograph, taken in a booth when they had gone to the seaside for the day, but of a good likeness of her, with no creasing or frayed edges.

Sally could now see the entrance of the hospital, it had taken hardly any time at all, for her to relax, and then start the out of the body journey to where she now found herself, which was on the opposite side of the road, facing the main entrance.

As she watched she could see much the same scene as they had witnessed that morning. Woman pushing prams and sitting in the shelter talking among themselves. There was something wrong about the scene in front of her, but she could not see what it could be. Everything seemed to be exactly what one would expect to see in a maternity home, when the sun was out and shining. Mothers out in the open air with their new born babies. She moved around the area of the hospital but not too close to be sensed by those she was watching, but could still not see anything that would be of interest to those back at the cottage, or Marcus. After quite a long while, she decided she had spent enough time observing the place and could see nothing coming of staying any longer. Perhaps she thought to herself, I might try again later on in the evening, or again tomorrow.

The return to her body was without any problems, as she awoke, or came conscious of her surroundings she saw Choco leaning over her, holding a glass of water in his hands, and offering it to her she took it from him, and while taking a sip from the glass thanked him.

"How did it go, did you see anything helpful to us?"

"Not really Choco. Just about the same as we saw as we drove past the entrance this morning."

"No one there you thought could have been Rene?" Choco looked at Tim who had been with him as he watched over Sally while she lay on the bed.

"I could not get close enough to be able to distinguish their faces clearly, but, there is something not quite right about what I saw. That much, I am sure of!"

"How do you mean?"

"I can't say exactly. It was just a feeling about what I was seeing, it was as if there was something missing."

"How many mothers and children were there around the place, were there more than we saw earlier? Could you see anything of what might be going on inside the place from where you were?"

"No, nothing! I tried moving around from the out side but there was no way I could see anything of what might be going on inside. I was thinking it might be an idea to look again tonight. But I think I will have to get in closer, it is of no use to us if all I can do is watch from the out side, no use at all."

"I don't know if that would be wise. You know what Marcus has told us about being careful, and not taking chances."

"What if we take a look in a more conventional way inside the building, or at least from the outside of it anyway, just by looking through the windows and listening."

"No way Tim. Remember those who have already disappeared, and the reason why we are here with Sally."

"What about driving near the place parking up, and see if there is anything to be gained by a quick squint around, or even talk to one of the women with a pram when they are out and about, you said yourself about the feeling you had when we passed the woman when we were in the car."

"That was just it Tim, the feeling I had and the way she reacted when we were near her, doing that sort of thing could give our presence here away, better to do it the way we have done up until now with Sally."

Sally had returned later that evening and had positioned herself in the same spot as she had earlier, there were no women around as there had been when she had last been there. The sky had become over cast and a rain storm was immanent. As she watched, she saw an ambulance arrive, and park outside of the front of the building. The drivers of which had got out and entered the buildings front entrance. A while later they came out accompanied by two women, carrying, carry cots who then climbed into the ambulance. As the ambulance drove off she decided to follow it. Leaving the City outskirts it drove for at least twelve miles or more, before turning off of the main road it had been travelling on, onto a side small country lane, after which it stopped in front of a five barred, field gate, the lights were switched off, the back doors opened and the women got out of the vehicle totally naked, climbed over the gate and started walking away from the ambulance towards a fir tree covered hill. The next thing was she saw was the lights then the engine started and the vehicle drove away. Curious as to what was going on she did not know whether to follow the ambulance or the two women. The children were not with the women, but still in the vehicle.

In the end she decided to follow the women after watching to see which direction the ambulance had taken when it had left and returned to the main road again.

The woman walked quickly but silently towards the fir tree wood, as they were almost there, she saw two men who were waiting near the entrance. They were just standing, waiting seemingly oblivious to the rain which was now coming down in torrents. The two women walked past the men as if they were not there and seemed to be completely unaware of their presence. Entering the wood the women continued walking, then stopped as if unsure of the direction they should take. Then, as if they were somehow under instruction turned left walked a little further and stopped. The men who had followed a little distance behind them stopped also. As she watched the women, they just keeled over and fell to the ground. As they did, she turned to see the men had not moved since they had stopped. Making sure they were not going to be near enough to either sense, or be suspicious of her presence there, she moved closer to where the women were on the ground. What she saw took her completely by surprise. Although it was within the darkness of the woods, with the dark and rain filled clouded skies, she could see there was something taking place with the bodies laying on the ground. There was movement on the bodies, their flesh she could see was moving, ripples of movement along the face, arms, legs, and torso. Although the darkness around her made her vision of them impaired gradually the flesh became more clearer, and as it did so there was a sound similar to someone sucking and slurping a thick drink through a straw. She watched and listened as the sound continued and the flesh began to some how, disintegrate in front of her eyes, until in the end she was staring at the white bones of their skulls, ribs, legs, and arms. Then she could see, as the rain continued to fall onto the white bones they seemed to just disintegrate as the rain hit them, as powder would when mixed with water, and then seeped into the wet and sodden ground leaving not a trace of colour or what was once bone. All that was left behind, were two unatural heaps of the internal organs of the two women she had followed. While she had been watching the action of the rain on the two corpses, and not really being able to believe what she had seen. While just standing there, and observing the horrific scene before her, the two men had started to walk towards where the two women had fallen, and they were almost upon her before she realized the fact, quickly she moved away from the immediate vicinity. But not before one of the two had sensed something, or some presence was nearby. He stopped suddenly, seemed to concentrate on his surroundings, and tried to feel around with some kind of mental ability for the direction in which some sense within him told him there was a in some way a witness to what had taken place. Immediately Sally willed herself away from there and in an instant she was down near the gate where the ambulance had dropped the women off.

When she had gone both men then walked to one of the trees picked up two spades, walked to the two piles of human remains and prodded them forward into a hole which had lain unseen by Sally due to the dark surroundings and then began to fill in and cover the remains with the earth taken from the hole and replacing the grass turf they had cut when they had earlier dug it.

CHAPTER 43

"Well at least the journey there has not been a waste of time, which at one stage yesterday I was beginning to think it would turn out to be." They had pulled into a transport cafe on the last stages of the return journey to Taunton, and were at the time sat at a table in a corner far away from any one else in the place. They talked in low tones so as not to be overheard.

"What do you make of it all Charlie, and why have you been so quiet and thoughtful looking since we started the journey back this morning."

"Oh! It might not be anything really, but I have had a few thoughts about what Sally has told us about what she saw happen to the two women she followed into the field, and what she described happen to them." He indicated he wanted to speak no more on what he had been thinking, by inclining his head and using eye language towards Tim. Choco still none the wiser, but understood there was concern in his communication for Tim, spoke no more about it and casually changed the subject.

"How far did you say the ambulance travelled when you followed it, after the incident in the woods with the two women Sally?"

"All of fifteen miles, it stopped in a village named Chilliton. A small place really, no more than about thirty houses and a few shops and a post office. They took the two babies to a large house at the far end of the place. The notice I saw there, said, it was a private adoption agency. I just watched them take the two babies in, and then returned to the cottage."

"What was the name of it?"

"I can't remember off hand, but I have written it down, with the rest of the notes I made when I returned to the cottage last night. Perhaps it will be on one of the discs Marcus has, we can see, when we return later this afternoon."

****

When they arrived at the home of Marcus they were surprised to see his car park full and, had to manoeuvre Dixie's van around to be able to park, leaving enough room to be able to get out of it."

"What's been going on here while we have been away I wonder?" Charlie muttered more to himself than the others with him.

"Must be something in the wind, for all of these cars to be here, that's for sure!" The Door bell was answered by Sean.

"Well, nice to see you back. Everything go well for you?"

"So, so, Sean, but glad to be back here again."

"Come on in, and it's a packed house we are. Your man's away at the minute, to see someone, took off from here just as I arrived with Molly. Said something about going to meet someone, and that it was important or some such thing. Did not have time to say much more, left here like a bat out of hell. It seems the world and his friends have turned up since he left. When he phoned, he said to come around here as soon as we could, and be sure to be here before eight o'clock tonight, and that it was important. Perhaps, the someone who he had to meet is connected with it!"

As they reached the interior of the house there seemed to be standing room only. The place was packed to over flowing, and any chance of making for any of the rooms they had been in before was impossible.

"Why did he want all of these people here, I wonder? More to the point, how is he going to speak to everyone? Has he got some kind of communication system set up? Because that is what it will take to talk to everyone here at the same time. There has got to be at least seventy or eighty people here. Some have come from quite a distance Choco."

Choco looked around and saw some people he had seen before, but the majority of those he could see there, he had not."

While Tim and Dixie made their way with Sally and Sean in an attempt unsuccessfully, to find somewhere in the house which was not so crowded. Choco asked Charlie what he had meant when he has said he had some thoughts on things, and had indicated he did not want to speak of, while Tim was with them.

"Can you remember the redhead, when we were in the manor, and how I told you I was unsure whether she had come to my bed or not that night. Well now I am sure she did, and I believe there was a reason other than just sex."

"Can't think of any other reason she would want to get into your bed, other than sex, when she did not want to know you afterwards the following morning. Seems to me she had what she wanted, and the next thing we know she was off to pastures new, and with a couple of other male studs who went with her to boot."

"That was just the thing I was thinking about, all the way back from Canterbury today, and did not want to say anything because Tim was at the table with us."

"Don't worry about it there's plenty more pussy about than her, redheads, brunets, blondes, and with the hair styles around now-a-days you could even get hold of multi-colours of all kinds."

"Jesus! Can't you see what I mean Choco. With her it was not just a case of a quick jump, and then away. That maternity home with the women and children, they were not possessing the kids and mothers, just possessing the mothers so they were able to breed the kids using the sperm from men like myself to make them fertile. Then once the child was born and weaned, they kill and dispose of the women. Why using the method they did, that, I don't know! But, there must be a reason, for doing it in the way they did."

As the significance of what Charlie had said hit him Choco's eyes turned in the direction of where Tim was talking to Sally and Dixie.

"So...What you are saying is, that what Sally saw happening to the two women last night, could have already happened to Rene, do I catch it right?"

"Well, since I heard what Sally told us of her experience last night, and the thoughts I have had today I think it to be the only conclusion applicable in the circumstances."

Anne Farr arrived with Dave Mitchell, as darkness was falling, and were as surprised as everyone else had been, to see so many people at Marcus's home. As she came in she saw Sean and the others talking together, and made her way over to them.

"What's going on Sean, is Molly here with you?"

"Yes she is somewhere around, she was with, Alice, Peter, Abigail and Leonard Seers in the sitting room." He looked at his watch .

"We have been here for almost four hours now, where is Marcus, and why was he so persistent we should all be here before eight."

"Yes he told me the same, I had to cancel an appointment with someone I had made ages ago."

There were a few more people who arrived after Anne and Mitchell, as they came in they commented casually that there was an early fog beginning to form, and how cold it was getting outside.

Shortly after, Marcus arrived and, by the look on his face he seemed as surprised as every one else was at the number of people he saw when he came through the door. Anne went to meet him.

"Hello Marcus, when you said that there were going to be a few others here as well, when you telephoned me, I never expected so many as have turned up." He stood stationary looking around the hall way and with just a glance could see there was at least twenty people standing and busy talking together, then his eyes fell on Sally, Choco and the others, puzzlement written all over his face.

"How long have they been here?" He asked.

"They arrived about an hour and a half after you left, according to Sean, I asked because I was wondering what time they arrived back myself."

Marcus looked at his watch, and saw it was just coming up to eight o'clock in the evening. "That's more than three hours ago! What time did you say, I said to be here?"

"Eight o'clock Marcus." He looked at his clock again colour seemed to drain from his normally flushed face.

"I never made a phone call to anyone saying to be here for eight o'clock. No more, than it seems, Sally told me to meet them urgently at the motorway services alone, they said they could get there at about six thirty, and not to tell anyone where, or who I was meeting this evening. I waited until seven fifteen, but they never arrived there, so I came on back here."

"What does it mean Marcus?"

"I am afraid it means, they have duped us all into being all in the same place at the same time, for the purpose, that they only know, but whatever that purpose is I think it will not be to our advantage."

Marcus immediately knew he should act quickly, summoning Sean and the others who were nearest to him, telling them to spread the word that he wanted to speak to all the leaders of the various circles, and especially for Choco and Co. to attend, to see if any help might be forth coming from their direction. He also suggested they clear everyone out of his study as quickly as they could, so that he could speak to them in there, and for them afterwards to relay to those who were not in the study what they would be deciding to do.

In a very short space of time the study had been cleared and Marcus had told the others there what he believed had taken place, and how they had all been tricked into coming to his house at the same time. Also, how he felt they could be in grave danger now from those at the manor house.

Some one asked how they had known how to contact them all, or even known how many of them there were to be contacted. To which Marcus answered that, that, was now unimportant the fact was they knew about all of them and, with the situation they were in now, they had to prepare themselves for what ever they had planned to do against them.

While Marcus had been speaking to those he had asked to see in the sitting room, Charlie, Choco and the other two had been getting feelings of uneasiness among them, and were already trying to find out the direction and source of them. They had sensed there was something going on for a while, before, Marcus had spoken of not having made any phone calls, or of thinking he had had one from Sally, and found the opposite was in fact the case.

While the facts that had come to light of them all being lured to his home were being discussed, with the leaders of the developing circles, they were already making their way to the study room door. Sensing things individually but moving as one.

No one had noticed them leaving the room except Marcus, and he did not draw any ones attention to them, knowing they were working together, and could at least may have some idea of what was necessary to find out some how the reason that every one there had been duped into turning up on false calls from him.

Choco was the first to feel the direction of something menacing and evil, and beckoned for Tim to come over to where he was. As they had come out of the sitting room they had started to walk in different directions of the house, in search of whatever it was they could all sense. As Tim turned and began walking in the direction of Choco, he felt that whatever it was was coming from the direction he had already been walking in, and silently signalled the fact of what he was thinking. They were all within sight of each other and all immediately became convinced that whatever it was that was a threat to them all, seemed to be coming from the direction each had had been taking.

All four simultaneously then came to the conclusion that whatever it was seemed to want to divide them up, by taking them in different directions. They immediately regrouped in the centre of the the hall, and facing the main front door of the house. As they did so Charlie felt a sudden compulsion to open the door and look outside. He walked forward grasped hold of the handle and turned it, when it was open, what he saw took him completely by surprise. Instead of seeing the steps and driveway to the house, all that could be seen was a dense thick black swirling fog.

It was unlike anything he had ever seen before.

It was as if a dark curtain was surrounding the whole of the house with no visibility what so ever, and as the light from the inside of the house radiated out to it, it just seemed to absorb it without giving any reflection. All he, or the others could see was a pitch black area where the light should at least have illuminated but there was not a centimetre of penetration anywhere. As they tried to peer into it they had the sensation that there was laughter. Laughter of a most hideous nature, and the feeling that whatever kind of fog it was. It was alive in some grotesque way. As they gazed at the darkness, there was a feeling there was someone beyond the doorway, and out side of the house in danger but as the feeling came so it immediately disappeared. All accepted it was all part of the process of what those at the manor intended to use against them, to illiminate all of them, from being a thorn in their side.

They also knew that whatever it was they were all perceiving inside the house, was tied up in some way with the fog surrounding it. They decided it would be better for them to return to the study room and to let Marcus and those with him know what was happening around the house. Then see if they could identify what they had been sensing and, locate where it was, in the place.

As they were returning to Marcus's study they passed the sitting room door, they could see that there was a change in mood of the people clustering around the doorway and, those inside, who they had passed only a short while before. Some they could see, were becoming quick tempered and angry. The gist of things as much as they could tell was, Marcus had told those he had first telephoned, and then asked them to get in touch with every one else, and to tell them that it was important for them to be there before eight o'clock that evening. Some, because of the importance, and insistence Marcus had placed on them to be there, had accepted and complied with his request without question they had rearranged schedules, and even cancelled other plans they had already made so as they could be there. Then they found they had gone through all of the inconvenience and messing up the evening, all they seemed to be doing there was chit chatting to one another while Marcus was in his study talking to the others, without any reason so far given to them of why he had wanted everyone there so urgently.

"Well, I suggest to everyone we leave now, and let those in the study with him to carry on chatting to themselves, because it seems we are not so urgently wanted as we have been led to believe."

Charlie and the others had heard the words spoken as they came to the doorway, and forced their way into the room. Charlie was the first to react. He made his way through the door way into the room.

"What's the matter with you people, you can't leave for the moment, and the others will be out of the study shortly to explain to you about what is going on. The one thing I can tell you, is that Marcus has not made any telephone calls to any of you and has also been duped into the same situation as the rest of us." As he finished speaking, and looked at those he had been speaking to. They seemed to take his words with distaste, and with disgruntled murmuring, a few began to leave the room by the door, and as they did so others were edging their way in the same direction. Choco and those with him tried to stop them leaving by telling them they would be in danger if they left at that moment. He could see there was no sign of them listening to them and walked after those who had already passed him as they made their way to the front door. He stopped for a moment, to still try and reason with them not to leave, and saw his words seemingly had no effect on them as the were prepared to force their way past him. He turned and opened the door to show them what it was they would be facing if they went through the door.

But it seemed to make no difference to them, Choco and the others could not understand why, when he had opened the door for them to see the swirling black fog for themselves, they could see no change in them and, how they still insisted on leaving. "Come on let's go! I would sooner be at home by the fire, than standing here looking at a bit of harmless fog." Words of agreement came from others near him.

Choco heard the man speak. He looked towards where the voice had come from, and recognized a man who seemed to be the leader of the crowd pressing forward. He had seen and spoken to him at earlier meetings. It was too much for him to understand. Then he realized something strange about him, before, on the occasion when he had spoken to him, he had found him to be very quiet, and of quite a shy disposition, nothing like the person he saw at the moment. It seemed some how he had undergone a complete change in personality, and in some way had been influenced, he just knew, by those at the manor to try and entice or rather lead everyone there out into the fog, and there could only be one reason for that, they wanted them all to enter the fog out side. Which they could only see as being an ordinary every day, light fog. The man continued to press forward, and as he did so Charlie seeing his intention made a grab for his arm but could not hold on to him, and he walked through the doorway out into the fog. As he did so he seemed to melt into it, or merge into the blackness out side, without a sound of any kind.

The others, those who had been closest behind him and about to follow were now held back by Dixie, Tim, and Choco allowing Charlie to close the door and lock it with the key, and putting it into his pocket, so as to stop any others from leaving for their own sakes. As he did so things were beginning to get strained and the aggression seemed to be increasing. It was at this time they could see everything seemed to be getting out of hand, and it needed something to halt the proceedings, before aggressive pandemonium broke out. Things were becoming worse due to another individual who also seemed quite determined that they should all leave there and go home, and forget any inconvenience caused to them, by coming there that evening and continued to stir the others there by saying it was obvious they were not needed there, he continued to try to get others nearest the door to get the key off of Charlie, to open the door so that they could all return to their homes.

Call it a hunch or some sixth sense he knew he had experienced before, and had acted on. He was unsure of what it would mean, but the one thing he was, sure of, was that there was more happening here than they had understood with the surrounding fog, they could see, but all the others could not.

He moved close to Dixie.

"The one that went out into the fog, just now Dixie! You were the one answering the door as the people who were late came in, did he come in with anyone else?"

Dixie looked around him before answering, his eyes peering around the room.

"Come on Dixie it's important, was he with anyone?"

"Yes he was." He inclined his head towards the middle of the room.

"Him! The mush, with all the mouth, he was with him, and t'other one next to him, the three of them came in together. Why, what do you know?"

"Not to sure yet Dixie but, perhaps we might be about to find out the answer! Some how I think they have been taken over by whatever evil is within the fog, and surrounds us, and is influencing the minds of the others, making them rebel against Marcus and, trying to entice them out side and for whatever reasons they have planned for them, and it is down to us to stop them."

Charlie quickly turned to make his way towards where the men were standing. To do what, he was unsure. The first thing which came to mind was to open himself up, as he had done before, then see what happened, and then take it from there. But as he approached them, he saw their features begin to change, it had started before he was on his way over towards them. As if they had both realized at the same instant he had made a decision to do something. As he came closer to them their features seemed to melt in front of his eyes, in the same kind of wispy and smoky consistency as the black fog they had seen when they opened the door exit to the outside of the house. Swirling around the forms started to quickly decrease in height until there was a flowing dark and thick misty mass flowing about six inches in height across the floor of the room, while at the same time it was moving towards the door of the sitting room. As it did so the room began to take on a completely different atmosphere, the cold that was there seemed to disappear, and it was not until then that anyone except for Choco and the others had realized there had even been a difference in temperature since they had first arrived in the house. The mood and perceptiveness of the others, who moments before were, strained and angry, changed in mood and the aggressive behaviour of which they had no control over had now gone.

Suddenly they were all looking in amazement and, a little fear, as they saw the dark and thick wisps of fog travelling quickly across the floor in front of them, afraid and jumping out of it's path as it came near to them on it's way to the front door of the house. When it reached it, it just carried on flowing out of the place under the bottom of the door.

As this happened all four friends gathered together and began discussing what it was that had been actually happening, and for what purpose, and came to the conclusion that it had all been part of a ruse to get them out of the house and dispose of them in one go. The attempt had failed but they knew there would be more attempts before the night was over, of that they were sure. Charlie and the others also realized that with the discovery and departure from the house of whatever the three forms were the others there could now also see the thick black fog surrounding the house, as Dixie had opened it after the fog and travelling evil it contained had left.

The leaders of the various circle's who had been in the study with Marcus, had finished discussing the various aspects of the situation they had all found themselves in. Choco, and the others had told them of the situation with the fog surrounding the house, explaining the status in the sitting room, which had developed while they had been discussing what they should do about the situation of the telephone calls which had got everyone there at the same time. All were in agreement that the situation against those at the manor had now reached a critical state and they could not afford to take any chances with the situation, what so ever. That in mind the idea occurred to one of the circle leaders, that perhaps the rest of the discs Marcus was in possession of, could hold the key which would help them in their present plight. The suggestion was made that he go through them and see if there was anything he could discover which would be of use to them.

CHAPTER 44

Marcus had been left alone in his study, alone, except for the times when there would be someone going in to check he was all right left on his own, because, of what he had said to everyone else, about being with some one at all times, and to see if he needed anything. So intrigued was he with what he had discovered, on just three, of the sloppy discs he had almost forgotten about the situation they were in. But as time passed and he began to discover more about the people at the manor and their followers, the more disturbed he was beginning to get.

After he had gone through just the third disc, he knew that whatever there was left to be found on the rest, the situation they were now in was far worse than any one could have realized.

Also he began to think and feel for the first time, that the chances of them coming out of the situation alive, seemed, by the information he had now gained quite slim. He sat musing over the facts that he had discovered, before, deciding he would have a break from the screen and make himself a hot drink, and while doing so tell the others there what his conclusion was. Or at least discuss with Choco, Charlie, and the other two, before deciding whether it might be a little unwise at the moment to put the rest there, fully in the picture with the information he had found out.

Coming into the sitting room he could see that everyone there was in a sombre mood and very quiet. Fear was more than evident among them everywhere he looked, except for Choco and the others. They were sitting together on their own, and were talking over what they should do, and what the next step those against them would make.

It had been almost four hours since the fog had been discovered outside of the house and the trouble with the three men which had followed it. Since then nothing else had happened and Choco and the others were beginning to become a little puzzled over that fact. To them all it seemed strange that they had not tried to gain entry into the house again since the last time they tried.

"Why haven't they tried again Choco?" Charlie asked.

"I don't know, but don't think for one minute they have given up on us. You know how it happens, first there is nothing happening, and then we find ourselves in the middle of whatever they are trying, it's been the same from the start of this thing."

As they continued talking among them selves Marcus came over to them.

"How have you got on Marcus, anything come to light yet that might help us?"

"I have found out a few things, but whether they will be of any help to us I am just not sure about."

"What kind of things are we talking of. Could any of it be to do with why they have not tried again since the last episode?"

"No I am afraid not. But I would welcome your views on some of the things I have found out, due to some of the information I have found on the discs you managed to get from the D.H.S.S. offices. I am about to make a drink for myself, when I go back to my study, can you all make your way there, unseen by anyone?"

"I just can't figure it out Charlie! What I have been thinking about is the same as you. They have managed to get us all here at the same time, and with everything they have managed to do up until now, and why is the outside of the place surrounded by that fog. I keep asking myself why have they stopped when they have managed to get whatever it was that took on the form of those three men into the house so easily, the other thing is why did they leave so easily without giving a fight of any kind like they have always done in the past?"

"They were already changing into that fog stuff before Charlie had gone over towards them, I noticed it before he had even started walking over to them."

"Yes, I thought that was strange, after it happened, and they did not seem to want to make a fight of it at all, like they usually do and, there was no blaspheming. Why do you think that was?"

The same question had been running through Marcus's mind, and he was beginning to get a little puzzled himself over the fact that they had done nothing more to gain entry to the house since the last time. What he thought could be stopping them? With everything they had accomplished in the past that he knew of, why were they stopping short of getting into the house now. He was sure they had achieved the task of getting them all together for the sole purpose of their destruction in one stroke and when he thought of the attempt they tried earlier it seemed a little bit on the pathetic side when he knew there were far more effective ways they could have employed. The more he thought on the matter the more sure he was they had all missed something, something which, for one reason or another they had not realized or had even missed about the efforts they had tried so far. Could it have anything to do with Choco and the others, he remembered the times that the four had interceded in the past to save situations which at the time were deemed, as past saving.

"Maybe!" He thought. "Maybe!"

The kettle began to boil and he poured the water into the cup with coffee and sugar, then a splash of milk from the almost empty milk jug. Coming out of the kitchen and looking across the the sitting room, he saw the four had now been joined by Anne, Mitchell, Sean, Molly, and Sally. All were in deep conversation, and as he watched they were in the process of rising from the table, as they were doing so they saw him looking in their direction acknowledged the fact and then began walking towards him.

Charlie was the first to speak.

"Have you noticed what time it is Marcus?"

Puzzled by the way he had asked the question, he looked at the clock on the mantle piece, and could not believe what he saw. The hands indicated it had just turned eight thirty, he looked at his wrist watch and found it read the same.

"We know! We have been through the house and all the clocks are telling the same time, we first realized it only moments ago, and thought to ourselves it just cannot be right, we have been here more than half an hour, because of all the things which have happened. Then when we went into the hall and saw the clock you have there, with the twenty four hour digital time, day, and date, we noticed something even more strange, by the time and day it says we have been here for twenty four hours, not just half an hour, or as it has felt like, even four and a half hours it has been over twenty four hours."

"It cannot be. How can we explain it?" He looked towards Choco and the others for an answer, which was not forth coming.

They thought it better not to speak any more of what they had found out in the sitting room in case of being overheard by the others there and not wanting to install any more fear into them than they were already showing, they made their way to his study.

When they arrived there the first thing they noticed was that the screen on the computer was blank, which it had not been when Marcus had left the room shortly before. Marcus tried to get it working but for some reason he could not get anything, it was as if the hard drive was somehow stuck, he took out the disc he had been using, and inserted another, but the same thing happened he could bring nothing up on the screen.

"I don't understand, it was working perfectly well when I left earlier."

"What information did you find out from the discs you have already seen?"

"Quite a lot, that's why I wanted to see you here without anyone else knowing." He looked at Anne, and those with her who had followed Marcus, Choco, and the others into the room and had not known of the fact Marcus wanted to speak to them alone, but as they were there and seemed to be in a little brighter spirit than most of the others there thought they might as well hear what he had found out, which was making him concerned for their well being, and the final outcome of the situation they were in.

"The first thing you should know is the reason for Kalleshin House, Private Maternity, home, is as you have already said Anne, not quite what it seems. Oh! yes it's a maternity establishment that much is true. A little of what I am about to tell you has some guess work I have had to do to fill in a few things I have not got the information for, but, with the information on the discs I believe I have found the real purpose of the maternity part of the operation, and when the realization of my conclusion became clear it filled me with dread and a profound disbelief of what has actually been happening. It seems that the initial possession of people has been but a starting of something far larger and on a scale so vast no one could have ever contemplated such a thing was even possible, but, with all intent and a purpose, they have achieved more or less, everything they had intended since they returned to this earth plain, and we might be to late and too inadequate, to even make a dent in what they have so far accomplished."

"For glories sake Marcus, stop beating around the bush and, tell us what we are up against, and how we might be able to defend ourselves, or what part Choco and his friends can do to help us."

"I am sorry Sean, but the truth is I don't know the answer to your question. Also, speaking of what I have found out, I don't know if they will be able to help us, or not."

He looked for his note book in which he had made notes on what he had discovered on the discs.

The children you saw with their mothers, I think they are in actual fact brought into the world for the precise purpose to be able to be used, for the rebirth of those who have possessed the mothers, and the spirit of the evil possessor of the women, then transfers from the host mother into the infant, as soon as conception has taken place, and then the host is then possessed by another entity until the birth, and then they are disposed of.

This I believe, is so that they are reborn into a earthly body, rather than using a possessed person. Which as we have seen, by such people as Charlie and others, can be exorcised. With an earthly body they are the same as us, but with knowledge of evil which they invariably use to fulfil their aims."

"How long did you tell us, that this thing has been going on Marcus?"

"I have worked out from the dates on the discs that it has been going on for upwards of ten years now, and from it's infancy, to the stage it is at now, with just the names on the discs I have seen, there are upwards of at least ten thousand who have come onto the earth plane using this method in this country alone."

If anything could be described as a loud silence then, this must have been the one and only occasion. The silence in the room as they were all standing there with, their own thoughts on what had been told to them, while at the same time they were privately and in their own way asking spirit for help and direction.

"We have to deal with the time first. Why has the time acted in the way it has, and why did tiredness not give anyone the clues that there was something not quite right before the time, that Anne said they noticed something was going on?" Charlie then turned to Choco.

"If they have managed to change time and, have confused us or led us not to think of time as it was passing. Why? What is their purpose in doing it. They must have known that we would have realized it happening one way or another in the end. It could be just to confuse us for confusion's sake. But another reason could be to buy time for themselves, at our cost. Also I think there is more to the black fog surrounding the place than we can make out for now. When was the last time anyone looked at the fog? If the confusion over the time we have been here is of significance, then perhaps the fog is not still there." Choco made a move towards the study window pulled the drapes and there it was, still swirling, dense and black.

Charlie was still troubled by the way things were happening. The fog, the time distortion, the computer malfunctioning.

"Why?" He thought! "Why had all these things been happening and how could they be have been caused? Find the reason for them! That's the answer. Find out the reason before it becomes to late to do anything about, *what ever it is* , they are planning." He tapped Choco on the shoulder excused himself to Marcus, and the others.

"Let's just go and take a closer look at the fog by the front door. There is something in my head about it, that just won't go away!"

Both men walked to the hallway and then made their way towards the front door. It was as they reached the centre of the hall facing the door, Choco stopped, and caught hold of Charlies

arm stopping him from going any further. They both stood still, Charlie looking at the expression of concentration on Choco's face, while standing still not moving an inch."What is it, what did you hear?" He looked around but could see nothing to account for his friends behavior.
"What is it?" He asked again, in a low whisper.
"Nothing! That's just it! Nothing." He whispered back.
"There is no sound, listen how still and empty it is out here. Can you can feel the cold and the silence it is not normal, there has been a change taking place out here."
"What shall we do now go back and tell the others about what we have discovered?"
"No wait! What was the reason we came out here for in the first place?"
"I wanted to see if the fog was still as black as it was when we last saw it, when we had the trouble with the entities."
"Well lets go and open the door and have a look before we go back to the others. They walked towards the door, both were feeling uneasy, although each was doing the best not to let the other see it, and as they did they gained confidence from each other. Standing in front of the door Choco reached forward and grasped the handle, while giving a side long glance at his companion, pulled the handle down and opened the door. Contrary to it having gone away, it had become even more dense and had taken on the appearance of a thick tar looking substance, pitch black and now had what seemed to them red and brown looking like veins running through it, altering the appearance completely, as they looked some kind of life forms within it giving it a kind of potency, the more they watched the more it seemed alive, pulsating and while doing so giving off a terrible stench which hit them all at once. It reminded them both of decaying flesh and green rotting vegetables. Moving quickly, he closed the door and retreated away from it, retching as he did so.

As they both reached the door to the sitting room, Tim was on his way towards them with Anne and Mitchell in tow.
"I have been thinking." He said as they reached him.
"Maybe we have been looking at things from the wrong angle, just think for a moment, we know that they have done something with time, delaying it in some way, but we have all been still able to function as normal within the house, I don't know how it has been accomplished or why, but as you have said if we try to think of what they hope to achieve by doing it, then we might be able work out the purpose of it. What do you think,"

There was silence as each pondered what was said. Then someone came up with the idea that it was possible that, by slowing down the time within the house, perhaps meant that whatever they were trying to do would take longer than a normal time span would allow. But then the question was raised of the reason why the watches and clocks in the house continued in the original time frame continuum. Although they talked on the matter for quite a while, no one seemed to come up with the answer that made sense to them except they knew whatever the reason it would be detrimental to all of them within the house.

Choco could not get the words of Tim out of his head.
"Maybe we are looking at things from the wrong angle." What was it they could accomplish by slowing time down for those inside the house. The more he thought about it the more it baffled him. He looked across the room to the clock on the mantelpiece. Something was dogging his mind. but it would not come to the surface.

Marcus had returned to his study to see if he could get any joy with his computer, hoping against hope he would be succesfull. It was useless, and in the end, he decided to give up, and perhaps try again later. As he sat in front of the V.D.U. pulled out the disc from from the machine and was putting it in the metal box, he heard footsteps from behind him, turning he saw Anne, Dave,Choco and Dixie, coming through the study door. They all seemed to be fed up over the position they found themselves in, and felt a need to at least try to do something, in some way about the circumstances which seemed to be becoming one sided more and more as they were there.
"Marcus!" It was Anne who spoke.

"There must be something that we can do instead of just waiting here for them to make their next move against us all. Why is it that since the last move they made against us, that they have not tried since? It so long now, have you any idea's at all? They have us all here together it just does not make sense, why are they so hesitant about trying again?"

He was silent for a while, took his glasses off and began to rub his eyes with a tissue.

"I just wish I could have the answer for you, but when we look back on everything that has happened, there has been very little in the sense of logic that we would be familiar with when we are dealing with the situation we are in at this moment in time.

"What I have learnt from the discs only in most ways, confuses and confounds me. What we now know of them so far, we would still be working against them blind in a lot of ways. As we all know for the moment they are holding all the cards. Until that is, we find out what their next move might be, and only then will we know if we can stop them doing whatever they have in mind for us.

"I have a thought!" Choco had not stopped thinking since his return from the hallway."

"No one has thought of seeing if it was possible to leave by going into the fog. Just think, is it really there, or is it another part of their mind games they have been playing with us. The thing that has just occurred to me is....."

"That's weird!"

Choco looked across at Dixie, he was looking at the others there, and down at his wrist watch.

"What is it Dixie, what's the matter."

"Take a look at your watches!" He indicated he was addressing Dave and Anne.

All except Choco who was not in possession of one looked to see what Dixie was on about and seemed puzzled as they did not see the point he was trying to make.

"Look at the second hand on my watch then look at your own, in the span of half an hour the second hand from not working is now working, I thought it was broken the last time I looked, it did not seem to be working, but now it is. At least it is moving slowly, but it is moving. From not being able to see any movement to seeing it now moving must signify something."

"He's right the hand is moving, very slowly but it is moving and his date is reading yesterdays date and show six hours adrift of those in the house. Why should his watch show yesterdays date when the one in the hall shows its a day later." Choco and Charlie were both now looking at his watch.

Marcus stepped across to look at Dixies watch, and then noticed his watch was also showing the same as Dixie's, three hours behind the clock on the mantle piece.

"What can it mean?" He asked the others.

Anne and Dave Mitchell looked around the room and drew the drapes back to see if there were any more changes they could notice taking place, but everything appeared the same as it had, before the discrepancy of the watches and house clocks was noticed was noticed, and with all thoughts on the matter they could see no answer, to what seemed to be happening. Charlie was also not wearing a watch, but had not really been thinking about the discrepancy in the different time pieces, but trying to think of the cause, then it suddenly hit him. Time had been interfered with by those at the manor house but not on the scale they had been thinking, the holding and slowing down of time had been localized just to the humans within the house, and was now being allowed to catch up with the actual time outside. But why now, had they completed the task of whatever they needed to delay the time for those within the house it's self.

Before anything could be said about his theory a voice broke the silence. It was Peter and Abigail Jones.

"Come quick some thing is happening near the front door!" Their faces bespoke the nervousness which was evident in the voice of Abigail. After speaking, they turned and beckoned for the others to follow, an urgency apparent, by their actions.

Without more a-do they followed them through the sitting room where there was flow of intermittent conversation in progress, and whatever it was, that was happening, they were obviously unaware of it. As they continued from the sitting room into the hall the two in front began to slow down so the others could catch up with them.

When Choco and the others drew level with them, there was no need to say, or indicate, what it was they had come to inform them of. For all could see what had brought them there. All around the door frame seemed to be a living pulsating mass of light, which was slowly, very slowly, seemed to in some way to be devouring the wooden door. The light if that is what it could be described as, had similar variations, as if one was looking into the glowing embers of a fire, except the colours were green, purple and brown, and as they watched they almost became mesmerized, until the stench that Charlie and Choco had smelt earlier, hit their nostrils almost choking them and making them move back in the direction they had come from.

"Oh dear! Now What's happening?" Choco and the others turned around to see Marcus standing behind them. What it was they had no idea, and no words were forthcoming from any of them.

As they gazed at the phenomenon they noticed that there was more than just light around the door taking place, as they watched the door seemed to dematerialise and then materialise again with a kind of flashing on and off varying in intensity, similar to the old flashing of film projectors of the early part of the century. It was also noticeable that with the flashing occurring there was not the slightest of reflections of it on the wall or floor what so ever, the brilliance of the flashing seemed to have no reflective qualities at all ,but kept up the intensity of light within it's own area in and around the door.

Choco was looking directly at the door, and started to squint his eyes, not from the brilliance, but because within the sequence of flashes he thought he could see forms and movement beyond the doorway, and was trying to focus on whatever it was he thought he saw. After a short while, he could definitely make out there was movement beyond, and within and seemingly beyond the area of the doorway, but could not see clearly enough to distinguish distance or clarity of the forms he could obviously see were there.

Everyone moved further back from the sight and smell in front of them, and were confused over what they were seeing. "You know what, does it seem strange to you that with all the flashing and movement which we can now see is going on, there is not the slightest of sounds coming from what we are seeing. It's as though we are watching from a distance and cannot hear the sounds of what we see yet."

"It was David Mitchell, who had spoken this snippet of observation in a calm and matter of fact way, while the others there agreed with what he had said in a calm but apprehensive toned voices. "But calm, or apprehensive, was not the tone of Marcus's voice, to the words which had just been spoken. "It's the time, as we have all reasoned. Time is the key to what is happening, we have said if we find out the reason for the time discrepancy we have experienced, we would probably only then know why they had to do it. This is, I am sure the reason, they had to somehow suspend or delay time to enable them to do what we are seeing now, and whatever it is now happening is what they have planned for us all the time we have been here. They have had to think of a way to keep us here to achieve whatever is now happening."

While the others went to return to the sitting room at Choco's suggestion, and advising that Tim and Dixie should accompany them back, he stayed with Charlie watching the doorway. They both had no sense of fear whatsoever now, the minds of both men were working overtime, sensing they had to come up with answers to what it was that was happening in front of them.

Charlie watched as the others were walking away from them, noticed for some reason the sparkle of the bangles, on her ankles, as Sally Parsons walked away from them, with the others. But it was the shoes she was wearing, which made something scream out to him from inside his head, something was not as it should be, there was something missing he could not understand what that something was, until it hit him like a thunderbolt from a clear and cloudless sky. Sound! There was, no sound. No sound as her flip flop sandals were hitting the ground there seemed to be a delay of the sound as her sandals hit the ground, the sound was out of time, he watched closely, saw her feet rise as she took a step and fall, but the sound came almost as she lifted the foot to take another step. He looked at the others as their feet walked and there was the same reaction. He lifted his own foot and stamped hard on the floor the sound was instant as he brought it down. He did it again with the same result. Choco watched him as he did it a few more times. "What's the crack Charlie, something wrong with your foot?" He watched and could see there was something Charlie was trying to work out.

"What is it?" Charlie then told him what he had noticed, and asked him to walk away from him stepping hard on the floor as he did so. Choco was puzzled but could see his friend was serious, and walked away from him stamping his feet hard on the floor as he did so. Within a couple of steps Charlie could hear a difference as the sound of choco's footsteps came a fraction behind the time his feet touched the ground and, the further he walked away from him, the more the delayed sound of his footsteps became. He turned and faced the door again, then had an idea, Choco was by then on his way back towards him, he held up his hand attracting his attention.

"Stay where you are Choco, and listen, when I stamp my foot!" He shouted to him.

"Did you notice anything strange when I brought my foot down on the floor?"

"No!....Why?....Should I have and, if so, what was it I was supposed to have noticed?" As he spoke charlie, then knew beyond any doubt he was on to something.

As choco had spoken, there was a definite delay in the sound of his voice, from the time his lips moved, only a fraction but it was about the same time as the time taken with his footfalls.

"The sound of my foot hitting the floor." He raised his leg and stamped his foot on the ground again.

"What did you hear then, Choco?"

"Your foot hitting the floor, is all! What else should I hear?"

"Does it sound strange or anything?"

"What the bloody hell are you going on about Charlie?" Choco was beginning to think, that perhaps the place was starting to have some kind of affect on him.

"Come on Charlie snap out of it, lets go back and join the others."

"I'm all right Choco and, not not going Ga. Ga. Come over to where I am."

"What?"

"Just come over here and, stand where I am. Come on Choco, humour me just for a moment, that's all. Choco joined him.

"Yes, now what?"

"Stay there, look and listen carfully at my foot steps, while I walk away, until I reach the point where I shouted to you. Then tell me if you notice anything, anything at all!"

"Go ahead then."

Choco watched and listened, and immediatelly realized what Charlie had meant, when he heard and, saw the same as he had.

"Now stamp your feet and listen." He did so, and the sound was exactly the same as Charlie had realized when he had listened at the time he had done it himself, the sound of impact was immediate, as his shoe's hit the ground. But there was no time delay from the distance which could be heard by Charlie as, he did so. It was the same as when he himself had done it.

He began to think he had indeed discovered some strange anomaly and, it was all related to sound and distance why, why was it everything seemed normal while he stood near the front door and, became distorted when anyone moved away from it. Find that out he thought and, the answer to a lot could be forth coming. He contintinued watching as Choco walked back towards him. Listening to his footsteps until he reached him. He turned around and looked once more towards the door had been. It had to be due to what he could see happening there. Choco saw him look at the door, the changing colour and, the moving distortion of the shapes of whatever was taking place behind them and, which they just could not make out.

"Come on Charlie let's get back and join the others. There is nothing more we can do about what is happening here. We just have to wait until whatever happens next, and try to take it from there." Charlie reluctantly agreed and, both started walking towards the sitting room area.

Marcus and the others listened to what Charlie had to say about the discrepancy in sound in the place, even to the point of demonstrating what he had discovered in front of the others.

"It is all connected with what is going on out side the front door and around the house."

Everyone there, pondered on what had been told them, and were as baffled as Charlie and Choco had been as to what the purpose was to the time lapse discrepancy.

"We will just have to figure out the reasons for this to be happening, and what it could mean to us!" Charlie muttered, more to himself than anyone in particular.

Tim was thoughtful for a while and seemed as if he was weighing up something in his mind. "You know, it's like watching an aircraft go over head and then hearing the noise of the engines when it is going faster than sound, without the sound of the sound barrier being broken. You know, first the movement and, then the sound comes."

"What's that got to do with the price of fish and what has been happening here?" Choco asked, while leaning cross legged against the table and, scratching the back of his hand with his finger nails.

"Well it could be that it is not the slowness of time which is causing us confusion over the situation here from the time of the unrest when it was discovered Marcus had not telephoned for us all to be here. But something that may have happened to us ourselves, and time is as it has always been. I know it might sound stupid, but could it be that all this confusion of what is happening could perhaps be to get us confused and talking and questioning what has been going on is a decoy, for us not to realize something else, which has needed time to prepare, before being built is going on. Because except for it being noticeable there is nothing else that makes sense about it is there? Also let us say, just for arguments sake, that all the unpleasantness we had when no one other than us four could see the dense black fog, while everyone else seemed to be being encouraged to leave the place, and were only stopped from doing so by Choco and those of us who thought we could see the difference out side, until the entities left. Then, and only then, could everyone see what we had been seeing and, then later on the changes that were taking place towards what we now see at the door were taking place. On reflection perhaps what we were seeing was only what we were meant to see, and at the time there was not anything there that could have done any harm to anyone, it was just a ruse to use us as unknowing pawns, to keep everyone here while there was some thing else being built at the doorway, until it is as we now see it and, I think it is almost ready to be used for whatever it may be they have in mind." The reasons and consequences of what Tim had spoken of seemed to more than hold water and, if true showed the four how they had been fooled completely, and to what extent the cunning ways of their foes had been so underestimated by them all.

CHAPTER 45

Charlie had been quiet up until the time Tim had finished talking, and had taken in everything the others had spoken of before that.

"Well where do we go from here? They seem to have accomplished everything they have wanted to, while we have been able to do nothing against them. It looks to me as if they are holding all the aces and, we could do with having the proverbial Joker up our sleeve!" He was feeling as perplexed as the others there but, had an overwhelming feeling that whatever was to be done for the good of everyone, there had to be some decisions made and, quickly, to be ready for whatever it was that was to happen next.

To him it seemed that the evil from Gowendene Manor had so far accomplished getting the upper hand over them, and seemed impervious to anything they could possibly do against them. Whatever it was those at the manner planned to do against them, he felt the best thing to do now, was to discover in some way how to find out what they could do against them. Up until the moment of the fog surrounding the house and, there was some thing that was tried by those at the manor to harm them in some way, one of the four seemed to be capable of releasing some power against them which always seemed to thwart their efforts to harm any of them.

Choco it seemed was thinking along similar lines, as was Charlie. At that time Marcus was rising from his seat.

"Let's get everyone together in the sitting room as quickly as we can. Whatever they have done in relation to time, whether it be a decoy, or a ruse of some kind to get us confused, as, has been suggested, they have not destroyed the unity of everyone here and, I just know that what ever it takes to beat them, it will be that unity and faith in ourselves and, in what we believe will eventually be the weapon that will free us from the jeopardy we find ourselves in.

As everyone in the sitting room saw Marcus and the others enter and stand together,and as he gestured for their attention. A slow hush descended over the crowded room, making the silence take on an emptiness, making each individual feel a sense of vulnerability and panic run through them. Wondering what else may have happened and, he was about to tell them of. Every eye followed every movement he made as he walked to the centre of the room, to speak to them all. "I am not sure of what it is I wish to speak to you of, but I am sure you must now realize that we find our selves in a very uneven and precarious situation. The power of those against us, as I am sure you are also aware of is of a powerful and evil nature, and how we will be able to subdue it, and then defeat it without any casualties while doing so I must admit to you is on the very best forecast of events to come I feel slim. I feel the only hope of doing so is for us to remain firm in our faith with spirit in the knowledge they will be by our side through out the coming conflict as they have told us they would be on numerous occasions in the past since we have known of what was to come. We have had but a small measure of success with what we have been up against in the past, but I feel what we are to be faced with in the very near future will be far greater than has been faced before. As I have said before the only thing we can do is to keep our faith and place ourselves in the hands of spirit. I just hope and pray that things are not too late for us to do anything against the evil of the menace we are facing.

As Marcus was speaking Choco could hear a noise which seemed to come and go, he was trying to fathom out where it was coming from, but did not want to move while Marcus was talking to the others. He caught Charlie's eye and could tell that whatever it was he could also hear it. The expression on his face changed as he looked behind him, towards the mantelpiece. Choco looked in the same direction to see if he could see what had made his friends expression change as it did. As he did so he saw immediately what had caused his friends altered expression. He could now see the second hand of the wall clock above the mantelpiece move, and as it did the tick of each second was instantly loud and clear. He immediately realized that what ever the purpose for the time discrepancy was for, it had now been completed, and whatever the reason was for it, it bode ill for all of them.

The silence in the room continued while Marcus spoke on, except for the ticking of the clock above mantelpiece. To those close enough to hear it, it began to have a grating effect on them as every tick seemed to take a physical tug out of their nerve strings.

Marcus was at a loss now to answer most of the questions which were being asked of him, it seemed he had very little in the way of answers to what was happening. Charlie was quiet himself, and immersed in his own thoughts on the plight of himself and of all the others there. Why and what, he asked himself, was the purpose of him and the others to have come together, if, as Marcus had said they had a purpose and the power within them all to carry it out, and be of some benefit to the others there. Why only when there was a period of immediate danger to them all, did it manifest itself? Why was it such as the periods of impending doom they had experienced did any knowledge come to any of them, even to the point of not actually being aware of what they were doing? He could not understand any reason for it. He moved closer to Choco and the other two and told them of his thoughts and if they might have any answers of their own they could come up with, and while talking moved closer to the sitting room door so as they would be able to talk more freely on his and their thoughts on the matter away from everyone else there.

After a short discussion on the matter, they decided to return and speak to Marcus about what they had discussed to see if he might be able to throw a little light on the matter they had talked of. He suggested they speak to Anne Farr to see if she might be able to throw a little more light than what he had been able to. All four then made their way to her. She was standing with a group of others who she was in conversation with.

"I just don't know what to suggest for you to do. With everything that has happened to you since the day of us meeting since the time of Father George's death in such horrific circumstances, I have never in all my time as a medium seen anything even close to what I have witnessed with the four of you in the sense of your psychic abilities. The only thing I can suggest is for you to try and meditate together. I understand that the circumstances here are far from perfect, but if it is possible and you can, I can only suggest you trust to your intuition, and act upon it as you have been doing up until now."

Since the conversation with Anne Farr, the four friends had decided to go to a room in another part of the house, to try to see if they could meditate. With further advice from her that it might be prudent for them to take someone with them who could try to lead them into a meditative state of consciousness, seeing as how they had not had much practice of such things before they had met Marcus and the others. To this end she had suggested they might do very well if they asked Sally Parsons to sit with them, to which when asked she readily agreed.

Sally watched as the four seemed to be in a complete state of meditation, from the start of the session they had been still and breathing easily and there had hardly been any movement at all. She was about about to break the silence and bring them back from their time within themselves, when there was a sound of rustling, such as leaves would make on a tree when the wind blew through the branches, then there was a fragrant odour that began to waft around the room. Not a pungent or heavy, but more of the fragrance of fresh spring flowers. The kind of early morning freshness one would smell on a spring morning.

As she listened the rustling died away, and as it did so, so the odour increased, and one by one the friends began to come out of their period of meditation. All that was except Tim, who remained eyes closed and breathing easily. As the others came back and became aware of their surroundings, they began to sniff with their noses as they also began to take in the fragrant scent of flowers in the air. They looked directly towards Sally in askance to what they could smell and what was going on. She could sense there was something about to happen concerning Tim and motioned them to remain quiet.

Tim began to straighten up in the chair, and as he did so his mouth began to move, his features on his face began to change slowly, seeming to become overshadowed by someone else's features. It was only when Tim began to speak, and a gasp of astonishment from the other three, as Sally was also taken by surprise. The voice was Tim's, but the accent as he spoke the words, was anything but. The voice spoke to them in turn and, by name, identifying himself as Father George, with all of his charm and humour.

There also came with the voice a calmness they had not felt for a while, reminiscent of the time when they had all first met up with each other. Along with the greeting there was the usual feeling and warmth they had known from him when he was living among them. But after the greeting was done, the tone and content of conversation took on a graver tone. But with also a smattering of hope for all present.

"I Know you are all curious as to why you are all here together, and what you can do to save the situation you all find yourselves in. The first thing is that you are well equipped to do what you will have to have to do. The gifts of awareness, and other abilities you possess, are due to many varied periods of lifetimes you have experienced from the dawn of your spiritual birth. Many lifetimes of failure's and triumphs along the spiritual path you have trodden. But of these gifts I have spoken of, are nothing, compared to the greatest gift and weapon of all, which is; the true faith in spirit and for you to hold fast to that faith and the genuine love for others, with these alone you can win through. If you look on the evil against you as if it was in the body and of the substance of quicksilver, and can understand the properties of your own personality as solid matter. Once your earthly body has been destroyed and disposed of, your spirit within you will not die. It, also, has a similar property but does not die or decay. You stay as you are now, except you become part of the power of all creation immersed in total knowledge and love. But, within that state of knowledge and love you remain as individual as a grain of sand on a beach but, not any less than the whole. As long as you remember this you cannot fail to win against the power of your adversary in the coming conflict. All I can say to you is, put all your faith in the power of spirit and you will never be defeated, all though there can be many stages of defeat in battles there, but can only be one true winner of a war.

When you have to fight fight with your heart, remember love and compassion for all, for at times we have to use both, while discounting how you might feel at the time. Also remember, that which is, will always be, nothing can be destroyed forever, but each of you have the time necessity, and ability for rebirth.

I must leave you now and bid you fare well until we should meet again. Remember my words and you will come through."

They stayed in their seats for a short while, Tim's eyes opened and he looked at the others, there seemed to be no confusion in him at all after what had just taken place. He looked at the others and smiled.

"Man do I feel good." Was all that he said.

"Do you remember anything of what has just happened?" Choco asked.

"Every word, it was incredible, I have never had an experience like it or even near it. I was standing a little to the left and above myself, and watched and listened and heard everything. I could see and hear Father George and the light with him was indescribable."

After the talk and manifestation of Father George, there was a difference in the temperament of them all.

CHAPTER 46

It was roughly an hour later that the first signs that there was something happening in the house appeared, up until then, the time waiting had made most of those in the house start to become complacent over the situation they were in. Nothing had happened for so long and the confidence of them had been rising, as the house did not seem to have been breached as they had been expecting because of what had been seen going on at the front door, especially, as the time had become normal since the clock's seconds were heard ticking in the sitting room.

One of the people there had come to Marcus and had informed him that some kind of disturbance was taking place in the room next to the main entrance. Moving quickly he made his way to the hall in front of the door where the lights and phenomenon were stll taking place. As he looked at the door, there seemed to be no change from the last time he had seen it. He walked over to the door at right angles to the entrance which he had been told of. As he reached it he could hear sounds of babbling voices, whispers, and sounds of bumping and scratching, sounding as if there was someone the other side of the door scraping their finger nails hard against the paintwork. He knelt down outside of the door and listened but, could only make out the babbling and bumping. It seemed to become louder as he knelt there listening, what he could hear was unclear and, muffled, as though whoever was speaking, had their mouths covered with a thick cloth material and were trying to speak through it.

He stood up and waited facing the door. His heart pounding as he felt the perspiration which had formed and was now dripping down his face, one droplet hung from the end of his nose. While at the same time his spectacles were half steamed up with the heat and vapour from the perspiration. The palms of his hands were hot and sticky, he moved his hand with a nervous hesitation and trembling, towards the door handle. As he grasped hold of it to open the door, there was a searing pain which ran from his hand to his shoulder. His hand went cold and his arm seemed to instantly freeze in the position it was in as he had grasped the handle. There was no feeling as the cold which now travelled deeper into the very bones of his arm, and then to the rest of his body. At that moment, to him, the time seemed to slow down, but while it did the pain increased aching and throbbing as his heart still tried to pump the warm blood through now frozen arteries, only for it to freeze as it did so.

Even as he watched he knew there was nothing he could do, his mind in a semi confused state, as he tried to rationalize what had happened, the laws of physics had, it seemed, been rewritten, and redefined. Crystals of ice were forming on his hand which had frozen to the brass door handle. A paralysing cold stiffness began to spread from his shoulder to his neck and downwards into his chest. The freezing cold ate away at his very being, as he tried to scream, so intense was the coldness and pain, that all sense of rationality went due to the pain and frozen rigidity of his body. He could look neither to his left or right. All he could do was watch his hand and arm, any other movement for him was now impossible, next came the tightening of his chest and then the sudden heavy thudding blow to the left side, under his ribcage, which came so suddenly it has passed as he had felt the initial pain which had come with it. After that came darkness and a release from the cold and pain. He never felt himself fall and strike the side of the door at an angle, his hand still frozen and gripped around the door handle.

Those around him could do nothing but watch in stunned silence but, what they had seen, differed considerably to what Marcus had seen and felt. They had seen him take hold of the handle and almost in an instant his face hands and all visible parts of his body was covered in a frosting of ice crystals, and underneath them they could see that his skin had turned a deep dark brown colour, his body as it hit the side of the door seemed to make a crunching sound, such as thick ice on a pond would make as one stepped onto it and, it gave way cracking and giving off the abrasive sound as it rubbed together on top of unfrozen water. His hand, still attached to the door handle, while his cracked and ice frosted spectacles hanging over the cheek of his face and, hooked over one ear, gave the scene they saw before them a grotesque and evil mockery to the ending of the life of the man known, loved, and respected, as Marcus De Clare.

"What is that room used for?" Choco, Tim, and Sally Parsons were standing at the door after being summoned by someone who had witnessed the death of Marcus. He turned to Tim.

"Ask one of the people here to go to the toilets, and wait for Charlie and Dixie when they have finished. Tell them, to let them both know what has happened here, you had better stay with me to see what is going to happen next, and perhaps it might take the two of us to keep things on an even keel. He looked around him at the others there who seemed to be getting panicky about the situation after what they had just witnessed.

"It was just a small room Marcus used for storing which had to be cleaned whenever he did any amateur archaeology, it was another of his many interests. All that is in there is only a sink, cupboards, table, and cleaning tools, and chemicals. As I say it was only a small room." Anne had tears in her eyes as she spoke.

"Surely we cannot just leave him here, laid on the floor like that. If it's a case of being afraid to touch him , can't we at least cover him with a blanket, a sheet or at least something?" Sally parsons spoke to Choco, while sobbing and fighting the tears back from her eyes as well.

Just then Charlie and Dixie appeared, making their way through the people crowding the immediate area where the death of Marcus had occurred.

"Oh my God, it's true then!" He moved closer to the body.

As he did so Choco held out his hand towards him.

"Don't touch him Charlie!"

"What the hell happened here?"

"I am not sure but, hell has more than a little to do with whatever it was."

At the same time as Choco was talking to Charlie, both Dixie and Tim began getting feelings of uneasiness. Without saying anything to the other two, they both started to physically move with their hands, everyone around them out of the area of the hallway where the body of Marcus lay, and into the sitting room.

Seeing the urgency in their manner Charlie started to do the same. The crowd had moved about seven or eight feet away from the body that was once Marcus, when something, a dark shadowy form was seen to come through the front door which seemed to dissolve around Marcus's body. Every one there could see the form, and as they did so a state of panic started. Making all except the four friends scramble through the sitting room doors. Then moments later a noise from the direction of Marcus could be heard.

Charlie and the other two then returned to Choco's side just in time to see the body of Marcus begin to move. It began to shudder and twist, as if in a fit of convulsions. Then there were sounds like the creaking of leather. Such as a new leather jacket would make, when being tried on for the first time came from the body of Marcus. His legs, body, and arms, began to stretch, his hand then came away from the door handle dropping to the floor. His glasses dislodged from his ear fell to the floor also, the glass and plastic frames brittle from the cold breaking, the pieces of the broken glass made a soft tinkle against the leather sounding straining, as what once was the body of their friend, began to alter in shape and appearance, growing longer and filling out into a far more bulkier and a leathery reptilian form. The face, and head changed, although keeping roughly to human features, to a rough leathery hardened countenance.

As they watched they knew what ever it was taking place, they would only have moments before what ever it was taking place would be ready to do whatever it had come for. All four then moved quickly into the sitting room to join those who were already there, slamming the door closed and locking it behind them. As they turned Sean and Dave Mitchell came over to them. Worried looks on their faces and a questioning look in their eyes.

"What's happening out there Choco?"

"Don't know exactly, but something is taking over the body of Marcus and it is changing in form. Into what I don't know, but we had better be ready for it when it's completed the transformation."

Before anything else could be said, the sitting room door burst open and, standing there was what was once the body of their friend. But there was no way that if they had not known of the events that had happened before, could they have recognized it for the person everyone there had loved and respected. For Marcus was no more, and in his place stood an abomination of the most bestial of creation, which had ever entered into the earth plane of existence. The eyes yellow with vertical slits for pupils, nostrils wide, beneath a broad, squat nose, opening and closing, as it drew breath into it's being, a lipless mouth devoid of any precise shape, with teeth yellow/brown, angular, and uneven, a revulsion from the lowest region of the spiritual plains which had invaded the body of a spiritual seeking being, and had now entered the physical realm of the earth plain.

Whether it had always been so, defied any reasoning, or laws of understanding. As it stood there one could feel emanating from it essence of pure evil. After bursting the doors open it just stood there watching those inside with unblinking eyes. It stood to a height of above seven feet, it's head held erect, the leathery skin was now completely visible, with parts of Marcus's shirt hanging around in shreds on the arms and shoulders of it.

It moved slightly, and as it did so there was movement behind it, then into view came a man and woman, dressed in immaculate clothing. A smile of total confidence and smug supremacy showed on their lips and in their eyes of the immediate situation, indicating and infusing into those in the room they had total control over their present plight.

"We have not, all, met before but, now is as good a time as any, to get to know each other, especially in present circumstances. Before I discuss anything more with you, allow me to give you a small demonstration. Just to give you some thought of what is possible for you to enjoy, or even participate in, of course what you will see will not necessary be the way you will enjoy leaving here. But we will do our very best to speed you on your way, with a little pleasure thrown in for ourselves of course.

He turned to the thing that was once Marcus, mumbled something and pointed a finger towards a person on the left hand side of the doorway. In an instant the creature had moved with incredible speed for something of such size. Towards the now terrified figure of Leonard Seers, grabbed him by the back of his shirt and, frogmarched him, his legs almost off of the floor to where the man was standing, accompanied by the woman.

Look who we have here, someone I do know, and who better to demonstrate your situation for you, should you not accept the proposition I will put to you later.

Everyone looked towards the terrified figure of Seers, and though their eyes saw what happened, their minds could not accept the *demonstration* they were to witness next. The long taloned fingered hands turned the poor man around holding him by the neck, drew a finger down his back and hooked the mans shirt away from him throwing it ripped and torn onto the ground, in one fluid movement. Then taking the same taloned finger started to draw a line down his back, the sharp talon as it moved drew blood from a deep cut following the line of Seers backbone. Then it quickly drew another line around the base of his neck in the same manner, causing, what could be only described as a necklace of blood, made to look even more gruesome, by the trickle of blood patterns running down in uneven lines towards his chest. After the first inscision which had drawn cries of pain from the lips of Seers he seemed to become immobilized but, remained upright, still screaming with the pain which was being inflicted on him. The next act of the scene they saw before them to all intent and purpose seemed an impossibility to achieve. The thing caught hold of the skin above the shoulder area of Seer's body and began to wrench it downwards with a forwards movement and tore the skin away from the upper body leaving the back of his victim completely exposed showing raw flesh, blood, and yellow/white lumps of fat. His arms the skin of which had been partially removed and remnants of which hung down in lacerated folds around him, the loose skin of his back hanging down in skirt fashion over his buttocks. The room was echoing with the screams Seers was making during and, after, the horrific so called demonstration. To finish, the thing of evil turned his victim around and drew back a long fingered taloned hand and, plunged it deep into the chest of Seers, the snapping of ribs could be heard all around the room as it did so. With a twisting motion, while it's hand was inside the chest cavity it was withdrawn holding the heart of Seers briefly in the air as if it was a trophy for all to see, it then ate it, moved back to the man as dog returning to it's master.

Seers fell heavily to the ground with a dull thud, the blood from his body forming a deep crimson pool on the rooms floor.

CHAPTER 47

While the unholy episode with Seers had taken place, Choco along with everyone else in the room was totally mesmerized, but as the sound of the tortured body fell to the ground, there was an instant awakening within him and, the other three. They knew that what they had witnessed moments before was only one facet of evil in it's true form, and knew they had to react to it in some positive way before the person who was accompanied by the woman and the creature could do more to those in the room who at that time were in real and absolute terror over what they had just witnessed. What they could do, each was unsure, but they knew they must do something, and quickly.

The man spoke and then waited until he had everyone's attention.

"What do you think of the small demonstration? Is he not incredible, of course there have been a few failures before we perfected the transference of what you now see here, and far from the realms it inhabited, and you can tell how happy it is in it's new environment, and it is so loyal to us who have accomplished the task of bringing it here.

As the man had been speaking Tim had been seething as the memory of what he had just witnessed and, remembering the the thing that stood before him using the transformed body of the person who had endeared himself to everyone who came to know him.

As the man finished speaking, he reacted with a lunge forward towards him, somehow he did not even reason what he was about to do but, he also felt no fear at the same time. His only concern was for his three friends and the people they were imprisoned with.

The man it seemed was taken completely off guard, so confident was he, that the demonstration had completely cowed everyone there with fear of him, and the creature. But the overwhelming anger over what he had seen happen to first, Marcus and, then Sears welled up in him. The attack when it came was fast and furious. As he reached out to the man landing a solid punch to the head and each side of the ribs, knocking him backwards. The attack had come as a complete surprise and Tim continued hitting while they were both sprawled on the sitting room floor. The aggression within Tim continued and he was more than getting the upper hand, it was then the creature intervened, catching hold of Tim by one arm he lifted him bodily and threw him across the room as if he were no more than a large rag doll, knocking over three or four others there before hitting the sitting room wall. After which he slumped motionless on the floor, dazed, but otherwise uninjured but, partly satisfied at his futile attempt to redress the situation.

Choco meanwhile had moved forward and stood out in front of the others in the room, closely followed by Charlie and Dixie, who had moved on his example. There was just a distance of five feet separating them from the three administrators of evil. He had by this time realized who the man was, from the account given by Father George, it was, he was sure, the man who had questioned him and, then sent him to be tied up next to the altar where they had rescued him.

"So, it seems, we will have to try a little more persuasion on you all." The man, his eyes blazing with anger, and his face contorted, which seemed to change his whole appearance. He had got to his feet, and was adjusting his cloths which had been dishevelled in the encounter with Tim.

"What do you think you can do against us? Through the stupid action of your friend you will all now pay even more dearly.
.

Charlie, standing by the side of Choco, had the appearance of some one completely relaxed, and seemed un-bothered about the situation they were in. He stood seemingly absent minded while scratching his chin.

"You are so sure of yourself, with all this talk of power and all. He turned to those behind him. I know what he is, besides being in the clutches of the evil he has surrounded himself in, he is still in essence, just a puffed up ego maniac. The power he talks of is not his but, on loan to him, he uses it for his own rewards, and is allowed too, for the time being, because, it suits those who give it to him to do so for their own ends. When the time comes, and it will, and, his use to them wanes, he will be discarded in the same way as he does to those who follow, and are subservient to him who he decides he has no further use for. Everything he controls he controls through fear. Just as he does as he pleases, at the detriment of any one who might oppose him and, his temporary position of power. I say temporary, because that is all it is, temporary, a tempory position of power. His so called followers, fear him. Before the attack on him from Tim he was, I am sure about to offer all kinds of earthly riches if you would renounce your belief in the goodness of love and the trust in the good teachings of spirit, and, if you do not, then your fate will be similar to what we have already seen so far, since we have found out about their return and existence on this present earth plain. We all have free will, it is just that we need the courage and faith enough for them not to be a threat to our very souls. He says we have no chance of winning against them, well, I don't know how but I believe him and his cohorts have lost already, and they will lose every time people like you and I keep faith in what we truly believe is right or wrong, and as long as we believe and keep faith, there is nothing they can do, without digging a deeper hole for themselves."

Choco glanced sideways at Charlie as he listened to him speaking. "What was it?" He thought was making him speak with such confidence, especially when he had seen what had happened to Marcus and Leonard Seers. But somehow as he listened to what he was saying there seemed to be a growing feeling within him he could not explain. It felt to him that there was more in the words that Charlie was speaking than he had realized and, before his friend had finished speaking there was within him a inner warmth and strength that he could not fully understand, but, above all he knew that he and his friends were not alone. Use your intuition, go by your intuition, that was the best Sally had told them she could advise them after the meditation session they had, had. "Open up!" He thought. "Open your mind to the situation you find yourself in."

His thoughts were interrupted, it was as if there had been someone listening to what he had been thinking, and had tried to send some kind of confusion into his thoughts. Looking away from Charlie his attention was immediately on the woman standing slightly behind the creature, with the man in front of them both.

She stood eyes closed with a tense look of concentration on her face. Instinctively he knew what her function in the proceedings was, and made a guess that it was woman Father George had encountered when he had been offered the chance join their group and had tried to fool them, when he had said he was willing to become a follower of their group, the woman could read other peoples conscious thoughts and, that was how they had known he was playing for time, in the hope there would be a chance to escape at a later date. He immediately decided to put his theory to a test and see if he could get any reaction from her. Without thinking about anything in particular he just tried to blank his mind out any way he could. He focused his eyes and all his willpower on the hallway behind where the three were standing, he was only consciouse of the man talking to everyone there but did not take in anything of what was being said by him, eventually he focused his thoughts solely on a tall standard lamp shade which was visible from where he was standing. As soon as he had decided on the object of his choice and while looking had concentrated as hard as he could. Within a very short space of time he could sense more than see, her move her head, and at the same time felt her eyes were open. Still he kept up the concentration on the lamp standard shade. Then he felt her look in the general direction of shade, but he was not sure whether it was the shade she was looking at for sure. Then something unexpected happened. He heard inside his mind, clearly, the words of her thought's "Why is he so interested in that lampshade? Is there something there I cannot see and does not want me to know of?" She then looked directly at Choco.

He, looked straight back at her and, then directed his thoughts towards her. "There is nothing there that would interest you, but you have answered my interest in you!"

The woman was visibly taken aback, she had not expected, *her mind, to be intruded by anyone. but much more than that, he had also communicated by thought to her.* It gave her a shock and un-nerved her for a moment or two.

Choco also noticed her reaction when he had thought the words and, had casualy directed them towards her, not realizing that what he did so casually, would have such an impact upon her.

But he had, communicated in that manner, and made him immediately understand that perhaps it would be their opponents could be the instruments for them understanding of what they could achieve, could it be that they would set the level and they must retaliate and surpass whatever they were going to try against them. Was it possible that what ever they were to do then Choco and Co. would have an antidote for whatever they could try against them, and perhaps more.

The woman turned to her companion, spoke a few words to him, then returned her gaze to Choco, a kind of nervouse twitch played around her lips. As she did so the man turned his attention towards Choco and the others. "Well now, it seems that we have been fooled to a certain extent as to what or who we were to deal with. It now appears, that there are some among you who have been capable of understanding our ability to practice arts of a covert nature, but let me assure those of you who are not in possession of such things, whatever things these few among you who may have capabilities similar to us, you will not succeed in overthrowing the might we are able to put against you. We have learnt our craft well during the time we have had to prepare for our return at this time. For us now there is no such thing as death, until the time we are reborn into this world as children, we have the ability to move from one host human body to another with very little inconvenience what so ever. For the want of a better phrase we are immortal beyond your wildest immagination. Against us anything you may be capable of doing will only prove futile, our legions are too well established now for anything you could do to stop us, and we have established control of all the major governments through out the world, with the few we have not taken control of, even those, will eventually succumb to our will. Any that might in any way oppose us will simply be disposed of."

"Consolidate, consolodate. Every one together now." The words entered Choco's mind like a fast flashing beacon. While at the same time he saw Dixie from the corner of his eye pick up a tea cup from a nearby table and mutter something. As he did so, the creature made a sudden move towards Choco, but before he could reach him, Dixie threw the remains of the cups liquid at the creature, and as it hit it there was a crackling sound, followed by a roar from the creature, it reared up and almost caught hold of Choco who had seen the movement coming as the creature reached out towards him, and had instinctively moved to one side while the action of Dixie gave him the few seconds to get himself out of the way of the deadly assault. By now Tim was on his feet, and could see what was taking place, picking up a nearby wooden chair he threw it in the direction of the creature catching it with a solid blow to the side of the head allowing time for his friends to move further back and out of range.

What followed was a relief and a surprise to them. Where the liquid from the cup had hit the creature there had been a blueish phosphorescence and, what looked like white smoke accompanied by a hissing and crackling sound, which gradually became louder. As the male and female watched the scene before them, they began to move backwards towards the hallway door, with the first signs of real concern on their faces, which was still present with them as they had gone hurriedly leaving the room and slamming the door closed.

The creature was wreathing around, on the floor then managed to get to it's feet, it's arms waving and lashing around, while at the same time stumbling backwards and forwards without any clear sense of direction it wanted to go. One arm smashed into the side of the wall next to the door, making a large area of plaster come away exposing the brickwork beneath it. The thing of evil roared and screamed, and as the seconds ticked by, the phosphorescence increased in intensity, and could be seen spreading over the things body, and as it spread the leather like skin began to burn and peel, with bits falling to the ground and continued sizzling and crackling. The smell as it was happening was atrocious, smelling of rotten and decaying fish. Eventually the creature fell to the ground in a heap, the arms and legs trembling in its lasts throws of death. The last gasps for breaths of air were taken and then there was silence, a matter of just seconds later there was nothing left but a stain and a pile of ashes left on the sitting room floor where the creature had fallen.

Silence reigned in the room after the scene that had been witnessed by those there, no one there seemed to know what to say to each other.

"What was that you threw at it to make it burn like it did?" Charlie asked of Dixie.

"Originally it was cold tea, but I asked for it to be blessed by Father George or whoever there was who could do it from the spirit world, I was unsure really what to do, I just had a hunch to do it, and did not really expect the results we got, but I'll leave it at that. It was a blessing in more ways than one, and that's for sure, perhaps we have a chance against them in spite of all the shit he was giving us about them being so powerful." He inclined his head towards the pile of ashes on the floor. "It really is surprising what a cup of tea can do for you, ain't it!"

"Well it certainly got us out of a hole and that's a sure thing." Tim gave Dixie a pat on the back as he spoke. "It might do as well to get a couple of buckets full ready and, ask for it to be blessed the same as the tea, while we have time too."

"I have my doubts for some reason as to whether it would work a second time, but go ahead it might be handy who knows. I suspect things might be a little different the next time they try something and we have to defend ourselves. They were not prepared for what happened just now, and we caught them unaware."

Tim finished speaking and turned to walk over to where Choco and Charlie were looking at the remains, of what had been the creature, and before that Marcus. As he did so he saw the concern on the faces of Anne, Sally,Sean and others with them.

"I don't understand something Choco!"

"Yea! What would that be, after so much happening that we do understand." His words were spoken with a hint of unruffled sarcasm.

"We all saw what happened to Marcus's body after he was dead right."

"Yes...."

"Why is it that when the cup of liquid was thrown over the creature, and it burned or, whatever it was that happened. Why did it not change back into the body of Marcus, instead of ending up as the ash we see here now?"

"I don't know perhaps that thing only happens in films, or on T.V.. Whatever the reason it does'nt make a lot of difference to Marcus now does it! So I would'nt pay much bother to it for now, we have more pressing things to think of at the moment."

"What are we going to do now?" A solitary voice called out from the middle of the room, but not really addressing anyone in particular.

"That's a good question Choco!" Tim commented as he reach them both.

"I don't quite know yet, but I don't think we will have a lot of time to debate on the answer. We know that they have somehow managed to get inside the house, and I don't think it was through the front door, probably the window in the room where Marcus met his death, outside of the room in the door way. Whatever! They have made a breach into the house now, and now they have managed to get in here I don't think it will be very long before they will be confronting us again. What I would really like to know is, what the purpose is, for what is taking place at the front door, and why it seems to be taking so long! What we have to do is to be ready for them when they try something again. Because when they do I think they will be coming in greater strength and with more power."

"What do you suggest then Choco? Do you, have any ideas?"

"I am not sure Tim, for some reason while the last episode happened I was being impressed for us all to get together as one. To consolidate. That was the impression I had."

"Perhaps a prayer or two might help the situation." Anne Farr spoke up. "Perhaps that would be one avenue to go down. It cannot do any harm, can it! I just feel while we have a little time we should all *consolidate in prayer* and, ask for help from spirit. So what do you say shall we pray for salvation from the evil that now exists here?"

"Can't think of anything else other, than buckets of holy water, so I suppose we might as well."
"I hope your praying is a little more positive than your enthusiasm is showing at the moment Choco." Anne Farr smiled, although, she could tell by the under tone of Choco as he had spoken, there was more concern about the situation than his words seemed to hold.

Every one in the sitting room were sitting down anywhere they could in the over crowded room. Heads bowed, they had been led in prayer by Anne and she had finished, they stayed there after praying in their own way and in their own words for salvation from the situation they were in. After everyone had finished with their private thoughts on how things were, and feeling a small boost to them they were feeling a little elevated. When there was a tremendous sound of crashing and banging, so much so the walls around them seemed to shake.

Anne and the rest of her friends, who's friendship had been built up over quite a number of years began to feel unsure and talk among themselves what part in the coming conflict, they, would be able to play, if there were anymore creatures, or worse, as the one they already had encountered. It seemed to them that with every thing that had happened up until now Choco and his friends were instrumental in defeating what ever they had encountered. Admitting to themselves that it was only due to Choco and friends that they were still all alive. They were also becoming afraid that they might be becoming a liability to them. They had been overheard discussing the fact among them selves by Tim, who had immediately relayed the information to Choco, Charlie, and Dixie. As time continued to pass the noise outside of the room became more louder and the banging more of an uneven and hollow sounding rhythm on the walls. Charlie was the first there to come up with a suggestion for them all.

"It seems now that things are going to get a little hairy, and we still don't know what they plan to do against us! They know now for sure we have some defences and are capable of fighting them on our level, what we don't know is exactly how and who of us is capable of doing what?" He then went on to explain to the rest of them what he had experienced with the woman, and how she had been shocked at the moment when she had found out what he had managed to accomplish, in the terms of telepathy with the intrusion he had managed on her mind, and how after the first intrusion into his mind when he had begun to think of the purpose that she had accompanied the other person. He felt it was a slim chance but it seemed that only by what they tried to do to them, they would some how know between them what to do against the attacking evil force. To which he added, he was sure would be coming again sooner rather than later.

Peter and Abigail Jones, had from the start of the time when they had first met everyone in Marcus's home who were also in the same Jeopardy as they were themselves, did not seem to get involved with the rest of Anne's friends. They attended every meeting that had been held, but kept themselves very much in the background. They were both of a quiet nature but very deep thinking. Never very often speaking about the things they had witnessed, or heard, content to let others do the talking and putting their own views, and ideas on any matters being discussed at any particular moment. They would then talk to each other, about anything that might have puzzled them at the time of any discussions. Sometimes they would agree on an answer to subject under discussion and, sometimes they would agree to differ, but always ready to try to see each others point of view on any subject they would discuss. One thing had puzzled both of them more than anything else in the last few weeks, and that was; why had everyone there come together at that particular moment. The way everything seemed to have come together, seemed to them, a lot more than just coincidence, and seemed to have the ring about it of a greater plan when all things were considered objectively.

Things such as Choco, Charlie, Tim, and Dixie, meeting in the way they had, and in turn how they had become involved in the present situation and meeting everyone else after the death of the priest. With so many things bringing them all together, at this present and crucial time. The four of them, had been regressed and, although they had only met a short while before the things they had found out about which were happening at the manor and later, the rest of the things they had witnessed, it seemed to them both they had one common factor which over rid everything else, it was, according to the regression, and since things that had come to light later, to verify what they had said in the regression sitting with the others present, they were connected through one major event in time, and that was, at the time of the crucifixion. Could it be they had asked them selves on more than one occasion the rest of them had been also been involved in things at that time, but had no memory of it as the other four had not until they were regressed? No memory of a time so important in the Christian calander.

If there was a reason then what could it be? Through the ages from the time of the crucifixion and before religion had almost, always, been at the centre of wars and persecution of people, or used within a method of stirring up hate and oppression. It is as still bad in many ways now, as it has always been. But also it was always those who held the mantle of power, more than often used it for their own advantage to obtain what ever it might be they desired, with those subservient to them but within the echelons of power and, position, have used money, laws, and the esteem they falsely acquire, through different means to forward their own ends. How many in the past have been ridiculed when they have stood up for their own kind through conscience, over what was right or just. No matter what religion one was born into or, to what station of life one attains, there is but only one truth in life, it is only the bane of life and, human failings that the truth differs and, it is within that difference that the inner soul, or conscience cannot come to terms with. Because things do not conform to what they wish them to be, and it is altered to suit an individuals needs for a false or, none existant conscience.

Peter and Abigail had been discussing these things together, and while going through everything again, they had come to the conclusion there was more to the situation than anyone had realized to start with. Namely the culmination of two thousand years of prophesy and, perhaps they had all better think quickly about what they had learned in that time, if it was not too late. "What do you mean?" Enquired Charlie as he heard them speaking, and had caught the gist of what they were saying, as he stood behind where they were sitting with their backs to him.

They were taken back by his voice as he spoke to them, and for a moment seemed a little embarrassed as he waited for them to reply.
"Come on share it with me, any theories or suggestions you might have might be something of importance we could use and, if you keep them to yourselves, they will not do any of us any good."

The husband and wife looked to each other unsure which one of them should speak. Eventually Peter was the one who began to try to explain what they had been discussing, and as he did so Charlie pulled up a chair which was free nearby, and sat next to them.
"What we were saying was, what is happening now could mean the end of the everything in world as we know it, the more in the way of political influence they have the less control everyone will have over their own lives. What we also mean by that is the evil around us will eventually alter the system of things forever. In other words we think that they are about to create hell on earth.

Just think about what they themselves have said to us of their aims. They have told us that their aim is total domination over all things, and then creating chaos, and in the end the world will revert to a state of disordered and formless matter, in other words Armageddon. That I believe is the reason we are all here at this time, and I just can't accept that everything that has happened to bring us all together at this time is just a coincidence. I don't know how, and am not sure for what purpose as yet but, I am convinced that we have at sometime and in some-way agreed to be in these circumstances, and it is of the highest importance that we find out for sure if it is true, and if it is, then we must find out what it is we have agreed upon before it is too late. I also believe it might be the last chance of redeeming our souls for things we have done in past lives, and somehow I don't believe it is just for our own sakes we are here, I don't think it is just us but every living soul on earth at this time will be eventually tested, and I just hope that whatever the outcome none of us will be found wanting."

Abigail was quiet while peter had been talking and her remarks when he had finished made a completion of everything that he had said.
"What Jesus said all that time ago was; No one would know when the time would come, the day, the hour, but that it would come was certain. Look what is happening in the world today, are there

not all the signs that the time is about ready. We have to place our trust in spiritual matters, seems to be what has been spoken to us all the way through the time since we have known of the situation before us."

They had not realized at the time when Charlie had sat down with them others nearby saw him do so and curiosity as to what was being said overcame them and gradually there were quite a few others there listening to what had been said by the couple.

Those who had been listening to what had been said by them, were silent, not one voice asked a single question from them when they had finished speaking. But everyone was thinking in their own minds and could see there was a certain amount of logic in what had been said.

Eventually the silence was broken by some one as they said;
"We keep talking spirit, and us keeping faith in them. If things are so bad as you have said, why have they not intervened some way on our behalf, lord knows we could certainly do with some divine intervention, with what we have experienced up until now.

It was only a short time later that things began to take a turn for the worse. The first thing to get everyone's attention was a terribly loud and hollow sounding crash as the sitting room door disintegrated, in what could only be described as an implosion. The door seemed to have been sucked into the hallway, shattering into a thousand pieces. As everyone looked in that direction they could see shards and splinters of wood which from the force of the shattered door had impacted into the floor and walls giving a porcupine effect. That had been bad enough but what held everyone's attention was a creeping darkness, which as they watched was moving slowly towards them. As it advanced the air began to become oppressive, then when it had reached about six or so feet from the sitting room doorway they could see it becoming thicker and blacker blotting out any light from the hallway as it advanced, upon entering the entrance to the sitting room it halted.

Tim Who was nearest to him whispered to Choco in a low and cautious voice. "What now mucker? It looks now, if we do have anything to fight with, we had better find out what it is now!"

But before an answer was forthcoming there came from the left of them and nearest the doorway, a terrible scream, as Sally Parsons was lifted off of her feet by some unknown force and lay for a moment prone on the ground, then by what seemed to be by an unseen hand, was jerked up high into the air, and while there seemed to be, punched, or hit with something with great force, then with groaning and screaming she was twisted in the air, the sounds of her limbs could be heard breaking amid the screaming, then her head was twisted and turned completely around, before hitting the ground, her tongue protruding grotesquely, and opaque and unseeing eyes stared blankly at the others who were around her. She lay still for a moment, and then suddenly sat up, her hands dangled at her sides and then she gave a shudder then moved in a crawling movement just as a puppet would being worked by a puppeteer. Her hands and arms still loose as she moved towards the darkness in a jerking movement, her bangles clinking as she did so, making the unearthly drama before those watching seem so unreal. As her head and torso entered the darkness with her legs dangling so unnaturally, there could be heard a chomping and what could only be a tearing of flesh.

So suddenly had it happened it took everyone there by complete surprise. The horror was brought home again resoundingly when the sounds of depraved laughter was heard coming from within the darkness. Fear spread among everyone in the room, fear of the unknown and fear for themselves and, all who were left in the room.

Seven more were taken in similar circumstances, repeating the macabre scenes they had first witnessed with, the death of Sally Parsons. Then after the last of the seven had been taken with nothing being able to be done, to stop the evil which was outside of the door way, there came a silence and a halt to the slaughter of those remaining. A coldness entered the room and with the coldness, forms began to start to take shape in the doorway, shadows at first, and then the shadows began to take on a gradual physical appearance, Humanoid but not human. Then as the forms became more solid they began to disperse around the room. Those inside began to move away from them, as they did so until in the end, the forms were all around the walls of the sitting room with Choco And every one else there, in the middle.

The fear among them escalated and as it did so the odour of fear was undeniable, every one became more tense, as the forms had taken on by now a completely solid and indescribable menace, emitting from them the smell of rancid and decayed matter, each looked different from the other. The smell only made things worse for those in the room as, it became mixed with that of fear.

Then amid the horror and putrefying smell of flesh there was a voice loud and clear, starting to pray and as it was heard more voices joined in. Charlie and Choco for the want of anything more began to do the same and pray along with the rest. As he stood there Choco felt a hand catch hold of his and looking saw Molly and Sean by his side he reached out likewise catching hold of some one he did not really know and held tightly praying in earnest as he did so. The creatures then began to slowly close in on those who were on the outer edges of of the crowded room. Gripped hands were broken, then cries of pain were heard and then bedlam seemed to erupt in the room. As the creatures of evil started to do as they willed with the people in the room, as there seemed nothing could be done to stop the source of the evil onslaught of carnage.

Charlie felt a burning on his throat as on of the abomination's caught hold of him, he lashed out with his arms, twisting at the same time, but it was to no avail the more he struggled the more the thing tightened it's grip on him. As the breath was leaving him he cried out for help, but nothing or no one came to assist him. He felt a coldness creep into his bones, and in his mind he was screaming, the thing looked into his eyes and what could only be construed as a grimace, then turned him allowing him to see his friends who were also going through the same as he himself was experiencing and were being forced to look towards each other by their captors. Choco his arms well and truly locked behind his back with only what could be described as a demon, although on a large scale. While he was being held another was opening him up through his chest, as the thing with Sears had done, to him. As he continued to gaze around him as his pain and injuries that were being inflicted on him began to take their toll, all around him he could see just a sea of blood and entrails from the rest of the fallen and dead in the room. Then the last thing he felt was the long sharp talons of the beast enter his throat and the tearing of sinew as his windpipe was ripped and torn out.

CHAPTER 48

Charlie opened his eyes, blinked, and then just stared to his front but, not really seeing anything. There was silence, not a still silence, but a silence when one is actually listening for sound, and the straining in listening takes part of the stillness away. Then there was movement, just slight, but movement just the same, he tried to focus in the direction he had seen it, following the different colours he had seen when his eyes first opened. Then he saw that all the colours seemed to be slowly moving as well. "Where am I, who am I?" He thought, then, as he thought this, there was more movement to his side he looked in the direction his eyes now focusing more clearly and could see someone raising themselves on their hands and knees, then he saw them sit on their haunches, and their arms began to feel around their body, they seemed to finish and just sat where they were for a moment before slowly struggling to their feet.

"Charlie, Charlie, he could hear some one whispering loudly, the name sounded familiar, then suddenly it all came back to him.

He felt a hand on his shoulder, it gripped and then shook him, he rolled over onto his back and saw as he did so saw Choco, with Tim kneeling next to him.

"You all right?"

"Yes, I think so. What happened? He looked around him from where he was laying, and saw the colours he had seen were all moving now, and had changed from the blurred coloured shapes into bodies of people laying on the ground as was himself. All were the same as he had been, confused and, puzzled as they began to remember the last thing that they could remember happening to them. He put his hand up to his throat, and felt, there was no sign of any injury of what he thought he could remember had happened to it.

"Come on Charlie, up you get. Let's see if we can find out where Dixie is." Choco and Tim helped him to his feet, although he felt that they did not need them to, for he felt fine and as he rose he realized he was still in the home of Marcus. As he looked around he could see there was everyone there who had been there when the blackness had come into the hallway. He looked over to the door and saw standing there, Sally Parsons and some others standing with her, and as confused as he had been when he had first come around. He looked out of the window and saw the sunlight streaming through it, the curtains which had been torn down were now in place hanging tidily as they had been before the evil which had entered the room and had caused mayhem.

"Choco? Choco! What has happened, are we all still alive?" The voice of Dixie came from behind the three, they turned and saw him looking around the room with the same baffled expression as everyone else there.

"I can distinctly remember one of those creatures taking me appart, and definitely recall you and Charlie laying dead and Charlie had his throat torn out. How can we be still here alive?"

"Dunno, Dixie, could be we had some of that 'Divine Intervention' Marcus and the others were always on about, perhaps our prayers were answered, just as he said they would be when we were in mortal danger, who knows? Or perhaps it has all been some kind of dream or mass hypnosis, by those at the manor. But why.....?"

A short time later everyone there had accepted that something, or some power, must have intervened, to save them when they had asked for help while they had prayed before, and during the onslaught of the evil that had invaded the house, and it had not been a dream or mass hypnosis of any kind. It seemed as if whatever had taken place they had been spared for some reason.

Then some one mentioned Marcus and Leonard Seers were nowhere to be found. All accepted that, that, part of what they could all remember had not changed, and that they, were not with them. Then there was a movement by some, towards the sitting room door as some had decided to leave now that things seemed normal again. Cautiously they walked through the door and into the hallway towards the front door, everything was as they had remembered when they had arrived at Marcus's house. The Door was as it had been closed and normal. The pictures were still hanging on the wall. As the door was opened the sunlight shone into the doorway, bright and cool, as it would be on a late autumn morning. As they looked upwards there was not a cloud to be seen.

Everyone there felt elated and relieved, with a strange feeling of fresh vitality which seemed to run through them all, some individually thought it must have been due to the relief of coming through the recent conflict intact, and they really had come through the ordeal safely, and bodily intact.

Those at the front started to walk around to where the cars were parked, but saw the car park was empty of any vehicle, also as they did so they could hear sounds of birds singing, it felt wonderful to be alive. They continued walking down towards empty carpark puzzled over what had happened to the vehicles, and could only assume they had been taken away by those from the manor, they then heard what sounded like cheering voices in the far distance, then as they looked in the direction it seemed to come from, the sound of a dog could be heard barking.

Peter Jones who was among those in the front of the crowd saw running towards him a familiar friend bounding over reaching him, he saw not aged as he had been when the last time he had seen, and lost him. Tramp now looked as he had in the prime of his life.

He stopped, reached for his wife's hand, the dog came nearer, uncertain, confused, and yet he felt as if what he was seeing was as natural and, as normal as everyday life. Then tramp was barking and jumping up at him, nuzzling as he had always done before he had met and married his wife. Confusion and the state of puzzlement he was in suddenly left him as the realization of the situation hit him......, the dog then turned from him, ran a little way and stopped and looked towards where he had come from and seemed to be waiting for them to follow, barking excitedly, while at the same time there were sounds of other dogs running with the same sounds of excitement towards those who were behind him, then among others who were now beginning to appear into view as if coming from nowhere, he saw his mother, father and who he took to be his brother Max now grown tall and waving with the others to him.

Those who had seen what had happened were more than a little bewildered, which was soon to changed into total amazement as they could see one figure, and then another begin to arrive from behind the parents of Peter Jones, and from behind the bend of the drive which led to the house, walking towards them. There was hesitated movement towards the figures as they were recognized. Mothers, fathers, brothers and sisters, and relatives, husbands and wives who had passed into the world of spirit years before, and who were now appearing before them.

Then suddenly Tim all thoughts of rationality for the present saw walking towards him his Rene waving at him, accompanied by Father George, and as he did so he ran towards her, a thousand things going through his mind. Choco alone now, looked behind him and could see the house Marcus had lived in, seemed to be fading from view, to be replaced by landscape. He then went forward following those in front as they were being joined by their loved ones, who it seemed had known of their arrival.

Suddenly a voice spoke, "Come with me Choco, Charlie, you too, and where is Dixie?"
Choco turned, and saw the smiling face of Father George, but not only that, he knew him also as someone else, in another time and another life, memories came flooding to the fore and, as the recognition, and realization came so did the reasons and the meaning of what they had all gone through in this latest life, and all those before, but the difference was that this last life had not been just a learning process. But to gain the right and total knowledge and understanding for the start of the new world and life everlasting for them all, they had but completed a mission they had agreed to undertake, and to face the final conflict that only they themselves could undertake, but a mission that would leave a mark and, new understanding to help his fellow beings who followed them, as they themselves entered the new and final world where there would be peace, love, and compassion. Where greed, wealth, and power of, one over another, would be none

existent. Entrance to it would be with compassion and inner peace, and undying love and understanding and an extending of an offered hand, for those who were not advanced spiritually enough, and who could not allow themselves to enter the highest realms of the spirit world at this time, but to go to the realm they themselves had earned in their journey through their many and varied earlier lives, their last being the final earthly one, but eventually they would learn that they would have to know to look within themselves to seek the truth of spirituality on the lower plains that they would have to find there, and until they found themselves not wanting, and to be their own judge of their own lives within their own appointed spheres, and to submit to their own conscience and of the consequences, of their own judgement of themselves, with the eventual knowledge of the true and positive reality of life eternal. Gradually the three friends walked with Father George as those who were with them in the final conflict, began walk in different directions but with an understanding of purpose in their step of where they were going why, and how.

A last turnaround saw Tim with his Rene arms around each other looking in their direction, a smile which came from their hearts told them an inner knowledge told them they would meet again, and that when they did the future would be different for them all.......

THE END

Then I saw the new heaven and a new earth... The first heaven and the first earth disappeared, and the sea vanished....Then I saw the holy city.....There will be no more death, or grief or pain. The old things have disappeared.

REVELATION. 21.